beautiful things evil people do

kailee reese samuels

WARNINGS
are like cups of tea.

This warning is here for a reason.
This book is a work of fiction containing explicit, graphic,
and violent material.
If you're not 18+, put it the *fuck* down.

Please practice safe sex.
Safe, Sane, and Consensual (SSC)
and
Risk-Awareness Consensual Kink (RACK)
practices in BDSM.

Communication is key and I do not believe anything should be swept
under the rug - sexuality, gender orientation, race, age, or religion. If I
help stir the cauldron of conversation and provide an escape for a few
hours, I have done my job.

Play hard and have fun.
Be good and love one another.
Enjoy the ride!

Without further ado, here we go...

BTEPD PLAYLIST

Listen to the music that inspired Beautiful Things Evil People Do on Spotify

There are those who randomly feed my muse.
And never know.

BTEPD is for many souls,
in the dark,
naked and bare,
running from the demons
wanting a chance
to dance
in the light
just one time.

Just one time.

For Angela
Without you, this never would've happened.

"Nothing says I love you baby,
like beating a man to death."

In your hands is Beautiful Things Evil People Do,
a dark romance.
*More specifically, it is a **dark + romance**.*
*Do not make **any** assumptions after the first chapter.*

Go in blind.
Please keep reading.
Trust me.

Thank you again for everything.
Chase the happy.
Love hard.

peace
k xx

CONTENTS

1

ASSUMING THE POSITION

ECHO

"YOU'RE FUCKING INSANE," SELIA MUMBLES, CRUNCHING on her carrot stick. "This will never work. You're going to end up dead in a ditch somewhere."

"No, I won't." Sipping on my sweet ginger tea, I thoughtfully stare at the blinking cursor. "I will have an excellent final research paper that will be the envy of everyone."

"There are countless women you could ask," she harshly scrutinizes. "You're going well beyond what is expected. Write the damn paper on something that isn't a calling card for every serial psychopath this side of the Rockies. Anything else. You aced your dissertation; you don't need this bonus paper for the analysis class."

"Not the same." Tapping my nails on the desk, I consider her concern for all of two seconds before spinning in my chair to argue her accusations. "This is a fetish scene experience. I want it, like this...*not planned*. I don't want to sit down over cocktails and negotiate, only to ruin the surprise element."

"... Go to a club?" She waves her hands about and snorts. "Your surprise element may be a body bag and a toe tag."

"Selia," I whine, wishing she hadn't walked in as I was mid-thought. "You don't understand. I am a twenty-two-year-old virgin with a Bachelors, an almost completed Masters, and my one true experience was Daniel Turnip asking if he could hold my hand at the sixth grade Sadie Hawkins dance. I have never even been kissed."

"I may be more concerned you held the hand of a guy named Danny Turnip."

I laugh. "Fuck you. He grew up to play collegiate ball."

"Echo Turnip would've been priceless."

"One of my many mistakes," I reply, swiveling back and forth in the chair. "Help me."

She shakes her head. "There is no way you can handle this," she garbles, using her half-eaten carrot stick as a pointer. "You're asking for too much. One slip from the tongue, and you will run like the wind."

"Bullshit!"

"I just don't get why you want your inaugural spread to be via a ravishment scene."

"Because I am sick and tired of using any number of toys stuffed in plastic bins under the bed. I want a real guy, a warm, hard cock, and a heartbeat."

"You could date and fall in love like a normal person," she bluntly suggests.

"I do not want to fall in love," I scold, growing irritated. "I want to get screwed. Banged. Pounded into next year by one unforgettable man."

"And then what?" she questions as her eyebrows lift with great exaggeration. "You know what happens next? One hit from the D, and boom! You're only going to want more. Dick is like a drug."

"One hit will be plenty," I assure without any basis for my reasoning. "One time. One scene. One moment where I am lost."

"And you may never be found again," she points out. "I revert to my original diagnosis—fucking insane."

The ad read simply enough:

RAPIST WANTED

Collegiate student, 20-something female seeks any race/age/profession of male for a sexual encounter. Platinum blonde. Hazel eyes. Works at The Village. Physical passed. No drugs/diseases. Psychological screenings passed. Records available upon request. Protection by you is required. Obviously, due to the nature of the request, no references are available.

"You should take off records available upon request. How are they going to contact you? You have no references, but you're offering records? You start involving documentation, and the precious elements of surprise and fear diminish."

I hit the delete key.

"… Should I include no anal?"

She stops and stares with a blank expression. "Girl, you want to be raped. If you think rape victims don't get assaulted in all three holes, you're further wrapped in the cuckoo nest than I thought."

I watch as she flops on the sofa. Selia has been my best friend for years, and we've shared an apartment since our freshman year. She's finishing her Masters in kinesiology with a focus on rehabilitation; I'm getting a Masters in psychology.

"You think it's a bad idea…"

"I think," she says, getting up and reading the ad over my shoulder.

"That you're getting in over your head. If you aren't careful, this will destroy you. It's a kamikaze mission."

"Kamikaze or not, I want this."

"You're looking for this guy to do this, but somewhere in your mind, you're hoping to find a long-term relationship with him. The problem with that is once you fall in love, you'll lose your fascination with his savage tendencies. It's all over after hello..."

"I don't want a hello. Or a name. Or an address. Or a text message. I want eight-inches of hard manhood to rupture my sheath without care."

"Dear God, I need to call someone for an intervention," she remarks. "You're asking for the impossible. You won't be finding some wealthy as fuck playboy to whisk you away in his private helicopter to a remote island where you will be pampered and praised. You're stuck on some societal romantic bullshit. You're asking to attract degenerates and low-lifes. And believe me, they'll show up in droves to take a number. You won't just get one eight-incher, but sixty-four feet of them. One after another. You'll be like a drive-thru."

"Jesus." I slump in the chair, shifting my lips back and forth. Selia doesn't have the same issues I do. She is a gorgeous blend of Portuguese and Chinese. Her dating habits tend toward the perfectly sculpted African American male. More precisely, she only dates Black men. She prefers football players, but in the past, she has been known to date everything from a runner to a gymnast—not only was Spencer black, but he ended up being gay and became one of our best friends. He lives next door with his flavor of the month.

My social life isn't even worth mentioning.

After my four-year high school crush deteriorated, I ran off to Northern California for college in hopes of finding Mr. Right, but my Southern charm and happy, bright attitude rendered a slew of do-gooders.

Flowers and kisses at the door led to my wanting more of a wise guy and less of a nice guy. I went through every sordid movie and dark romance book with my collection of vibrators in hand.

I didn't want to be a submissive, sexual slave, or bottom because those all required some form of communication and consent. I wanted a thoroughbred of a real monster.

I didn't want the choice.

With an inability to locate such a male, I subsequently gave up dating by the end of my freshman year.

When Selia agreed to share my apartment, she was convinced I'd *turned* queer. One night after a round of tequila shots, I confided the truth. I didn't want a woman. Nor did I want a nice guy to take home to Alabama—this was before my parents moved to Florida.

I wanted a beast—a calculating and manipulative man to lay claim without warning.

Her suggestion of visiting seedy bars only proved a line-up of suitors that I found less than appealing. I didn't want a man who had let himself go only to force his hatred of women upon me.

I wanted a stand-up anti-hero, full of complex dynamics, artful persuasion, and subtle control. I wanted a genuinely well-balanced guy with a kink, so we put up an ad on one of those dating sites with the title—*Hot Girl Seeks BDSM.*

She conducted interviews, and eventually, I agreed to a date with one—Master Kirk—he called himself. He was a decent looking lawyer, but when he showed up with a thick leather collar dangling on his finger, I knew he wasn't the one.

As it turns out, I didn't want to call anyone Sir, or God forbid, my boyfriend because I didn't care about their name.

I cared that they knew how to work their tool and their 'tude better than the collection in the nightstand and under the bed. Possessing intimidating confidence was just as important as knowing how to thrust the ding-a-ling.

The complicated problem wracks my mind as I swivel back to stare at the ad on the underground website. Even the idea of seeking out a rapist was outlandish with an inherent instability. Writing the ad caused the wiggle of my hips in the chair.

"... What if you get a child predator?"

"They don't profile the same," I dispute, tucking my fingers under my chin as my elbow rests on the arm of the chair. "It's not like I am advertising for that, but I should add in the word adult."

"You already say twenty-something..." she adds as I twirl towards her and roll my eyes. "You're right though, twenty-something doesn't mean adult."

I read it out loud. "God, maybe I am insane."

"If you don't think you can do this, you shouldn't post it. People know The Village, and I guarantee some of these nerds on campus are on the dark web looking at these ads."

Her assessment was accurate. Everyone in our small collegiate town did know about The Village, the hub of upscale retail, dining, and entertainment. I worked at the wine store, and while not obvious, if someone paid close enough attention, they would know.

"By nature, and my definition, the ideal suitor is inherently a stalker."

"No, shit." Her slender fingers brush over mine. "Let me repeat this one more time since you seem to have lost the ability to comprehend basic English. If you do not think you can go through with this, don't do it, Echo. Research paper or no."

I bite my lip on cue. "You know me too well."

"I know this rapist/stalker/criminal mindset is what you're searching for, and I understand the motivation for it as well, but you're asking to be violently assaulted. You're young, beautiful, and intelligent, but you're soliciting for some egregious corrupt male to stick his dirty dick in you. And I won't deny the notion is impressive, albeit crazy, but you're playing roulette with your life. You're basing the underlying safety of a sexual assault on your ability to read a person in less than one breath. You're good, Ekky, but I don't know if you're *that* good."

I ponder her words but focus on the phallic element. "Geez, I hope he can *use* that dirty dick."

Tossing her head, she laughs. "You mean, what if you acquire the perfect rapist who can't fuck?"

"Yeah," I mutter, hitting the spacebar to stop the screensaver. "What if he doesn't know his tool from a table?"

"It's a possibility," she snickers with a shrug. "You didn't say, *Wanted: Rapist Able to Give a Good Ride on His Bountiful, Engorged Cock. Must perform above standard.*"

I giggle. "If I humor the guy, and we get to that point, then it happens."

"I don't think you fully understand the magnitude of what you're asking for—*you will not have a choice*—regardless of what you say. You're spreading yourself for a hotbed of villains. These guys may end up drop dead gorgeous and drool-worthy, but their psychological assessment will infinitely remain categorized as a scumbag."

"And you warned me I might fall..."

"If the right bad boy comes along, you might," Selia argues, sitting on the edge of the chair near me and locking her fingers together. "And you cannot deny that as a possibility. If you find the ideal, gratifying violation, you'll want round two."

"Because he'll know how to move better than a vibe?" I giggle.

"No, because I know you." Her expression hardens with sharp angles. "You've spent over three years during the day dissecting assault cases, and at night, you lay on your bed and pet the kitty to images most people would rather never see."

I blink dumbfounded. "You're saying I'm off."

"I'm saying that this isn't a joke, and you're making light of the situation because you're completely aware of that fact. You're scaring yourself into a silly reverie over a paper."

"I'm posting it."

"So do it, and forget about it. Or it won't work."

The Paper she referred to would appear more like an audition for the FBI or police, but the exact opposite was true. I didn't want a job on the state or federal level.

Ultimately, I wanted to be sought after by a private security team, running profiles, and chasing down leads with an investigative unit. Still, they wouldn't take ho-hum in the highly competitive industry.

My resume and *The Paper* needed to show talent, creativity, and exposure to danger. I thought my idea was brilliant.

Brilliantly dumb, perhaps.

But it would garner the attention I coveted, warrant a one-way ticket to a psych facility, or put my ass permanently horizontal—either option I deemed acceptable when I hit publish.

Men would love the idea; women would say I just committed suicide.

But it was my life.

My decision to make.

"Just promise, if I end up dead, you'll burn the research."

"I promise, if you end up dead, I will end up in jail being Betty the Butch Mama's lover."

I crack a smile. "Why?"

"Because I will kill whoever hurts you."

JYNX

"I DON'T WANT TO GO TO THIS MEETING," I COMPLAIN TO my co-worker and best friend, Wang, on Friday afternoon.

His name isn't Wang, but Wendlin Rile. We call him 'Wang' because his standard lunch fare usually includes skimpily dressed waitresses and wings drowning in thermonuclear hot sauce. He doesn't dredge them in a dressing to cut the heat as most human beings do. His steel tastebuds must be void of sensing any flavor.

He's commonly late after lunch because he's dipping his dick in the secret menu item of creamy goodness in a utility closet.

Wang has a way about him.

Ladies love him.

What the fuck am I talking about?

Guys love him too.

He's the epitome of a best friend, the guy to bail your ass out of jail and bring you a twelve-pack just because. No reason is needed. He's *that guy.*

I am not that guy.

I am a proud, card-carrying member of the asshole association.

Hit it and quit it.

Care about one—myself.

And do not, under any circumstances, get involved with anyone.

"You have to go to the meeting, J," he says as I drop my credit card on the table. "You're the boss' son."

"The boss is in Europe." I roll my eyes and gulp my tea as Sweet Sally saunters over to swipe the card. She shakes everything the good Lord gave her in hopes of a bigger tip. I'm certain my colleague could accommodate her needs.

Wang pivots in the booth to catch a glimpse of that ass in those shorts, which aren't exactly shorts at all. Coverage is at a bare minimum, and last time I checked, I wasn't wearing shorts like that to walk my dog in.

Not that I have a dog. That would require care, much like a woman.

And I do not care enough to care.

"She's got so much ass, man," he mumbles under his breath, and I snarl. "I cannot wait to tap that one."

Let it be known; Wang has *tapped* almost every waitress in the joint since we started the Dower contract in Phoenix three months ago. Thank heavens, we're over halfway done because he's almost out of waitresses at all the wing joints.

It's not that I'm immune to Sally, Monica, or Renda's womanly prowess, but their version of getting it on included *verbally* communicating, which I do not do.

Hit it and quit it.

Don't chat it up.

In and out, and...*bye-bye.*

"Why can't I just send you?"

"You want your father to skin you alive?"

"I'll owe you for the next year," I bargain.

His eyes spark like I said the exact wrong thing. "Enough to warm up the temptress in the tight ones?"

"I'm not foreplay."

"You're no play," he cackles as the waitress slides the leather folder with a bright smile and a slight bend to show off her cleavage.

Implants. Eyelashes. Boobs.

Fake. Fake. Fake.

"Don't go there, W."

"When was the last time you got laid?"

I contemplate if his inquiry even deserves a response as I scribble my name, leaving a respectable tip and slam the book shut. I grab my jacket, put on my sunglasses, and head for the door.

The weekend meeting is a celebration of this expansion project, and it just so happens to be in Vegas in two months. Eight weeks away. I am counting down the days.

I used to love Vegas, but not for the reasons Wang does. I loved the glitz and glamour—the lights, music, and noise—the addiction to blackjack, partying until dawn, and the smell of whiskey that caused irreparable damage. I gave up gambling and booze over a decade ago. In exchange, I took up working out, green shakes, and reading thrillers.

Wang is hot on my tail as I exit the building and light a smoke. The heat in late March in Arizona is not yet unruly.

When we finalized the contract last August, the temperature was terrible, not like South Carolina, where a pervading humidity dampens everything in the summer—a warning before the imminent, oppressive swelter.

Pulling out my keys, I click to unlock the doors of the sports car. It's a rental and a piece of shit that has been dogged out worse than the stretched out pussy of one of Wang's wild ones.

I can't wait to get back home. I've got plans that involve my quiet, secluded house, and no hot wings for the next year. Wang will return to the Windy City, and I can get back to being me.

I wouldn't have taken the gig in the Devil's ball sack, except I sometimes like my dad. He runs a respectable, affluent, international IT consulting firm. I know computer architecture, understand the importance of reliable infrastructure, and how to make shit work right, the first time.

As a bonus, he trusts me more than the twerp with three degrees who couldn't hack into his own thermostat if he had to.

He notices the bag packed in the backseat. "Is *she* getting serious?"

"I like the club in Tucson," I answer, blasting the air conditioner as Wang sits down.

"… Another random?"

With a side-eyed glare, I ask, "Does it matter?"

"Do you even know her name?"

"I don't need to," I say, backing up. "And I don't want to. She changes every weekend. I plug in, play, and move on."

He gives a sympathetic gaze like my motherboard just fried in one of my custom machines. "At some point, you have to grow up."

"Like you?" I snicker. "A couple of long-term, a string of diseases, and no life? No, thanks. I'll keep my ever-changing weekend menu."

"So wait," he eagerly says. "If a proper girl presented herself, would you hitch her to the altar?"

"Proper girls don't exist in the seedy world I hang out in."

2

ROOM SIX

JYNX

THE HYPNOTIC, SENSUAL ENERGY IN THE PRIVATE CLUB IS unreal on the weekends. I only know because when we first arrived in Arizona, I was desperate for a fix, but decent, upscale fetish clubs are rarely listed on any website. They're hidden in the underground or in towering skyscrapers, but they are not spoken of in the neighborhood bar by strangers.

The way in is by knowing someone who knows.

I called my "brother" in the Reckless Rebellion MC, who also happened to be my cousin, and he recommended the place.

With a grunt, he exhaled, "Where are you again?"

"Phoenix."

"Tucson has a nice spot," he said amidst the clattering of tools. "They do lots of rope work."

"I need an eager ass to tan with zero commitment, Cruz."

"Go to Tucson. Madame Tilda's place. I'll send you the address. Tell them I sent you."

Leave it to that crazy fucker Deacon Cruz to know where to go.

I had taken a sabbatical from the two-wheeled lifestyle since taking over my grandparents' place when my gramps died last winter.

My younger biological brother, Axel, is also a member of RR MC. He is watching over the farm while I do Dad's dirty work in Arizona.

Axel is everything I am not. He lives in eccentric opulence with his gold toothbrush and marbled toilet paper holder.

Life on the farm is probably destroying his mental state with Grandma's shabby chic junk finds. I snicker at the thought.

I need a dependable truck—*Ford F-250*, a fast car—*Mustang*, and a bike to make the girls squeal and guys drool. I collect Kawasaki Ninjas, having bought and restored over twenty, buy Maker's Mark by the case, and love a good cigar.

I enjoy hunting and fishing, relaxing with a spectacular bottle of wine while preparing a fine meal, and getting off on girls who like it rough.

This is the extent of my lavishness.

I have no need for excess in anything.

Despite the name conjuring up grungy images, Axel is a complete nerd set to run Monroe Consulting alongside me.

His real name isn't Axel, and mine isn't Jynx, but we hackers never talk about that. These bitches don't need to know what we stand to inherit.

That is mine.

Not theirs.

Thankfully, Axel feels the same way I do about relationships and women. The only difference is he routinely plays with the same half dozen girls.

At thirty-four, the bastard likes them young—college age. I have no desire to play with or train someone under the age of thirty. I am thirty-six, set in my bachelor ways, and relishing in the peacefulness of my life.

I hand over my card to the girl at Madame Tilda's place. "Good evening, Mr. Monroe."

"Is Katie here?"

The pretty woman leans over the counter and peers into the club. "She is with Joker."

"Fuck," I mumble, and she giggles, offering up an alluring smile with a twinkle in her eye.

Don't think it, J.

She is too fucking young.

"I'm off in fifteen if you want to play, Sir J."

Humored by her assertions, I grin. "I'll meet you at the bar."

"I'll be ready." She winks. "My name is..."

I drown it out because it doesn't matter. She wants to sign over consent; I'll do the deed. It won't be nice, but it will provide the release I need.

The regulars all know I don't play sweet.

I am Master Jynx and have developed quite a reputation for presenting a challenge to the most seasoned participants.

I disappear deep into the club, past the exhibitionists engaging in any number of sport sex shows to the dimly lit mahogany bar that serves as the dividing line to the private rooms.

I have never been much for performance. I don't need the approval of the crowd to find the arousal. I can do it and have done it in the past, but it isn't my forte.

I prefer one-on-one.

No double kneeling subs or sharing with another Dominant.

No swinging. No gray areas.

Just one malleable girl and me.

I like it clean and neat, just like my beach house on the coast of South Carolina—sterile, uninvolved, non-committal. Crisp lines of folded linens. Cords tucked away. Shirts starched. Everything organized.

Maddening to many, but the only way I know how to exist. I cannot breathe in disarray. I function just fine in chaos, as I do at my grandparents' place, but I prefer a system of order, including recognizable rules with self-imposed boundaries that I refuse to cross.

I was wild once...*years ago.*

I'm recovering without any need to relapse into my reckless youth —*not the addiction which surfaced from being wild.*

Alcohol is doled out incrementally while the crux remains in the leather I am about to palm like it is a part of my body—*like I was born with a twelve-foot bullwhip in my hand.*

The bartender provides my order—*the same as it is every week*—and the smell of bourbon hits my nose with a pleasurable numbing sensation. The agony is all there—*between the scent and the lip*—where the source flourishes. The taste, swallow, and subsequent manifestation in my body are far less important factors in determining a decent consumption.

Just like in slaves.

I genuinely don't want whatever hostess girl's name is, but perhaps the sub standing in the corner talking to her girlfriend and eyeing me is worth considering.

I check my watch, knowing time is of the essence, demanding and depleting far too quickly to properly scope out the club. I don't want to foster any notions the young hostess might have. The thirty-some older woman understands better than most. At the very least, she'll listen without needing to learn.

I never claimed to be a teacher.

Polishing off my two shots, I give her a subtle nod and grab the keys sitting beside my empty glass. I casually stride over to the sub decked out in her best fetish gear.

She needs this night as much as I do.

We'll find a mutually beneficial high and enjoy the time well spent. Tomorrow morning there won't be any need for a phone call or a text message because we understand this isn't long-term. This is a brief moment without any strings attached.

I demand.

She supplies.

And it's just that easy.

I brush her auburn hair from her shoulder and whisper, "Room six if you're interested."

"And if I'm not, will you stay there alone all night?"

"Hardly."

She blushes, knowing it's true. My parents' genetics blessed me. This face....this body...they aren't ever lonely. But I often am.

Very alone by choice.

Her friend disappears into the fray as she inquires, "What are you into?"

"Discomfort."

Her eyes drop to my side. "What's in the bag?"

"Room six."

WITH THE RANDOM JEZEBEL SUSPENDED ON THE ST. Andrew's cross, I thrash the whip to her backside for one final round. Her pale skin marked up nicely in the backless frame of her harness. Pinked with a few red splotches from my overindulgence, she wasn't kidding when she walked into the room and declared herself a *pain slut.*

I've heard it so many times.

But it is rare to find such an accommodating sub who truly means those two words.

Many say it; few prove it.

Nine times out of ten, I end up with a safeword being called. I always abide by the limitations, respecting boundaries.

If I desired to possess my own girl, I'd push her further, but most of the club subs aren't seeking a push—they're searching for a rich playboy with a kink and hoping to take him home with a ring for the win.

Ignoring my arousal, I unhook her wrists and ankles. "Thank you for the night."

"You're welcome, Master J," she replies. "I'm the one fortunate enough to have had the experience with you tonight before your departure."

I have eight weeks left, which feels like eternal hell. But I get it; I don't ever play with the same girl twice. Packing my precious implement into the satchel, I snicker, "Word got around."

"It did. You're coveted," she laughs, draping the sheer black cape over her shoulders. "I understand not to expect anything more."

"I don't take it further."

"I'm aware," she says, smiling. "Be careful out there. Girls are looking to score a cock."

"Nah," I reply, shaking my head. "They're looking to get a rock."

"Fair enough." She extends her hand. "If you're ever in the Midwest, give me a call."

"Where are you from?"

"I'm based out of Kansas, but I travel all over the States with work."

You're talking too much, J.

Shut the fuck up before this turns into coffee, pancakes, and bacon at a diner.

"What do you do?"

Her blue eyes flicker in the lights. "I do product showcasing for various companies. We design, implement, and maintain window dressing and product display on a broad scale level."

"You own it?"

"I do," she informs. "If you're ever in the neighborhood and looking for some willing flesh, hit me up. Dissolving is good."

I'm humbled by her offer of a repeat, even if I will never take her up on it. "I should be going."

We shake hands and part ways.

Cold. Delivery. System.

It works.

In the club, I spot Katie taking a public lashing from Joker. Damn shame. She's better than he deserves. We've been drinking and flirting for weeks but never had a session. I had my fingers crossed that Katie would happen tonight.

I pass by the nameless hostess, grinding on some guy's lap. She glances over and drunkenly grins. I barely make it outside when I hear her yell, "Jynx!"

I briefly close my eyes and sigh, knowing I wasn't fast enough to escape her jealous wrath. I reluctantly turn around. "... Yes?"

"Five hundred for the night?"

With a broad grin, I shake my head. "No."

"What's your deal?" She asks, poking me in the chest. "You've been showing up for weeks and never taking anyone home."

Nice of her to be paying such close attention to my goings-on. "I don't need a girl half my age to be babysitting me."

"Five," she repeats, sloppily grabbing me. She can't even stand up straight. Her drunken sludge is similar to a mudslide. Not clean or neat. Read: *not my type.* "And the babysitter swallows."

I almost spit, laughing in her face. "You've got some nerve. You seem to be missing a key point," I calmly reply. "I don't need to pay anyone to suck my dick. You would have to pay me, sweetheart. And frankly, by the looks of it, I'm out of your price range."

Champagne taste on a beer budget.

Not even craft.

She lifts her hand to swat at my cheek, but I swiftly back away. "Not going home with me now, Bella."

She gasps, shocked. "You know my name..."

"I'm not deaf, nor am I dumb," I sternly reply, catching her off guard. "Just disciplined."

I walk to the car and drive to my hotel where I will stay the night. I reserved it for two, but after Bella's outburst, I doubt I return tomorrow. She'll be lucky if I don't call up Tilda and complain about the harassment. Not every Dominant who walks into the club wants to get their rocks off.

The subs have a choice, and so do I.

My hotel room is an upgrade, but not a suite. I order room service and take a quick shower before the food arrives. I watch the news while eating my medium-rare steak and scanning the latest on the dark web.

"What the fuck?" I mutter, setting down my fork and wiping my mouth. I pull the machine closer and reread the title of the ad—thinking my eyes must be messing with me. *Rapist Wanted.* I click the link and stroke my chin. "What the fuck are you thinking?"

I grab my phone and call my brother. "Hello! How is Azi—*roner?*"

"Did you see this ad on Gray Market?"

"You mean the twenty-something wanting to get alley ripped?"

"Yeah," I say, reading the ad over again. "Any idea who she is?"

"Not a fucking clue," Axel replies. "I can dig if you want me to. You going to do the deed for her, bro?"

I might.

But I don't need to confirm that with Axel. He knows what a bad guy I am. "Nah, I got this," I contend, looking up her profile. "Do you think she is serious?"

"In Northern Cali?" he quizzes. "Anything is possible."

Scanning over her name—D4RK4NG3L—I snicker. "How is life on the farm?"

"Disgusting," he groans. "I'm hiring some of the Ag boys from the high school to do this shit. I don't know why we don't sell the live-stock, have an estate sale, and put this place on the auction block."

I type away and casually mention, "Because we spent all of our childhood there."

"And you're a sentimental schmuck."

"Don't tell anyone," I cackle, studying her profile and contemplating the best way to break into her account. "As I ponder violating this poor girl."

"Softy rapist."

"I will be keying your car for that one when I get home," I joke, chuckling. "I'll make sure the lines are nice and straight. You can have them filled with 24-karat gold paint."

"Asshole."

"Trust me. If Dad ends up selling the business off, you don't want me to be anything but…" I suddenly stop as a feminine voice fills my ear with more than I needed to hear—my disgusting baby brother is getting his dick washed in her mouth while on the phone with me. "You enjoy the skank of the night. I am out. Bai, perv!"

"Later, J."

I lean back and stare at D4RK4NG3L's profile. It could be bait, but Gray is reasonably good about cross-checking. Still, it's not worth the risk. "Who the fuck are you? And why are you so stupid?"

I send a text message to Wang. "Where is Theodore Dower's son's wedding at?"

"At their farm, about an hour out of San Francisco," he quickly replies. "Why?"

"When is it?"

"Four weeks."

"Send an RSVP," I peck with determination. "J.A. Monroe will be in attendance."

"Cool. So will Wendlin Rile. Champagne servers…"

"You. Are. So. Bad."

I set down my phone and grab my laptop as I walk over to the bed. I click off the light and hit the link for the live feeds. I scan over the names until I find Christy.

The night will end up costing a pretty penny, but I won't have to wake up with a random girl asking a thousand questions and hoping for more…

Because that will never come.

Unlike me—*who is about to come several times*—with Christy writhing naked on my screen. With obscene thoughts of my whip lashing skin, my hand fists around my dick.

3

LAZY DAYS

ECHO

BY LATE APRIL, I EXPECTED MY RESEARCH TO BE completed.

It wasn't, and I ended up writing *The Paper* on Women's Fantasy of Sexual Assaults, an in-depth case study of giving up.

My professors loved it.

I adhered to the basic formulas; up to half or more of women's sexual fantasies involved being taken in some form.

With the burden of guilt and shame during fantasy dub-con/non-con scenes placed on the male, the female is finally free to explore her sexuality. Few women wanted to admit it, let alone discuss the fantasy versus reality element.

Blah. Blah. Blah.

The paper was a disheartening personal let down, but I managed to get an A and planned to graduate with honors in May.

I was putting in extra hours at the shop, and soon, I was promoted to maintaining inventory, shipping, and receiving. I wasn't responsible for stocking but ensuring the guys who did the stocking handled the bottles with care.

I was about to complete a Masters in Psych with a Bachelor in Gender Studies, and yet I was counting wine corks and printing shipping labels.

I slipped into a bit of a mental slump, but I needed the job, which paid remarkably well, to pay for the six years of college loans. Nonetheless, I was quickly approaching the point where I needed to determine whether or not going for my Doctorate was even worth it.

Another two years at the wine store, I—*Dr. Abigail Maines*—would end up managing the damn thing.

Selia was beyond busy, taking an apprenticeship at a physical therapy place, along with keeping a few clients that she did personal training for. All-in-all, life was good, and while I hadn't forgotten about the ad, I didn't fret over it.

As for the naughty little bit of words, I hadn't gotten any stalkers —*at least that I noticed*—but plenty of anonymous-no-way-I'm-revealing-myself likes on the site and a few personal emails, mostly asking— "Are you serious?"

Immediately, those went to the trash.

If they had to ask, they didn't have it in them to know.

I received two from irate sexual assault victims—and I do mean victim by the wording of their letters—and one from a survivor.

Through a series of emails, I discovered she was a former student bullied by her gang of assailants. She praised my efforts and wished me good luck, but not before informing me of all of her fantasies centering around that night.

She was brutally hurt, but she admitted to craving the attention she received during those hours. Her reality had evolved to the primary subject of her fantasies. I wanted to further our conversation, but after her last email, she never responded again.

I followed up but still nothing.

She proved the case and point of the problem—*expressed control becomes like a drug*—and cravings begin, which can never be duplicated.

It wasn't Stockholm Syndrome, but a replication to seize the loss of control, thereby regaining control.

She didn't want to befriend her attackers or meet them again, but the feelings of free-falling generated by their will over her body proved insurmountable by her psyche.

She longed for the loss of control.

Her answer was found in the confines of subservience, under a Master, as a house slave, but that did little to provoke my thought.

Our correspondence ceased around the time I received another email—"Do you want to be a house slave?"

I didn't want to be a submissive.

Submissive equated the delinquent word of consent—and it indeed was delinquent to me. I didn't want to negotiate a contract, define limits, or discover my triggers to avoid them. I wanted to be pushed —*hard, unapologetically for hours.*

The sting of my teeth bites my lip as I watch the porn video. There are plenty of good ones out there, but I'm a bit particular.

I don't like the circle jerk assaults in the bathroom or girls who look like they put every ounce of makeup on that they own. I prefer the innocent victims—*the unassuming, shy ones*—the ones who look like me. I also don't necessarily need a guy buffed to the max on steroids.

A penetrating pair of eyes will work just fine.

The rustle at the front door causes me to jump and drop the vibrator against my ass cheek. I pause the video. My bedroom door is open since Selia is gone for the night at a family gathering in San Francisco.

All of the safety latches on the door are fastened, including the deadbolt, but I hear the key flip over the mechanics with a distinguishable thud.

I wonder why she is home when I hear her try to open the door. "Hold on. I'm coming."

I was about to, too.

In my oversized shirt, I toss on my panties and rush for the door. "I'm so sorry, Selia." I spot the door open a few inches with only the two chains securing it. I peer out the crack and see nothing. No signs of Selia. No signs of anyone. "Selia?" I call out, shutting the door and throwing the deadbolt. I run back to the bedroom and grab my phone from the nightstand. I check her GPS location—she's in San Francisco. "Fuck..."

This is it.

Slowly, I venture closer to the sliding glass door in my room, which connects to the balcony. I glance down and drop to my knees, trying to catch a sneak peek beneath the curtain. I don't make a sound. I don't touch the fabric. My heart races when I open my eyes to see nothing but the black frame.

I anticipate having some horrific attacker behind the curtain, trapped behind the glass of our second-story apartment. He'll smile wide, break his way in, and attack me. I wipe my clammy hands against my shirt, drying them.

I never thought I would feel so...*anxious.*

On edge.

Fucking scared as hell.

'Just do it, Abs,' I think to myself as I rip back the curtain and see nothing but a few plants, chairs, and our small orb-shaped barbecue grill. I pivot fast and sprint back to the front door, madder than hell.

I swing off the chains and pop the deadbolt before stepping outside. There are three other apartment doors on the landing. One is empty. One belongs to Spencer. And the last one is occupied by a little old lady, Lillian Nakamura, who stashes about ten cats in her overly decorated space.

It's lovely inside, really.

She invited me in for tea once, but I know, she is in bed at this hour—*this hour being nine at night.* She is a person instilled with routine, gets up at three-forty-five, has a cup of matcha, runs either on her treadmill or the perimeter of the complex for an hour and a half. She also goes to bed by eight every evening.

I look over the back rail, which leads to green space. There are plenty of lights, but no one is around. I spin and run into a strange man. "… Hello?"

"Hey, girl," he says, sounding as gay as the day is long. His turquoise suit is flamboyant and clashes horribly with the orange shirt. Style isn't always sexual preference specific. "How are you doing?"

I don't bother with a greeting as I point. "If you're looking for Spencer, he's in that apartment."

Carefully, I tiptoe down the cement steps to the parking lot. Maybe Selia forgot her phone in San Francisco and had an armful of items. It wouldn't be the first time the postman piled her brother's packages from Hawaii in the mail room.

I scout the lot in search of her car. She doesn't have the reserved space under the awning; that is mine. But her older sports car is missing. There is nothing odd going on. A family across the way is piling into their minivan, probably going for ice cream. A few couples are out holding hands and walking their dogs. A car zooms fast toward the gate.

With the building surrounded by lawn on two sides, I decide to go back inside. I'm halfway up the steps when I hear the rev of an engine in the lot. I turn around to see a motorcycle zipping past. Again, not unusual. A few of the collegiate boys have them.

On the landing, I notice the apartment door ajar next to Miss Lily's place.

That's odd.

I cringe at the sight of my door left wide open. "I'm so stupid," I whisper as I overhear the moans of Spencer and the man. "Well, at least one of us is getting lucky."

I jump at the sound of Lily's door opening behind me. "What was all that racket?"

"What do you mean?"

"Someone was next door to me, banging on the wall, and woke me up!" she angrily yells. "I called security!"

"It wasn't me," I mutter. "I thought Selia was back."

"Damn, kids need to find something better to do besides ransacking empty units!"

Sneaking inside of my apartment, I mutter, "Goodnight, Lily."

"Sleep well, Echo."

I quietly close the door and press my back against the frame. My heart pumps on the verge of exploding. I worry he may have snuck inside. I click on all of the lights and scurry from room to room, frightfully checking in closets and peering with worry under the beds.

"No one is here," I whisper on my knees as my phone rings, and I hop up. "Hello?"

"Hi!" my mother says. "Just wanted to let you know we'll be there for your graduation. We reserved our flight."

"That's great, Mom!"

"You sound tired," she sympathetically remarks. "Did I wake you? I figured you would still be up with the time difference."

"Yeah," I excuse. "I am up."

My parents live in Florida since leaving the family property in Alabama to my older brother when his longtime girlfriend wound up pregnant. They got married, and my parents gave him the house and land. She lost the baby, and two years later, they divorced.

Now, Brandon has an enormous bachelor pad and a drinking problem. My younger sister still lives with my parents near Tallahassee.

"Call me back tomorrow," my mother replies. "Get some rest, Abigail."

I drop the phone on the nightstand and shut my computer. I double-check the door and click off all of the lights before flopping on the bed. My mother is right about one thing; I am exhausted.

In the middle of the bed, I stare up at the ceiling. My skin tingles with nervousness as I tuck my fingers inside my panties and touch myself. I'm soaked by the fear as I arch and moan. My fingers clench the sheet as I hold out as long as possible.

I think of waking to find him standing at the foot of my bed, staring at my bare skin, and stroking his cock steadily and slowly. He falls on top of me, pinning my hands with one of his, and guiding his dick to my wetness.

He thrusts inside with ferocity.

The fantasy is all about his wants, needs, and desires through every buck and pulse of his rhythm.

I don't fight because he feels too good.

With my fingers circling my hardened bud, I need more and pull open the nightstand to grab the thick dildo. I shove it deep inside and close my eyes to pretend it is him.

My fingers fall from my clit, hoping to extend my release a bit longer. I reach under my shirt and twist my nipple as I fuck my pussy with—*his hard cock*—taking and claiming.

What woman hasn't wished for more hands at this point?

I'd have fingers on my clit, up my ass, and on both tits. I might even have a couple gagging my throat or cinched around my neck, choking me.

More. More. More.

My mind is on fire with thoughts of his jacket zipper sawing against my nipple with each thrust. The burn of my pinch comes on strong, and I drop my hands low. One hand rubs my clit, and the other pumps the cock without remorse.

"I'm going to come…"

And he'll say, *"Admit how much you like my hard cock, baby girl. Say it. Let me hear you say it."*

"I love your dick…give it to me…take me…please," I beg between pants. "Use me like your slut. Fuck me like your whore."

I'm going…to come…

Within minutes, I erupt, gushing on my hand as tears drip from the corners of my eyes onto the pillow, and I whisper, "I saved it all for you. I saved it all for you."

I thought I had him. I thought he wanted me. I thought he would stay forever.

I pull the fake plastic cock from my body and roll over with a nauseating feeling. And I cry myself to sleep, alone, again.

4

THE ABCD'S OF ME

Echo

THE NEXT MORNING, I ROCK BACK AND SWIVEL IN THE chair with my feet up on the desk as I ponder the ad. I tap the mouse, hovering over the EDIT button, with my toe. The cursor blinks on the screen at the letter R.

I finish my coffee and mumble, "... Why won't anyone respond?"

Sitting up, I set down my cup and let my fingers hit the keys. I write what I want him to be.

Considering my additional details, I shrug and pick up the phone to call Selia. "Do you have a minute?"

"We're on our way to an art exhibit," she happily informs.

"Just listen," I warn with excitement. "Don't say anything."

RAPIST WANTED

Vibrant collegiate student, 20-something adult female seeks any race/age/profession of male for a sexual encounter.

You are a:

Dominant. Alpha. Male.

I am a:

Blonde. Hazel eyes. Looks like the All-American girl next door, cheerleader type. Physically active, runs the park loop in the evening. Social gatherings downtown every weekend. Works at The Village. Physical passed. No drugs/diseases. Psychological screenings passed.

Obviously, due to the nature of the request, no references are available.

If interested...

If interested, please do not contact. Find me.

"Get rid of the double if interested..."

"I know, I know! Stop editing me!" I rebuke. "I was thinking and typing at the same time, but how does it make you feel?"

"That's kind of quirky, but you're still fucking crazy," she giggles. "But I mean, what could it hurt?"

I laugh. "Exactly! Thank you! Have a beautiful day!"

"You, too!" Selia says. "Oh, and when did you bleach your hair again?"

"Last night," I giggle.

Feeling good about my updates—*or lures to catch a monster*—I take a quick shower and dress for work. I dry my hair, put a few curls in it, and dabble on a bit more makeup than normal. The new blonde has me feeling alive and free—a real partygirl.

I arrive a few minutes before I'm expected at the shop.

Upon walking in the back door, I spot José. He's the beer guy, a good looking American Latino, and about my age. Unfortunately, he falls under the nice guy header.

"Good Morning, Echo! How are you?"

"I'm good," I reply with a smile. "How are you?"

"Better now." He winks and walks away with the empty dolly. I take a quick count of the cases of beer and know he'll be here for a few minutes. I strategically plan to be bent over and putting my purse in the locker when he returns with the next load of suds.

I hear the snicker under his breath as my very short skirt leaves little to the imagination. He neatly stacks the cases and says, "You're such a good girl."

Hmph.

I'm somewhat insulted by his tone, kind of like a girl saying a guy's dick is cute. I understand he means well, but his words snag in my brain. I meander to the front of the shop where Morgan is counting out her register before we open. I smile, but the harshness of José's assessments hit home as I furiously stomp to the back room.

"What is that supposed to mean?"

"It means the face doesn't match the attire," he says, unloading the dolly as I follow him out to the truck.

"What does that mean?"

"You're untouchable, Echo."

My hands raise with a marked sigh. "… Untouchable?"

"You're like a wedding cake topper. The girl guys are supposed to marry, not have a good time with if you know what I mean."

A look of horror washes over my face as I mumble, "Ewww…"

Loading another round of beer, he snickers, "Not exactly. But you aren't the dating type. Or, for that matter, a one-night stand."

"So, I'm stuck? In limbo? Until Prince Charming comes along?"

I don't bother to tell him how dark that prince needs to be to earn my attention.

"Hey, José," Morgan says, standing at the backdoor. "Can you help me move this display?"

"Sure thing," he says, staring at her ass as she walks away. He peers down at me. "Marrying type," he instructs, and then with a nod to Morgan, he adds, "Fucking type."

"I don't want to be the marrying type!"

"Then you need to change," he assesses, tilting the full dolly.

"... What?"

He grins—a beautiful, white smile—and quips, "Everything."

"No!"

A chuckle escapes from his lungs. "Make it believable, and we'll talk Echo."

I cross my arms and prop against the edge of his truck. He is as right as Selia. I have reached a desperate point in my dating career. I pull my phone from my bra, click on my ad, and hit disable.

I don't give it another thought as I pull my hair down and fluff the long blonde curls that cascade onto my blouse. I undo the top two buttons and await José's return.

He does.

Glistening with sweat and looking good enough to eat, José pulls off his ball cap and wipes his forehead on his sleeve. He cracks open the water bottle, undoubtedly a gift from Morgan, and downs half of it. He smirks at me. "What?"

"Dinner and a blow job?"

He laughs. "Dinner and a blow job?"

"Yes," I maintain, feeling frustrated, and knowing I need a companion—anyone will do at this point. "You take me to dinner," I whisper, leaning forward slightly to show off my cleavage. "And I'll swallow."

"What do you like to eat? I mean, besides dick."

"Italian? Japanese? Thai?" I suggest avoiding the obvious cultural twist. "Burgers and Fries?"

"Korean. And you eat Mexican," he teases with an impeccable grin. "Six o'clock."

"Done," I say with a smile as I bounce off the back of the truck with a hop. "See you then."

"... Hey, Echo?"

"Yeah?"

"Try not to look like you just got out of Catechism class."

"José?" I reply, giving him the bird. "Fuck off."

With his hand perched on his hip, he laughs. "That's better!"

I HATE TO ADMIT HOW MUCH I LIKE NICE GUY JOSÉ.

I spend the better part of the day training with Morgan as we have a staff of ten in the store. She is a nice, middle-aged woman who manages the shop—the job I imagine taking after two more years of school.

I have a good deal of respect for Morgan Pellister.

After I worked a year at the café next door, she got to know me and offered to take me under her wing. I spent the first two years, under-age, in the back of the wine store. She hated doing the books, preferring to be out on the floor and working with the customers. I didn't necessarily enjoy crunching the numbers, but I was good at it.

Midway through the day, we sit in the backroom over salads from the café when I ask, "Do you date?"

Setting down her tea, she laughs. "I do."

"Haven't met *the one*?"

"You're assuming I want to meet *the one*. Not every girl grows up dreaming of a white fairytale gown and a prince, and that is okay. Someone should tell all the little girls in the world they can be more than enough without the guy. The guy should be a choice, not a societal necessity."

Knowing very little of Morgan's personal life, I politely inquire, "What about kids?"

"I have two."

I almost drop my fork. "You do?"

"Yes," she giggles. "A ten-year-old boy and a five-year-old girl."

"… And no, husband?" I question, almost sounding condescending. I hate to think of myself as the judgemental type, but her evident eschewing of romantic relationships perplexes me.

I am damn envious.

"I have *lovers,*" she heavily annunciates the plural. "Of both genders."

Oh. Morgan.

You kinky bitch.

I don't want to pry, but I long to know how she managed her life without *the one.* The moment I think it, the stark reality hits—*she is the one.*

She chose herself before a man…or a woman.

However, she wasn't a radical feminist, either. She was just a woman—happy and content in her existence. She was the only child of the shop owners with two kids and multiple lovers.

I bravely ask, "What is your goal?"

"Right now?" She peered up with her big greenish-blue eyes. "I'm trying to master hydroponic gardening with my father. I'm planning a vacation in June to New Zealand, speaking of which, I'll need you to attend to Dower wedding because I will be in Seattle that weekend. I don't always attend the events, but this one is huge, with dozens of our cases. I need to make sure it runs smoothly."

I ignore the fact that I have to go to a wedding and blurt out, "Are you going to New Zealand alone?"

"I'm going with Ravi."

I blink. Both genders. Multi-cultural. Two kids. Life. Happy. Goodness.

I am so fucking jealous.

During lunch, my new idol appeared before me in the form of my boss.

"Ravi is a banker in New York. We meet a couple of times per year. Last fall, when I took a few days off, we went to Tulum. He loves his work and life and doesn't want any of it to change. I'm the same. We meet up, and sparks fly."

"But no talk of marriage?"

"Why would we ruin a perfect thing?"

I ponder her choices as they inspire my hope of finding someone to do to my body what I yearn for. And maybe the old saying that *there is someone for everyone* isn't that far off.

I lower my voice and ask, "How many do you keep?"

"Currently, I have about a dozen I rotate depending on my mood."

... A dozen?

... A dozen lovers?

My eyes and mouth open wide. "I can't even get one."

"Because you're a hot mess trying way too hard," she informs, blotting her lips on a napkin. "You're never going to bait the kill if it knows you're hunting. Stop hunting. Go back to the drawing board, listen to some music, have a glass of wine, get lit. Find out who YOU are. And I guarantee they'll find you."

Little does she know, I'm hunting for a bear to maul me.

Proverbial bear, not literal, unless he has a great beard.

God, beards...

"Reverse the situation..."

"Exactly! Think of it like making yourself marketable. We have lavish displays in our store windows, not wine, but moments —*moments create memories.* Make your moments, and the customers—*or lovers*—will bang down your door to get in."

"Thank you," I whisper, finishing my salad. "Really."

"Years of experience, Echo," she replies, piling her trash into the plastic container. "But be careful about who you choose. Don't take them all. The best one will be the next one."

"How will I know when to stop?"

Standing up, she grins. "Oh, trust me, you will know when to open the door and take aim. Or spread your thighs. Or open your heart. Right now, focus on *you*."

She wanders back to the front as I mull over her unexpected lesson in dating, love, and life. I twist my hair up into the clip and refasten one button.

No need to go overboard.

I glance at my phone and the message from Selia. "I've met someone. I may be an extra day or three. And likely won't be capable of walking when I get back. I'll need ice for the tub. Lots of ice."

I smile and snicker. Selia practices Morgan's theories, but I missed a lecture—*putting myself as the one.* I see another message from my mother. "Brandon is going to rehab. He'll miss your graduation, but Daphne will be with us."

My brother. Alcoholic. Player. Trouble.

I have an honest moment where the words change. Brandon is a depressed, lost soul. And then, it hits. He isn't alone.

We were the alphabet siblings.

I inherited sadness from my mother.

My psyche was the sole reason for my studies in psychology. My eldest brother, Alan, died at three when he fell into a neighbor's pool and drowned. Brandon was one, but instead of my parents going onto C with the next baby, they put me back at A—Abigail Renata Maines. Renata, meaning born again, and also my mother's maiden name.

No one calls me Abigail, except for my mother. It's a curse.

And myself—*Abs*—when I am scared shitless.

My father nicknamed me Echo after his Korean grandmother, who I never knew. My father was ethnically blended with a Korean mother and an American father. My mother was Scandinavian. When I told Selia I was part Korean, she didn't believe me until I introduced her to my parents.

"Your father looks Korean!" she shouted as soon as we arrived home.

I laughed, "Yeah, no shit."

"And you look like a white girl!"

"Good thing you didn't study genetics. Bottle blonde goes a long way."

My sister, Caroline, would be born next, but my mom miscarried.

My parents went on to D with Daphne.

I carried the burden of Alan's death for my entire life, and my mother's grief led to my attempting to earn her attention by being the super-achiever—straight-A student, book worm, head cheerleader, and soccer star. I was popular but quiet...*until he came along.*

He slipped into the perfect snow globe I had created.

I fell in love.

And then, he shattered it.

I MEET JOSÉ AT MY FAVORITE KOREAN RESTAURANT, AND WE end up talking for hours. During our conversation, I accept the date will not result in the expulsion of seminal fluid in my mouth but cups of tea in my apartment where I confide my sinful study of the male mentality.

"You've got to be kidding," he chuckles after I reveal my tactical strategy. "No guy in his right mind will respond to a rape ad."

"I think you're wrong," I argue, curling my knees under my bottom. "If women have the fantasy, so do men."

"Yeah, but you're talking about a guy as rare as you," he points out. "Most women won't admit it, and neither will men. You'll either find a real creeper or hit the lottery but not both. That said..." He runs his finger beneath my chin. "Keep up the innocent look."

"... Does it work?"

"I don't know. I'm not a rapist, but purity looks good on you."

In short, we become friends as my one meager attempt at dating ends up going nowhere. I'm put off, full of despair, and frankly, done with romance. I'm not getting anywhere.

I know it is one date. But better to pull out (no pun intended) now before I have a dozen, leading to a downward spiral of my unworthiness. It isn't confidence or even a self-esteem thing. The lack of men I find attractive on multiple levels is a real problem.

Take José.

He's good looking, friendly, and employed, but after speaking with him for several hours, he is way too metrosexual for my tastes. Almost gender fluid. A better fit for Spencer than me.

And that is the problem.

Everyone knows exactly who they are and what they are looking for these days. Subsequently, it's like looking for a needle in the manure stack. Hay is way too kind of a word for what we're dealing with. It isn't just the missing puzzle piece; the piece was never made.

Dorky guys ignite my mind; buff guys bring on the waterfall between my thighs. Having that—*in one package*—together? Near impossible. Needle. Shit pile.

Unmanufactured puzzle piece.

Something is always *missing*.

José is absent of the masculine bravado I desire to sweep me off my feet. His lack of understanding old school courting techniques is a no-go, which means I may as well return to soliciting for a monster.

His attraction to me was about as fleeting as mine for him. He thought I was pretty but real chemistry? We didn't have it. He managed to compliment my physique by telling me I had a nice rack and ass. I told him he had a nice smile. He's a pretty boy who would do well in a gay disco with tight pants and a g-string.

But that's the thing.

I can assess what everyone else needs, but knowing what I need?

Fuck it.

After washing our cups, he departs with a hug and words that would haunt my mind for hours. "Save your dick sucking for someone who earned it."

Would my rapist earn it?

It doesn't matter. At least, not in my mind.

Spencer and his flavor of the month (the one on the landing) are heading for dinner and a show. I note the twinkle in Spencer's eyes; he is checking out José.

Great.

A love connection.

Just not my own.

The three chat for a minute. Flavor's name is Rod. I think I'll stick with Flavor. Or maybe expand it to Flavored Rod. I have no doubt there will be a lot of banging going on next door.

Gay ménage, anyone?

I'll get the rundown from Spencer in a few days. The odd thing is in the cluster of Spencer, Flavored Rod, and José—José proves to be quite the man. Dare I say, gentleman? It's weird. He'll extend his arm for them but refuse to open a door for me.

Interpersonal gender dynamics are fascinating.

One girl's trash is another man's prince charming, or something like that.

I can break it down even further.

My baby sister, Daphne, is the apple of my mother's eye. They're best friends—lunch dates, hair appointments, trips to the spa, and vacations for the two of them.

Mom and me?

We barely know each other's names. She'd never go on a luxurious European train trip with me or have our nails done together while we gossiped over the latest headlines on the trashy magazines.

Sadly, I'll sit with Brandon and analyze the hell out of our existence over a whiskey bottle because that is who I am. Bran is my person. I didn't know about rehab, but I knew he was considering it when I brought up the ad.

He knows.

And he thinks I am crazy.

I think he is crazy for following our Dad's genetic trait—*both of them*—booze and philandering. We grew up with the knowledge of our Dad's affairs. They started after Alan passed when my mother essentially died. Brandon has a few memories, those precious moments, where he remembers her happy and whole.

Alan's death broke my family.

I should have healed her, but fate wasn't so friendly, and it would be five years later before the presence of Daphne would cauterize the wound.

I seek refuge in a hot bubble bath with my favorite explicit piece of fiction. It was written by (presumably) some girl online and always brought waves of pleasure to my aching core.

Not tonight.

Tonight, I want the real thing.

Tonight, I want dick.

But not just any dick.

A certain special kind of wielder.

I toss the papers from the edge of the tub and watch as they scatter to the tile floor. Tears brim in my eyes as I scan over the typical dating website. Far too many of them begin with—*Good Looking Guy Seeks Companion*—but one catches my attention—Lost Soul Hoping to Find Another.

I click the link and read his appealing spiel but no picture, no way.

My toe pulls the drain plug as I leave the dating site and click my want ad back on. I'll find someone, or I'll find a grave.

One or the other.

And either is okay with me.

5

BE STILL

JYNX

SITTING AT THE DOWER WEDDING'S OVERCROWDED outdoor reception, I smile at the bride and groom dancing. They're a cute couple appearing as though they belong together. I attended the hour-long service, which was beyond boring—a stupendous snoozer of splendor. I have been at the reception for thirty minutes when I decide I cannot take anymore fake.

Just fake—everything.

Fake conversations. Fake smiles. Fake hairpieces. Fake shelves packed into fake knock-off dresses made by fake legal workers—undoubtedly children—in some factory in a foreign country.

Fucking fake—*I can't stand that shit.*

I have made an appearance, and that is enough to say Monroe Consulting cares.

We don't.

And neither do I.

That's fucking fake as well, and that makes me a hypocrite because I happen to enjoy the authentic dollars they put in my bank account —*so I fake it.*

Perfectly sensible, right?

Wang is causing all kinds of trouble with the bridesmaids, and I think he may end up taking all nine of them back to his hotel room for an old fashioned gang bang.

Despite the lackluster attendees, the reception's remote location is fantastic, with a cliffside view of the ocean and big beautiful trees dotting the landscape.

The white waves draw my attention.

I'd rather be out on a sailboat than hobnobbing with this elitist bunch. I do not need to stay for the cutting of the cake—overpriced and rather gaudy—or the toss of the garter—probably fragrant with plenty of hoe-logne.

While I have been known to dance, I won't amongst this crowd because no one is worth the honor. I polish off my second bourbon and depart from the table with proper niceties.

On my way to the nearest exit, I loosen my tie and undo a few buttons on my shirt before popping my sunglasses on. The sun is too bright, too happy, too cheerful for me.

A white delivery van blocks the main path as I rush to detour around the back and bound my six-three frame into a petite woman carrying a full case of wine.

Who am I kidding?

She's not a woman; she's a girl—a damn kid.

"Excuse me! Shit! I am so sorry," I mutter as her enormous hazel eyes flicker with intrigue. They're mesmerizing spheres of wonder.

Her blonde hair is piled high, but a few stray tendrils have fallen to dangle upon her shoulders covered in a sheer white blouse. I notice the peek of white lace in the dip of her cleavage. Her plentiful handfuls bounce as she jars back from unexpectedly running into me.

"I'm sorry!" Her soft feminine voice whispers through the air like a calming breeze soothing my senses and easing my stress. "I parked in the path because I had so many boxes."

Please don't ever stop talking.

She's stunning but far too young. A worker, part of the catering team—*the help*—and very fucking real. One glimpse of her tiny frame, and I question her ability to carry an entire case of wine alone. I'm not a gentleman, but I am a decent human being.

"Do you need assistance?"

Get away from her, J.

"Nah," she mutters with a smile trapped beneath the most innocent pink pout I've ever seen. "Thank you, though."

"You don't even look old enough to drink," I absentmindedly mumble. She giggles as I notice the logo on the back of the van—*The Vinery at The Village*. My mind conjures up the possibility of her being the crazy ad girl. I don't ask about the box again. I carefully remove it from her hands and take the situation into my own.

"I was supposed to have assistants, but they called in sick."

"How many more boxes?"

"This is the last of fifteen," she says, leading the way to the kitchen.

And no one thought to help you?

Stop caring, J.

Cease, now.

"Lot of work for one," I say as she opens the door. "I'm sorry none of these bastards helped you."

She generously grins. "Thank you so much."

"You're welcome," I reply, setting the box down. "Anytime."

Do not go there, asshole.

Following me out, she chirps, "Have a good day!"

Dammit, she's pleasant.

Stripping out of my jacket, I walk to the rental car, trying to put the girl with the mesmerizing eyes out of my mind.

Do not turn around. You know she's staring. Do not do it.

Glancing back, I catch her waving and smiling. I do nothing but speed away to the nearest gas station with shaky hands. I buy a pack of smokes and a lighter before moving the car to a crowded grocery store parking lot.

Stepping out, I light my first cigarette in almost a decade.

It's long overdue.

"You can't look it up..." I mumble, sensing how right my intuition feels. "Hell!" I breathe, pulling my phone from the console and putting in directions to The Village. It's less than half an hour away. "Don't do this, J."

The phone rings in my palm. It's Axel. "How was the wedding?"

"Disgustingly loving."

"Did you get laid?"

"No, fuckface, I left early."

"I've been watching rape girl," he says as I roll my eyes and lay my arms on the roof of the car and rest my head in my hands. Sometimes my brother has a unique way of wording things.

"I don't want to know, do I?"

"She took the ad down at one point," he informs what I already knew. "Edited and reposted. This poor girl will end up dead or sold."

I close my eyes and see hers. "No shit."

"You need to stop," he warns, detecting the conflict in my voice. Axel knows me way too well. "You cannot do this."

"How do you even know I am thinking about it?"

"Because I know you, Jynx, and you're in Northern California," he replies, snickering. "This one is screaming your name, but if you go back to being the guy you were at twenty-five, then you might as well give up everything you've worked for because you will lose it all."

"She's too young," I excuse, wanting to believe I can stay true to the lie. "I haven't even thought about the ad."

I don't bother to tell him how much I already know.

Or that I haven't been back to Madame Tilda's because my leased apartment in Phoenix looks like a stalkers haven.

Or that she didn't bother to hide her IP address, and I know her entry point, and therefore, her address.

Or that I've been in Northern California every weekend for the last month.

I already used up all of my saved tokens in the jar for this one.

And I'm the only one who understands—*it's too late to stop me.* The hunger, the craving, the desire—it's already there. I have been *watching* and waiting.

"Have you seen her?"

"No," I say, snarling. I tell myself that the girl at the reception wasn't her, even though I know it was. Pure accident. Fate. "You seem to think I want to go back to the slammer."

"You've had some issues in the past."

Issues involving one specific girl over a decade ago.

I should've swiped her when I had the chance.

But by that point, it was too late.

I was arrested for stalking.

Her name was Celeste Albatross, and I had been watching over her for years. To most, she was just another nameless nineteen-year-old girl from the wrong side of the tracks.

Four days after my incarceration, a group of guys brutally raped and murdered her in the woods.

I wasn't a killer.

I was a stalker.

Problem?

I ain't got one.

At first, I was accused of her murder until the dumbasses realized the timeline didn't add up. Three days post-mortem, the coroner finally released their estimations that she had been dead for twelve hours when they found her body, and I was behind bars at the time of death.

For three days, they badgered and harassed me.

Three days they could've been chasing down the real killer.

Three days they gifted to that bastard.

He escaped.

That son of a bitch got away with it. Enough money and power in Daddy's back pocket—*disappearing wasn't a challenge.*

Charles "Chuck" Tullen, Jr.'s father was a senator. And Chuck was also my best friend. He hasn't been back to the States since, and Celeste wasn't significant enough to warrant his extradition.

The bandwagon of bad boys—Chuck, Fitz, Vice, Axel, and me— had been hanging out and causing mischief since high school. We broke into empty houses, stealing whatever we could get our hands-on, and selling pretty pills to the kids on campus.

Fitz's father was the police chief, and he was more concerned about his wife's deteriorating health battle with MS. His son's behavior fell by the wayside as he turned the other cheek and looked away.

We agreed from the beginning that we'd never have girlfriends unless we would share. We liked to party—booze and drugs with one hot girl and our five. Typically, the girls were more than willing because we ran the fucking town and had since high school.

I was the instigator, the leader of our bullying brotherhood—stupid teenage boy shit that carried on into young adulthood.

At fifteen, Celeste was the most beautiful girl in town. Unfortunately, she was just as reckless as we were. She loved a party, and I started keeping an eye on her.

Celeste always resisted our advances as a whole, but privately, she and I became friends. She wanted more, but I refused.

For one, I was six years older than her and a troublemaker. And two, I didn't want to have to share with my heathens.

Instead of dumping my fake friends and having a real relationship with Celeste, I kept an eye on her, which morphed into stalking to keep her safe.

A good guy shrouded in bad.

At night, I fantasized about abducting Celeste, having her all to myself. I quickly found release in private, but I kept my shit in check publicly. I never would've hurt her like they did because I was very much in love with Celeste.

Out of spite from my rejection, she reported my valiant, dedicated efforts to the police for the third time—*the last time*—and Fitz's father randomly decided to act on it.

Before the night of her murder, I—*alone*—determined who, when, and where we would hit. My gang should never have been anywhere near Celeste.

Chuck kidnapped Celeste with Fitz and Vice in tow. He drove them out to the woods, where they proceeded to rape, stab, and strangle Celeste. Fitz and Vice confessed to the rape and ratted out Chuck to receive lesser charges. Chuck committed the gruesome killing.

I don't know if I believe them.

I don't think about it much anymore.

My brother wasn't involved in the ordeal because he was busy trying to figure out how to bust me out of jail from the stalking charges. Our parents were living a luxurious life in Europe and building my inheritance—Monroe Consulting.

He wound up calling our drug supplier, Victor Cruz, who was also Deacon's father and President of the Reckless Rebellion MC. Uncle Victor hired my defense team, but I managed to spend eight months behind bars because I liked to fight.

And at that point, I was pretty damn angry at all that had gone down. My attorney convinced the judge that I was of no danger to anyone because my sole obsession was deceased.

After I was released, I hooked up with a group that ran for RR known as the Tennessee Twelve and never looked back. I took Axel's ass with me because he didn't need the bullshit of my parent's life-style any more than I did.

I put in the work.

I sobered up.

I cleaned up.

And I stayed the fuck away from any serious relationships by learning to crack code. I traded stalking for hacking, learning a lot along the way.

When I discovered one of Dad's trusted employees skimmed off the pot and could prove it with hard data, Dad finally forgave my roughshod youth and hired me.

That was eight years ago.

I never broke the oath in our pact of thieves. I never told the police that my friends premeditated the torture of Celeste that night out of revenge.

Chuck was jealous because Celeste was in love with me. He killed her to hurt me and prove that he was a big man.

Big man on the run is what he is.

Love sucks.

And I refuse to ever fall again.

6

HIT THE VEIN

ECHO

THE DAY AFTER MY GRADUATION, I STARE AT THE AD ONE final time early in the morning as my duffel sits packed for the trip to Las Vegas with Selia. We have front row seats for a show tonight that I don't want to miss, but she is taking her own sweet time in the shower. I pick through my makeup, tossing more into my purse than I will ever need. She opens the door, and I hand her a towel.

Touching my shoulder, Selia asks, "How much longer are you leaving the ad up?"

"Only until fall term."

"You accepted the invitation for your doctorate?"

"I did," I reply with a smile. "Dr. Abigail Maines."

"You're doing the right thing," she says, drying her hair. "Are you ready to go?"

I glance at her ridiculously athletic figure. To say she is a buff is an understatement. The girl could enter competitions if she wanted to. My hourglass isn't bad, but I'm not Selia. I'm mortifyingly top heavy. I typically wear baggy sweaters and hoodies, keeping the girls covered unless I'm at work. Morgan prefers her employees to look professional in white shirts and slacks.

"Yeah," I respond, feeling a tad insecure. "But I suggest you put on some clothes."

"Are your parents leaving?"

"They're at the airport now," I mutter, disheartened. "Fly in late Friday night and out by eight on Sunday morning."

"I am sorry, Ek."

I hold back my tears. "Don't be. They cannot stand one another. Mother must be shopping, and Dad must be with one of his lovers, or they make everyone miserable."

"Why do they even bother to stay together?"

"Because Dad feels like he owes Mom for dealing with Alan and Caroline's death. Little do they realize, we all would've been better off if they'd split years ago."

She drops the towel and rummages in the closet. "What about Daphne?"

"She's headed to Alabama, starting college over the summer, just to get away from them," I inform. "And poor Brandon is stuck in damn rehab."

"You should go see him and help your sister out."

"... Me?"

"Yeah," she suggests, dressing. "We'll go to the show in Vegas tonight and have a good time. I'll fly back. You drive to Alabama and take care of your siblings because you, my dear, are far better than either of your parents."

I repeatedly blink. "... You want me to drive to Birmingham?" I sound like the idea is kooky as she nods with a big grin. I pick up my phone. "It's over two thousand miles and two days of hard driving!" I whine as the idea flickers in my mind. While intriguing, I'm not the kind of girl to drive across the country on a whim. That's Selia. Maybe I need to loosen up. Morgan said I needed to get to know myself. "I can't do that!"

"Why? You have a brand new car that Daddy bought you. And you have driven, what? Two miles a day for four months? Get out on the open road. Clear your head. See your brother. Help out your sister. You have three months before you have to be back here."

I scramble to find excuses. "What about The Vinery?"

"Morgan will give you time off," she persists, pulling on the skin-tight jeans and slipping on the stilettos—*for the boost*. I understand all too well. We'll end up destroying our feet by fifty just to have thirty-five years of slightly less than average height. "She adores you. Tell her you have a personal family issue that you need to tend to."

I don't know what to say.

If Brandon ever stands a chance of healing, he will need the support of family, and I'm quite possibly the only one who cares enough to visit him.

"Fuck," I mumble as she tosses her extra-large suitcase on the bed.

"Pack your shit while I finish getting ready so we can get the fuck out of here. An overnight bag to Vegas will not cover a couple of weeks in Alabama."

Another minute passes, and I whisper, "I love you, Sel."

"I know you do," she says, putting on a blouse with no bra. It doesn't matter because she has no cleavage. "And I love you, too. Now, trust me on this one. Take your pretty new gas-guzzling 4x4 SUV, your Daddy's credit card, and drive."

"He'll kill me," I mutter, glancing at Selia.

We both shake our heads with mischievous grins and simultane-ously cackle, "No, he won't!"

"He was so proud of you," she adds, smiling. "There is no way that man would say two words about his dear daughter doing anything. You're the star in his eyes."

"I should call and tell him."

"You can do that on the road tomorrow," she says, blotting a little makeup on. "I'm going to be waiting for you if you don't start packing!"

"I'm on it!"

"That's my girl!"

And I hit publish—*one final time.*

RAPIST WANTED

Vibrant college graduate, 20-something adult female seeks any race/21+/professional male for a sexual encounter.

You are:

Natural Dominant. Alpha. Male.

No nerds, truckers, wannabes, virgins, or bikers. Professional-types, athletes, and bad boys welcome.

Pure ravishment, abduction, and torture scenes. No personal communication is necessary.

I am:

Brunette. Hazel eyes. Looks like the All-American girl next door, cheerleader type, innocent. Physically active, runs the park loop in the evening. Social gatherings downtown every weekend. Works at The Village. Physical passed. No drugs or diseases. Psychological screenings passed.

I offer my body for use at your discretion with complete confidence. Again, no exchange of names or personal information is required. I do not wish to know your name, your dog's name, or your prior relationship record. I am not looking to date, have an affair, or engage in a romance.

All that is required by you is a willingness to control the scene and a hard cock.

No authorities will be involved. All reward, no risk situation for the right suitor appreciating violent sexual encounters.

I agree to struggle, play the role of victim, and provide you with a challenge. You agree to use protection, not bruise any flesh above the neck or below the wrists, and incite fear in me. If I do not entertain your advances, I will cause a commotion, using any means to show non-consent, and do anything in my power to flee. Again, no authorities will be contacted.

Obviously, due to the nature of the request, no references are available.

If interested, please do not contact me.

Just surprise me.

JYNX

UNDER THE LIGHTS OF THE CASINO, I SMUGLY GRIN AT THE ad she updated hours ago. I've managed to rack up quite the stack of chips at the blackjack table. "Are you out, Sir?"

I snicker and shake my head at her ending hook—*Just surprise me.* I check my watch. "I've been here for the last eight hours. I should grab some food."

She whispers, "I'm off in an hour if you're interested."

"Thanks, Millie." She is cute, but her type speaks of missionary and not much more. "I appreciate it, but I may meander The Strip for a bit."

"You're welcome, Jynx."

I've been quite the naughty boy since attending the Dower wedding. I went back to Phoenix, packed up all my shit, and prepared for the contract to end. We had a grand time Friday and Saturday celebrating, even though all I could think about was attending *her* graduation—her in nothing but the cap, gown, a sexy pair of heels, and riding me for hours.

Congratulations, sweetheart.

Here is a present of my cum.

Nah, I'm not that much of a douche. If I was her suitor—*not that I do such ever*—there would've been jewelry with amethyst—*her birthstone*—and loads of cum. Diamonds and amethysts if I planned on hitting all three holes.

But I wasn't that guy.

Boyfriend material.

Gag. Kill me now.

Wang already took his flight back to Chicago this morning, but I decided to stay for a couple of extra days to indulge—trip to the spa, a few bottles of bourbon, countless chips. She graduated with her Master's in Psych, and I'm celebrating—for a girl I don't know.

Life was good as I attempted to drown the thoughts of a girl I could do nothing about.

I was trading problems again, but I was good at it. Empty glasses and stacks of money offered up a pleasant reprieve. I had hacked into her—*Abigail Renata Maines, who they call Echo*—but what could I do?

I found out from the friendly wine shop manager, Morgan, that the source of my stumble and subsequent remission from all logic would be visiting Vegas for a few days with her friend. I wasn't sure what I was hoping for, but the rush of adrenaline was intoxicatingly delicious. I hadn't felt this alive since I was twenty-five, spying in a window at a naked teenage girl in the middle of the night.

I was losing my shit fast.

But fuck if I was about to stop now.

After all, I had come this far. I was damn steadfast in my downward spiral. If I was circling the drain, I was determined to hit rock bottom at supersonic speed and end this with a fabulous assault.

What can I say?

I was born bad.

But was I *that* bad?

What I didn't know is if I could get away with it. Her ad said no authorities would be informed, but what were the odds?

I had to trust the girl trusting the untrustworthy.

In the evening sun, I light a smoke and walk toward her hotel. I'll play a few rounds and scout it out. I end up grabbing a burger and finding a relatively secluded spot to watch the passing crowds.

I don't give off the aura of a deranged psychopath in my black slacks and starched shirt. I appear like a damn white collar, which I guess I am on the surface, but the truth is I cannot wait to be home— barefoot in jeans and a t-shirt. I've spent far too many weeks in dress clothes.

About forty-five minutes later, a horde of people emerges from the performance hall. They're all glammed up and ready to lay it down on the tables. The energy is infectious amongst them as I note the two young girls giggling.

"Oh, Jesus," I mutter, wiping my mouth. "There she is..."

I throw my half-eaten burger in the trash as I follow her from a distance. Her new hair color—a frozen chocolate hue—sets off her pale skin and incredible features.

Crap, I'm losing my shit.

What am I thinking about doing?

If possible, she's even more lovely than before. And far more innocent looking than I remember.

What the fuck am I doing in Vegas stalking this girl?

They stop and play the slot machines, but I hang back and observe her from a distance. God, I would love to stick my dick in her wetness and be the one to give her exactly what she wants. But how?

You're pushing the sanity limit, J.

"Shut up," I mumble under my breath.

I catch myself smiling when she wins. She is cheerful, joyous, and happy.

And you're the asshole that is going to hurt her—forever.

I think about my internal dilemma—someone could make her unhappy for the rest of her life as long as the ad is up. That much is guaranteed. Some putz will take advantage of this poor girl, just like Chuck hurt Celeste, and Echo may not live through it.

Her precious smile will vanish.

God, J—what are you thinking about doing?

Reasoning with myself, I pace between the boutique and the pizza joint. If I do the deed, she will likely pull down the ad, but I am a stalker. I get off on the thrill of the hunt and the pursuit of the chase. I've never actually caught—*kidnapped or abducted*—anyone. First time for everything, right?

God's honest truth is—*I've never raped anyone.*

I can be violent with belligerent males, but nothing like this.

Never toward a woman.

Jesus Fucking Christ, what am I thinking about doing?

Nothing I haven't thought about a million times before.

I sit down, feeling slightly lightheaded, and contemplate my next move. She cannot keep doing this, but persuading a twenty-two-year-old girl to do anything else will only cause her rebellion. I know; I was twenty-two once. A very long time ago.

Shit.

With my elbows on my knees, I bend my head down, only to look up and spot her, making a beeline for me. Her friend walks over to the slot machines, and Echo stands still, staring in my direction. I hope she doesn't remember me, but I note the tilt of her head as I shake mine once.

Don't do this, girl.

I've been close to guys who do the shit you're begging for—*don't do it.*

Please, I'll beg you not to go through with it.

I long to sit with her over coffee and tell her how perfect she is and that she doesn't need a scheme because plenty of great guys would kill to have a chance with a girl like her.

She could be my fucking daughter for chrissakes.

We're fourteen years apart; she will never listen; this will only land my ass back in prison.

I rack up the excuses trying to talk myself down.

She hasn't met the one yet.

He is on the way, but she has no patience because of her youth.

Just wait, pretty girl.

I beg, plead, and bargain with the devils in the darkness, knowing they're my brethren—*my kind.* The perfect guy will show up when she least expects it. Just hold on for a little bit longer.

I can't decide if I'm rooting for her to hook up with a random guy. Or praying he isn't me.

One very bad man is considering doing something horrifically vile to save you.

She smiles and turns away, not knowing I know or that I've cracked into the system and been stalking her for weeks.

I'm the fucking villain.

I stand and spot her checking me out; I'm the guy she should be running from, not flirting with.

Run far away, girl!

Don't grin at me.

Don't taunt the wicked.

We're so far apart...so far away...so many years.

I'm almost forty, and she's barely over twenty.

I know better.

And that is why—*I cannot do this.*

7

DON'T MAKE ME

JYNX

I CHECK OUT OF THE HOTEL AND GRAB A CUP OF COFFEE. I need an open road to prevent suffocation. I have to get my head on straight.

I don't want to be in a crowded airport waiting on an overbooked flight with that much obtuse energy surrounding me. I want away from it all, including my mind.

I put my bags in the back of the sports car. I brought the old dogged out girl up from Phoenix. The rental company won't give a shit which location I leave it at as long as I pay the damn bill.

I sit down, situating everything—from putting my coffee in the holder to opening my water bottle. I crank on an eighties rock and roll mix, roll down the windows, and open the roof. I put my sunglasses on.

I must drive to exorcise the fucking demons manifesting inside of me.

Backing up, I notice her waiting on the valet.

"Where the fuck are you going, Echo?" I pull off to the side and wait as she nervously shifts her weight between her feet. "Why are you so anxious?" She smiles as the black SUV pulls up. "Mama-mobile," I snicker. "You should go, J. Forget that hot piece of ass that you shouldn't have anything to do with and get the hell out before you drown." I shake my head, arguing with myself. "But if I leave, she's as good as dead."

Fuck it.

I light a smoke.

I'll pay the fucking cleaning bill.

She zips out of the lot like a damn race car driver, and I hit the gas. I don't know where the fuck we're going, but I follow her ass. She drives like a maniac, whipping in between cars and heading out to the freeway.

South on 93, we do more than 90.

We're going to get pulled over.

"You sound like such an old fuddy-duddy," I laugh, knowing I have a suped-up drag car sitting in the garage at home. I wish I had some clue as to where we were racing. She's veering through traffic and finally gets into the fast lane. By accident, I end up directly behind her ass.

And the bitch brake checks me.

I have a good mind to flip her off and dust her because she won't keep up with me. We're stuck behind a semi, doing seventy when I spot her a car length distance and swerve into the right lane. I wait for her—not because I am a gentleman—but I'm having a damn good time fucking with this girl.

She dodges in front of me and floors it.

I never knew a Mama-mobile could do that in those hands; I stand corrected.

I'm chain-smoking and losing ground because if I keep following her so close, she's bound to know. Hell, maybe she already does.

Again, I say—*fuck it*.

Only this time, I whip past her and take the lead. "I ought to brake check you."

She grins at me.

Yeah, she knows.

I tap'em.

And she flashes her brights at me.

Goddamn, she's a piece of work.

The traffic clears up when we hit I-40, but she is still shadowing me. The problem is—I have no idea where in the hell we're going. She's zipping around as we hit a good open road. "What are you doing, girl?"

She darts around my car and flashes her damn tits. *Jesus. Help. Me.* I grin and point for her to take the lead.

We're driving, with me following and having a grand time for several hours. She is bouncing in her chair, probably singing, while I play watchdog to make sure this poor girl doesn't kill herself. I don't know what the fuck I am doing. I'm taking it as it comes, on the fly, and crossing my fingers.

Half an hour out of New Mexico, she slithers over to the far right lane and exits. "Shit."

Her car screeches at the curb of the shoddy looking gas station, and I lurk off to the side in the parking lot, waiting on her. "I gotta pee!"

Keep in mind, this girl doesn't know who the fuck I am—but she also doesn't seem to care. As she opens the gas station door, I bravely step out and yell, "Give me your keys!"

She tosses them, and I catch.

I move my car and hers to the gas pumps and fill them. I check her tires and wash her windows. "What the fuck am I doing?" I ask myself again as I scrub her back window.

"I don't know, but thank you."

"Where the hell are you going?" I ask, drying the edge with a paper towel.

"Birmingham."

"Why?" I ask, not looking at her. I can't. She's too damn beautiful with her hair pulled back in a ponytail.

"My brother is in rehab. How old are you?"

"Thirty-six, child," I reply with a grin, dropping the squeegee in the bucket and pulling out my phone. "Let me drop this bitch off in Albuquerque, and I'll help you get there. I can fly home from Bama."

She giggles, "Where is home?"

"South Carolina."

"You're native Southern," she guesses, wrongly. I don't bother to correct her. I reluctantly glance up at her as I remove the pump from her tank. She's chewing on her lip. "Do you have a name?"

"Not one you need to know."

"So you want me to let you drive my car to Birmingham, but you won't tell me your name?"

"Call me J."

"Okay, J, I am A."

Liar.

She hands me a water bottle and a bag of sunflower seeds from the black plastic bag on her arm. "Do I look hungry?"

"You look like the kind of guy who eats sunflower seeds," she replies, getting in the car. She shuts the door and quickly rebounds back to my side, grinning at me. "You have my keys, J."

"I do." I grin, opening the bag and taking a mouthful of seeds. "You want them?"

"Please?"

"Are you going to trust me?"

"Yes."

"Why?"

"Because you keep showing up—the Dower wedding and Las Vegas —was it coincidence or purposeful?"

I arch my brows and defiantly smirk. "Wouldn't you like to know?"

"I would," she says, grinning. "But you're not going to tell me."

"Nope," I reply. "I gotta piss. If you're interested in having me get you safely to Birmingham, don't fucking leave, E."

I wink.

ECHO

SITTING IN THE CAR, I WAIT UNTIL HE DISAPPEARS INSIDE. My hands tremble with the suspicion that he knows about the ad.

God, he's freaking perfect.

I hit the gas as I spot him in the checkout line. He shakes his head.

"How bad do you want it, asshole?"

I enter the freeway and soar. I could take an alternate route, but I have never done this—*any of this.* I call Selia and explain the whole story of the wedding until now.

Her only response, "Is he cute?"

"I don't fucking know!" I yell, spotting the sports car several cars back. "I haven't gotten close enough to him to know. He's mysterious, dangerous, and sexy as hell."

"You're a fool if you do not find out what this guy wants," she scolds. "You've been waiting for some low-life to have seedy sex in all your holes, this guy buys your fucking gas, and you ghost his ass? What the fuck is wrong with you?"

"I'm scared," I whimper as my palms slick on the steering wheel. "He's big."

"Hopefully, in all areas, if you know what I mean."

"Selia!"

"You didn't say—I want a little rapist. It would help if you thought about that earlier. From what you've told me, he more than fits all of your criteria. I say get on that D and ride until it ejects you."

"You're of no help."

"Look, you're the one who wanted someone to assault you. You knew, you even said, he would be a stalker. This guy is clearly stalking you. You got exactly what you asked for!"

"No," I say, crying. "This guy is right behind me and grinning from ear to ear, Selia."

"And if you recall, I told you, one slip of the tongue and you would run like the wind, which is what you're doing. Stop freaking. Have some fun with the guy. Loosen up. He bought your gas. He's not going to chop you into bits."

"But I'm alone!"

"Uhh," she stutters. "You were going to be alone in an alleyway being raped too, sweetheart."

"How do you know he's not going to kill me?"

"Because it is quite apparent that he has a working heart, and he cares," she assesses. "And again, you're a fool if you let this one go."

"Shit."

I hang up the phone and drive for another two hours to outside of Albuquerque with a strange man following me. I zip off on a farm to market road and stop in a deserted parking lot. I step out, and he does the same.

"I will let you take me to Birmingham."

"You left," he chastises, slowly approaching me. "Why?"

"Because you scared me."

"Did I scare you, or did you scare yourself?"

"Both," I honestly reply. "Lead the way to the car rental company."

I feel his steady gaze on me, but I can't look up. His finger lifts my chin. "I'm not going to kill you."

"… Is that a promise?"

"Yes," he says and I nod. Surprisingly, he pulls me into his arms, holding me close. My God, he smells divine like musk and sandalwood with a hint of spice. "I've got you, Echo."

It's perhaps the greatest words anyone has ever said to me.

"You know my name."

"I know many things," he says, smirking and walking me to the car. He opens my door. "Follow me."

"You're a gentleman."

"Hardly."

Why do I do it?—*I don't know.*

There is something about him that I trust. Gut instinct or stupidity. I feel that we're together for a reason, and if I don't try, even if I get hurt, I will regret it for the rest of my life.

I would find someone or find a grave—*and I believed it.*

Half an hour later, we drop his car off, and I pop the tailgate for his bags. He sets them inside of my car before returning the keys to the office. He jogs around to my door and opens it. "I'm driving."

"Okay," I reply, getting out, as he lights a smoke. "You can do that in my car."

"Are you sure?" he confirms, walking me to the other side. He opens the passenger door. "Don't call me a gentleman again."

"Yeah," I giggle, sitting down. "Selia smokes her weed in here."

He darts around the front and plops in the driver's seat. "If you're sure."

I pull the special ashtray cup out of my door compartment and stick it in the console where my bottle of water was. "I'm not sure of much anymore."

"I gathered that much," he replies, tossing his sunglasses on the dash. His blue eyes spark at mine. "What's your brother in rehab for?"

"He's an alcoholic. A surprise visit from his sister."

He nods and looks away. "Been there. Done that." We sit for an awkward minute of silence. "Are you hungry?"

"I should probably eat."

He surveys the area filled with fast-food establishments. "Taco?"

"That's fine," I say, smiling as he grabs my hand resting on my thigh. I stare at the setting sun, casting an ombre drift of yellow to pink through the sky. "Thank you."

"Do you want to stop for the night?"

I open and close my mouth several times as the blush rises on my cheeks. "I...I don't know...that's up to you."

"I'll get us a couple of rooms in Amarillo."

"How do you know I won't leave your ass?"

"I can catch a plane," he informs, without any emotion. "You won't catch another me."

I lick my lips, knowing he's right. "One room is fine."

"Okay," he says, tugging his phone from his pocket. "I'll feed you and provide shelter."

"Sounds like heaven."

JYNX

I BOUGHT HER DINNER—THREE SUPREME TACOS THAT SHE scarfed down like a starving child—and she passed out as I drove into Texas. The roads were relatively empty, which was a good thing because I needed to figure out what I was doing with her.

If I left her in Birmingham, which a gentleman would do, she would end up back in Northern California with her ad still posted while I was in South Carolina.

See my problem?

She's sawing logs while I smoke, drive, and think. I can't let her go back to California. That's a death sentence. Even if she survives a rape, the act will destroy her innocence. She didn't ask me to be her hero, so I must be the monster. We wound up together by fate, but I cannot let this one go.

She may ruin me.

But rewards don't come without risks.

A win with her is worth it to me.

I pull up to the hotel and run inside to check us in. When I return, she's awake. "Sleep well?"

"Yeah," she whispers. "I can't thank you enough for all of this."

She won't be saying that very much longer.

I'm about to be the dick of a lifetime, but in doing so, I might get through her thick skull that what she thinks she wants isn't what she needs. I park near our room and grab our bags. "My name is Abigail, but everyone calls me Echo."

"I know," I reply, scanning the room key over the reader and opening the door. "Abigail Renata Maines."

"You know a lot."

"More than you think." We quietly ride the elevator up to the fourth floor and locate our room with one queen bed. "It was the best they had on such short notice."

"It's fine, considering."

"I'm not raping you," I inform as the door shuts, and I set down the bags. "Take a shower, change your clothes, or whatever. I'm going to smoke and get some ice."

Outside, I call Deacon and explain the situation. He only says, "Meet me in Lafayette tomorrow."

I don't argue that Lafayette is a bit out of my way, but I trust the guy. He's got a solution. Still, there are many hours between here and there, and somehow, I doubt the magic pill to her sleepy time is always three tacos.

I could be wrong.

I'll accidentally get lost in Texas and end up in southern Louisiana. Or maybe we jolly ride. Or who knows. But I will not let her go until someone says otherwise.

When I return to the room, she's brushing her damp hair and wearing cute pajamas. I set down the bucket of ice and grab a pillow for the loveseat. With concern, she says, "You're going to kill your neck on that thing."

"I'm not sleeping anywhere near you."

ECHO

I'M HURT BY HIS WORDS AND CRY INTO THE PILLOW AS I wrap the blanket around me. I'm so black-hearted that even he won't pursue me. A few minutes pass in the darkened room when he asks, "Why are you crying?"

"Because you won't sleep with me."

"I won't," he callously replies. "You're right."

"Not even have sex," I argue, sitting up and clicking on the light. I blink several times, adjusting to the brightness and staring at him. His inked, scarred arms and masculine chest sprinkled with hair prompt swoon worthy butterflies. "Holy shit…"

He tosses his feet to the floor and stands up in one swift move. My mouth gapes open as he steadily approaches. His ripped abs undulate with every breath, leaving me speechless. He clicks the light off, bringing on the pitch blackness.

Without warning, he dives on my body, pinning my hands down with his as he spreads my thighs. I can't stop him because I'm in too much shock. I long to lift my hips in exploration. I feel his warm breath hit my lip. "Is this what you want?"

"I've never had a guy on me."

"Wait…" he mutters. "You're a virgin?"

"I am," I admit as the tears stream down my cheeks. "I had a crush on a guy in high school. I was so focused on my studies and him that I never dated. He was a good Christian boy, vowed to abstinence. He ended up being valedictorian and was headed to some Ivy League school. I woke up the morning after we graduated to learn that he killed himself. Dating will never be my thing. Love will never be my thing. I need one time with a guy to take this fucking thing from me because I do not want it anymore."

"That's pretty warped."

"You don't understand," I cry. "The few friends I do have all talk about their sex lives, and I have nothing to compare it to. I need to know, so I never have to experience it again. I can't find a guy to fuck me to save my soul."

He snickers, "One and done?"

"Yes!" I say, laughing through my hysterical sobs. "One time."

"So, get a boyfriend?"

"You're not hearing me," I reply. "I don't want a boyfriend. I don't want any emotional commitment. I cannot handle that. I want a monster to breech the band, and I never want to see him again. Feelings only get me hurt. And love only gets me harmed."

"Echo," he mutters, petting my hair. "You need help."

"Just fuck me."

"I won't do that," he whispers, laying his forehead against mine. "But it's not because I don't want to." He moves, grinding his hips slightly against me. I feel his erection and bawl, knowing he refuses to use it on me. "I'm not the guy you're looking for."

"You're a guy with a hard dick," I say, sniffling. "You're *exactly* what I'm looking for."

"No, I'm not. I'm the bad guy, baby."

"Then you're the bad guy with a big heart."

"It's been an empty cage," he informs, rolling off of me. "For a very long time."

I cannot stop crying, but he doesn't leave.

He quietly lays beside me.

When I finally settle down, he holds my hand, which is more than anyone else has ever done for me. "Thank you, J."

"You're welcome," he mumbles. "Just don't call me a gentleman."

8

MENTAL MUTINY

Jynx

I WAKE UP IN THE HOTEL ROOM BEFORE DAWN. HER BODY IS way too close to mine—a few more inches and she would be clinging to me.

I quietly get up and glance at the clock—4:55 AM. I go to the bathroom and lock the door because I don't trust that she won't just magically appear in my shower out of desperation. And I don't know that I will be able to resist her advances again. I step into the steaming hot water, needing to clear my mind before an accident happens.

It took all of my willpower not to claim her last night.

I review the facts, once again, drilling them into my head. She's not my type at all. She's a bubbly dark cauldron, a chaotic mess of highs and lows, possessing zero stability. She's way too young with fourteen years between us; even if she has a particular maturity, that doesn't negate the life experience difference.

I was five-fingering shit out of houses when she was in diapers.

And that matters.

About the only thing she wins me over with is the fact that she is clean and neat. From eating her tacos in the car to abiding by a bedtime routine, this girl understands self-discipline and self-care but fails miserably on self-valuation on a social level.

It is non-existent.

Not even low.

Where someone should have filled her with love for herself, she holds a blank space.

Empty.

Vacant.

An assault is her solution, but after spending a few hours with her, I know that a random rape will decimate this girl. She isn't strong enough to handle the trauma.

What the fuck am I going to do with her?

I don't have a damn clue.

I didn't plan on raising a twenty-two-year-old girl into adulthood, but some greater power seems to believe I need Echo Maines in my life.

I grab the towel and wrap it around my waist, realizing in my rush to disappear from the bedroom that I forgot clothing. I take a deep breath, opening the door and hoping she is still asleep.

I am not getting that lucky.

Sitting up in bed, she smiles, holding a cup of coffee. "I made you one, but I didn't know what you liked in it."

"Black is fine," I gruffly reply as I feel the heat of her gaze on my body. "Thank you."

"You're welcome."

"Are you ready to go?"

"I will be as soon as I throw on some clothes," she says, tossing the covers and getting up to rustle through her bag. With her back to me, she pulls the shirt over her head, and I marvel at her swirling ink from her left shoulder blade running diagonally to beneath her shorts on the right side. She's full of surprises—*read: bubbling dark cauldron.* She glances in the mirror at me. Her forearm covers her breasts. "You want to see what you're missing out on?"

"No." I should look away.

Turn around, J.

Don't do this.

She bends and pulls down the cotton shorts, exposing everything.

Fuck.

Do not breathe.

Do not inhale.

Do not fucking move, bastard.

Her arm drops from her breasts as she straightens up, providing a full frontal view in the reflection—my dick throbs with determination beneath the towel.

"You're struggling with me."

"And you're not helping matters," I curtly remark, sipping my coffee. "Nice ink."

"Thank you," she says, pulling her hair down from the messy bun. The tips skirt the top of her ass.

"I would so pull that," I absentmindedly mumble. "I would jerk it just to hear you cry."

She spins, facing me. Her breasts offer a generous roundness with pronounced nipples as her waist tapers significantly, indented by abdominal muscles and a small belly button. Her gloriously full sex holds plentiful amounts of dark curls that intrigue my senses. Taking a step closer as my eyes drift over her graceful curves, she taunts, "You should, or prohibit your eyes from having sex with me."

"I can't," I admit with barely a whisper as she crawls on all fours to the middle of the bed. "Don't do that."

"Fuck me, J," she begs from her swollen, dampened lips. "You know you want to. I know you want to. And I want you to."

"I will not be putting my dick in you, Abigail."

Her eyes well with tears. "… Am I not enough?"

I move my arm that was concealing the shadow of my erection under the towel. "Do you see what you do to me?"

"So use it."

"No."

"Why?"

"It's not that simple," I respond, finishing my coffee. "Just because you are wet and I am hard doesn't mean that we should…that I should…take your virginity. You just want sex."

She sits back on her heels. "And you cannot say that you aren't the kind of guy who hasn't fucked just to have sex. You've used women. So use me."

"You're assuming a godawful amount."

"Tell me I'm wrong!"

"I can't," I say, stepping closer. "I have used multiple women in a night, but I will not use you."

"Why?" she screams as the droplets fall from her eyes. "Am I so grotesque that you won't do the deed?"

"I won't do the deed because you aren't a slut or a whore or a one-night stand."

"No," she snickers, shaking her head. "I'm not a fun girl. I'm the girl guys want to marry, not fuck."

"You act like that's such a bad thing."

"It is when all of my friends are getting it on!"

I furrow my brow. "You don't see how rare you are. How special you are…"

"I'm just a girl."

"No, you are not just a girl," I argue, standing at the side of the bed. "I'm just a guy. And you're so far out of my league. You don't want to be where I am."

"So I'm a mutant," she says with determination, sulking, as I put my finger under her chin and tip her head up. She avoids looking at me. "I should just become a nun."

Trying not to laugh, I smirk. "You're something else. Get dressed. Wear something comfortable. It will be a long day."

"This was our one chance."

"Don't be fatalistic."

"It was," she rallies. "We are alone in a hotel room. We won't get this chance again."

"Chances happen all the time," I inform like a wise old owl. "But that doesn't mean you need to take every single one. It will help if you have faith that more opportunities will show up, and they'll be even better than this. There is a perfect guy for you out there somewhere. But he isn't me. And I won't take what is his."

"Fuck you, J."

"Hate me," I sneer, wishing she would look at me. "It's the most passion you've shown."

"A naked girl is sitting in the middle of your hotel bed, and you won't fuck her. I don't know what that says about you, but if that's not passion..."

"It's not passion," I interrupt, scowling. "That girl is misbehaving, and you're a demanding cunt because she isn't getting what she wants. Throw a tantrum, babygirl. I'm not sticking anything of mine in you."

She lifts onto her knees and swings at me. I catch her arms, and we are face to face. "Take me home."

I narrow in to her supple lips and whisper with a low growl, "You have no idea what it is taking for me to not throw you down on this bed and have my way with you, do you? You're fucking beautiful. But I am not yours. And you damn sure haven't earned me."

Tears cascade down her rosy cheeks as I release her, walk away and cross my fingers that I did enough emotional damage to exhaust the girl.

I'll feed her and pray for her dreams.

ECHO

AFTER WE DRESS AND LEAVE THE HOTEL, I REALIZE HOW embarrassed I am by my actions. He is an absolute gentleman in my book, whether he acknowledges it or not. He opens my door, making sure I am comfortable and secure.

Selia is right; he cares.

He would never admit that, though.

"What can I feed you?" He starts the car and rubs his hands on his jeans. "Are you a granola/oatmeal type or a biscuit type?"

"I'm a bowl of cereal girl."

"Fair enough," he says, backing up. "How many bowls?"

He grins, and I do the same. "Depends on the mood. Sometimes one, sometimes three."

We laugh. "Favorite kind?"

"Frosted Flakes."

"Alright," he replies. "And juice or coffee?"

"Sparkling water, preferably fruit-flavored, no lemon."

"Got it," he says, pulling across the street to the large gas station. "I'll be right back. Do you eat sunflower seeds?"

"I prefer jerky or pork rinds."

He gets out, shuts the door, and quickly returns. "What kind of milk?"

"Whole or almond," I say, smiling. "I'll even do chocolate with Frosted Flakes."

I watch as he makes a dash for the entrance and holds the door for a woman carrying a baby. Glancing at the clock, I know Selia probably isn't up at 4:54 in the morning, but I call anyway. Surprisingly, she answers.

"Why are you up?"

"I haven't been to bed yet," she giggles as the water cuts off. "I am in the bathtub. Ben is here."

Oh. My. God.

"Shit is getting serious," I excitedly mutter. "You're falling..."

"Like you don't even know," she readily admits. "Problem is he is moving to Houston to play college ball."

Ben is eighteen to Selia's twenty-three.

They've been knocking boots on and off for about six months. He even took her to his senior prom. I understand the gap, but Benjamin Grant doesn't act like a typical teenage boy. He's more mature than me and brilliant beyond reason. His parents are both surgeons in San Francisco, and he is a heavenly biracial mix with a Caribbean father and a Thai mother—which is quite unusual for Selia. She generally avoids Asians—*her own kind*—like the damn plague.

"Did he ask you to go?"

"He didn't ask, per se, but we are talking about long-term plans."

"You have to go!" I blurt out as I stare at J, checking out. His chiseled biceps tease in the loose gray workout shirt. I shouldn't know that they hold magnificent swaths of ink. "He is thirty-six."

"And the problem with that?"

"I don't need a Sugar Daddy," I mumble, strumming my fingernails on the console. "And he doesn't need a kid to raise."

"You're not a kid, Ek. You've got your shit together except for that one little impromptu rape post, but you wouldn't be where you are if you hadn't done that. Is he offering to be one?"

"A rapist? A gentleman? Or a Sugar Daddy?"

Her exuberant laugh echoes in the bathroom. "All three!"

"He isn't offering anything but cereal and driving skills," I sass as he pays for the items. "But there is something about him."

"You want him."

"I don't know that I don't," I confess too quickly. "He's overcast with this dreamy, enigmatic magnetism."

"Enigmatic magnetism," she repeats, letting it flow sensually off of her tongue. "I like that. So I should go to Houston with hopes of becoming Selia Grant, and you should hang out with your stalker boyfriend until he reveals what the fuck he wants."

I laugh and find myself smiling. "I think I might. I'll call you later. Get some sleep."

"Love you!"

"Same!"

He returns to the car with two bags full of stuff. "I bought you whole milk."

"Thank you," I giddily say. "I'll give you some money."

"I don't need your money," he replies, opening the milk and cereal before handing me a spoon. "I want you happy. What kind of music?"

"Usually, alternative stuff."

"Today, you're listening to country," he says, giving the bowl to me. "And feasting on flakes."

"What are you eating?"

"Protein shake."

I wrinkle my nose as he takes a swallow. "Have you ever had it?" I shake my head. "Try it. Just a sip. It's not what you think."

I take a taste, twitch my lips, and pour some in my cereal, making him laugh. "I bought three. Do you want one?"

"No," I reply, grinning. "I appreciate the offer. Let's drive. But take your time."

"Are you on a schedule?" he asks, turning onto the frontage and heading for the highway.

"Not at all," I answer, eating my cereal. "I'm free until school starts."

"You like Cajun food?"

"I've never had any authentic Cajun, or Creole, for that matter."

"No jambalaya or crawfish...sucking heads?"

"Ewww!" I squeal and giggle. "Why, are we going to Louisiana?"

"Do you want to?"

"I would love to!" I eagerly say. "I need to call my boss, Morgan, and my dad. I already called Selia."

"New Orleans, here we come!" He winks and smiles. "I'll get a room in the French Quarter, and tomorrow morning you will be dining on fresh beignets and Café Noir."

"Why are you doing this?"

He tilts his head to look at me, but I quickly turn away. "Because I have spent five months in Arizona working my ass off, and you seem like you could use a vacation away from everything for a few days."

"You're right. I could. I have probably even earned it."

"Yes, you have earned it, Echo. Every bit of it."

Jynx

WE SPEND THE NEXT FOUR DAYS IN THE CRESCENT CITY, seeing the sights and eating incredible cuisine. I spoil her rotten, buying her clothes, art, old records, and anything her heart desires. She bubbles with happiness and light like I've never known.

I hold her hand as we stroll Bourbon Street, more as a safety precaution—I tell myself. I lie. I want to hold her hand.

I want to do everything *for* this girl.

I need to do everything *to* this girl.

But she's warped.

Good thing I am too.

Lighting a smoke, I drive North on 59 from New Orleans up to Alabama. We pass through Birmingham, and I glance at the sleeping angel. My assessment of bubbling dark cauldron was way off.

Ain't nothing dark about Echo except one thing.

And that thing doesn't sit right with me.

She's too good to desire harm from a stranger who doesn't deserve her in the least.

I should mention, I don't think I deserve her, either.

My only goal is to persuade her to want more for herself.

Someone should've raised her better and warned her—there would be guys like me, residing in the shadows and prowling in the night; creepers breathing in the darkness, craving her light, capsizing her into the abyss.

Her yearning for dark recesses wasn't a good thing.

But a very, very bad thing.

Someone never taught her the rules.

The difference between good and evil, beautiful and ugly—light and dark.

I intentionally wore her out over the last few days—*early mornings and late nights*—and she gulped down the morning protein shake loaded with sedatives like a good little girl.

Crazy fucker Cruz understood my problem way too well.

Ten hours from now, she'll wake up in South Carolina.

I will show her an evil, ugly darkness that she never imagined.

This didn't start as a sweet romance.

And we won't end as one either.

9

THE BATTLEFIELD

ECHO

DARKNESS CLOAKS THE SHED AS SOULS SLUMBER WITHOUT regret. Owls hoot in the woods, where I long to be, running away—leaves and twigs skirting under bare feet as I cross the water rushing in a creek with no recollection of what happened. I'm exhausted, but I must thoroughly reexamine his behavior again.

His unapologetic nature festers, inherent in his sins.

I will forget if granted—*an escape.*

Never to look back.

I make deals with God, the Devil, and Saints—

Please save me.

Get me out of this.

I am far too young to die.

Stop thinking like a victim, Abs.

I uncurl my fingers on the dusty floor as my eyes peer open, just a sliver, a minimalist peek. Filthy clothes enshroud my skin, stained by his achievements.

The dank and musty dwelling reeks of mildew in a dampened closet. I linger with an unappealing odor. The rusted chains attached to my ankles scrape along the crumbling cement floor.

The moonlight catches my eye as the rickety door cracks and squeaks to allow his passage. Time to slop his swine trapped within his cage. He notices the untouched lunch tray on the shoddy table as he brings in dinner.

"You didn't eat," he mutters, lifting the lid. "You must eat."

"Your five-star meals don't matter when the only place I can rest my head is the floor," I openly protest, expecting the worst. "I need a bed."

He snickers, walking closer and squatting down. His fingers move my straw-like hair from my eyes. "Are we negotiating, pretty girl?"

"Whatever makes you happy."

"You eating and drinking are my chief concerns," he says, sitting cross-legged on the ground when I note the frays of fabric surrounding his knee, near my nose. My mind is a blurry haze, and I don't want to think about this man—the same flirtatious, good looking guy racing with me on the highway—as being a perpetrator. I want to forget, not remember. Freedom would bring immediate compulsory amnesia, self-induced.

Never to look back.

God, how I fucked this one up.

In overpriced ripped jeans and a black concert t-shirt, he doesn't appear like I ever anticipated my offender would. In the shadows, I marvel at his strong jawline, cerulean eyes, and curly chocolate mop. Maybe Selia was right. I'm not good enough to profile on the fly. A sexy smile and charm tricked me. He grins.

The bastard grins.

Straight white teeth, clearly cared for with appointments to dentists and orthodontists. His crisp, clean scent hints of aromatic woods and musk. "You want money?"

"If you want to know whether a ransom would release you, the answer would be no."

"What will?"

"Time," he replies, pulling his knees up to his chest and wrapping his arms around them. "With you." His expensive silver watch sparkles in the moonlight and catches my eye. "That is the only way you are getting out of this."

"I need some guarantee that I am not dying."

His lip twitches. "... Is that all you care about?"

A laugh erupts from my mouth. "Pretty much. Will I get out of this alive, or are you a sociopathic killer?"

"You're in captivity to keep you safe from predators."

"Like you?"

He laughs. "People never pay attention; they just turn and look the other way. I'm a wild animal—*untamed and savage on the loose*—and you're a young, vulnerable host."

The callous delivery of his statement infuriates me. "Do you plan on taking shelter in me? Finding nourishment? Invading my dwelling like a low-life squatter?"

His hand drops, and I jolt away, afraid of what his touch will bring. For days, I've wanted this stranger to inappropriately touch me —*molest me*—and now, I can't even look him in the eye. Grazing the back of his fingers over my cheek, he whispers, "I promised you days ago—you will live. I'm not a murderer."

I breathe a sigh of relief and make a bold accusation, "... Rapist?"

He smiles again.

I wish he would stop doing that, gloating like he has the upper hand, which he does. But I am offended, insulted by his arrogance. "There are worse things in the world than rapists, Sweet Pea."

"Like crazy guys who chain up women like beasts," I scoff as he firmly vices my cheeks between his forefinger and thumb, forcing me to look at him.

"Like sadists."

My breath quickens. "Are you going to torture me?"

"Does the idea turn you on?"

"No!" I spit, nailing his high cheekbone. He releases his grip and pulls a handkerchief from his pocket. Spreading the fabric flat, near my face, he removes his watch before running his finger through the spittle, smearing it onto his tongue. His eyes close as he savors my saliva.

"You're..." I stop, unable to form a coherent thought.

"I'm what?" he snorts. "Tell me. Because I've heard it all before. Twisted? Maniacal? Deranged?" His brow arches with a suggestive innuendo. "Tell me how you feel because you're lying."

"I want a bed!"

He rolls his eyes and smirks. "If I bring you a bed, will you eat?"

It's a taste of power—raw and alluring. I haven't lost, and he hasn't declared victory. His willingness to bargain is akin to swapping secrets on the playing field. He's rigging the outcome in his favor, assisting my moves, benefitting his long-term strategy, and yet, I whisper, "You want the challenge."

"It's part of the fun," he cackles, peering over me. "But eventually, you will need upkeep."

"How long will my abduction last?"

"Over the summer," he informs, dropping clues. "You start school in the fall. I won't hold you back from your education."

"Is this your idea of a hot summer romance?"

He licks his lips and smirks. "I don't romance."

I sass, "... Fling?"

He chuckles. "Unlikely."

"Why are you doing this?"

"Because you asked for it," he informs. "You deserve this. You earned it. Good job!"

"You're an asshole."

"You'll be calling me far worse by August." He leans over and kisses the top of my head before standing up. I latch onto his sneaker and blink, hoping to play into his perversion. "You should pray you're in the house by then. The cottonmouths can be problematic."

"The only snake I'm concerned with is the one slithering in front of me."

His lips perk with a suggestive simper as he cackles, "You're too young to win and too smart to forfeit."

"I hate you, J."

"I'm not surprised," he remarks. "Nor do I care. You're being punished whether you like it or not."

"I'll give you head," I randomly blurt out. "You can have your way with me."

"I plan on it, Sweet Pea," he assures, staring at me. "But we're doing this my way. You should be patient. Slow...methodical...disciplined...until you know better than to do what you did. Until you learn that sometimes the serpents in the grass bite back with an intoxicating venom."

I sniffle as tears flutter in my lashes. "I never wanted this."

"You did," he growls, rummaging in the darkness of my soul like a thief. "You asked for this."

Taking a breath, I toughen my resolve. "What do I have to do to go inside of the house?"

"Prove you're not feral," he growls. He is unmoved by my desperation to please—in whatever way he demands.

"Days with me didn't prove that?"

"Not now," he argues. "You won't stay if I set you free. I'm not a fool. You will run right back to California and put the ad up again. You will end up six feet under. And I can't let that happen."

"I didn't ask you to save me."

He strokes his chin. "You didn't need to ask."

"You're not some fucking superhero!" I angrily yell. "What do you want from me?"

A simper lifts from his lips. "It's not what I want from you. It's what I am taking...*stealing*. I'm only borrowing you for a little while."

"For your own selfish needs!" I shout. "Dick!"

"Is that the best you have?" he rebukes as I'm unable to avert my eyes from his bold intimidation. It would greatly help my plight if he were gnarly and jagged-toothed. The difference in behavior versus physical appearance is outstandingly deviant—a deceptive lure I'm confident he has used before.

Fuck.

I'm such an idiot.

"Do you have a name?"

"Not one you have earned the right to know. If you want these things, you need to behave. Now, release my foot." I reluctantly let go and clutch my stained fingers around the watch band. I press the cold, hardened steel to my lips and a wave of his scent hits my nose. "Eat," he commands, pulling the journal out from under the platter. "And write. Document it. All of it."

Rolling onto my back, I gawk, upside down, at his lean, well-kept physique. He isn't some podunk nightmare or an uneducated disaster, but a monster to remember—*a man to never forget. Shit.* I will never get him out of my head. My lips part as I defiantly hiss, "You're giving me what you think I want in a fucked-up fairytale."

"Not at all," he calmly growls. "I'm giving you more than you ever bargained for—*to teach you a lesson.*"

"If I pass your test, will I go unharmed, Professor?"

"Do no harm doesn't exist in my vernacular."

JYNX

"... J?"

In the doorway, I turn toward her lying on the floor—helpless and mine. "Yes?"

"You carried the box of wine, bought my gas, found hotel rooms, fed me better than I've ever eaten, and lavished gifts upon me. You fucking held my hand, so why am I on the floor of a shed?"

I stroke my overgrown scruff. "You wanted to be raped. I won't let that happen. I'm teaching you a lesson that you will never forget."

"This isn't who you are."

"You don't know me, Echo."

"You have a heart, and you care."

Too much.

I care too much.

I step inside and crouch near her face. "Do you want me to show you how little I care?"

"Whatever gets us to the end faster."

"The end is when you change your thought process," I inform, brushing my fingers over her matted hair. After three days, she stinks. I should take her up to the house for a bath since I sent Axel back to his place in Myrtle Beach. I don't need his assistance with my summer project. "I have never killed anyone. I don't plan on you being the first, but you must realize bright girls like yourself shouldn't be holding up flashing, pointing arrows for the nightmare to come to you."

"Just make this stop."

"I won't do that," I thoughtfully contend. "Most people give anything to dream. But I would do anything to stop the nightmare."

"I cannot help you if you're treating me like an animal."

"Precisely," I reply. "Posting that ad, hunting for a criminal to hurt you, that was acting like an animal. Stop acting like an animal. And I will stop treating you as one."

"Will you let me go then?"

I stare at her hazel eyes darkened with circles from exhaustion and dehydration. "You need to eat, drink, and take care of yourself, Echo. You wanted the lessons in the darkest mindset, and I'm giving it to you."

"Let me go, J."

"I can't, Abby..."

"God! Don't call me by my name."

"... Is it that bad?"

"Yes, it is that bad," she confirms, crying. "So, stay with me until we've purged my demons."

"Prove to me that you are worth my time."

"You've already declared when I'm leaving," she reminds, clutching to my wrist. "You're letting me go back to school."

"I said I had never killed anyone, but I'll take us both out if you don't change your ways. Because I cannot walk this earth knowing that a sweet, decent girl like yourself is soliciting evil. I know my kind, Echo. We won't just consume you; we will force you to be one of us. Change the mentality. Learn a new dialogue. Have some fucking self-respect."

"Why are you doing this to me?"

Glancing at the chains, I grin. "Because I can? Because it was way too easy to play you. To lie to you. To bait you. To convince you that I was a nice guy."

She cries, "But you won't rape me."

"I'm not into bestiality," I confirm, unmoved. "Even a guy like me has his limits, babydoll."

"Great, so I'm stuck here until you decide I'm worthy of being a human."

I nod once and blink. "Pretty much."

"... And if I behave?"

"We move up the ladder from the hell you put yourself in."

"You're rebuilding me," she muses, crying. "You're breaking me to turn me into something I'm not."

"You're right, I am," I challenge. "Because you're not human."

"I'm starting to regret that I ever met you."

"That's better," I praise, standing up. "You shouldn't like me." She latches onto my ankle and sinks her teeth into my flesh. I don't react as she glances up and hisses, "Fiend."

"Sick fuck!"

I walk away, laughing. "Eat, drink, and behave, Sweet Pea."

IN THE HOUSE, I STRIP OFF MY CLOTHES TO TAKE A SHOWER. I stare at the reddened bruise on the inside of my ankle. I'll bend her will, but keeping Echo will require more patience than I have ever possessed.

I desperately want to run to the shed, bring her up to the house, and care for her. I want to bathe her, brush her hair, and put her in my bed—but she is wild, like one of the many stray, rabid animals I brought home and begged to heal.

My mother never would.

When Dad thought we were safely tucked in our beds asleep, I would hear the gunshot ring out in the stillness of the night. The moon cried with the loss of one of her furry children as I did.

Every creature deserved a chance to survive.

And when it proved to have enough fight to overcome, I would teach it to thrive.

Grandma understood my spirituality, empathy, and kinship to life. She never once took it for granted, and I ended up staying with her more often than my parents.

At her farmhouse, we tried to save countless souls.

From stray cats and dogs hit on the road to my best friend's— *Chuck's growing drug problem*—and the girl I favored—*Celeste's promiscuous nature*—Grandma blessed them all with her healing hands and home-cooked meals. She gave until there was nothing left to give.

She tried.

And trying counts.

We lost two humans.

I won't lose three.

I won't lose Echo.

During my eight-month incarceration, Grandma died of a massive heart attack, and I gave up. I swore I would never try to save another human after Chuck betrayed me and Celeste refused to listen.

Being a good guy never helped anyone.

I was stalking a girl to watch over her, and she was fucking murdered by my best friend. And if I took that stalking too far—well, at least she was alive with my eyes on her.

I started stashing credits for people I walked away from who may have needed help, or a hand, or a bit of advice. I ignored all their requests, demands, and pleas because I shut down.

I was the bad guy.

People died when I stopped.

Instead of saving the dying animal lying on the side of the road, I became the guy that would run it over again to make sure it met its maker.

I was that guy; I was that asshole.

Hit it and quit it.

Care about one—myself.

And do not, under any circumstances, get involved with anyone.

In Tucson, I read the ad, and something triggered deep inside of me.

I wanted to rape this girl.

I wanted to own her.

I needed to claim her and make her mine.

But one night wouldn't cut it—*I wanted a whole fucking lifetime with a girl as fucked up as she was.*

I am fucking starving on the hunt.

And I can't stop.

I can't turn off my predator now.

Echo will die if I stop.

I'm too far gone, spending all the years of credits on one girl—*one feral kitten wanting to be mutilated*—in my shed. If I have to pour every ounce of my soul into her to convince her that she alone is worth fighting for, then I will. But she cannot give up; she cannot quit.

She must survive.

And if she doesn't, then neither will I.

In saving her, I redeem myself.

If I lose her, I am done.

Hit it and quit it.

10

TERRIFIED WITH THE LIGHTS ON

ECHO

First entry, the fourth day

I hate him.
I'm so fucking lonely.
And stupid.
Stupid, stupid, stupid.

"GOOD MORNING, SWEET PEA," HE SAYS FROM THE doorway. "Did you eat?" He lifts the lid and tilts his head. "Not bad."

"The broccoli was good."

Setting down the tray, he smirks. "Thanks. The farmer's market always has the best. This morning, we have your favorite." He lifts the lid to a mammoth bowl of Frosted Flakes. "Enjoy."

"What if I agree to stay put and let you do whatever you want?"

"I'm not having sex with you, if that is what you're asking," he replies, propping the door open wide with a rock from outside.

"But you want to."

His eyes shift back and forth. "I would be lying if I said I wasn't attracted to you. And I won't lie to you again."

"What's changed?" I ask, holding a spoonful of the cereal.

"You're safe here with me. No one is going to hurt you here on my property."

I swallow the bite and hold the spoon in my trembling hand. "... How big is it?"

He pauses, unusually long, staring at me. I meet his gaze. "Big...*really big*."

I lick my lips and smirk. "You're a flirt."

"With the right girl behaving like a girl, I can be quite the charmer. You act like an animal, and I will react accordingly, handling you like an undomesticated wench."

"... Is that how it's going to be?"

"Pretty much," he says, walking to the door. "I have a present for you. Eat."

I keep munching as I hear several loud thumps. He returns to the entryway, shirtless, and wearing a tool belt. I drop my fucking spoon on the floor because he is too masculine for my meager mind. "Fuck."

"Where do you want this bed?" He dives to pick up the utensil. "You're lucky. I have an extra in the truck."

"You have extra silverware in the truck?"

"I have lots of things," he admits, promptly returning with a clean spoon. He holds it in front of me but refuses to release it. I lay my hand on top of his, and he pulls back, pressing my hand to his lips. "Trust me, Echo."

"You can call me Ekky."

"Eat, Ekky." He smiles. "My name is J.A. Monroe."

"You're not going to tell me what the J.A. stands for."

"Probably not, but you can call me Jynx."

I'm stunned he told me his name. "Jynx Monroe?"

"That's my name," he replies, shooting me a glare. "And if you don't eat, your name will be Red Assed Ekky." He points as his eyes widen with a scowl. "Where do you want the bed?"

"I don't care," I garble with a mouthful of cereal. "Anywhere."

"How about this corner?"

I nod and continue eating as I attempt to avoid paying too much attention to my captor's gallant efforts. He disappears outside and carries in pieces of an antique metal bed frame. "That's beautiful!"

"It was my Grandmother's as a child," he informs, carefully setting out the pieces. "It's been in storage for far too long."

"Were you close to her?"

"Yes," he replies, bolting the frame together. I finish my breakfast with occasional glimpses at him. He finally stands and asks, "What are the odds you're running off?"

"Do you want the honest answer?"

His blue eyes peer down at me as a slight smirk lifts his lips. "Be transparent."

"I'm not leaving," I reply. "You promised I would live. And I trust you."

"You've been overly trusting of me."

"Yeah, well, I'm a dumb *wench*," I say, arching a brow.

"Can you help me?" he asks, pulling the key for the chain out of his pocket. "If I let you loose?"

"Will it earn me a shower?"

"Maybe." He winks

Kneeling, he undoes the chains from my ankles, rubbing them. His touch sends a shockwave through me. "Don't leave me. We've got work to do."

"Is there more than putting a bed together?"

"Quite a bit," he says, smiling wide. He has dimples, but they're hidden by several days of shadowy beard. "We have to feed the farm."

"What do you do?"

He pops a mint, the red and white swirly kind, in his mouth and offers me one. "Legit?"

"In all ways...be transparent."

"I do computer stuff for my dad's business, and I hack into shit for fun."

"That's how you found me," I mutter, understanding. "Because I never expected a smart stalker."

"They're not all dumbasses."

"Girlfriend? Wife? Anything?"

He shakes his head. "I have no interest in caring for anyone."

"You realize," I point out with a wave toward the bed. "That everything you say about yourself from not caring or being a gentleman, you're disproving in practice with me."

"You're special," he snarls. "I'm an asshole. Trust me."

"If I run off, will you hunt me down?"

"Good question," he seriously remarks. "I'm hoping you will stay on your own," he admits, licking his lips. "But I don't know that you're ready to get to know yourself as much as I want you to."

"I'm living in a stranger's shed. Unrestrained and not struggling. Even though he readily admits to being a stalker and an asshole. Who doesn't want to get to know themselves here?"

His eyes roll-up. "Fair point."

"You're incredibly cute."

"So are you," he confesses as I study the sharp angles of his high cheek bones. He is the looker here, not me. "Which is what started all of this. I don't pursue anyone really, but I avoid twenty-somethings."

"Why?"

"Are you aware of how much work you are?" he rebukes, and I laugh hard. "You're stunning when you smile."

"And you want to fuck me."

"Yes," he finally affirms. "I desperately want to fuck you into next week."

"But, you won't."

"Nope," he says, grinning. "Not until you truly believe you're worth more than what you think. We have to get to work."

"You're segueing."

"I am," he replies, standing, and offers his hands. From the chair, I stare at his noticeable protrusion in dark gray sweat pants. "Avoiding even, because sex complicates everything."

"What are you going to do with that?" I ask, flicking my eyes to his and taking his fingers.

"Use what you're holding."

"But you don't have to."

"Do you want me to throw the tray, splash the milk on the floor, and screw you on the table?"

"Yes!" I giggle. "That is exactly what I want."

"You don't learn anything then."

"Fuck!" I yell, unable to stop smiling. "You're infuriating! Kiss me."

"No."

"Hug me?"

"No."

"Asshole," I mumble with a pout as his hand releases mine and tucks beneath my chin. "Say it. Be brave."

"I'm breaking the rules for you," he confides, dipping down and breathing against my lip. "I lost years of sobriety and sanity to taste you. But I'm a grown-ass man, and I will not gulp you down like a parched man walking across the desert. I will sip, savor, and devour every last drop because I'm disciplined in my convictions."

With every ounce of courage I have, I confide, "I want to break you."

"That feeling is mutual," he whispers as I consider stealing a kiss. It would be offensive to his position, though, and I hate that, but I respect it. He softly smiles. "Let it naturally evolve."

"Are you saying there is a chance you may care about me?"

His full-blown grin smacks my heart with the force of a hammer. "I'm warming up to the idea, but don't push it. I'm still an asshole."

His hands drop, and the intense moment passes. He turns to the bed frame. "I need you to hold that steady while I screw it..." His words suddenly fall silent as he stares at my naked chest. "Where are your clothes?"

"If you're going to walk around here, taunting me with all that raging manhood, I'm doing the same to you."

"Damn you, Ek." He licks his lips and lowers to bolt the bed together. "Hold this."

"Are we alone?"

With his battery-powered screwdriver in hand, he fastens the bed together. "Yes, except for Tuesday and Thursday afternoons when the Ag crew arrives."

"For what?"

He grabs my hand, leading me outside. "Welcome to the farm."

"Oh, my God," I gasp at the dozens of peacocks and chickens running wild. I briefly forget how self-conscious I am over my breasts, but when I remember, I tug away. With a subtle smile, he refuses to let go as his eyes skim over my flesh. "I smell water..."

He keeps a firm grip on my arm, dragging me to the edge of the shed where a spacious lake comes into view. "This is gorgeous."

Picking up the pack of smokes off the tailgate, he releases his stronghold and lights one. "I'm glad someone else sees that. My brother, Axel, wants to sell the whole thing."

"Is this your house?"

"No, I have a beach house about an hour from here," he says, exhaling. "You're smitten."

"I grew up in Birmingham. I went to school in California. I know small town, but not rural like this."

"You should see the stars at night."

"Will you show them to me?" I excitedly question, and he nods. "Can I go jump in your lake?"

"Are you going to swim away?"

"No," I say in awe. "Are there fish?"

"Yeah," he says as I notice the bag of sunflower seeds. "And snakes. But the peacocks usually keep them at bay."

"Peacocks..." I susurrate, believing in a blissful nirvana that I wasn't sure existed. His looming presence shrouds the unimportant, allowing my focus on the basic needs.

We walk closer, under the canopy of oaks and cypress laden with Spanish moss, as he extends his hand. I lay my fingers into his palm, and he clasps them.

"My grandparents bought this place back in the fifties. Shortly after they moved in, Grandma found a cottonmouth—a water moccasin— up on her back deck. She went into town and asked the local feed store owners what to do about them. The man knew she had bought the place and recommended the peacocks and peahens."

I watch his expression shift from a toughened leather to an indescribable mourning. "You miss her."

"Like you cannot believe," he whispers, breathing through the agony. "She was my person, Clementine Eudora Merco Monroe. Anyway..."

"You don't deal with emotions well at all," I interject, assessing.

"Not at all," he knowingly admits with a smirk. "She went out and bought a flock. They all ran off or died. So, she bought another flock with a coop. And she kept trying until she had ninety-six when she passed four years ago."

"Paternal Grandmother. Spanish?"

"And yes, on both counts. My mother's side is Danish."

"... Parents names?"

"Montgomery Merco Monroe and Laverne Howser Monroe."

"Siblings?"

"Just Axel, he is two years younger than me," he replies as I let go of his hand. "Are we playing twenty questions?"

"We might be," I say, undoing my pants. "Do you have any questions?"

A look of awe fills his eyes as he asks, "Only why would such a magnificent girl want something so horrific to happen to her?"

"Because I have a problem," I caution, handing my rank pants to him. "I don't want normal."

I run for the water, and he yells, "What does that mean?"

"Find out, stalker!" I dip into the warm water and emerge with a splash, tossing my hair back. Water drips from my skin as I pace back toward him. "You're the sleuth."

"Would you like a shower before feeding my peacocks?"

"Yes," I say, grinning. "I would."

"Up to the house." He points. "Go in the back door, past the kitchen, first entry on the left. Your bags are there."

"You're trusting me?"

"You won't leave," he arrogantly boasts. "You're too enchanted."

I take my pants from his arm, and he startlingly plants a peck on my cheek. "You're right, I am. We're alone?"

"Four hundred acres."

"Shit," I mutter, comprehending that he has me invisibly tethered. "You're damn good."

"I try."

JYNX

I FINISH PUTTING THE BED TOGETHER, DRAGGING THE mattress to the room, and making the bed with vintage lace coverings, which all seems so futile because I want this girl in my bed. I finish and catch her, staring at me in the doorway. She is wearing jeans and a tank top with her wet hair pulled into a ponytail. Her arms are crossed over her chest.

I smile and ask, "Feel better?"

"I did some thinking in the shower."

"I bet that's not all you did."

"I already did that on the shed floor several times," she openly admits. "You want to teach me a lesson. If I agree to stay, will I go to the house?"

"Eventually."

"When you can control yourself?" she questions, pushing. "Or when we reach said point of my training?"

"Don't use that word."

"You're the one who said handle me like an animal," she says, revealing the lack of undergarments on her chest. "I assumed that meant training one as well."

"You don't want to be submissive."

"How do you know?"

I snicker as she follows me to the truck. "Get in."

"... No door opening?"

"I'm not a gentleman," I reply, smirking. I drive around the property to the large metal barn. "We're talking and working."

"You have horses?"

"They're out grazing the front of the property."

"How many?"

"Four," I reply, putting a rake in her hand. "Stalls. Scoop. Shit."

"You're kidding."

"Sure, you want to stay?" I rebuke with a snarl. "I know you don't want to be submissive because I have your ad memorized. You're looking for violent sex. Nothing more or less. You don't want a boyfriend or the likely boring missionary sex acts he would bring. You want a sexual savage to Dominate the scene."

"You've got it!"

"I'm a fucking genius!" I sarcastically chime.

"But you won't do it even though you admitted to being a sadist."

"I won't do it because I am a sadist," I reply as she rakes, and I fill the buckets with fresh food, hay, and water. "Being a sadist naturally implies that I am seeking a masochist. Someone willing to surrender to my demands. You're not a submissive or a slave. You're just fucked up."

She laughs, and I grin. "Is it that bad to have this fantasy?"

"Ravishment is great, but not the way you went about it. You opened a barrel of cottonmouths, quite stupidly, I might add."

"I wanted the surprise."

"Well, surprise," I joke with a tilt of my head. "You've been abducted by a monster."

"You're not a monster," she cattily sasses.

I move closer, using my height to intimidate. "Are you so sure about that, Sweet Pea? You've been with me less than a week. Do you know who I am?"

"Yes," she assures. "I do."

With one swift move, I latch onto her wrist, and the rake falls from her hand as I push her into the back wall of the stall. I press my sweat-laden body against hers and breathe on her neck. "I suggest you consider your answers more cautiously."

She shivers beneath my weight. "You want to hurt me."

"Like you cannot believe."

"So why haven't you?" she whispers through ragged breaths. "If you're such a deviant, why not attack what is on your property?"

"Because I *am* stalking you, sweetheart." The clean sweet smell of her skin permeates my nose as I involuntarily buck my hips to her ass. She would feel so good...so tight on me. "You have no idea what I am capable of...*I will ruin you.*"

"But you won't do it," she mumbles, arching her hips back to greet me. I push against her, making sure she understands what she is doing to me. "Because I'm not submissive."

"You aren't anything but mine."

Her teeth vice her lip as my hand slides up under her shirt and gropes her breast. Her soft flesh melts against my calloused fingers. She whimpers, "For three months."

"Unless I send you away before then," I mumble against her flesh. "You offered your body for use at my discretion with complete confidence."

"Fuck," she rants, fully grasping the negligence of her actions.

"Oh, you can bet your sweet ass, we're going to do that too."

11

PAY THE BOUNTY

ECHO

Second entry, the fourth day

I am alone again.
Back in my shed of a prison cell.
We worked all day on the farm, feeding the animals and
catching up on all of the stuff that Axel let slack off
while Jynx was in Arizona. I didn't mind helping
because I got to spend time with him.
I understand what he wants to accomplish with me, but

there are extenuating issues that provoked my ad. He
doesn't know about my freakish tendencies. He may
be a Dominant, but that isn't what I'm interested in.
I'm way out in left field on the violent sexual fantasies.
He pushed me against the wall of the barn, and I
practically came in my pants. I wanted him to take it
further, but he won't let himself because he's
"disciplined."
Little does he realize how undisciplined I want my perfect
suitor to be.

I TOSS AND TURN FOR WHAT SEEMS HOURS. THE relentless sauna lingering in the air is terrible, and the box fan offers no reprieve. I lace one hand around the bed frame and skim the other into my panties.

I'll pass out with an orgasm.

Thinking of how his back muscles shimmered in the late afternoon as he brushed the horses down, I dip my fingers inside and dampen my thighs with every thrust. I want his body, mind, and spirit to be mine. I need his passion inside of me. A crack of thunder sounds in the distance, but I ignore the storm for the flood coming within me.

"Fuck me, Jynx," I beg, gripping tightly to the frame. "Please..."

I come hard and fast as lightning flashes outside the window. I don't care. I drift off to dreamland with my only thought being of Jynx Monroe.

I'm on the football field in my violet and white cheerleading uniform. When
the crowd dies down from winning the game, a few friends gather round as
we head out for our victory celebration at someone's house. I'll sit in the
corner like I always do, quietly observing it all.

Instantly, I am alone on the field when the lights shine on me.

I wander off the turf, past the concession stand to under the bleachers,
where I spot a girl—my mirror image, a complete doppelgänger—strapped

down to the table while he has his way with her—which is me. Her sparkling hazel eyes demand my attention as she moans beneath the man.

I step closer, wanting to get a better look.

He tosses a glance over his shoulder to me. "Took you long enough to get here, Echo."

The area overflows with the attendees of the football game. They're laughing and pointing and saying horrid things about the girl lying on the table.

No one understands.

No one but him.

I sit up in bed, sweating buckets, and grab my book. In the glow of the nightlight, I jot down a few notes.

Third entry, the fourth day

Close your eyes.
Don't look around.
Don't peek down.
Don't read what they say.
Don't ask me my name.
Don't listen.
Echo.

"Why is my foot wet?" I mutter, flicking the light on. A continuous waterfall pours onto the end of the bed from the shed's ceiling. "Oh, my God!"

I tug on the wrought iron bed, but it's too heavy to move alone. I spot the bright headlights beaming through the window and the curtains of rain crashing from the heavens to the land.

With a smile, Jynx busts in the door. "I guess we put the bed on the wrong side."

I giggle at his easy demeanor, rolling with any catastrophic situation. He's the guy people want on their team—the problem solver with a great attitude and cheerfulness to match.

"I think so."

"Grab your stuff," he commands, shaking the water from his long chocolate curls. "This is only supposed to get worse. There is a super-cell headed for us. We need to hurry."

"What about the bed?"

"Fuck it," he dismissively says, extending his hand. "Your safety matters more than the bed."

I grab the journal, wrap my jeans around it, and tuck it close to my chest. "Let's go!" A series of earthshaking booms deafens me as we rush to the truck. He opens my door and holds my bottom, ensuring I don't slip on the wet running bars. "Shit!"

He drives like a madman toward the house. "Are you okay?"

"I'm sorry," I mumble, upset.

"Why?" he asks, clutching my hand. "I'm the one who should be apologizing. I had no idea the shed even leaked, or I wouldn't have put you there. I guess you're staying in the house with me now."

An upgrade I hadn't planned on occurring quite so soon.

With a smirk, I tease, "You said you wouldn't kill me, but you tried to drown your captive."

He laughs. "We're soaked to the bone."

"I want to soak around your bone," I carelessly say, grinning as he parks the truck by the garage. He cuts the engine at the exact moment a bright bolt hits a tree at the front of the property. Gold dust flutters, surrounding where lightning hit as a small flash fire breaks out. It quickly dies in the pouring rain as the thunder roars, and the lights go out. "Uh, oh!"

He doesn't flinch in the darkness. "Why do you want to have sex with me?"

The obvious reason is attraction, but it's shallow and not the answer he is seeking. "You seem competent."

Wrong answer.

"Try again," he hastens, getting out of the truck and running to my side. Before I know it, he's tossed me over his shoulder and carrying my ass inside. He sets me on the kitchen cabinet. "Why do you want to have sex with me?"

"Because you do things like that."

"That's a better answer than being competent." He lights a few candles and grabs a couple of towels from the adjoining laundry room. Without concern, he proceeds to pull off my drenched shirt. He doesn't ask; he does. "Hold onto my shoulders." Reaching behind me, he slides my panties off and hands me a towel. "Keep going. You aren't done. Why do you want to have sex with me?"

"This is hard under the gun," I reply as he tosses his wet shirt in the sink with my clothes and grabs a bottle of wine from the fridge. "It's 2 AM."

"Do you have somewhere to be tomorrow?"

"No."

"Then," he says, grabbing two glasses out of the cabinet. "We're drinking."

"I'm sitting here naked," I remind as he hands me a glass of white wine.

"Technically, you're not." He takes a sip of his wine and proceeds to drop his sweat pants—my mouth waters. I gawk at his chiseled musculature in the orange glow of the candles. His ass is perfectly plump with sculpted thighs and calves. He wraps the towel around his waist before accidentally showing off his big, delicious secret. "Problem?"

"Do you like turning me on?"

"I was being polite," he mutters as his lip lifts suggestively. "Would you prefer rude?"

"Yes, I really would," I quip. "You ask why I want to have sex with you, but have you seen yourself?"

He scratches his cheek, pausing to collect his thoughts. "But what you don't know is I don't see what you do. Much like you. I am an average guy."

"There is nothing average about you, Jynx Monroe."

His lips pucker. "The lights could be out for days. I'll get the generator running for the essentials."

"I don't mind."

The back of his fingers stroke my cheek. "If you need to go, you can leave tomorrow."

"And what if I want to stay?"

"Anything could happen," he informs stoically. "I can't promise anything but honesty."

"Why do you want to have sex with me?"

With his hands propped on either side of the counter, he traps my tremulous body beneath his sturdy frame. "Because you're the most beautiful, witty, and charming woman I have ever met."

"And why won't you?"

"Because I want to make you uncomfortable," he confirms, easing closer. His blue eyes peer into the deepest parts of my soul as I force myself to meet his steady gaze. I'm just realizing how truly massive this man is. He's tall and broad with hefty, sinewy cords practiced and worked over. I've never been around a man this buff. A noticeable tremor shudders through my body, aching for more than I fear he will ever provide. "I want the tension so tight that my dick is continuously weeping with a built-up wanton lust for you."

"You're holding back on purpose?"

"I am," he admits with a smirk. "But you're making it very hard."

"... Freudian?"

"More than a slip," he concedes. "I've never done this."

"But you've been with women."

"Countless, nameless, faceless women who I couldn't tell you a damn thing about," he replies, uncaring. "And that makes me an asshole."

"Sheltering your heart for one doesn't make you an asshole."

"No," he agrees with a raise of his brows. "But what I long to do to you does."

I reach up, touching his cheek and breaking through the barrier for the first time. We've held hands and brushed against one another, but I've not set forth with a purposeful intent of touching him until now. I quiver with what may transpire. "Tell me."

"I don't need to tell you," he growls, closing his eyes. "I want to show you."

"Jynx Monroe, I offer my body for use at your discretion with complete confidence."

"You're handing a monster the keys to the kingdom, baby."

"Pillage and plunder," I whisper as he narrows in on my lips. "All reward, no risk situation for the stalker appreciating violent sexual encounters. I'll struggle, act the role of victim, and provide you with a challenge."

His unshakeable focus unnerves me as he probes, "Do I incite fear?"

"Yes," I breathe against his lip. "You do."

"And are you struggling?"

"More than you know." His intense gaze seizes all that I am as my skin tingles with apprehension. "Hurt me, J."

"You don't understand what you're asking for."

"Please," I beg, curling into his frame and laying my hands on his hair covered chest. "Don't think."

"I will cause permanent damage to your heart."

His teeth snap to my bottom lip, and his large hands press against my hips. "Hold me."

"I can't," he says, fighting his demons. "I won't let myself."

"Because you're afraid of loving me."

"Because I'm already falling," he confesses, shaking his head and backing away. "I need to get some sleep. There will be broken limbs come morning light."

"Don't go."

"I can't stay," he mutters as I cling to his hand until he's out of reach. "Sleep well."

I watch as he disappears through the house. I want to cry, but what good will my tears do if he isn't here to catch them?

I carefully slide from the counter, grab a candle, and walk to the bedroom where my things are. My luggage is gone. I check the chest of drawers where my clothes are neatly folded and put away. I twist to the closet where the rest of my clothes are hanging.

On the nightstand, I spot my phone and computer.

I am a prisoner by choice.

I should pack my things and leave this fucked up man to resume his miserable life alone. I can do nothing but disrupt his psyche.

Just as he has done to me.

Dropping the towel in the middle of the room, I grab a pair of pajamas and curl up in the bed. I open my laptop and sign onto the site where the ad is posted. I hit the unpublish button on the post when a message pops up on the sidebar.

> $T4LK3R: I am sorry.
> D4RK4NG3L: I should go.
> $T4LK3R: You should, but you won't. And for the
>   life of me, I don't know why.
> D4RK4NG3L: Just your charming cynical self.

I cannot stop grinning as I see the dots and know he's typing. I bite my lip and patiently wait, letting him lead. Mostly because I don't want to. I wouldn't even know where to begin. Dating, relationships, sex—it's all out of my league, but he's older. And for reasons I don't fully understand, I trust him to take me where I want to go.

> $T4LK3R: Click into the private chat room I just
>   made.
> D4RK4NG3L: Will it get me dick pics?
> $T4LK3R: Quite possibly, if you will stay.
> D4RK4NG3L: That's bribery, Mr. Monroe.
> $T4LK3R: I'm trying here, Echo.
> D4RK4NG3L: I know. :)
> $T4LK3R: But I only know one way.
> D4RK4NG3L: This.
> $T4LK3R: Yes.

A minute passes with no dots, and I think that we're through. I fluff another pillow behind my back. I wait for so long that I worry he may have fallen asleep.

$T4LK3R: Turn the camera on.

Taking a deep breath, I press the button, but I see nothing. We clearly aren't on the same page or level, which is fine. The smile plastered on my face is starting to hurt.

D4RK4NG3L: Can you see me?
$T4LK3R: Yes.
D4RK4NG3L: You aren't allowing me to see you.
$T4LK3R: Take your shirt off.
D4RK4NG3L: You realize you're on the other side
    of the house?
$T4LK3R: Do it.

I pull off my shirt and look into the camera, making sure he can see my breasts. Boldly, I ask, "Does this make it...*easier?*"

$T4LK3R: The space between us makes me very
    hard.
D4RK4NG3L: You're jerking off.
$T4LK3R: I am.

I mutter out loud, "To me."

$T4LK3R: Yes, Echo, I am.
D4RK4NG3L: What should I do?
$T4LK3R: Pretend like you're never going to see
    me again.

In disbelief, I reread his words again and again. A good five minutes passes with not another word sent between us. I'm panicking that this is his goodbye. He's seriously fucked up.

He's right; I should go.

This isn't healthy.

I bite my lip, and sadness blooms from the corners of my eyes.

I don't like his game.

It hurts as the tears fall onto my chest. I want to curl into a corner and forget any of this ever happened. I'm in California with my vibrator in hand. I flashback to the aggressive images on the screen.

He is getting off on hurting me.

I hysterically cry, realizing this is what I wanted all along.

My strange stalker is my fantasy coming to life.

This is real.

$T4LK3R: god... don't stop.

Babbling with drool, snot, and more tears, I whisper, "Jynx... Give it to me."

$T4LK3R: babygirl...I'm going to...come...

He leaves the chat room.

I blow out the candle and stare, stunned by the callousness of his actions. I shut the laptop and slump into the bed, lost and alone.

My bedroom door bursts open, and I question, "What are you doing?"

"Open your mouth."

Terrified, I bellow, "Jynx!"

"Open your fucking mouth, bitch!"

"Jynx, please," I beg, desperate for my knight in shining armor to return. "Don't do this."

I stay covered, shivering with fear under the blankets. He rips the linens, my only shield, from my hands as his savage sword takes centerstage. I cannot do combat with this man. His magnificent weapon stays hidden in the shadows, but I gasp at his sheer size.

In the darkness, his dick is fucking huge.

And I don't mean the male anatomical part, but how he behaves,

BEAUTIFUL THINGS EVIL PEOPLE DO | 113

shifting from gentleman in the light to monster in the night. I'm learning as fast as I can, picking up his crumbs of clues to assemble who and what he is.

I don't wish to tame him.

I want to know him.

In an authentic Biblical sense.

I glare at his shrouded silhouette with my breasts exposed and feel the jostling, pumping motion of his arm. He aims, moving faster and harder as he hovers over the top of me until finally groaning, "God! Yes! Abby! Take it!"

He said my name.

And as he releases his cum all over me, I soak the sheet beneath me.

12

THE LIGHT OF DAY

JYNX

AFTER THE INCIDENT, I LEFT THE ROOM WITHOUT A SOUND and went to take a cold shower. I didn't sleep much. I went for an early morning run around the property, surveying the damage from the storm, but more so to clear my head.

I cared about Abigail Maines.

And I had to get to a place where caring was okay.

I wasn't there yet.

Soaked in damp grass and dirt, I stripped down in the mudroom and walked naked through my house—seemingly forgetting, or just not caring, that she was here with me. I had a resident—an invader—a captive.

I had said I didn't know if I would chase her, but I accepted the truth after my ninety-minute run. I would do whatever was necessary to keep her here with me. I took another shower and dressed in jeans and boots for the long day of clean up ahead.

The French toast sizzles in the pan when she emerges from the bedroom. Her hair is damp from the shower. Her eyes are reddened from my actions. My dick throbs with the reminder, and my heart pounds, trapped beneath the layers of guilt and regret.

"What's on the schedule for today?" she stutters out, her voice hitching as she avoids the emotion.

"A lot of branches broke," I politely say, flipping the toast. "I need to go into town to get a new chainsaw blade. I thought you might like to ride with me after breakfast."

"I'll go."

"I'm rude," I boast, grinning. "Sit down. Would you like coffee, juice, or some water? Can I get you anything?"

"Bottle of whiskey," she giggles as I plate the toast and add a few pieces of bacon. "And a cigarette."

"How about coffee with Bailey's?"

"Love it!"

I pour her coffee into a large mug, add a splash of half and half, and a generous double shot of the liquor. "You're welcome to have a smoke."

"Can I have more bacon?"

"Of course," I eagerly reply, grabbing her two more slices. I peek over at her, twirling her finger, motioning for more. "That's six."

"Perfect!" She rubs her hands together.

"You're a good time," I praise, setting her breakfast on the table. "In more ways than one."

She hastily snatches a piece of bacon. "I will need two more pieces of French toast and some butter."

"Anything you want," I offer.

"Some water."

"Keep going."

"Tell me we're okay," she mumbles, cutting into the toast and stuffing a mammoth bite into her mouth. I set the butter dish by her plate. Her insecure eyes blink up, searching for a life rope in the tumultuous seas we spin in. She needs a source of stability. I must provide all she will ever need and more.

I grab her hand. "We're great. Just don't leave me."

"Don't leave me," she counters.

"I don't plan on it," I insist, filling her a reusable water bottle. "Do you want some syrup?"

"Is it real or fake?"

"Everything is real in my life." I gaze over at the grazing beauty. "Including how I feel about you."

"How do you feel?"

I squat down. "Like I don't want you to go."

"You're kind of messed up," she assesses, feeding me a piece of bacon. "More French toast, please."

"I'm on it!" I press my lips to her hand and proceed to grab the syrup from the pantry. "You'll need to wear boots and jeans today."

"I don't own any boots."

"We'll stop at the tack store and pick some up."

I dredge more pieces of bread in the egg batter as she stares in my direction and asks, "What happens when you get tired of me?"

"That will never happen."

"How do you know?" She swigs back a generous gulp of the coffee. "Wooo! You know how to make a drink."

"It'll take the edge off. And I won't tire of you because I've never been like this with anyone. I don't bring women anywhere near my life. For the last ten years, any sex I have had has been in a hotel room. Women aren't welcome here. Until you showed up and changed the game."

"I am a woman."

"No, you're my abductee." I mischievously grin. "Big difference."

"Does your brother know I am here?"

"No, but my cousin does," I openly admit. "He's the one I got the sedatives from in New Orleans."

"Does he have a name?"

"Deacon Cruz," I reply as she finishes her first round. "Do you always eat like a horse?"

"Yes," she says, giggling. "I am barely five feet tall, weigh 115 pounds, and eat like I'm starving most days. If you order pizza, get two because I won't share."

I chuckle. "So, you can pack a steak away too?"

"Oh, yeah," she alleges. "I can eat more than most men."

"Have you always been this way?"

"Since I was little, I've always had a huge appetite. My mom used to complain because there were never leftovers in our house. I would finish my plate and anything Bran or Daphne had left on their plates. My dad is the same way, but he would finish whatever Mom didn't eat."

"Is he short?"

"Yes," she says, nodding and smiling. "But Brandon is almost your height."

"You're kidding."

"Daphne and Brandon are super tall. My mom is about five-nine, and at one point, she modeled over in Europe, which is what Daphne wants to do. Dad disagrees with her decision, so she decided to move to Alabama and start school early. Your turn."

"I was born in Connecticut."

Her hazel eyes blink in shock. "You're not Southern?"

"I got here as fast as I could."

She asks, "How old were you?"

"I was six months old."

"You're practically Southern," she quips.

I give a broad smile. "Dad's business took off in Savannah, and we eventually moved to Milsap because my grandparents had the farm. My maternal set lived in upstate New York, but we rarely ever saw them. My parents are a mess. Mom is a trophy wife and a raging alcoholic. Dad works all the time, makes a fuckton of money, and battles his addictions daily."

"What is his addiction?"

"Mostly, women. Very young. Barely legal."

"Shit," she mumbles, pausing with the frightening reality. "That's scary."

"Yeah, I don't ask. I don't want to know because I already suspect. Axel inherited the gene, and I avoid twenty-somethings like the plague because of it. You're the last."

"You shouldn't say things like that..."

With a deep breath, I steer the conversation back to the facts I believe she needs to know. "He is considering mergers, selling off the business, or handing over the reins of Monroe Consulting to Axel and me."

"What do you want?"

I plate her second round and deliver it with a kiss to the top of her head. "I don't care either way. I wouldn't mind running it, but I'm not strapped looking for work either. I have plenty of income without Daddy's money. Speaking of which, Monroe Consulting is having a party mid-June at headquarters in Savannah, a big hoopla, black-tie kind of a thing. Would you be my date?"

She drops the bacon on her plate as I grab a protein shake from the fridge. "You're serious about this *thing*?"

"I'm very serious about *you*."

"I'll need a dress and shoes."

"We can go shopping. It's not a problem," I stress, fearing rejection. "I work from home. I can go anytime."

"Are you sure you want to show off your captive?"

"I have no opinion either way," I shrug, amused. "I'll happily introduce you to friends and family. You're not a secret I need to keep, but if Axel or Dad gets anywhere near you, you'll see a side of me I don't often show. We can stay at my beach house when we go to Savannah."

"This beach house is literally on the water?"

"Yep, seven thousand square feet, over fifty acres right on the water between Savannah and Charleston. Gorgeous piece of property."

Slowing down on her feast, she swivels in the chair. Her lips wiggle as she tries to form the sentence. "Go on, ask the obvious."

"If you know what I'm going to ask, just answer."

"I've made a lot of money in a couple of lucrative investments."

She shakes her head. "That's not what I was thinking. How does this guy who presents better than average end up with such a deviant kink?"

"I don't have an answer for that."

"Have you always been this way?" she asks, holding her coffee in her lap. "Or am I your first *deviation?*"

"Um, you're the first I've drugged, which I'll never do again," I thoughtfully admit. "But I was willing to do anything to bring you home with me."

"You could've just asked."

I snicker, "Would you like to spend the next three months being my..."

She walks over to me. "Yes, I will spend three months with you, Jynx Monroe. Whatever that means."

"Just know, whatever happens in the dark..."

She interrupts, "The dark stays hidden in my heart."

"Don't make me want to kiss you more than I already do."

"You should," she whispers, "consider doing that sometime. You might like it." Her serious expression diminishes as she offers a wide smile. "But what do I know, I've never even been kissed."

"You know, you're asking me about my kinks, but what is the deal with your chaste behavior?"

"I was always busy with school, and most boys bored the fuck out of me. I don't want what has been offered."

"What do you want?"

A light blush rises on her cheeks. "I want a real man. Boots and jeans. Grit and spit. Sweating. Cursing. Smoking. No frou-frou drinks. Able to shoot pool, but knowing how to shoot his gun is even better. Aims and throws punches. Employed and doesn't need me to entertain him. He carries a normal wallet, not a checkbook holder, or God forbid, a bag. He drives a truck, looks damn fine in a three-piece suit, and understands chivalry. And he's not afraid to take little bitty me over his knee. I want a filthy fucking gentleman." She winks, and I grin. "Do you have any idea how hard that is to find in a single, willing to be monogamous form?"

"That's a helluva request."

"I'm a helluva high maintenance demanding chick."

"Where does one apply for such a position?"

"Oh!" she elaborates smirking. "He would have to audition with an adequate response to my rape ad."

I chuckle, picking her up. She straddles her legs around me. "Are we doing this?"

"We're testing the waters," she teases.

"I'd like to test your waters."

She giggles. "May I have rhinestone boots?"

———

ECHO

———

I HOLD HIS ARM IN MY NEW TEAL-COLORED BOOTS WITH pink stitching and plentiful bling as we walk through the small hardware store in town. He waves at a couple of people. "You know a lot of the townsfolk?"

"I grew up here," he says, studying the chainsaw blades. "They know me."

"Was Axel raised here?"

"No," he says, undeterred. "Mom raised Axel."

"Why did she not raise you?"

"Because I was always a radical firebrand," he chuckles, turning to face me. "And my grandmother adored me."

We check out. He buys me a Dr. Pepper, a bag of pork rinds, a wide-brimmed straw hat, and a pair of sunglasses. "Do I need cheap sunglasses?"

"Yes," he replies, opening the truck door and biting the tag off of them. "Put them on."

I ask, "What kind of trouble?"

He gets in the driver's seat and licks his lips. "Dad caught me following in my mother's footsteps at a very young age," he mutters, glancing down at the dash. "She had a thing for pills and booze. He took Axel and me to his Mom's—Grandma. Axel was a Mama's boy, though, and after about two days, he threw a pissy bitch fit, which he still does. My brother is a piece of work—the kind of guy you would shun in two seconds. If he has to work for food—*cracking crab claws, sunflower seeds, pistachios*—he deems it beneath him. Says he is not a savage male," he informs, and I giggle, popping open the pork rinds and offering him one. "Anyway, Dad came and got him. I stayed with Grandma, off and on until she passed."

"What do you mean taking after her?"

"I was drinking with my mother when I was six."

"Jesus!"

"Yeah, she is also a unique piece of work," he says with a deep breath. "I stay on a fairly even keel now, but I'm always one drink away from what I consider losing sobriety."

"But you drink."

"I do," he admits. "But I'm careful to know where my head is at before I start. I try to keep my shit in check now. At one point, I didn't give a damn. I wound up in jail."

I blink. "... For? Don't tell me! Abduction, rape, and murder?"

Glancing out the window, he explains, "Stalking a girl I was trying to protect, but I was bad, breaking into houses and selling drugs. I'm not innocent. I've never raped or killed anyone. Or abducted anyone until you."

"First times," I playfully say with a wink. I'm unscathed by his history because no man that will drug a woman is an angel. But I don't need an angel or a saint. "Where is she now?"

"My best friend, Chuck, murdered Celeste," he begrudgingly mutters. "Can this therapy session be over?"

"Yes! Drive!"

I quietly munch on the pork rinds with occasional glances to check on his well being. We're doing tough stuff—real, hardcore emotional shit. It's not going to be easy on either of us. As much as he wants to correct my frame of mind, I want to heal his bleeding heart. He's not bad, just a misguided lost boy due to environmental circumstances. We stop at a hole in the wall Mexican restaurant on the outskirts of town. "Stay here."

He quickly returns. "A dozen tacos and a gallon of tea, my dear."

"There can never be too many tacos!"

Spending all afternoon on the tailgate of his truck, I feast on tacos and slurp down tea while watching my stalker chop up tree limbs. He's disgustingly dirty. "Okay, feed me a taco."

"Is this a sexual innuendo?"

"No, Ma'am. Feed me. I need food."

"I have eight left." I unwrap one as he pulls off his hat, gloves, and sunglasses before dumping my bottle of water on his head. "It's ridiculously hot out here."

"Tell me," he says, biting into the taco. "Fuck, that's good. More."

"What are you doing with all the wood?"

"Building you a bonfire on the Fourth of July," he replies, promising a future—at least until Independence Day. With a wide smile, I scoot to the edge of the truck and spread my legs around his torso. His truck is jacked-up with a lift kit and oversized tires. He had to help me up into the back. "What? Do you want down, Shorty?"

"No, Jynx."

I shove his last bite in my mouth as he rants, "You thief!"

Taking another, I offer him a bite, but the playful look in his eyes is almost more than I can handle. I squeal and kick my legs. "Eat that taco!"

"I'm so going to get you."

I lean closer. "I'm hoping that you will."

He pulls my ass to the edge and brushes his lips against mine. He slowly backs away like he cannot believe we just kissed. His blue eyes rush over my face as he places his hands on my cheeks and does it again. His gentle tongue swoops over mine for a brief tease. "Thank you for taking care of me."

"I could say the same thing to you," I whisper, staring into his blue eyes.

"Will you take the truck and fetch me more water?"

"Who was your bitch last night?"

"You," he declares. "But I'll never call you that in the light of day."

"I know." Tasting his kiss on my lips, I hesitate, "That's why I didn't take the keys and my packed bags and leave."

"You packed? You're leaving?"

"I was," I painfully cite. "And then it dawned on me that would be the biggest regret of my life. The greatest mistake I could ever make would be not to know how this story ends."

"You should stay with me," he suggests with a flirtatious twinkle in his eyes. "I'm a filthy fucking gentleman."

13

THE DARK OF NIGHT

JYNX

I FINALLY FINISH PILING THE BRANCHES IN THE CLEARING and hop into the truck just a little after dusk. The night is coming on way too fast.

She's driving because I'm damn exhausted. The property had significant damage, with over a dozen trees having major breaks. The giant limbs are cleared and chopped, and I plan on having the Ag boys finish the smaller shit.

"You need a shower," she softly says. "You should let me make dinner or go get something from town."

"I wanted to make you a steak."

"I could grab some Chinese or pizza."

Do I trust her to return?

"How do I know you won't leave?"

"Jynx, if I were going to leave, it would've been after last night," she replies, parking the truck where I always put it. *Damn, this girl.* She kills the engine and lays her hand on my thigh. My pulse skyrockets. "I'm not leaving you."

With a nod of my head, I extend my hand, and she easily crawls over the console and sits on my lap like making a wish to Santa. "Spread your legs."

She straddles over and lays her hands on my chest. "It's dark outside, but I can see you."

"I know," I mutter, running my hand from her delicate jaw down to her slender, feminine neck. She would look fabulous in a collar with that long neckline and her hair up. I hold her close, tightly against my chest. I'm beyond nasty, but she doesn't resist my advances. "Stay."

"Trust me, J."

She wiggles just enough to turn my issue into a significant problem. "What are you doing?"

"Putting ideas in your head."

"I don't need any more ideas," I mutter like a crass motherfucker with one thing on my mind. She kisses my neck. "I sweat all day, baby."

"I don't give a shit." Her mouth works its magic, sucking and biting as my hands slip to her ass, and I grind once, adjusting myself against her heat, imagining I'm sitting deep inside of her folds. A moan escapes from my lungs, and my eyes close as she slides onto the floorboard.

I back the seat up all the way. "What are you doing?"

"Basking in your masculinity."

"I fucking stink."

Her eyes sparkle in the incandescence of the house lights. "I need time to explore the male anatomy. I've never done any of this. Humor me."

I lick my lips, and a smirk elevates. "I will give you as much time as you need. I will be your guinea pig. Your plaything. Your toy."

"And at the witching hour..."

"I will show you what your wild womanly ways do to a man." Staring at the bulge, she coyly blinks as if needing permission. "You don't have to ask, sweetheart. I'm not an isolated Dominant."

"What do you mean?"

"I mean, if you want to touch me, you can. I won't react unfavorably. Some Doms want all of the control both ways—they can touch you whenever, but you have to seek permission to touch them. I am not a one-way street. I don't have Mommy or Daddy issues. I have issues because when I thought I was in love with a girl, she was taken from me. Feel free to mess with me. Flirt with me. Play with me. Touch me. I won't reject you."

"Go back there," she whispers. "You *thought* you were in love with her?"

"Knowing how I am starting to feel about you," I tenderly say. "I don't believe that what I felt for her was real at all. It may have been young lust."

"You care about me."

"I care about you greatly, more than I wish I did because I was certainly not prepared for you to vault into my life."

With a jagged breath, she inches her trembling hand up my thigh and rests it on my erection. "Holy fuck..."

I snarl at her gullibility. "Can I see it?"

"No."

"When?"

"In time."

"So, there are limits?"

"There are," I correct. "But, I think you're too afraid to come after me boldly."

"Would you stop me if I unzipped your jeans?"

"Yes, because I'm grungy, and you deserve better."

Mischief ignites in her expression. "What if I snuck in your room and mounted you in the night?"

"I don't know what I would do," I say, smirking. "I'll be sure to lock my door now, though."

"Damn!" She snaps.

"You're a Southpaw."

"I am," she says. "You're not."

"Only in some things," I tease. "I like holding your hand with my left."

"Go take a shower, Jynx. I'll get your dinner."

"You're amazing."

"I am just a girl smitten with a man."

Something about the way she says the words force my inquiry, "Are you trying to impress me, Miss Maines?"

"I am," she whispers, trailing her fingers over the length of my denim-covered cock. "Is it working?"

"Very much so."

———

ECHO

———

WITH A SLIGHT NERVOUSNESS, I GO TO TOWN AND PICK UP Chinese food. His truck is massive, but I manage to wrangle the big bitch with ease despite a few patrons looking at this tiny girl hopping out of the beast. I order way too much food and pay for it with the credit card that he insisted I take.

I stop at the corner store and pick up a twelve-pack of beer, a carton of smokes—Marlboros, and every flavor of sunflower seed that they have. I drive the twenty minutes to his grandparents' place set back in the boonies.

Pushing the button for the gate, I notice one of the peacocks out in the driveway. He's cutting up, making all kinds of noise at the intrusion. Jynx tries to make sure they all return home to nest for the night, but some of them are stubborn and prefer to roost up in the trees. They're loudmouths—*at all hours*—amidst the frog, owl, and bug symphony.

Jynx's rural existence is a far cry from being in a sleeper suburb where police and ambulance sirens carry on like a triumphant jazz band through the night. I'm slowly adjusting to the difference. I step out of the car to howling coyotes in the distance.

I grab the two bags of Chinese food and head inside. Jynx doesn't surface, so I bound back to the truck for the beer and haul from the convenience store. I shut the garage and lock the door before tiptoeing through the house. I haven't been upstairs in the three-story Plantation Home. I take the curved grand staircase in the foyer up to the landing.

I have no idea where his room is.

There are four doors, three off to one side, and double doors on the opposite side. I try the three doors first, all bedrooms, similar to the one I'm staying in downstairs. The rooms are decorated in a shabby chic style, each with their own bathroom. I head back across the landing to the double doors, which are locked.

Hmph.

I eye the spiral staircase up to the third floor, which is rather scary. The wrought iron artistic focal point is suspended above the foyer with vast open space and a glorious view with the wall of windows. The step groans with my weight, but I reason that if Jynx takes his big frame up the steps—*he probably clocks in around two hundred pounds*—my ass can climb up it.

On the third floor, I find another set of double doors at the end of a bridge walkway. Again, suspended above the first-floor foyer. Upon closer inspection, I note one of the doors is cracked open. I peek inside to the enormous four-poster canopy bed with a sleeping Jynx sprawled out on the white chenille and lace bedspread.

I step inside.

His hair is damp. His snug midnight blue boxers provoke my fantasies. I grab the wet towel off of the bathroom counter and inhale the scent of him in the room. The mixture of body wash, cologne, and aftershave is Jynx. I note the almost full hamper and toss the towel in before carrying the whole thing down the two flights of stairs.

Once downstairs, I open the washer to discover his nasty clothes from the day. I pick them up and sniff them. He claimed he was gross, but something about a man smelling like a man turns me on. I didn't realize this until in his presence. He liked to play hard and dirty outside; I prayed that would remain true in the great indoors as well.

I start a load of laundry and put the beer and food in the fridge. I should probably eat something, but I'm restless and beyond curious about what is behind the double doors on the second floor. I scavenge around the drawer where my car keys are and find a single key on a green piece of silken string.

I rush upstairs and try the key in the lock. It slides in easily, and I open the door without a sound. The room is massive with the height of two floors and more BDSM gear than I ever imagined a man like Jynx possessing. Racks. Kneeling benches. A padded table. And a bed that looks like it belongs in a dungeon because...*this is his dungeon.*

I close my eyes as the reality divulges more than I can handle.

"He doesn't bring girls home," I mutter, spinning right into him.

Boink.

Oh. Shit.

With a curious expression, he demands, "Why are you in here?"

"Explain this to me."

"No," he says, shaking his head. "It doesn't concern you."

"You have an entire wing devoted to your fetish and yet claim that no woman ever comes here? I'm not buying your lies. You're just like everyone else."

He lowers his head with a perturbed look. "I don't need to explain anything to you because I've done nothing wrong."

"I'm leaving," I remark, feeling sick and rushing past him. "Which is what I should've done last night."

His fingers seize my arm. "Abigail!"

"Don't call me that," I sass, struggling against him. "I hate it!"

"Why?"

"Because my mother always calls me that when she is angry or judgemental or just herself. It makes me cringe."

"Last night," he mutters, stepping closer with an effortless bravado. "Abby fell from my lips, and it made you come."

"I'm not ever coming again with you!" I cry, knowing I cannot escape his grasp. "You lied to me! You promised you wouldn't lie! That you lived in the real and not the fake."

He tosses me over his shoulder, and we leave the room. He sprints up the spiral staircase with me bouncing along on his shoulder, dangling three flights up in mid-air.

I hysterically scream when he tosses me onto his bed face down in the darkened room. Quickly, he locks my hands together with a pair of thick brown leather cuffs and tosses my shoes across the room with a thud. He tugs my jeans and panties from my body as I attempt to roll away from him.

I'm an idiot to wrestle with a monster.

Not only is he fucking psychotic, but his mammoth size prevents my leaving.

"Stop fighting me!"

"You're using your size to bully me," I snarl and kick his hard wall of abdominal muscles. The force of the kick only propels me back, and I hit the floor because of my stupidity. He lunges across the bed and topples onto me.

The swing of his arm is nothing compared to the burning sensation of his palm on my bare ass cheek. He grunts, lashing out and spanking my ass red. "I did not lie to you!" He plops on his butt with his back against the bed and pulls my body across his lap. More smacks. More tears. "I promised you I would not lie to you!"

"Jynx!" I wail, losing my ability to process what is happening. "Stop!"

He doesn't listen.

I've never been spanked in my entire life. I'm humiliated and mortified, but I feel the upsurge of his arousal pressing into my belly.

The more I fight, the more his monster surfaces.

He slides my body over his mighty thighs and opens the fly of his boxers. "Suck me!" Pushing his hard cock into my mouth, he firmly grips my hair, forcing my mouth to welcome his engorged dick. I'm gagging and crying as he bucks like a savage and thwaps my ass. "Faster! Tighten your goddamn lips and suck me properly, wench!"

I'm a blubbering mess, not having the faintest clue as to what I am doing. Selia says this is natural, but there is nothing natural about this man driving his colossal member repeatedly into my throat while swatting my ass like he's serving a volleyball.

Somehow, through his guidance, I slowly find the rhythm, stiffening yet softening my orifice to provide an accommodating service. I moan as tears drip from the corners of my eyes and drool pours out of my mouth, cascading over his sack and thighs. His hand rubs my stinging rear end, and he teases my entrance, blotting in the dew with his finger pad. He refuses to penetrate me.

Bastard.

In my peripheral vision, I watch as he brings it to his nose, breathing in the soppy scent of my youthful vigor and tasting the richness on his tongue. His thrusts increase as I gulp him down, and he maintains a vigilant clutch of my hair.

"I'm going to come, baby. Oh, God... you're going to make me come." He explodes in my mouth, coming with a ferocity and holding my head down. "Swallow me, Abigail. Swallow *me.*"

And I do.

14

PUSHING THE NEEDLE

ECHO

AFTER DOWNING HIS SPUNK, I LEAVE HIS ROOM. I MOVE THE laundry, swipe a beer, and peel open the carton of smokes. I remember seeing a lighter in the junk drawer with the keys. Grabbing my journal from the bedroom, I step outside and sit on the wicker loveseat overlooking the lake.

Fourth entry, the fifth day

He is an asshole.

An utterly deranged dickhead.
And I think I have real feelings bubbling up for him. His
salacious ways aren't sugared with kisses but
perversely bittersweet.
I want to be in his room. I want to be tethered down and
tortured for hours by him without regard for my
feelings on the matter.
I desperately want him to conquer me.
Fuck getting raped.
I want his absolute Dominion over me.
Claim me. Take me. Use me.
Til the end.

I cry warm tears of anguish.

I asked for this—every bit of it—but it's a lot to accept. I'm not expecting him to indulge my sadness or even express concern, and when I note his standing in the door, I'm left speechless.

He's trying, and so am I.

We're meeting in the middle and finding the missing pieces to make this thing work. Because—*we like each other.*

We speak the same peculiar language.

"You got another one of those?" he asks, sitting down beside me and twisting the cap off of the beer for me.

I hand him my cigarette. "I don't smoke. I'm just doing it to look cool."

He grins, and I laugh. "You don't need to look cool. You are cool, Ekky."

"I'm not sure what the fuck we're doing, Jynx."

"... Are you happy?"

My face contorts. "Happy? One minute we have a remarkable intimate bonding, and the next thing I know, shit is spinning out of control."

"But do you like it?"

"I want you to fuck me."

"So you do like it?" With a chuckle under his breath, he beams a smile at me. His fingers gently brush my hair over my ear. "You should probably know a few things about me before we go any further. I'm not the kind of guy who would ever use my fetish as an excuse for violence."

"But it is inherently violent."

"It is, but there is a hard line. I won't ever be genuinely angry and take it out on you."

"You're not mad about my snooping?"

"Fuck no," he says, shrugging. "Make yourself at home."

"Why did you spank me?"

"Because I saw an opportunity to fuck with your mind."

"And I fell for it."

"You did," he cockily snickers, laying his hand on my bare thigh. "But I would never truly hurt you. I'm a bastard and an asshole in the confines of a scene, but filthy fucking gentleman pretty much nails who I am. I like my kink. And I like it dark. And fucked up. And uncomfortable. And painful."

"You're a sadist on every imaginable level."

"And I told you I was," he reminds, taking a drag from the smoke and rubbing my thigh. His hand keeps inching up—higher and higher. "I wasn't lying. This is the tip of the iceberg for me. But if it's already too much, then maybe you do need to go. I won't rape you. I'll push your limits hard and even go beyond them, but you also need to know that I would never cause serious harm. I don't want to disassemble your sanity. I need to take care of you, making you better than you already are."

"You're already harming my heart because I don't know how you feel," I allege, taking the beer from his hand and swigging back a gulp. "During the day, I feel like you're the boyfriend I've always dreamed about, but when the night comes, you're a damn pornstar with a sharp edge."

He bumps into my shoulder. "Don't give up on me."

"I'm not," I promise, wishing his fingers would dip into my hollow. "I just want to know where we're going."

"Someplace wonderful and warm, if I have my way."

I set the bottle down on the side table and take the cigarette from his fingers. I smash the butt in the ashtray and crawl onto his lap. "You mean that?"

"I mean every fucking word, Echo."

"Sleep with me."

"Literally?" His face lights up. "Sleep?"

"Yes, my room, your room, I don't care. I want every remaining minute of this summer to be spent with you."

He leans back, rubbing his hands over his face, and mutters, "Fuck."

JYNX

"DON'T FALL FOR ME."

"It's too late for that," she says, restraining her emotions. "I was falling for you when we raced across the country. You're everything I've ever wanted."

"I'm not, though," I assure with trepidation. "I'm trying to teach you that you're worth more than an attack. Don't fall for what you cannot have."

"Is that all this is—*you playing professor?*"

"I cannot plan out my life," I say, setting my jaw. "My brain doesn't work that way. I take things as they come."

"But you promised a bonfire," she rallies, arguing her point. "That is planning."

"I mean long term," I elaborate, staring at her and wondering how we wound up here. "I can give you three months. I can't promise what happens after that, and to tell you the truth, I don't even want to think about it. If I plan it all out—this idyllic masterpiece—and it doesn't happen, I will end up in an awful place. And so will you. My job is to protect not only my heart but yours. Don't make this harder than it needs to be. Enjoy the days. Relish in the nights."

"So I only get this big bad Dominant in the middle of the night?" she asks with increasing irritation. "What if I want you like that all the time?"

"I refuse to let the darkest parts of me out in the day. I'm like a vampire. The sun will burn my monster and consume me without a way to diffuse the endorphin load."

"Let him out again."

"Right now?"

"Yes."

"I don't perform on command."

"Then I'm leaving because we aren't in this as a team," she claims, caving into her fear. "We aren't fifty/fifty."

Running my hand over my hair, I shake my head. "I stalked, drugged, and abducted you. What part of that screams a healthy relationship? I am toxic. We are toxic."

"I want to be intoxicated by you," she cries, grappling for anything to hold onto. "During the day, you're so kind."

I blink repeatedly. "I'm a decent human being, and I will concede to your filthy fucking gentleman title, but I'm not your forever white knight. I'm serving as a teacher, a dark Master, who believes you deserve more than rape."

"What do I have to do to deserve you?"

"I don't want romance."

She squeals, "Liar!"

"Take your shirt off."

She pulls it over her head and throws it far. Her hair flutters back to her shoulders with the gracefulness of a butterfly. "Now what?"

"Masturbate."

Her eyes bulge wide like I've insulted and tarnished her soul. "... What?"

"Touch your pussy like you do when you're alone watching all those videos."

Covering her chest with her arms, she gasps with embarrassment, "… You know?"

"I'm really good at what I do," I marvel with arrogance. "And you need to learn to protect yourself online."

She skitters off of my lap, grabbing her shirt as the chase is on. Sprinting across the backyard, she darts into the shed and locks the door. I walk over. Fuck running. I lightly knock on the door. "Go away and leave me alone!"

"I have a key, Abigail!"

"Stop calling me that!"

"Open the door."

"No!"

"If you don't open the door right now, I will send a list of all of the videos you've downloaded in the last three years to your professors, Abigail."

She swings the door open fast. "You wouldn't do that!"

Lifting my brows, I fiendishly smile. "… I wouldn't?"

"Fuck you, Jynx!" She tosses a pillow at me. "I hate you! You're too good at this!"

"I'm thirty-six. I've had a bit of practice." She twirls away, but I grab her arms and shove her onto the bed. I lunge onto her naked flesh, securing her wrists in one hand as I flick my tongue over her lips. I nip at her neck and draw a wet trail to her nipple. I fastidiously suck and bite. "Touch your fucking pussy, like the slut you want to be. Show me how you make yourself come."

"I hate you!" she repeats, spitting in my face. I spread her legs and grip my dick in my hand, preparing to mount her and give her exactly what she wants. "You won't do it!"

I spring back at her accusation. "You think I won't put my dick in you?"

"No!"

"Bitch, I shoved my dick down your fucking throat! I can easily take your ass."

"No!" Her screams echo throughout the cabin. "Don't do that!"

I stick out my tongue and smirk. "Why, is your ass holy? Cause your mouth sure sins like a tart."

"Dammit, J!"

I gently swoop my tongue over her hardened peak. "Show me how you pet that beautiful kitten between your legs. Make her purr for me."

Her teeth are clamped so hard on her bottom lip that I fear she may have a bruise by morning. I lift on my forearms, hovering, planking, as her hand skids down to her slit. "I love the rough scenes."

"You like the ones when there is no consent or negotiation."

"Yes," she mumbles. "I don't want the choice."

"But you don't want to be taken by a low-life criminal; a man smelling of booze with bad teeth and a rank dick isn't going to do it for you. But somehow, you foolishly believe that you can dissuade his efforts of raping you. And that—right there—is where you are wrong. He will have his way with you and obliterate your existence."

"Not really, no," she finally admits. "I want an honorable man with a closet full of skeletons." She gasps as her fingers speed up. "He's gorgeous but capable of taking care of things. He's brilliantly sinister and knows my number." My hand grazes over the fullness of her breasts as my fingers lightly pinch and twist her nipples. "Oh, God...Jynx..."

"Don't you come yet," I warn.

"Don't stop," she demands, rocking for more. "Please." I toss her hand away from her clit and slip down between her legs. My tongue caresses the damp shell. I circle the ripe bud, sucking it into my mouth. My fingers don't stop, tweaking, and burning her nipples. Her hips wickedly buck to meet my demands. "Please, fuck me!"

I stop and slide off the edge of the bed.

She sits up in protest, but I push her down, whipping her legs onto my shoulders and swiveling her across the bed. "Don't say another word. Touch your fucking cunt."

Her erratic breaths speed up as I pound one-off between her legs and groan, "I want to hurt you."

"So do it!"

"That's giving consent," I enthusiastically praise, raising a brow. "Are you sure you want *that?*"

"I desire whatever you are willing to allow."

"You took the ad down," I mention, spitting on my hand and coating my dick. "I'm so proud of you." With one solid thrust, I plunge into her unyielding asshole, and she howls like I'm shredding her insides apart. I firmly cover her mouth with my hand, and she proceeds to sink her teeth into my palm. I love a good horizontal brawl. I don't fucking care. I cannot take it anymore. I'm getting off in this girl again tonight. I pound her body with a vengeance as a maniacal rage consumes me. "You wanted this."

I chuck her feet from my shoulders as I lean closer and remove my hand. I passionately kiss her, diving my tongue into her swollen mouth. She kisses me back with as much intensity as I bring. I reluctantly part from her, and she whispers, "Jynx Monroe, you're one fucked up son of a bitch."

Her eyelashes brim with tears as I come hard and fast, bucking with all that I have. "Cry for me, baby. Cry harder." I groan with pleasure as her body clamps to mine. "Do you know how much I want to take everything you're offering?"

"So do it," she mutters as the tears multiply, and I thrust my fingers into her wetness. I pump hard, wishing it was my dick she was blessing with her dew, but I'm not there yet. Taking her virginity is a commitment, and I want to earn the distinction of possessing the right to call her my girl. Her eyes shutter closed, and she pants, coming with a wave and saturating my hand. She blinks and breathes. "I won't let you down. You think I am too young, but give me three months to prove to you that I'm just right. I'm exactly who you need. I'll let you do whatever you want."

"I wasn't looking to fall in love."

"I wasn't either," she charges, brushing her hands over my shoulders. "I wanted a fucking one night stand."

My lips meet hers again in a delicious frolic of lips and tongue. "I cannot be your one night stand. I'm sorry. I can do many things for you and to you, but I won't do that."

"Then I admit defeat," she says, bawling in my arms. "I'll be your submissive."

"You don't want that," I caution, tempted by the idea. "I'm cruel."

Through her tears, she cackles, "Like randomly fucking my backend wasn't cruel?"

"I like getting off, and you're just so damn beautiful," I confess, blinking back my tears of conflict. I won't let them go, but they're damn sure there. I'm falling in love with this girl—Abigail Maines. She's damn twenty-two. And my fucking dick and heart cannot get enough of her. I almost hollered when she asked to sleep with me. "You're a brat."

"Does that make you my Sugar Daddy?"

"I'm not *that* old," I contest with a seductive grin. "But you're still a brat. My fucking beguiling brat."

I want her in my bed.

I want her on my dick.

I want my collar on her neck.

But most of all, I want the responsibility of keeping her happy.

"I want whatever brings me closer to you," she whispers, declaring her subjugation. "Master Jynx, with much respect, I beg you to train me."

And so we begin.

15

SHORTY

Echo

In the bathroom, I finish packing up a few things for the weekend away in Savannah. We're leaving tomorrow morning. Time is passing far too quickly. I want to stomp on the brakes to spend more time with him.

We've spent the last few days working sun up to sundown. The days are blissfully romantic as the night brings on a hot, sordid affair.

Jynx is outside right now with the Ag boys. A couple of them—Tommy and Jake—are going to maintain the farm while we're away for a few days.

Surprisingly, Jynx asked me how much to pay them. I was humbled that he asked, but considering they're closer to my age at eighteen than his, I understood. I had no idea, but I tossed out the idea of a few hundred, and he agreed. They're finishing the yard clean-up, letting the horses and flock out and back in. Two trips a day, but they live less than five miles away.

I glance at the party dress hanging in the plastic bag. We found it in Charleston at a lovely boutique. He paid way too much for it, but I'm trying to accept his gifts are part of the Jynx Monroe prize package.

"Are you aware of how incredible you are?" He asks from the doorway, surprising me. "I could stare at you for the rest of my life."

"And you wonder why I am falling for you!" I giggle, tossing makeup into the bag as he comes up behind me and wraps his arms around me. We stare in the mirror at one another. "I'm not ready for this."

"Yes, you are," he insists, spinning me in his arms and picking me up. He deposits me on the bathroom counter and rubs his beard. He pulls off his shirt and hands it to me. I bring the fabric to my nose as he flips on the electric razor and shaves. "You're watching me," he mumbles, turning on the hot water. His eyes dance to mine. "Am I that entertaining?"

"Why not use the electric razor to take it all off?"

"I don't like the feel of it. And I don't want to dull my blade with that much hair," he instructs, pulling open the straight razor. He whisks the lather and goos up his face. "And the answer is no. I will not allow you to do this."

"I wouldn't know the first thing about it."

"Lean against the mirror, spread your thighs, and arch your hips out."

"What are you doing?"

"Shaving," he replies, running the razor over his face. He smirks, and his dimples resurface. I blush as he encourages, "Trust me."

I patiently wait as he finishes his face, and he whisks more lather. "Are we going bare, Mr. Monroe?"

"Yes," he informs, pulling up the chair. "But purposefully. After we come back, I will be sending you to Rochelle for a proper waxing."

"Fuck," I yelp as the brush barely touches me. "It tickles!"

"Breathe," he urges, continuing. "And don't move. Arch up more."

"I feel like I'm at the gynecologist."

"I could conduct a thorough exam."

"Where did you learn to use a straight razor?"

"I taught myself, years ago, because back in the olden days," he cackles, gleefully. "We used to carry switchblades because we were bad. Being the kinky ass bastard that I am, I thought it would be cool if I learned to do this. I had taught myself everything else about being a man, so I figured what was one more thing."

I ponder his words and consider who taught me to be a girl. I learned a lot from my paternal grandmother. And strangely, Selia has provided many lessons. We raised one another from fumbling teenage girls to young women. "… Everything?"

"Pretty much," he replies, calming my nerves with his deep voice. "My dad was never around, and my grandfather was not the type to do anything that didn't involve golf. If you swung a club with him, he might have said two words to you, which meant you had a deep and meaningful relationship."

"Who taught Axel?"

"Me!" He booms, lightly nudging my thigh. "But as I said, Axel is a prissy little bitch boy. He would rather see Rochelle or whoever in Myrtle Beach. He's not in your league."

"Is he straight?"

"As the day is long," he says, running the razor over my tender flesh. "Don't even question his sexuality, or you'll get a sermon on his straightness."

"… What is *my league*, Jynx?"

"You want a real man."

"And you're a real man?"

"I am," he affirms, taking a warm washcloth and cleaning me. "Beautiful barren landscape."

Leaning in, he rolls his tongue up the slit. "Jesus! Warn a girl once in a while!"

"Perfection!" He proudly beams and helps me down off the counter before leading me to the bedroom. "Sit on the bed."

He disappears into the closet and returns with three boxes. "You will be wearing these things underneath your dress." He sets the stack of presents on the bed and crouches on the floor in front of me. "Big-box first."

I pull the red ribbon on the white box to find a luxurious black silken bra, panty, and garter set. The wide strapping speaks of his fetish. The next box contains a remote control vibrating anal plug. "You've got to be kidding! I'm meeting your parents!" His brows wag as I laugh at the seriousness held in his eyes. "Oh my God, Jynx!"

"My name is Jeremiah." I gasp at his sudden revelation.

"The weeping prophet," I mutter, remembering my religion classes in college. "A seething harangue."

"Yes, I'm quite angry," he laughs, showing off those precious dimples in his face. "If you need to safeword out, call me by my name, but do not ever call me Jeremy."

"I wish I had that clause."

"You don't get that clause, Abby." He winks.

"I hate to say how much I love hearing you say it," I admit, blushing and grabbing the last box. My eyes water as I stare at the diamond necklace. "This is a collar."

"It is," he confirms, standing upright and fastening the row of diamonds around my neck. Another long strand of diamonds dips between my breasts. "Hell, that's hot."

"Is it..."

"I don't do fake," he asserts with a crooked grin. "Ever."

"I should say your name now because I cannot breathe."

He takes my hand and drops to one knee. "My name is Jeremiah Abaddon Monroe. A pleasure to meet you, Miss Maines. Please call me Jynx."

"Hebrew," I muster out as he latches his fingers around mine. "Destroyer. Doom."

"Angel of the abyss," he adds.

"Who gave you such a wretched middle name?"

"My mother—she was sixteen and pregnant with me," he carefully says as we trudge through his bleak beginnings. "I interfered with her partying ways," he factually informs like a news anchor, but the sorrow in his words brutally stabs my heart. "And they had a king over them, *which is* the angel of the bottomless pit, whose name in the Hebrew tongue *is* Abaddon, but in the Greek tongue hath *his* name Apollyon. It's from Revelations 9:11. Also, don't ever say I have Mommy issues. My grandmother may as well have been my mother because the woman you will meet this weekend means absolutely nothing to me. She provided a cheap motel for nine months and nothing more."

"You're over it."

"I'm over her," he contends with utmost conviction. "I spent the better part of my reckless and wild youth, causing mayhem in acts of rebellion, hoping to garner her attention. It did not work. No matter if I was good or evil, she does not nor will she ever care about her first-born son. She never once came to see me in prison, and I decided when I was released, that I would no longer care about her thoughts or opinions. I call her my mother or Mom out of respect for my father. He's done a lot for me."

I cautiously ask, "Is that why you lash out at women?"

"No, I do that because it gives me a boner."

We laugh and smile. "You're too much."

"The room was my grandmother's."

"Your grandfather only golfed through..."

"And when the cat was away, that mouse played with all kinds of people." He leads me down the spiral staircase to the double doors where we step inside the hallowed ground. He clicks on the bright lights. "This is my grandmother's playroom."

Flabbergasted, I muster out, "Her dungeon."

"Yes," he reassures, popping a mint in his mouth. He places one on my tongue like a communion wafer in his sanctuary. I walk around with an innate curiosity, capturing the essence of the old equipment. I completely misjudged him. "I have never brought a woman here. Nor have I ever taken a woman to my beach house. Hotels—quick, easy, noncommittal. Clean and neat. Or a club for practicing my craft. Never here."

At a cabinet, he pulls open a drawer full of scrapbooks and memorabilia. He hands me the framed picture of a young woman in fetish gear. "Those black thigh highs go up to her crotch!"

Rubbing his smooth chin, he snickers, "Yeah, they do. They don't make them like that anymore, but I have several pairs of hers."

"This is part of who you are," I whisper, startled. "Who is the woman tied up in that picture?"

"That is my 'Aunt' Sadie," he says, smiling at the memory. "She wasn't really my aunt. She was my grandmother's *girl* for years."

"She's such a fetish provocateur." I lay my hand on the necklace. "This is more than just kinky sex for you."

"Yes, it is a spiritual place."

"I crossed you," I regret, understanding Jynx more than I ever thought possible. "I tread on the sacred—*your religion.*"

"Bingo," he comments, pointing at me, as the scent of clove wafts through the air. "I'm old. Girls don't ask to be raped. Rape is a crime, a punishable offense. Ravishment is more what I believe you're looking for, child." He winks.

"Thanks, minister of kink," I tease, immediately regretting it. "I disrespected something I knew nothing about. And I am very sorry. The ad is done. It won't ever go back up."

"When we go to Savannah, you will walk in on my arm as my date, my lover, and my submissive. Many people in attendance will probably know what you are to me because they know me, and they knew my grandmother. Don't let it unsettle you. I will take care of you and protect you as long as you're mine."

"... Am I yours?"

"You're wearing my collar," he admires, touching my neck, "which looks ravishing on you."

"How did your grandmother get away with this?"

"My grandfather kept a mistress for years at the old foundry he did the books at," he says with a touch of naughty. "The deal was, they could both do their own thing, but divorce was out of the question because too much money was on the line."

"Did they sleep together?"

"God, no! Grandma took over the third story suite and the game room. My grandfather stayed in the middle room on the second floor when he was here, but he spent most of his time with his lover until she died. I stayed downstairs in the room you were in."

"You grew up around Sadie?"

"And many others," he adds, studying my reactions to everything. "Lady Clementine was famous in these parts."

I'm awestruck by not only his story, but his sharing. I have so far to go in both regards. "When did you start?"

"Shit," he mutters, rolling his eyes. "I was probably fourteen when I first ventured out on my own. I'd go to the seedy bars with Sadie. She did comedy routines, and I ended up picking up some twenty-something."

"You don't remember her name?"

"Not a fucking clue," he says, aloof. "Might as well call her first wet pussy willing to ride me. I seriously don't pay attention to these things. I know your name because yours is the only one that matters."

I stick my tongue out with the mint on the tip of my tongue, and he sucks it up into his mouth. "Can I say it once?"

"Yes."

"Master Jeremiah Monroe."

A grin incrementally perks upon his lips. "Yes, my love?"

"Is it wrong that I want to be wearing leather shorts like Sadie with Clementine's boots on and having her grandson whip my ass?"

"Not at all," he says, pulling me closer. "It sounds like a heavenly dream to me."

"I will proudly walk into the party as yours, Sir."

I lower to my knees as he grins. "This is my first sinful act in this room."

"The first of many," I whisper as he unzips his pants and reveals his cock to me. It's the first time I've honestly gotten a good look at his manhood. He is everything I ever imagined—thick, long, and veined. "You aren't cut."

"No, because my mother was busy tramping about town on the eighth day," he confides. "Her very Jewish parents never forgave the act, which led to the disintegration of the relationship and subsequent loss of visitation."

"Are they still alive?"

"Yes," he replies, smiling. "Both of them. In the last decade, I've tried to make amends, but it isn't easy because they do not speak to their daughter at all. We share the same view of my mother."

"Are you close with any of that side?"

"My Aunt Trudy, and her son, my cousin Deacon."

"Do they practice Judaism?"

He considers how to answer the question. "No, they practice the same religion I do, Shorty."

THE QUIT

Jynx

IN A STUNNING RED DRESS WITH HER LONG HAIR CURLED
and piled high on her head, I escort the raving beauty into the shark
pit party in an upscale Savannah hotel. Under the twinkling lights, we
descend the steps with glances to my beautiful date. The annual event
is for the sole purpose of company morale.

Thank heavens employee morals never come into play.

Tucked in my pocket is the remote control for the butt plug I've
inserted into my lovely hostage. I'm starting to believe she is the
terrorist attacking my heart.

I wave and smile like I've rehearsed my whole life for this.

I should've been a politician.

God knows I'm crooked enough.

Before this night, I was the most eligible bachelor at company functions. My typical behavior included tossing back a few drinks and a cheap thrill in a hotel room with someone who I wouldn't be the boss of eventually.

I scan over the crowd dotted with about a dozen (very) young escorts. Dad's addiction is ever-present. I care about my father because he's helped my ass out of some tight spots, but the man known as Montgomery Monroe is a sleaze.

Spotting my drunken mother at the bar, I snarl and guide Echo away from the wreck waiting to happen. She doesn't need to encounter that cow.

Unfortunately, I end up running into Axel, who is always on the prowl. Echo clings to my side as he approaches up in arms. "We need to decide what we're doing. Dad is considering selling next week. If we want our legacy, now is the time to say something."

In a classic Axel-is-a-dick-and-a-prissy-bitch fashion, he doesn't bother to greet or introduce himself to my date, and I don't go out of my way to do such because the last thing my brother needs is more ammo.

"Who is he selling to?"

"Some new group out of Europe ran by women."

"Dammit," I reply, scanning the crowd and glancing down at the girl by my side. Her innocent smile fills my heart. I clear my throat. "Let the company go. We'll figure it out."

She tightens her grip on my arm, grounding me as my somewhat naive baby brother says, "Are you sure?"

He doesn't have the stability I possess, and he depends on me to make the big decisions. It's been this way as long as I can remember.

I lead; he follows.

I joined Reckless Rebellion; he had his prospect cut on within forty-eight hours. I went to work for Dad; two weeks later, Axel was in conference calls.

My lifelong shadow is a six-foot playboy with a penchant for shiny things.

I pray Echo powdered her entire body.

I give Axel a lot of shit about being slightly flamboyant, but I also know that if I needed someone to transfer crypto currency or bury a body, he would have my back.

Axel is a good person—*to me,* but he doesn't ever feel the need to man up. He'd never plunge a toilet or use a tool of any kind. I imagine he expects the women in his life to know how to operate his tool because that would simply be too much work.

Truthfully, I doubt he'd ever hit on Echo out of respect to me. However, he wouldn't think twice about killing someone if they hurt her—but he'd hire a hitman to do it.

I'd do it myself.

"Yeah, we got this," I reassure, trying to calm his nerves. Underneath his perpetual asshat-mode, Axel has an enormous heart. He's worried about the employees and their families because selling out like this is never good. "We'll get something going on. No worries."

"I trust you," he mutters, fidgeting and laying his hand on my arm. "This is a tremendous shift of where you and I planned on being, but I talked to Deacon, and he's onboard."

Of course, he is.

Because my Cuz knows I'll make him a shitton of money.

"If Dad has already overlooked his two sons," I rhetorically think out loud as I ponder the circumstances. "Do we want him backseat driving wherever we decide to take the company?"

Axel turns to look at Echo. "What would you do?"

"I don't know anything about this," she softly whispers.

"Certainly, you have an opinion," he stresses, taking two glasses of champagne from a passing waiter's tray. He hands her one. "Tell me."

"A long-term strategy based around your subservience to what I assume will be a remaining board member is not a good way to take over any business," she thoughtfully says, taking a sip of champagne. "If he's ignored you thus far, there is no reason to believe that will ever change."

Axel grins. "Where are you from?"

"Originally, Alabama. But I live in California," she answers, and Axel tilts his head at me.

I snarl, crossing my fingers that he keeps his mouth shut. He merely nods and says, "Take care of my brother. He's a snake."

"I plan on it," she counters with an uppity smirk. "His snake is easily charmed by me."

Damn, this girl.

"What's your degree in again?"

"I'll be working on getting my doctorate in psychology in the fall," she proudly informs. "Why do you ask?"

"Are you interested in coming to work for the Monroe brothers?"

Her brows tightly knit together because I hadn't brought up Axel's idea to Echo yet—we've been a little busy between farm work and kneeling practice.

It's like football practice with different balls.

Axel suggested her doing human relations and performance coaching for our new firm. Start it off strong and keep building upon that.

Her sharp glance discreetly warns of the trouble I am in. "We've been talking about it," she lies, on the spot, covering my ass. "It will all depend on Jynx's relocation and compensation package. I don't come cheap or easy."

Inside, I die laughing—*that is my girl*—while my dick throbs like an insatiable beast. The girl I have waited an entire lifetime to find comes in a five-foot, twenty-two-year-old, smart-mouthed package.

I want her on my team.

Not the company team, but Jynx Monroe's team. "Come to the beach house tomorrow. We'll figure out what our next move is."

"Over half of these people are being fired next week."

"I know," I reply with concern. I'm not immune to what is on the line, and it's been wearing on me since I left Arizona. "And they'll be immediately hired by J.A. Monroe Consulting."

Axel shakes my hand and smiles. "Good meeting you, Abby."

Fucking dick.

He walks away as I take a deep breath to regain my composure. With concern in her eyes, she whispers, "How does he know my name?"

"We need to go talk someplace privately."

"I would say so," she rebukes as I lead her outside to the balcony of the hotel bar. "What was that about?"

Lighting a smoke, I ask, "Which part?"

"All of it," she says, polishing off her champagne and stealing mine. "Start talking, or I start walking."

Shaking my head, I cackle, "Where are you going to go?"

"I can catch a plane too," she seethes, reminding me of the words I said to her. "I'm not a baby or a child, but a woman with credit cards and money. I don't need any lies or games."

"Axel knows your name because I told him," I remark, grinning. "I have nothing to be ashamed about with you. I have no problems putting you on full display in front of my family, friends, and future employees. If I did, you wouldn't be here."

"Gee, thanks," she sarcastically mumbles. "And what about my new job? I thought you didn't plan things, Mr. Monroe."

I'm caught red-handed on this.

I'm making plans for post-summer bliss with the girl of my dreams.

She doesn't know any of this yet, though, because I fail at communicating.

I politely suggest, "There are several good universities in South Carolina."

"... You're kidding, right?"

Dad steps onto the balcony and approaches. "Who is your lovely date, Jeremy?"

Her eyes widen at me.

"This is Echo Maines, Dad."

I SPEND THE NEXT TWENTY MINUTES FROTHING WITH RAGE at the bar while my father twirls and spins my willing abductee amongst the hopping crowd. I've lost count how many bourbons I've downed next to my mother, but it isn't good.

Shit is bad.

I want to return to the farm and our love bubble, where we were alone to be ourselves. Outside factors influence relationships, but I readily dismiss the environmental noise contaminating the current situation.

"She's quite young," my mother admonishes with a distinctly judge-y tone. "An unusual choice for you. I'd be careful. She may be a gold digger."

Ripping off my bow tie and undoing a few buttons on my shirt, I say nothing as I walk out onto the dance floor. The party is in full swing—on disco, drunk, and delusional as the DJ plays old school favorites—nothing like watching my dad and Echo making letters in the air while shaking their asses.

I tap the old man on the shoulder. "She's mine," I boisterously claim. "Now."

Leaning into me, she mutters, "About time, you showed up, Master." She winks.

With ease, Echo slips into my hands, and we dance—and I don't mean ballroom. We're jamming to Donna Summer, The Bee Gees, and getting down with deep rolls and grinds. "Do you realize this music is from twenty to thirty years before you were born?"

"I do! My dad is a musician," she yells. "You're doing a pretty fair job of keeping up with me, geezer!"

She sticks out her tongue, and I answer the challenge by swinging her out and dipping her. "Your point?"

"I have several, but I'm a little tipsy at the moment."

I laugh. "I could crank up the vibe for you."

"I appreciate you not doing it while your dad was doing the Y.M.C.A. with me."

"You're welcome," I chuckle, holding her close. "Shall we get the fuck out of here?"

She bounces around, grooving and snapping her fingers. For the life of me, I cannot stop laughing. My professional life is in shambles, but Echo manages to make me smile with genuine happiness. "You're going to be the Monday water-cooler discussion, Monroe."

I bust out laughing, "That is not something I want to think about, Maines."

"You know it's true," she says, shaking all she has next to me. "They're going to want to know when you found your long lost daughter and why you were getting your thrills on with her."

"Fuck," I mutter, raising the stakes. "Let's give them something to talk about."

I hoist her up in my arms, and we make out with a thorough tongue thrashing. I'll be lucky if my mother doesn't have a heart attack on the bar stool. My hands clamp on her ass as I realize what attracted me to her in the first place—*this girl is fun.* I mean, who the fuck in their right mind posts a rape ad? That alone says she's a little off her rocker, but the more I get to know her, I see the humor behind everything she does.

She's fucked up.

But so am I.

And it works.

It really works.

"If you plan on being my new boss," she hysterically laughs. "Does this mean you will be bending me over your desk for a little afternoon delight?"

"I swear I'm whipping your ass when I get you to our suite."

"Oooh," she coos, puckering her lips. "Whip me, Daddy!"

I seriously try to contain my amusement, but I can't. Axel snickers, shaking his head next to Mom, who stands up, pointing and complaining about our antics. Meanwhile, my father is surrounded by the teenage call girl cavalry of Monroe Consulting.

"You want to play? We will." I toss her on my shoulder, shortcutting through the crowd for the exit. I pull out my phone and hit send on the resignation letter I had drafted. At the elevators, I send the text to my father.

I quit.

ECHO

IN THE LAVISH HOTEL ROOM, I STARE OUT AT THE LIGHTS dotting the night sky. The cork popping sends an energetic rush through me. "Why did you do that?"

"Which part?" he asks, pouring the champagne. "The dancing or the quitting my job?"

"Both," I seriously say. "Tell me the truth."

"I don't need the bullshit of that life anymore."

"You just walked away from years of work after spending a couple of weeks with me."

"Put your logic away," he mutters, slamming the champagne. "I've got this. You just provided the fuse to spark the bomb."

"What else do I give you, Jynx?"

Stalking closer, he strips off his shirt. "A raging hard-on."

I creep back, taunting and teasing him. "You were a very naughty boy tonight."

"It's all downhill from here, baby."

He eases closer as his whiskey-tinted breath hits me. "What do you want?"

"Everything," he mutters, trickling his fingertip along the diamond leash between my breasts. "Give me everything, *you sweet, sweet bitch.*"

I sit on the bed and stare at his belt buckle. My tongue swishes over his abs before running along the edge of his waistband. I blink up. "Hurt me, J."

He picks me up underneath my arms and tosses me into the center of the bed. I crawl onto all fours, jetting my hips back and offering the roundness of my derriere for his inspection. I sensually roll my entire body.

His hands shove the hem of my dress up, and he admires the package. "Damn, you're trouble." Grazing over my cheek with his knuckles, he growls, "Breathe."

"Best plan on filling that back up," I request as he gently pulls out the vibrating plug.

"I would never dream of doing anything else."

"What are we doing?"

Snapping his belt, he snickers, "Drunk sex."

With one swing, he changes the course as I gasp and bite my lip. "Shit!"

He paces around the bed, pausing way too long. "... Are you okay?"

"I'll start thinking you care if you show concern," I challenge, grappling with my conflicting emotions. "Swat me, Jynx!"

The reassurance was all he needed to embark on a journey that I had shunned for so long. *I was not a submissive* was etched into my mind, but with every strike of his belt to my ass, he proved otherwise, marring the mantra until I no longer remembered a life without his control.

My fingers grip the sheet, twisting and curling as he proves to be a relentless bastard with countless lashes against my immaculate flesh. "I'm so fucking hard for you."

"Take it," I encourage, dampened with lust, tears, and drool. "Be my first."

He flops on the bed, covered in sweat. "Stroke my fucking cock and kiss me."

I stop, hiccuping on his request, "... At the same time?"

He laughs, "Yes."

"This is getting dangerously close to being a romance," I mutter, kissing his lips as he unzips and places my fingers around his dick. His enormous hand gently seals over mine, showing me how to stroke his cock. "You feel like velvet in my hand."

"Follow me."

He's teaching me.

Everything—how to behave, how to touch him, how to live, and how to love him. My tongue sweeps across his bottom lip. "I'm falling in love with you, Jynx Monroe."

"I will be your first and last in everything, Abigail Maines."

"Is that a promise?"

"Absofuckinglutely."

17

SO FIGURE IT OUT

ECHO

THE NEXT MORNING, WE DRIVE THROUGH THE
Lowcountry, which feels like deep boonies compared to Clementine's
house. Marshes and wetlands surround as we pull up to a rusted gate.

With unease, I ask, "This is your house?"

"Yeah," he says, smirking and sensing my fear. "It's fine."

"Uh-huh," I say as he hops out to unlock the chain and quickly
returns. "This is the moment when I die."

"Only after I torture you for a few years."

"I hate you sometimes."

"I know," he replies, chuckling and tossing his sunglasses up onto his ball cap. He pops the truck into four-wheel drive, and we ride the long, muddy path to an unimpressive shanty. Two giant trash receptacles sit in the yard. "Sorry about the construction."

"Um," I nervously say. "You're scaring me."

"Trust me," he says, giving a reassuring grip to my fingers. He rushes around to open my door and extends his arm. "They had to stop working on it last week because of the rain. Come on. I'll show you around."

He leads me down a weed-covered path past the house. Trees and bushes block the way as we trod through the grass to the main house. "This is my home, but as you can see..."

"There is no yard yet," I mumble, staring at the grand Antebellum. "Is it old?"

"No, it's brand new. The original was unsalvageable, so we located the blueprints and rebuilt it."

"It's massive!"

"Oh, yes!" We carefully climb the steps, and he covers my eyes with his palm. "Turn around." His hand drops to a breathtaking, untainted view of nature—trees, creeks, and the magnificent ocean. "The house has minimal furniture, and the echo is real."

I giggle at his pun. "What are you doing with the house out front?"

"Tearing it down as soon as we finish here," he informs, staring at me. I can't stop smiling. "My house is not done, as you can see."

"... Is it livable?"

"The kitchen is complete, as is the Master suite. Everything else is still being worked on and able to be decorated as however one might wish."

"This is crazy." It's all too much for my mind to process. I want to believe the fantasy I have running in my head that he is saying I could decorate, and this would be our house, but I turn numb. In awe, I guess, "It floods."

"You didn't ask if I was sane," he jokes, rubbing my shoulders. "It's been one thing after another to get the house this far. I've had the property for two years, and water will always be an issue."

"Are you going to live here?"

Are we going to live here?

Are you making plans?

"I was planning on it at one point," he says, tossing his sunglasses, ball cap, and keys on the counter. "I've got several offers from people who want to buy it." His seductive bedroom eyes urge with a passion that I haven't seen.

"Why are you looking at me like that?"

He smirks, almost blushing, and confides the truth. "Pretend for one minute that this thing works. Would you want to live here?"

I wrinkle my nose and glance around. "I don't know," I blurt out, unable to feel my toes. "Flooding makes me nervous."

Like the flood of love I feel in my heart for this man I don't even know.

What is happening to me?

"You like the old farm and the scary staircases better?"

"I do!" I giggle, needing wings to fly away. "Let's pretend," I slowly —*carefully*—muster out. "We end up having a family. I don't know that I would want to raise kids here."

I don't even know if I want kids.

Or to be your…wife.

My head spins with all the variables that I don't have answers for, and I need them. I studied psychology because I love the webbing of the mind. This must have a solution.

Everything has a solution.

I needed to have sex; I couldn't find an appropriate suitor; I posted an ad.

It may not have been the right solution, but it was, nonetheless, a solution.

And I'd like to note—*I still haven't had actual intercourse.*

All I did was attract this very good looking, strange man who abducted me.

"I'll sell it."

"Just like that?" I bellow, louder than I intended. "You shouldn't do that!"

I might want to live here if I decide to be your peculiar little wife.

"Yeah, just like that," he says, snapping. "But let me tell you why. For what I have on the table for this, I can easily invest in the business with Axel, so this decision matters."

"It's pressing," I acknowledge, feeling under the gun. My eyes shift from side to side with uncertainty. "You would sell this because I don't like it?"

"Yes."

"Let's go over this one more time," I insist, methodically. "You won't talk about the future, have even said several times that I'm leaving at the end of summer, but so far, you quit your job and are considering selling your house because of me. It doesn't make sense, babe."

"I'm in love with you, Echo. There is no falling. We're well past that. Falling was when you showed me your tits doing ninety. I love you."

Oh. My. Fucking. God. No.

I query, "Flat out?"

"Flat out," he declares with a serious glare. "There is no debate. I'm a middle-aged man in love with a beautiful young woman, and I intend to do everything in my power to keep her happy and by my side."

In your collar.

Under your belt.

With your greedy power plays.

I fake a grin, unsure of what to say, so I make light of it. "Must have been a helluva hand job."

"Oh, it was." He winks. "Best I've had."

Don't say that.

God, it was fun.

Stop and think about what you're doing, Abs.

He turns to grab a bottle of water from the construction crew's mini-fridge. "What if I don't want you to partner up with Axel?"

Pivoting back, he easily says, "I won't."

"Rape me."

"No."

"Dammit!" I pout, and he laughs. "So I'm allowed and encouraged even to make life-changing decisions for you, but requesting sex…"

"Not happening."

I blink, on the verge of crying or screaming at him. "I'm going to look around."

Meandering through the incredible house, I question how my stupid ad led me to this place. I'm in fucking South Carolina, in the middle of nowhere, with a man I barely know, and I want to fuck his damn brains out.

He stalked me.

He drugged me.

He abducted me.

He pushed the limits.

And God, it's so good when he does.

Think, Abigail!

I climb the elegant, broad curved staircase, trying to imagine a future with Jynx. And the truth is—I can't see the pages of our lives unfolding in the house surrounded by water.

I don't mind the water from a distance.

But this is too much water.

The reward isn't worth the risk for me. I can't imagine building our lives to have it swept away in an instant, and I understand that could happen anywhere.

Life is fickle.

Better not to get involved with life or anyone associating with life experience. It's full of a foul stench, a decay.

Easier to live than love; love hurts.

Move robotically from one task to the next. Do not think; do. Do not mourn the losses. Do not feel the pain.

Function.

Damn, my ass stings.

In many ways, Jynx is like an ocean. He rushed into my life with the rapid force of a hurricane, submerging everything I knew and leaving me stranded—*alone, safely*—on the island of his shoulders.

But I can only stay here for so long.

Out the back window, I notice a fancy truck pull up. Axel steps out, and I hear Jynx greet him. I'm not being fair, defining the terms of his business, yet this is the position he put me in.

We've known each other for less than a month.

Everything is happening way too fast.

Struggling in my turmoil, I sit on the top step of the staircase, staying out of their meeting, but I cannot help but eavesdrop.

"She's the girl from the ad," Axel chuckles. "I know what you did."

"I couldn't let this girl get raped."

"And you decided saving her was a better alternative?"

"Yeah, I did," he persists, convinced an abduction was worth the risk.

That makes me a reward.

I cannot be his reward.

"That's fucked up, brother."

"I didn't plan on actually liking her. I planned on changing her perception. She deserved far more than some dickhead taking advantage of her."

Axel snickers, "What do you think you're doing?"

"Treating her right," Jynx argues, unwavering with an escalating tone. "And if you insinuate otherwise again, you can get the fuck out of my house. Abigail is mine."

Shit.

Reward. Collar. Possession.

HIS.

My presence is annihilating his entire world as I await his blame and resentment, but the fallout of mine is his to claim. I cover my ears, not wanting to hear anymore. I know what I need to do as tears spring from my eyes.

But doing it will be the hardest thing I've ever done.

"YOU HAVEN'T SAID A WORD FOR HOURS," JYNX SAYS, driving the darkened road back to the farmhouse. "We need to talk."

"There isn't much to say."

"The whole weekend threw our trajectory off-kilter."

"Why?" I ask as he pulls into the driveway. "We cannot live the rest of our days at the farmhouse. We have to learn to deal with Axel, your parents, my parents, friends, jobs, social circles, and everything. We have to find a way to explain who we are and what this relationship is."

"Do you need to define for someone or yourself?" he angrily demands. "Because love needs no explanation."

He parks the car, and I hop out on my own. "I'm staying in the downstairs bedroom tonight."

"Fine," he replies with agitation before grabbing the luggage and unlocking the door. "When you leave, don't come back."

I sneer, "How do you know I'm leaving?"

Setting my things down, he walks off toward the staircase. "It's real fucking clear."

He's halfway up the steps when I accuse, "And Axel knows about the ad!"

Glancing over his shoulder, he doesn't say a single word. I run to the bedroom, yank my suitcase from the closet and shove my things in the bag. I have many items in his bedroom, but those will be a loss. I scan over the room, spotting the journal, and the tears come on strong.

I grab the book, shredding it with maddening fury and yelling, "You fucker! You never should've taken me! Dammit!"

Out of my purse, I grab the silken bag, holding the diamond collar, and toss it on the bed with the shredded notebook. I wipe my nose on my sleeve, click off the light, and swipe my car keys from the junk drawer.

With an overdose of adrenaline, I quickly carry my bags to the car in the driveway and glance back at the house. His bedroom light is on, but he doesn't honestly care. I was only a conquest—a willpower championship match with exact determining factors of Dominance and submission. I would never win.

The game was rigged.

"Goodbye, Jeremiah."

"When you start to care, you run like the wind," he mutters from behind, startling me.

I almost jump out of my skin. "What the fuck are you doing?"

"You're afraid to love, stuck in the absolute misery of loss."

"You cannot compare this to what happened with Colton!"

"Was that his name?" he asks with his arms crossed over his chest. "Colton, the kid who chose to commit suicide? You didn't do that. He did that. You're carrying his scars, but he's dead. How much sense does that make?"

"You're asking me to make decisions, but you won't even discuss the future!" I yell as he peers over his nose, remaining propped against the tree. "And how is this any different from what happened with Celeste? You've locked yourself away for a decade, but I won't be your prisoner!"

"You seem to think you have a choice in the matter."

"I'm leaving, Jynx!" He takes one mammoth step and pummels my body into the side of the car. "Don't do this," I beg, crying. "I won't put up the ad again. I'll go back to California, live out my happy life, and promise to forget you."

"You can say that," he growls in my ear. "But you don't mean it."

I close my eyes, feeling his hard body pressed against me. "I do," I whisper. "This was all a mistake. And you're nothing but a messed up gentleman. You warned me about the criminal mindset that I was attracting, but have you looked in the mirror?"

"You want to go?" he questions, loosening his grip as my lip trembles. He fucking opens my door like a goddamned gentleman. "Go. But you best be prepared to lie to yourself for the rest of your life because you'll always wonder. And after that nightmare stops, the real regret will come on relentlessly terrorizing your heart and punishing your mind as you question what could've been."

With great gumption, I dare to ask, "Why does your dad call you Jeremy?"

"Because he knows I hate it." His eyes blink up to the numerous glittery stars sprinkling the sky. "And since I fucked up and got thrown in the slammer, he has made sure I understood that the only reason I was out of jail was because of him."

"He held it over your head."

"Yeah," he mutters, clenching his jaw. "That is why I quit. You just gave me a reason to do it."

"... Me?"

He snorts. "Maybe you missed the part where I said I was in love with you. I don't need this job." The back of his hand caresses my cheek. "What I need is you—all of you, Echo. You're the beautiful light, full of goodness to my ugly, darkened evil. You balance me like no one ever has."

"For the next two months," I cry, sniffling and inconsolable. "You said you'd never raped anyone. How many times have you thought about it?"

"... With you?"

"Yes."

"Countless."

"You're so fucked up." I'm unable to stop sobbing. "God, I've so fucked up my whole life because of you!"

"I can't do this," he mumbles, releasing me. "Just go."

I slide into the driver's seat, start the engine, and hit the gas.

And I don't look back.

18

TO THE HOUSE

ECHO

"YOU JUST MADE THE STUPIDEST FUCKING MISTAKE OF your life!" Selia yells on the phone as I sit in the superstore parking lot in Columbia. "What the hell are you thinking! Get back out there and be his bitch, servant, slut, slave, hussy, whatever-the-fuck-he-wants girl!"

I blink through her chastising. "I didn't plan on getting reprimanded by my best friend for making a healthy decision!"

"For most people," she says, munching on something. "It would be a healthy decision—you, not so much. You're giving up a fan-fuckingtastic guy who is admitting he is in love with you. And why are you doing it?"

"Because I'm destroying his life."

"Change is equal parts destructive and constructive," she compellingly makes her argument. "You're changing Jynx, and he is trying—*God knows, I bet he is trying with you*—to change you."

I snort, "Are you saying I'm difficult?"

"Beyond."

"Great," I quip, wanting to cry again, but I'm all dried up. There are no more tears left to cry for Jynx Monroe. "I cannot go back there, Selia."

"You cannot come here."

"I'll go to Birmingham."

"That is the last thing you need to do," she scolds grumbling. "You need to drive your ass right back out to his farm, get on your hands and knees, suck his fucking dick, and beg for forgiveness for being such a damn idiot!"

"I really don't appreciate you taking his side on this."

"Because you're blind, Ekky," she stresses with an impassioned plea. "This guy is in love with you. Does he have some issues? Yeah. But you know what? So does every other person on the fucking planet! You're still looking to achieve perfection to earn your mother's acceptance. That is never going to happen. Give up on that notion, little girl! You must do for you! Stop living the life you think will make your mother happy."

I hate how right she is about that.

Not the Jynx part.

My phone buzzes. "He's calling me."

"Answer it. Love you. Bye!"

"Same."

I click to his call. "Hello?"

"We need to stop at the gas station because your left back tire is low."

I glance around, looking for his truck. "Where are you?"

Suddenly, headlights beam into my back window. He brought out his Mustang for this. *Shit. I am in so much trouble.* I close my eyes, knowing the hour-long trip home will be grueling.

Fuck.

I just called his farmhouse home.

"You should say something, Ek."

"I need to piss."

"Follow me."

He hangs up and zips around me. I do as he says because the alternative isn't really what I want either. California is the same old same; Birmingham is four years back with many bad memories I don't need.

South Carolina wins by a long shot.

We stop at the gas station, and I hurry inside before he has a chance to corner me. By the time I get back, he's aired up the tire and waiting in his car on the other side of the parking lot.

My whole life hinges on this moment of decision.

It shouldn't be this hard.

JYNX

I FLOOR IT OUT OF THE PARKING LOT AND ONTO THE frontage for the highway. Mama-mobile better bring her A-game. I must acquire this girl a more appropriate vehicle. She's twenty-two, not forty with four brats in the back.

No offense to forty or those four brats.

But a girl needs to be free when she can be.

Because responsibilities add up way too fucking quick, stealing youth.

Realizing my whole thought process, I pull off into an empty church parking lot. I light a smoke and get out as she comes to a stop mere inches from my bumper. I eye the difference, and her, with a lift of my brows.

"What?" she cattily mumbles, rolling down her window. She doesn't look at me.

Great, we're back to this.

Square fucking one.

I toss my keys in her lap.

"What the fuck am I supposed to do with these?"

"Drive my car."

She frantically bats her lashes like all the bugs covering her windshield just flew in her eyes. "That is your baby."

"Drive my car," I calmly say, though she is testing my patience tonight. The weekend was long and hard with lots of new emo-garbage to sort through.

Turning to look at me, she says, "Jynx?"

"You're so fucking beautiful when you're mad," I admire, stroking her cheek. "And I love you so goddamned much."

Her whole face twitches. "You shouldn't."

"I don't have a choice in the matter," I admit honestly. "Believe me, if I did, I wouldn't have chosen you." She scowls. "I don't mean you as in *you*...I mean, I wouldn't have chosen anyone. I didn't want a relationship. I only need an ass to whip. I didn't plan on falling in love with a damn girl."

"Woman," she corrects, staring at the dash. I tilt my head.

"Fine, young woman," I say, humoring her because I need to get off and soon.

"Better," she praises.

"Now, go drive my fucking car before I change my mind."

"... Jynx?"

"Yes, baby?"

"I can't drive a stick."

"Fuck," I mutter, running my fingers through my hair. I can kiss the tranny goodbye. "Come on."

"What are we doing?"

"Having a lesson," I reply, walking to my car and opening the door. I wait as she reluctantly paces toward me. "Get in the car."

"You're an asshole."

"I warned you of that."

THERE ARE TIMES IN LIFE WHEN WE ALL MAKE MISTAKES.
Teaching Abigail Maines to drive a standard was probably the biggest one thus far. She is an excellent driver. She is also an extremist.

One minute, she kills it.

The next, she zooms past the Mama-mobile flipping me off.

"I'm beating her ass when we get home."

The problem with that statement is we may never make it through town. Every stoplight, she kills it. At one point, she somehow managed to throw it into reverse and almost rammed the front of her car. Quick thinking on my part prevented an insurance claim.

From the farmhouse to Columbia, on a good night, maybe forty-five minutes if I'm speeding. It has taken us two hours to get home when she finally turns into the driveway.

Maybe she doesn't need freedom in a sports car.

A better solution is to lock the bitch down.

I understand what has occurred better than most. I kidnapped the poor girl, and she managed to escape. By luck, I charmed her into returning to prison.

Pretty good, if I say so myself.

She parks a reasonable distance from the house and truck. I whip her car into the garage. I'm fucking hiding the goddamned keys.

Standing by the Mustang, she waits as I sprint past her. "Get in."

"Where are we going?"

"Get in."

She clearly cannot hear tonight. Plopping in the passenger seat, she says, "I'm in trouble."

"How do you know?"

"You didn't open the door."

I lean across the seat, wrap my hand around the back of her neck, and kiss her hard with all of the love I have. My lips and tongue claim her attention. "I love you. And yes, you're in big fucking trouble because I had to drive five miles out of this hole in the wall to get your GPS to pick up. I didn't know where you were."

"You told me to go."

"I also told you three times to drive my car and twice to get in. The selective hearing thing will not fly with me. You listen. First time. Every time."

Her lips purse into a hard line. She's steaming mad, but at least she's back in my possession. She's my problem and my responsibility. "Yes, Sir."

Wow.

I didn't expect that. "You're to go inside, march your ass up to the room, take off all of your clothes, and wait for me."

She gives a brief, subtle nod and mutters, "This is punishment in anger?"

"No, this is discipline because I've been rocking a massive fucking erection since I smelled you," I reveal, and she briefly smirks. "Go!"

ECHO

KNEELING IN THE DARKENED ROOM, I WAIT FOR MY Master's disciplinary action. The door opens and closes almost silently as he enters. "Congratulations! You've graduated from undisciplined wench to a tantrum throwing bitch needing some rules. You should be proud of yourself. It is quite an accomplishment. That said, don't let it go to your head. Stand up."

I rise and whisper, "I didn't listen, though."

"You did when it counted."

"And that matters?"

"It does," he says as his eyes flash to mine. "I appreciate it when you listen. Let's get something straight. I'm never trying to be a dick to you. I'm trying to take care of you the best way I know how."

"You told me to go," I whimper with big eyes. "Why did you do that?"

"To let you have a minute to think about life without me," he brags, standing in front of me. He's shirtless with damp hair. My toes curl against the grain of the wooden floor. "You're going to be resistant. All bottoms are. You're particularly bad because of your age. But I want to take care of you. And more than anything else in the whole fucking world—you need to remember that."

"I would like you to take care of me."

"I didn't take you out to the beach house to confuse you," he implores, scanning over my face. "I took you out there because I wanted to know how you would react to the idea of more before I got my heart set on it."

"What is your heart set on?"

"You, Abby," he whispers, touching my cheek. "My heart is set on you."

"You want to rape me."

"I do," he divulges with a dangerous smirk. "More than anything right now. I want to pin you down, silence your mouth with mine, and stick my dick inside of you. I want to fuck you for hours until you can't walk in the morning. And then, I'd make you breakfast and set you up somewhere pretty with a good book and cups of hot tea all day."

"And tomorrow night, you'd do it all again. Your princess by day and your whore by night, but I don't understand where we go after summer. It all sounds great until the expiration date when the cliff drops off, and I lose you. Then, what the fuck do I do? I'm warped, conforming to your fittings, and no one else that comes after you will make sense. What do I do, post-Jynx?"

"There won't be a post-Jynx."

"How do you know?"

"Because..." He stops, scratching his brow and looking down. "I'll move if I have to. You want California; we'll go there. You want South

Carolina; we'll stay here. You want fucking Alaska; we'll go there. I'll go anywhere you want to go. I can do my job anywhere."

I cannot help but smile. "Dating you is difficult."

"You want some regular dates with all this other shit? We can do that too," he appeases, diligently trying to bridge the gap between us. "We can do whatever you want."

"Rape me."

"No!" he roars, refusing my demands again.

"One day, you'll say yes."

"No," he snickers, shaking his head. "One day, I'll just do it."

"You're going to be my first."

His brow tightens as he lights a smoke. The flame of the lighter illuminates his blue eyes and the shadow of scruff on his cheeks as he exhales and snickers, "It won't be rape, and we both know that."

"We'll pretend," I giggle, knowing he's right. I'd spread my thighs for this man—*even at his worst*—anytime. "What now?"

"I'm whipping your fucking ass," he casually mentions. "And I'm getting off in one of your holes because you've upset me. And then we're going to take a shower."

"… Together?"

"Yes," he confirms as the slickness of lust streams between my thighs. "And I'm molesting you in my bed, and after that, you're sleeping on my arm."

"Jynx?" I bravely mumble, reaching out and grazing his hand with mine.

"Yes, baby?"

"Hurt me like I'm a bad girl. Use me like you have other girls. Take what you want from me."

"I intend to."

JYNX

IN THE HOUSE'S SILENCE, THE RIDING CROP NUMBS THE unnecessary head gunk and promotes real intimacy. Her whole backside is inflamed with my fierce marks, but she has stood like a soldier, taking the blows without nary a tear. I'm beyond proud of her because I know—I'm not easy.

I throw another lash to her ass and rub my hand over my hard cock. I've been throbbing for over an hour since we started, staring at naked flesh, waiting to be used by my hands and will. I want inside of this girl—to break her and make her mine.

I need her confession.

Reaffirmation—that she wants this, so I don't feel like we're just passing the time.

"I need a drink."

She quivers and asks, "What would you like?"

"Something strong and a lot of it."

Soaked in sweat, I drop to the floor and raise my arms above my head. She asks, "Are you okay?"

"No."

"What's wrong?"

"I can smell your pussy, and it's driving me insane," I confess as her giggle sweetens the air. "Come piss on me."

Spinning around, she says nothing for a good half minute. I let it slide because this is a tough one—*a trial.* "Where would you like it, Sir?"

"My dick."

In the moonlight, I note the smirk as she bites her lip. "You're serious."

"Don't make me ask twice." I pop the button on my jeans and rip the zipper down with a tug of the denim. My hard cock springs free, demanding attention. I'm so worked up all it would take is one stroke to launch me. I've got it so bad for this bitch. "Give it to me, baby. Let me feel it. And don't hold back."

She slowly steps over the top of me. I lightly brace my hands on her ankles. "You want it low or high?"

I'm impressed she bothered to ask.

"You can go down there, but if you penetrate *my* pussy," I warn with a harshness. "If you take what is mine, I will never forgive you." Boldly, she lowers, barely brushing her lips over the head of me. "God, it's too much. Back up a smidge," I command, knowing I won't be able to control myself. She does as I request. "Fuck!" I grimace, agonizing in the dilemma of my self-control. "Go back down."

"You're really tempted by this."

"Like you cannot fucking imagine," I moan as she slathers over the tip. "Dammit, I want to fuck you so bad."

"Jynx, I'm going to go."

"Oh, shit," I yell, not thinking she would actually have the nerve to do it. I feel the warmth of her rushing over my dick. "Fuck yes, baby... do it..." Leaning up, I try and hold out, but her giving up all control is too much. I groan hard, coming in her flood. "Holy fuck!" I flop my head back and breathe. I'm stunned with delirious amazement. "Okay, I've never done that. You're fucking incredible. The best ending ever."

"That was fucking hot," she whispers, touching her cum covered lips. "I'm going to masturbate now."

"No, you're fucking not," I chide, sitting up and putting her on her back. I thrust two fingers hard and deep into her wet lips. She's soaked, sucking my fingers like a ravenous kitten. "Touch your clit."

She does, but only for a moment as her explosion erupts, and her body convulses on my hand. "I love you, Jynx!" She smiles as blown away by our chemistry as I am.

"We need to talk about protection," I sigh, laying beside her with ecstatic relief. "Like now."

"I've been on the pill since I was eighteen," she whispers. "And you're the only man I ever plan on being with."

"I like the way that sounds," I confide, smirking. "Are you going to let me make you Mrs. Abigail Monroe?"

She curls against my side and whispers, "In time."

"Good girl."

19

FEED OFF THE FEAR

Jynx

Life rapidly changes when least expected.

I took the beach house off of the market.

Axel moved to upstate New York to be near our grandparents.

My father sold Monroe Consulting, and my parents took a month-long vacation to Australia. The buyers immediately dismantled the entire operation, laying off over seventy-five percent of the employees. They kept the foreign clients but terminated all of their North American contracts, leaving them with a lapse of—*what the fuck do we do now?*

With Axel, who handled public relations, conveniently among the missing, and my parents out of the country, guess which Monroe everyone decided to call upon?

I answered the call.

Until it got to be too much.

"Let me help you," she begged on her knees with my dick in her hands and pre-cum gloss on her lips. "I want to be able to do things for you."

Oh, God, are you ever...

Now, I have a pleasant assistant in Echo to answer the non-stop ringing phone. She is my first line of defense, deciding the urgency of the call. I have teasingly named her, "My little phone sex operator."

She giggled and said, "Only for you."

She'll need to file harassment charges with HR by the end of the week.

The farmhouse resembles a cluttered office full of computer gear, racks, and equipment. Client files and Echo's honey-do lists are scattered between Grandma's owl figurines and collection of bones she found on the property over the years. Somehow, with a lot of take-out, we're making it work.

And it helps that she swallows nightly.

Busting in the door, Ek mutters, "I bought all the crap on your grocery list, but they didn't have a few of these weirdly named things." I grab the first load from her hands and kiss my girl. She hands over the keys to the Mustang. "Sorry, it took me a bit. Traffic into Columbia was terrible."

She's dangerous with a stick now.

And yes, I have extended her leash quite a bit—*out of necessity more than anything*. If she were leaving, she would have done it already.

"We're out of space on the dining room table," Deacon sighs, swaggering into the room. Echo's been gone since before the dynamic duo arrived, and her eyes widen at the appearance of one Deacon Cruz —ripped jeans, t-shirt, and sneakers—same as he's been since birth. "We're going to have to do something else. We cannot run your shop here."

"Fuck," I mumble, downing a protein shake.

"You're going to need more help to do this, and she needs help carrying in groceries." Echo glances at him, and he smiles politely. She starts to follow him, but he says, "I got it. Start unpacking."

She's probably wondering why there is a long blonde-haired biker in our home.

Her mouth opens. "Is that *your* cousin?"

"Yeah."

"The family resemblance is eerie, J."

He flew in early this morning to help assemble all of the machines we're using to run Peacock Consulting—the name and logo all due to the girl with the shocked expression. He brings in the last of the bags, and now he's helping load vegetables in the fridge. She's handing them off, and he's sticking them in.

These two are a pair.

"We're gonna need more power," Sal mutters, shuffling in and eyeing my girl, standing over the top of the crouching Deacon. She gives the Italian in the backward ball cap a once over, deems him acceptable, and returns to their tag-team efforts. The grocery list was a mile long because these two know how to eat. "There is no way you can do what you want to do, J. Psst, Ekky!"

Holding the single-serve packet of marinated olives, she smiles at his noticeable accent, "Hmm?"

"Pitch'em!"

"Can you catch?"

"Baby, I can catch." He grins, and she listens, tossing the olives to him. Deacon snickers. It may not sound like much, but she picked up on my respect for the pair. Her ability to listen delights the fuck out of me as he rips into the olives. "I'm Sal Raniero, by the way."

"Explains the accent and the olives."

He extends his hand, introducing himself, and she offers her fingertips—that's not a handshake, but I'll overlook it. "It's good to meet you, Echo." He switches his gaze to me. "You're gonna need another panel if you don't want to be blowing circuits left and right. There's not enough power in the old girl."

"We have so many people who need their shit maintained. I have so much to do," I whine, collapsing my arms on the counter and knocking Echo's two giant boxes of Frosted Flakes over. She rubs my back. "What the fuck am I going to do?"

"Let me think on that." Sucking on an olive, Sal asks, "What did your Dad do with the equipment in the building?"

"He liquidated all of it."

"Jesus fucking Christ," he mutters. "I'm sorry I cannot stay away from home for longer than a night, but I'm leaving Cruz here for the rest of the week to help you."

"Still not doing any better?"

"Bad topic!" Deacon segues, making a giant X with his arms. "Off-limits!"

"Sorry," I apologize as Sal shakes his head and disappears back to the dining room. "Did I..."

"Nah, you're fine," he mutters, taking a look at Echo. "You're a sweet little thing, ain't ya?"

She giggles, "I guess so."

"I'm this fucker's cousin. If he gives you any shit, let me know," he greets, boldly hugging her. He was always the sweet one. Pounding my arm, he reassures, "Sal will figure something out."

"... You're a biker?"

He beams a broad smile. "Yeah, I'm the president of the club he's in." She turns with a scowl at me, and I close my eyes tight, shaking my head. "Fuck. She didn't know?"

"No."

"You're the asshole who gave him the drugs to send me nighty-nighty," she accuses as my eyes open wide. "You caused my abduction."

With his head slightly tilted back in a cocky pose, he readily admits, "I'm the bastard who saved you. I'll take a thank you when you get over yourself."

"I oughta rack the fuck out of you," she sasses, and I smirk.

"You don't seem any worse for the wear, Darlin'." He lays a sympathetic hand on my arm as he passes by. With a wink, he stresses, "Spitfire."

"SAY IT AGAIN," SHE DEMANDS IN A LONG BLACK
sweatshirt and pink lace panties. We can't even have a sesh tonight
because we've been quibbling for hours in the playroom.

Straddling over the bench, I roll my eyes and repeat the words for
the fiftieth time, "You are a: Natural Dominant. Alpha. Male. No
nerds, truckers, wannabes, virgins, or bikers. Professional-types,
athletes, and bad boys welcome."

With her hands in the air, she yells, "What part about that descrip-
tion don't you fit?"

"I'm a hybrid—a nerd and a biker. They negate one another."

She's not amused.

"I can deal with the techno-geek in you, Jynx!" she roars loud
enough for Deacon and Sal to hear at the other end of the hall.
They're staying in the same room. I'm not bothered, but the idea
seemed to perplex her with a—"*What? They're lovers!*"—reaction. Not
everyone understands the attraction between the two pretty boys, but
I've already given up hope of dissecting what forms the bond between
two people. "But, I will not be some bitch in a club for everyone's
taking!"

"And you're twenty-two, not a submissive, and a virgin!" I rebuke,
feeling verbally assaulted as Deacon swings open the door.

"You two need to stop fighting," he scolds, stepping inside. He's
shirtless, inked, and my girl notices. "This is silly. Jynx, get over it
because she is a great girl." He approaches her and gently—*bravely*—
sets his hand on her back. "Look, I know what you think about club
life, and I get it, I do. But I promise you," he tenderly says, laying his
hand on his heart. "My club is not like that. And none of my guys are
going to pass you around. Or I will fucking kill them."

Sal pops his head around the open door. His mop of raven hair is a
wretched mess. "... You're a virgin?"

"Yes!" She squeals and stomps to leave as he quickly gives me a
thumbs up and closes the door with a thud. Deacon steps in front of
her. "Let me go."

"No," he declares. "You two need to work this out."

"He lied."

"I didn't lie," I argue with a shrug. "It just never came up."

She glances between Deacon and me. "I don't want to do this again. I was very serious in my wording. No bikers. None. I don't want that in my life, Jynx!"

I sulk as Deacon mutters, "Why?"

"Because my father was a VP in a club."

His expression tightens as he steps out of the way, and she walks out.

"I take it you didn't know."

"I didn't have a fucking clue," I mumble, rubbing my hands over my face. "I don't know this girl at all."

"It doesn't matter. Forget about all the shit. You like her."

"I love her," I interject, correcting him.

"You love her," he whispers, laying his hand on my shoulder. "And it is evident that she loves you."

"I have to go find her," I mumble, walking to the door. We step into the hall and peer over the edge to the living room where Sal and Echo share a box of her flakes. "Should I worry about this?"

"Nah, he's in love and," Deacon replies, nodding. "Age does wonders for maturity."

EARLY THE NEXT MORNING, I LEAVE ECHO SLEEPING IN OUR bed and head downstairs. Sal is already up, coffee in hand, and getting ready to go. "I thought you were staying the day?"

"I was going to," he informs, polishing off his java. "But I'm making a pit stop in Birmingham to check on Brandon Maines."

"... Do you know him?"

He shakes his head and washes his coffee cup. "Nup, but I'm gonna."

"Why are you doing this?"

"Because I've been where he is at," he says, drying his hands. "And she needs the reassurance."

I pick up the empty box of cereal. "You two, KO'd these."

"We had a long chat."

"Her father is MC."

"Yeah, he's a womanizing player of a man. That is her benchmark for all bikers. She blames her father and the club for destroying her family. She's scared, and you need to prove otherwise."

"Am I going to get that chance?"

"Ya," he reassures with a nod. "You are. And I'm working on finding you someplace to put all of the hardware."

"I owe you."

"You don't owe me," he replies, hugging me and planting a kiss on either cheek. "You owe finding happiness to yourself, brother." The horn blares twice in the driveway. "I gotta go. That's my ride."

"Uber?"

"Nah, Hannah went to visit with her adopted family in Buckhead."

"My other cousin is here?" I ask, following him outside as I note the pretty girl smiling. "Damn, Echo is right. The family resemblance is real."

Lighting a smoke, Sal remarks, "It's the Howser gene pool."

SITTING IN THE MAKESHIFT OFFICE OF THE DINING ROOM four days later, I watch Echo and Deacon rummaging through client files. We're slowly getting things back to a workable state. I've rehired half of those we lost from my father's negligence.

I've spent the better part of the week running on steam while assembling a business and accepting that I got screwed again. Dad left a mess for someone else to clean up.

I didn't necessarily want it but properly taking care of the clients we'd spent years forming relationships with and reinstating employees was the right thing to do.

I do care.

Sometimes too much.

I blamed Axel a lot in the beginning, but he knew it was coming. I won't hold a grudge for his running out of a burning building, but he can't diss me for trying to put out the blaze.

Two different approaches.

Neither is wrong.

Dad doing what he did was wrong. He passed off the entire HR responsibility to Axel, and he buckled under the pressure. I refuse to point my finger at him because I've been the guy running from personal relationships for years. I understood the hit it and quit it mentality, but eventually, I needed more.

Wanting to make Peacock Consulting thrive parallels with my need to make Echo and I work. I'm driven to extinguish the fires, not throwing additional issues into the blaze just to watch them burn.

But what I've realized is I cannot do it alone.

I need help.

Family need not be blood to be worthy. I always knew that being involved in the club, but choosing family is in my spotlight now. I never imagined that my cousin would show up with his computer guru geek boyfriend—*all to help me.* Or that Echo, who should be taking her summer off to relax, would be equally concerned about tending the stables and logging my accounts as sucking my cock.

I've functioned alone for so long that this past week has felt like a reunion with myself.

Axel and I took a sabbatical from the club because we needed to deal with the farm. Dad didn't want to do that either. We cleaned up the mess of the estate, and the bulk of that went to me.

Grandma raised me to be a healer, a giver, a caring soul. Sometimes, that gets taken advantage of, and sometimes, like in Echo's case, I use it to my advantage.

Axel is talking about rejoining the club. I don't know if I will follow in his footsteps, but what I do know is that he has my back— even if he chooses to step away from the firestorm. He's proven that over the last week with countless phone calls and messages. He's significantly helped from a distance.

Not everyone needs to be shuffling through papers like the two clowns laughing at the table. I grab my empty coffee cup and mosey into the kitchen.

"He's got a place for you," Deacon raves with a smile. "I told you not to worry."

"Don't tell me it's in Texas."

"That goes without saying," he replies with a wink. "Downtown Houston."

"Houston?" I say, slightly intrigued. "Not too far from the water."

Echo giggles. "You need the current."

"I do," I admit, stroking my chin covered in a week's worth of scruff. "Are you staying for the Fourth of July?"

"I can't," he regretfully says. "I gotta get back. My boy is feeling a bit overwhelmed with three under five."

Echo's eyes light up. "You have kids?"

"Three of them," Deacon says with a proud smile. "I'm catching a flight early tomorrow morning."

"Before you go…" Echo whispers.

Deacon shakes his head. "You're going to have to ask your boss about that, babe."

She smiles pretty and blurts out, "May Deacon please tie me up, Sir?"

My eyes bug out in the blast of her words, hitting hard like shrapnel tearing my skin from the muscle. "You want to *what*?"

Deacon interrupts, "We were talking about rope work, and I said I knew how to do it."

"You want to tie up my girl," I repeat for clarity's sake.

"Not like you're thinking," he snickers, making neat piles of folders. "It's an art in this case. I even tied up my sister, dude. And yes, she had on a swimsuit."

"His rope work is beautiful!"

I ponder the idea. "Where are you going to get the rope?"

She hastily volunteers, "There is a whole box of it upstairs in the closet."

"How do you know this?"

"I snoop on my stalker." She winks.

I am so sunk.

20

REBIRTH

ECHO

THE FLICKERING WICKS ILLUMINATE THE ROOM AS THE scent captures the moment, halting time. Burning vanilla candles will forever recount the rite of passage where we forgot the clock, leaving our souls undaunted by the ticking of hands and the lacing from his fingers.

The suspension within—*permanent*.

Tethered from the hooks in the ceiling, I adored their focused attention. At the first knot, I understood Japanese rope bondage's appeal—erotically ethereal with a sensual mysticism, and a tantric, transcendental seduction.

Cocooned within the womb stitched by his hands, I flew high in the out of body experience, providing more than the twisting of filaments. I was captured—*caught in the spider's web, the victim of his sustenance*—and entranced by his diligent efforts rendering me breathless.

There was no withholding.

There was no hiding in dark places.

Oh, Clementine, you kinky bitch.

Having a stranger tie me up was not as odd as I feared it would be. I crammed the lessons of Master Cruz in a study session constructed by madmen. His endless patience and delicate touch tutored my flesh with the most brilliant comeuppance.

My physical body was no longer my own.

I belonged to a Master.

A Master of disguise eclipsed in the darkness and determined to feed on the invisible light that I couldn't see in me. I was blind to its presence, but he revered the brightness like christening a newborn. The D words I believed to portray—*deranged, depressed, or diabolic*—he crossed out and drilled my soul with a new verse—a hymnal of one word I craved—*Dominance.*

And the one D belonging to him.

In a black leather armchair with old-style metal rivets, he rhythmically strummed his fingers as he sat directly across from me. His long sleeve navy blue shirt and gray slacks spoke of a mature soul. My Master readily took a lessor role as a pupil with a few fundamental lessons from Deacon. I was enchanted by Jynx's willingness to learn a new craft, and even more so when he became a spectator, leaving the practice up to his brethren.

Trust was imperative.

With a devilish smirk, Jynx growled, "Give me a show worth remembering."

I didn't know if he was talking to Deacon or me or both.

By the glossy haze of desperate hunger in his eyes, he meant me.

I wasn't a victim but an active participant in my swaddling. With every thread circling a limb, I unraveled my spirit that had been aching in tangles, suppressing me for years. The decision was always in my hands—*my control*—my power. And I finally understood why everyone contended I would never go through with a random assault.

I am too much of a fighter.

It would take me being bound to silence the demons, churning like hellhounds, biting with gruesome, slobbering fangs around my pointed toes. I dropped into their inferno, made myself at home, and put my feet up on the gilded pedestal they provided.

I reside in their dark shadows.

Deacon asking if I wanted to wear lingerie or a swimsuit was a strange glitch, jarring with authenticity, but after studying his reactions to those who did turn him on, I knew I was safe. I wasn't his boyfriend. Or one of the girls who called at all hours.

My answer arrived with immediate urgency.

I wanted to be naked without shame.

Apparently, I had it in me to be an exhibitionist, even with my over-pronounced tatas. I wasn't truly surprised, considering I wanted a rape in a dank alleyway, and Deacon's professional approach on the canvas of my flesh made things easy.

He is an artist; the rope is his medium.

I asked if we could take pictures afterward, and he agreed.

The intense longing stares between Jynx and I bring a realness to our romance. The more rope I wear, the more flirtatious he becomes, and the deeper the bond surges into the abysmal, sweltering lair where lust and love collide into one.

His trust in the girl trusting the untrustworthy never deviates.

Deacon is an outlaw; Jynx is a stalker; I am a college student.

"You let me return to the club, and I'll learn to do this," he offers, laying down the agreement as Deacon winds the threads round and round. "Let me have the family I know will protect us with their blood."

Deacon says nothing but glances over at him.

My respect for him becomes infinite in that second.

Respecting Jynx and Deacon, and even myself—often forgotten and overlooked—arrived without warning. With my deference, they promised I would recover from my self sabotaging ways, healing the blighted emotional wounds, as the scars that remained were nothing more than reminders for lessons learned.

Beautiful scars.

This scene thrives between Jynx and me as the artist practices his craft.

I would've said no to his reuniting with the club a week ago, but things have changed. His cousin is as impressive as he is, and I trust him.

Deacon licks his lips and backs up, scrutinizing with an assessing squint. I smile at him, and he catches me. "Say something."

He snickers, "What do you want me to say?"

"How am I doing?"

"You remind me of my favorite," he confesses with a smirk and a twinkle in his eye. "She's small too. It's a lot easier to tie up someone more substantial. Small people, smaller knots, less space to work with —the entire process weighs on precise skills. I could do amazing art with you in my studio at home."

I bluntly question, "You tie-up, Sal?"

"I do."

"Often?"

"Yes."

"Have you ever tied up Jynx?"

"Not yet," he chuckles, and Jynx laughs. "But I could. He's huge, though. I could tie you together."

"Oh, my God!" I squeal, wiggling my toes. "The possibilities are endless!"

Twitching his lips, he affirms, "Yes."

With a trembling fear in my voice, I ask, "… Would I be welcome?"

"In my club?" He peeps up with his ocean blue eyes. They're brighter than Jynx's, startlingly so, with an almost translucent quality. Jynx's are saturated with majestic admiral blue. "Absolutely." His brows tighten as he scans over me. "Where'd you get the scar?"

Jynx tilts his head with innate curiosity. "What scar?"

"This one," Deacon points out, lightly running his finger over the length from under my right breast to my hip. I shiver, not from Deacon's touch, but Jynx's penetrating stare that announces his staunch vow to protect me at all costs. "It's pretty."

"Pretty bad."

"No," he corrects, bestowing a sensitivity. "Pretty—a pretty scar symbolic of a past trauma that you survived."

"I was attacked," I confide, not expecting rope bondage to result in a much-needed therapy session.

I notice the upsurge of worry in Jynx's expression as he questions, "By who?"

My eyes dampen, and Deacon pulls out his handkerchief, blotting my eyes. "My brother was fourteen, and he was messed up bad on dope. He wasn't all there and pulled a blade attempting to kill himself. We struggled; I lost or won, depending on how you look at it. The next thing I remember, I was waking up in the ICU. I found out they had taken Brandon to juvie, and I lost my sanity."

Deacon mumbles, "You've seen some shit."

"I have," I whisper, acknowledging the heartache and not running from it. "It's not all been pretty."

"Beautiful things evil people do. Evil things beautiful people do," Deacon whispers. His words prick my flesh like needles as the time in his care darns the damage of the past. "There is always a balance."

"Light and dark," I whisper as a single teardrop falls from my lashes and splashes to his sneakers. "Good and evil. Beautiful and ugly. We cannot have one without the other."

"To eliminate one destroys both," he suggests, leaning in and kissing my cheek. "It has been a privilege to do this piece and a great honor to spend time with you. You're a precious soul. Thank you for your patience. This one was a challenge. We're in a constant state of metamorphosis, changing and evolving, do not hinder what is meant to be."

"A constant finger on the pulse of life," I answer, heeding his shamanistic narrative and regurgitating the exercise. He presses his hands together and slightly bows as I pass his test. "I'll never forget this."

With a silent step over to Jynx, he says, "If you need any help getting her down, come and get me. There are release points on either side, but she's light. I don't imagine you'll have any trouble."

This is his religion.

"Thanks, Cuz."

And like a performer, he exits the stage. "Make memories. Goodnight."

"Thank you so much, Deacon!"

He turns and nods from the doorway. "The pleasure was all mine, Echo."

He departs, and I glance up. "How good is it?"

"He's fucking insane," he proclaims with joy. "Why didn't you tell me about the scar?"

I counter, "Why didn't you tell me about being a dirty biker?"

He smiles. "Getting to know one another takes time."

"Yes," I concede, lightly swinging from the rafters. "Lucky for you, Mr. Monroe, I have all the time in the world."

"Is that so?"

"Mhmm," I reply, grinning. "Will you take pictures?"

"I'm about to," he says as a down feather glides to the floor. "Who knew why I was collecting all of them."

I giddily ask, "Am I a beautiful peafowl?"

"Like you cannot believe," he admires. "Innocent. Pure. Unstained. This is a defining moment for you. Thank you for trusting your Masters."

"I cannot thank you enough for the opportunity to surrender all that I am."

"May you find freedom in your rebirth."

JYNX

"HOW ARE YOU?" I ASK, AFTER SNAPPING HUNDREDS OF pictures. "Getting tired?"

"I'm amazingly high."

I stare at all of the virgin white peacock feathers interlaced amongst the rope. "The finite intricacy and meticulous detail are incredible," I marvel, appreciating his live art from the chair. "I'm not sure why he isn't doing more with his skills."

"The magic in his gift would be lost."

"You're the gift," I whisper. "Do you want to talk? Meditate? Get down? Tell me what would make you happy."

"I forgave my brother."

"I know," I reply, tucking my fingers under my chin. "I haven't traversed over your naked skin enough to know all of the markings, but I have every intention of memorizing each and every one."

"What are the ones on your left arm from?"

"Bike accident," I inform, glancing at my rippled bicep in the shirt. I have concealed most of the scars with ink. "I had two. The first one was when I was sixteen. I broke my left wrist. It was a fairly easy tumble where I hit the pavement wrong. The other one at twenty-seven put me in a medically induced coma for three weeks. I busted almost every bone in the arm. I believe the words the doctor used were—crushed and mutilated. I punctured both lungs, shattered my knee cap, and my blood pressure shot up because of the stress from my injuries. I tried to have a heart attack on the table before surgery. I almost died."

"Holy shit."

"Yeah," I say, recalling the months of rehab. "It was not a good time."

"How long before you were riding again?"

"It was a good year or more before I was up and going."

Her lips pout as she stares at the floor. "How important is the club for you?"

"Not as important as you," I honestly say. "If you gave me an ultimatum, I would choose you."

"I wouldn't do that," she replies, glancing up through the intense conversation. "Ultimatums bring resentment unless it's for your own good." Her air shifts to a lightheartedness as she boldly declares, "I like him."

"My cousin?"

"Yeah."

"Deacon's a good guy." I clasp my hands together. "Loves his family like a warrior doing battle with the world."

She takes a deep breath. "If you ever call me your old lady..."

"I would never call you that, bitch." I wink, and she giggles. "Seriously, I have no desire to cause harm or even piss you off. Now that I know there are extenuating circumstances and you have a bad history with bikers, I'll watch myself and be cautious of my behavior."

"Are you a bad boy, Jynx?"

"Yes, Ma'am," I confirm without hesitation. "I am."

"No cheating. No baa-baas. No drunken and disorderly excuses either."

I laugh. "You wouldn't be here if I planned on cheating. I'll take one precious peafowl riding my cock for the rest of my life if she'll have me. I'm loyal like a fucking dog."

"I'll have you, but you're still an asshole."

"Filthy fucking gentleman."

I walk over and gently pull a feather out of the harness. I brush it over her breast, arousing the bud to a peak. "Jynx..."

"Yes?"

"I love you," she whispers, crying as her mascara runs black trails to the white ropes. The pounding ache in my dick encompasses how my entire body yearns to be connected to hers. "Stalker."

I snarl and lower, flicking my tongue against the hardened nipple trapped between the ropes. "This is cruel."

"Because you can't get to me."

"Yes," I admit, wanting to touch her. "I never knew how intimate this could be."

"We should restrain me more often," she suggests as I slide my hand over her belly. The contrast between the rough ropes and her supple skin sends a sudden bolt through my spine as my hand slides low between her thighs. I dip my finger into her slit, mounting pressure against her clit with small circles, tighter and faster, until she gasps my name in praise, "Jeremiah, make love to me."

"That's an improvement!"

"Reflected by the love you give to me," she whispers, weeping. "You're going to make me come."

"I should stop." Her mouth gapes open with a frown as I gently scold, "Don't be disobedient now that you've come this far. There is pleasure in restraint."

I unzip my pants, pulling my dick out and stroking with dedication. With her eyes glazing over, she moans, "And the ropes have left you with none."

"Smartass."

"I have an outstanding teacher," she mutters with enlightenment. "If I were out of these right now…"

"I would throw you on the floor and have my way with your body for hours," I charge, pumping harder. I tighten my grip. "I would mark all three holes, claim you as mine, and leave you breathless and begging for more."

"It's too late for that. You already have, Jynx."

21

ACCEPTANCE

Echo

"HOW ARE YOU?" HE MUTTERS IN THE BATHROOM AS I stand in the pile of ropes. "Are you okay?"

"I've never been better, Sir," I reply as he turns off the water brimming to the edge of the tub. "Are you getting in with me?"

"Into your bubble bath?"

I nod, smirking. "Please." Lifting his arms, he tugs the shirt off from the back of the neck, revealing his body that I don't deserve. Well-defined muscles, sculpted with the blessing of an artist and kissed by Gods, urge my toes to curl beneath the blanket of bubbles. "You work out."

"I do now," he says, unfastening his jeans. "I was a fat little kid."

"You were?"

"Pre-puberty, I was," he confides, letting his pants fall. "I ended the sixth grade, no taller than you are and round as a ball. By the time school started in the fall, I was half a foot taller. And going into ninth grade, I was over six feet."

He steps into the other end of the antique clawfoot tub and lowers with my eyes glued to his body. His feet and legs ease around my bottom. We're facing one another with nowhere to run. "You're more than I ever imagined."

"I'm the bad guy." He smirks, extending his hand. I take his fingers in mine, and he tugs me on top of him. Sudsy water splashes out onto the floor, soaking the towels, clothes, and rope. Every bit of his wet, naked body wedges against mine. Our lips meet with slow, soft licks until they become too intense, and his tongue delves deeper into my mouth. I conform to his will, his body, his mastery. "We should not be in this position."

His growing erection rams against me, and I breathe in his kiss. "Too dangerous for you?"

"Yes."

"You want me?"

"More than I can express in words," he growls, rolling my body over like I'm nothing more than a twig. He sets me between his thighs and pulls me in close. His hardness is pinned between our flesh. I gasp.

"This isn't any better."

He groans from deep in his throat, "No, it's not. But at least you don't have to see the villain in me."

"What you can see, or what I can see, matters that much?"

"Yes," he hastens, lifting his hands from the water and letting the tiny droplets hit my shoulders. "It's the only thing that matters."

"We'll never have morning sex."

"No," he cackles, resting his lips against my shoulder. "I have limits. I was born in the dark. I live in the dark. Light exists for others."

"I will always be on the other side."

"Unless I sway you into the foreboding recesses."

The truth bites as much as the reawakening sensation in my skin. "I didn't belong where you were in the underground on the Gray Market. I was nothing more than a white peafowl set amongst a green landscape. I was easy pickings."

"You were," he admits, running the back of his hands over my hourglass curves. "But don't ever think I saved you because I didn't."

"No, you seduced me with the gentleness in your tone. You could talk me through anything. I could perform surgery with the expert guidance of your vocal cords. They resonate with a comforting strum. I fell prey to a monster with a good voice, kindness, and sexy window dressing. I bought the merchandise."

"There is no return policy," he confirms what I already know. I'm stuck—caught between titillating desires and the reality of wants and needs. We aren't real. He isn't real. This is lust in a costume of fake love. "I was afraid you would never figure it out."

His hands coast over my breasts as he gropes the fullness in his palms. His fingers graze over my aroused nipples as his other hand shoots toward my slit. I should've realized weeks ago that this was his skewed version of an acceptable crime. My voice quivers as I ask, "Why did you never rape anyone?"

"I never found the right one."

I fall into the trance of his sweet touch as my body betrays everything that my mind believes. *His fingers circle the bud.* My heart lies. *And my body blossoms with every pass.* This isn't love. *His wicked garden entices with glorious splendor.* This is so fucked up. *His fingers twist my nipple, burning hot, as his vampire taunts the sun.* I buck against his hand.

He's got me...

For fun.

For challenge.

To see if he could get away with it—*how far he could push his boundaries before giving in*—withholding sex to prove to himself that he's not capable of the violent sex acts. But with every kiss, caress, and intimate moment past, it's getting harder to resist the needle hitting the vein.

I know it; he knows it.

We're traveling up a deviant elevator with turbojets beneath our feet, rocketing to the skies, faster than I ever dreamed.

From I wasn't submissive to on my knees with his cock immersed in my throat, I plead for his plunge. I beg for his addiction. I solicit my body for his unruly consummation, and I will not protest. I will not fight.

"Fuck me, Jynx," I beg, gripping my nails into his thick forearm. His fingers slide inside of my unused sheath as his grinding rubs my ass against his hard cock. "Make your home in me."

He lifts my body like a feather and penetrates the departing gateway like a predatory animal with a vitriolic attack. His feral thrusts to my ass damper my resolve as his courting ways restrict my cognizance. "There is no exit."

With tears quietly streaming over my cheeks, I whisper, "When I leave, I'll escape through the entrance."

JYNX

I LISTEN TO THE SOUND OF HER BREATHING IN MY BED. HER fingers rest on my chest. I do not know how much longer I can restrain myself from having my way with her body. I have her mind, but it isn't enough. I'm a greedy son of a bitch. Her malleable, vulnerable side wraps to my will, but I long for her thighs to do the same.

I will break her spirit if we don't stop, switching off the light and forcing her to trust my hands in the dark, where I reside like a vermin in murky tunnels.

There will be nothing she can do to stop my advances. We're not riding the highs and lows of a roller coaster but spinning loops and waiting to fly off the tracks.

This love won't survive the accident.

But I don't give a fuck what she wants.

I will lose the girl I've fallen so hard for—yet, I want to accost her. And I've yearned to do such since I first saw the ad. My self-discipline is running out. If I give her what she wants, she will take my heart. So I lie to myself, still believing I can escape—*unscathed*.

It's too late; I lapped up the poison of her love.

I close my eyes, wishing I was drunk to the point of blacking out. I would awaken, and she would be long gone before I had the chance to fuck this up and hurt her beyond repair.

It's too late; she swallowed the toxicity from my sword.

Time and time and time again.

I'm stupid crazy in love with this girl.

This love should be easy, but it's not because I want to stretch her further than the elastic will allow. We will rupture, snap, and hurt one another. We are an impossibility.

Her phone rings on the nightstand. I spot the clock at—4:56 AM. And I answer. "Hello?" The woman's words fire off in a blur. "We're leaving now. Thank you for calling."

She sleepily asks, "Who was that?"

"Your sister," I murmur, stunned, as she quickly sits up.

"Jynx..."

"Your father had a heart attack," I whisper, watching the landslide of my needs skirt off the cliff to the valley below. I flashback to the wreck, laying on the pavement, unable to move with no one in sight.

I no longer matter; this is all about her—*my submissive.*

"Is he okay?"

"Daphne doesn't know," I say, bracing through the shifting tides threatening to submerge her—*my girl. The one beside me in my bed. The one I fantasize about assaulting.* The one I dream of marrying but know I never will because I'm nothing more than a trespasser, carrying the burden of her inclinations with my own. But something kicks in, something I don't expect—*I must protect Echo.* "We have to go."

WITH HER HAND ON MY THIGH, I DRIVE LIKE A NUT JOB IN a race car to Tallahassee. I make the six-hour trip in a little over four and a half hours. I never claimed her escort to the bottomless pits was of sound mind.

We turn into the hospital parking lot, and she whispers, "Thank you, Jeremiah." I blink several times, holding back the pain of hers that I feel. "If he dies..."

Stopping the car, I glance at her sitting cock-eyed in her seat. "I will take care of you."

I want nothing more than to be her partner in life, but the facts present with disparity. I'm a monster for her virtue. But I make the promise, signing my death certificate because that is what a gentleman does. I do not doubt that I will push her too far because that is what an asshole does.

She will leave.

And that will be the end of me.

"There's Daphne," she announces, laying her hand on the door handle. "I have to go."

"Wait."

She listens.

And I hate that she does.

Run away, girl.

I'm the bad guy.

Exiting the car, I sprint around to open her door as the day unfolds, suggesting a kaleidoscope of normal images that I am not sure I want—family and responsibility. Not to her, but to them.

I'm obsessed with caring for Echo.

The next few hours are a haze of lousy coffee, pacing, and running to the car to smoke cigarettes. I can't stop touching her—holding her hand, rubbing her back, and letting her know I'm accessible to ground the emotional upheavals.

When her dad makes it out of surgery, we breathe a sigh of relief. Her mother shows no reaction, which upsets Echo. I suggest taking a walk. She latches onto my arm, and we stroll the halls for a good half hour before finding ourselves in the chapel.

"Talk to me," I implore, opening myself up with an availability. "Please, baby."

"My disdain for her festers at the worst times."

"Because she isn't who you want her to be," I offer, calling her mother out. "You've got to give up this vision that you have. The longer the ideal in your mind doesn't match the reality, the harder this becomes. And believe me, when I say, it doesn't ever get any easier."

"Your father hurt you."

"Yeah, both my parents hurt me," I confide, trying to bridge the rift. "I would've been in jail long before twenty-five if it hadn't been for my Grandma. She raised me. She saved me."

"Who is going to save me?"

"I fucking am," I vow, making the pledge. "I will save you now, tomorrow, and for the rest of your life, but I've got shit in my head that needs repairing."

She grabs my hand. "Don't we all?"

"I love you, Echo," I profess, staring into her reddened hazel eyes. "And I'm terrified I will fuck up and lose you."

"The only way you're losing me is if you push me away," she contends. "You're going to have to break up with me and end this for good."

"You said in the bathtub that when you left..."

"Because I want to believe, just as much as you do, that we can get out of this and part ways. Neither one of us are cut out for relationships, but fate put us together so we can fight through it or throw in the towel, but it's a hostile labyrinth where we merge. You say you were a hit it and quit it guy, but what do you think I wanted in that ad?"

"Not this."

"No," she says, smiling and shaking her head. "Not this."

ECHO

———

WE SPEND THE NEXT THREE DAYS WITH MY FAMILY. Daphne likes Jynx. Oddly, my mother expresses zero reaction. My father is less than impressed. When he finally moves to a private room, he manages to corner me alone—even in a hospital bed and connected to countless tubes a father's love knows no bounds. While Jynx is on the phone in the waiting room and Daphne and my mother are getting lunch, I'm alone and left to play Daddy sitter.

"You don't need to get too involved with that man you're with," he says as soon as the nurse leaves. "He's not good enough for you, Echo."

I'm not good enough for myself.

I hear his words, but they mean nothing to me anymore. Not after the heartache his actions have put me through.

What right does my philandering biker father have to pass judgement on my actions?

"I love you, Dad," I properly reply, kissing his cheek. "I'll be careful."

"I don't think you understand. He is the type who presents as the perfect man, but underneath he is a devil in disguise."

"I should be fine then," I counter as Daphne and my mother return to the room laughing, carrying on with their doting relationship. "I'm used to that."

He latches onto my hand. "Ask yourself how much you truly know about him before you get heartbroken."

I nod as the tears form in my eyes. I was hoping for more, but no man will ever be enough for Daddy's Little Girl.

"We bought you a salad, Abigail," my mother says. She didn't care enough to feed Jynx.

That's okay.

I will.

I rush out of the hospital room, not bothering to say goodbye to my family, and run into Jynx walking toward the room. He has a concerned look in his eyes, and I ask, "Is everything okay?"

"I'm fine, but you're not okay. What is wrong?"

"Please take me home," I beg.

"To?" he whispers, uncertain.

I lace my fingers with his. "South Carolina, Jynx."

A RIVAL WORTH REMEMBERING

ECHO

WITH MY NEWFOUND FREEDOM IN MYSELF, I DANCE IN THE truck bed in my boots, cut-offs, and a hot pink macramé swimsuit top. "Be careful up there," he laughs, tending the bonfire burning a reasonable distance away. "No broken bones."

"Says the bad boy with a bike crashing problem."

"Do you need a reminder of who I am?"

After the adverse reaction of my parents towards Jynx, I accepted his care. I didn't leave with him to rebel, but I needed to breathe, and he offered silent empowerment.

With his maturity, he proved to have the magic elixir—the ideal antidote to heal the wounds their words and time carelessly inflicted. He was the oxygen in my smoke-filled lungs.

"No, Sir." I watch the flickering flames dancing in the early evening. "No need for any overt shows of testosterone-induced power plays."

"I'm sorry we couldn't do this on the Fourth of July."

"It's okay, Jynx," I reply lightheartedly. "I'm not expecting perfection."

"That's a joke if I ever heard one."

"If I set my bar that high, it leads to striving for the impossible and the sour fake flavor you hate."

"Well," he replies. "At least you learned real and fake."

"Life bends. We sway. We can choose to flow through the obstacles or fight against one another in the challenges. But I'm tired of battles. With your hand locked in mine, there isn't anything I can't do. I trust you. And we will get through whatever life throws at us."

"You're such a beautiful soul, Echo, but you need to stop lying to yourself," he mutters, climbing onto the tailgate. His arms wrap tightly around me. "You say all of this shit like you're reciting it from a textbook, but you don't mean a damn word of it. You are a perfectionist."

"Hardly," I dismiss, knowing he's right.

A few minutes later, he says, "We should've brought a blanket and a bottle of wine."

I swoon at the romantic notion as effervescent energy erupts in me. "Run and grab some. I'll be fine to tend your little blaze."

He glances back at the roaring fire. "Are you sure?"

"I am positive."

He kisses my lips and jumps onto the grass. Hoisting my body into his arms, he sets my feet on the ground. "I'll be right back."

"I know," I reassure as he hastily departs in the truck.

I meander near the flames as years of growth turns into ash. When it's all burned and cooled, he plans to scoop the remains and put them into the garden. The charred limbs will help the soil surrounding the tomatoes and beans that we will consume.

The revolution of a life cycle—*birth to death*—and back again.

I fear I won't ever get the chance to complete my evolution with Jynx Monroe.

I spot his tail lights in the distance as he stops to chat with the Ag boys —Tommy and Jake. They're doing a fine job at helping the farm return to a sustainable place. Not only did they clear branches, but they're working on repairing the old barn and hauling off debris collected over the years.

Clementine had little help around the estate, as was evident by her massive piles of junk stashed in the barn, garage, and attic.

With Jynx working so much at Peacock, his time is limited, and the two young men have proven more than capable.

Jynx drives to the house, and I expect the boys will return to the route down the drive, but they veer toward me. No doubt, entranced by the enormous fire.

They park the truck and walk toward me. I smile and say, "Just couldn't stay away from the fun?"

Tommy grins. "Couldn't stay away from you."

I blink with unease as they stalk closer. I don't bother to look for Jynx because I know he's conveniently disappeared and left me to deal with the two football players. "Motherfucker!" I whisper under my breath. "Don't put this test in front of me!"

I take off running as Jake rallies, "Damn, he called that."

"Let's get her!"

The games we play.

He's paying for this one.

I make a mad dash for the tree line where I can vanish in the woods. I've walked the property enough to know it. I pick up my pace as their footsteps and ragged breaths draw closer.

My boots splash into the creek on the other side where the house resides, and my hair falls from the clip as I leap over the short fence. One of the boys thuds to the ground with a groan.

Yeah, there are trees out here, dumbasses.

Why are you running, Abs?

Suddenly, I stop. I spot the lights on in the house as I detour to the gate of the backyard. I question—*why I ran?* After all, I was the girl who wanted an assault.

Jynx is testing me.

And winning by a wide margin.

The aroma of blooming honeysuckle fills my nostrils as I open the gate with the two hot on my tail. Jynx can see me from the house. And I know he is watching when I pull off my top and drop it in a lounge chair by the pool.

The boys wait just inside the gate as I spot Jynx in the kitchen. I kick off my boots and undo my shorts, letting them fall. Pulling my panties down, I bend, taunting their reckless youth with what lies between my thighs.

Those whippersnappers ain't ever met a vixen like me.

More than capable young, adult males.

More than capable of initiating and fornicating with me in my captor's backyard.

I catch a glimpse of Jynx smirking in the window as I sashay around the pool, and with a whip of my long hair, I toss a seductive smile over my shoulder to the man full of deviant delight. If he thinks I cannot play his games due to my age and naivety, he has another thing coming.

"You want to party?" I flirt as drool froths out of their mouths. My kinky minx is out for blood. "Filthy fucking *boys.*"

"Okay, fun is over!" Jynx informs, slamming the back door.

And there is my filthy fucking gentleman.

"Aww, too bad," I pout. "Maybe another time."

He tosses a robe at me and thumbs over a few hundred to them. "Thanks, boys. See you on Tuesday. Don't get any bright ideas. There will *never* be another time."

"But we could have a good time," I purr, seething inside, as the boys scamper off, rejected. "Problem, J?"

"You're something else."

"... Me? You sent those two clowns to rough me up in the woods,"

I counter, raising a finger. "Just to prove your point that I'm not cut out for what I'm begging for...groveling like a starving kitten at your feet...feed me your cock, Jynx. Just give it to me already!"

"I have to get back to the fire."

"Don't mess with me again," I warn, crossing my arms. "If you're pulling up to the table, you bring your best because I won't settle for less. And you better stay to play."

"Spitfire."

With a scowl, I brush past him. "Your Cuz nailed that one."

I almost make it to the door when he says, "Abigail."

Spinning on my heel, I reply, "Yes, Master?"

"Get your ass to the shed."

———

"Son of a bitch," I mumble, marching into the shed. "Who the fuck does he think he is?"

I flop on the bed and stare at the ceiling as the tears puddle in my eyes. His ultimate goal will always be to challenge me—test my resolve, pushing my determination to spur on growth.

Pruning lanky limbs, he sucks the burdens of undergrowth away, encouraging new life from me. I want to believe that there is an end to all of it. That this is just a phase, but I fear this is permanent.

He will forever be preening me.

His Sweet Pea. His Brat. His Girl.

I must accept his terms and conditions or default on the agreement. There is no further negotiation necessary. The deal is signed, sealed, and secured away someplace secret—*in our hearts as a silent love affair blossoms.*

The intimacy levels are incredible, but the switchbacks are cumbersome. His roller coaster isn't only up and down and loopy-loops, but the track dips below the surface to a pitch blackness. The questions manifest—Is this love worth this much trouble? Are we worth that much pain? Is the pleasure good enough to not renege on my heart?

The door kicks back as he stands in the darkness. "Get up." I slide out of the robe, striding over to him naked. "Touch your nose."

I do it, but he shows no reaction.

"Squat."

Again, I do it without question. He extends his hand to assist me up. "What are we doing?"

"Hands above your head."

I raise them high. From his back pocket, he pulls out a pair of handcuffs, locking them onto my wrists. "Babe?" I say with slight apprehension. "You're scaring me."

"And you still scare me," he rebukes with disdain. "Put your arms down."

Holding onto what remaining composure I have, I ask, "How?"

"With your behavior."

"What was the right answer?" I implore, struggling to comprehend the lesson. "Tell me because I don't know. What was I supposed to do? Let Tommy and Jake rape me? Scream for you to play the hero? What was the right thing to do?"

"Not what you did," he reprimands as we practice the intricate problem again. He'll go over it again and again and again until I finally get it right. And the worst part of it all, he never loses his patience. He never breaks. His resilience to my strategy is off the charts, unyielding, and damn infuriating. "There are no heroes here. Your only job is to execute."

"What am I executing?"

"Dependency. Need. Wants. Desires. Lust. Love. All of it is fucked up in your head. You're in love with the man who abducted you. You're willing to succumb to whatever anyone has in mind as long as you feel like you have the final say in the outcome."

"I don't," I mutter, crying. "You do."

"You want me to be everything for you, but how can I do that when your agenda is constantly conflicting with whatever I set forth. You're too independent. Too set in your ways of safeguarding one —*yourself*. You must give up."

"I can't!" I scream. "I don't know how!"

"Because you're not paying attention!"

"I didn't have a choice when I was young," I fiercely argue. "There was Brandon and me. Mom was always catering to Daphne's latest extracurricular activities—swimming, ballet, art, and piano lessons."

"You did those things too."

"Only as a bandage. Dad was at the club with the latest floozy of the month while my mother was cheering on her only daughter— Daphne. I was making boxed macaroni and cheese at six years old because we were hungry, starving."

"You're still starving!" He roars in my face as I curl inward and collapse at his feet. "We won't ever work if you keep fighting."

On the ground, I sob. "What am I supposed to do?"

"Fall."

I cannot control the laugh emerging from deep inside. "… Fall?"

"Fall. Fail. Fuck it up for once in your life."

"You make that sound so easy," I whisper, slobbering. "Like I can give up twenty-two years of independent thinking for one man. You're right—I'm a perfectionist!"

"If you can't…"

"What was the right answer, J?"

"To trust that I would not let them rape you."

"And what if I am in a situation one day where someone tries?"

"You knew I was fucking with your mind, though, and still, you go out on a limb with some creative, rather ingenious answer that I don't want or need. Stop overcomplicating the already complex," he points out, crouching low. His fingers run over the side of my cheek. "Does that bother you?"

"What?"

"That I take the independence you've fought for and wipe it away like a clean slate? I pick up a tablecloth with all the fine china and dishes prepared for hours and destroy them with one fell swoop. Does it bother you that I want to administer such care?"

The tears don't stop as my fingers clutch onto his boots. My sanity snags on the word—*administer*—like I'm nothing more than a patient seeking treatment. "This is so fucked up. You're twisted, and

I'm mangled. What if I give you everything you want and you leave me?"

He gazes down, gripping the bridge of his nose. "How many times have I told you to trust me?"

"Countless!"

"But you still don't..."

"I do!"

"But you don't! Or you would trust that I won't leave you," he mumbles, popping his jaw. "And if I told you to leave?"

"You told me to go, and I did," I report, grasping at anything to save whatever we have left. "You followed me!"

"Only because you were testing how far the extension of your leash would reach. Not me, I know how long my dick is," he callously quips. "It's you who needs to flop it out and take a measurement. Look at me! But you were never actually leaving. If you were, you wouldn't have stopped in Columbia. You wouldn't have called Selia. You wouldn't have rolled down your window. You wouldn't have gotten out of the car. You would've gone as fast and as far as you could and never looked back."

"Is that what you want me to do?"

"No!" He yells, "I want you to give up, dammit."

"I can't give up fighting."

"I want you to fucking admit that you need me—for more than just a pissing contest or a jolly ride on my johnson. You didn't ever truly want to be attacked either. You wanted to know if you could get out of this, and I'm begging you to consider what you're asking for before..."

Rocking onto my knees and standing up, I ask, "Before what, J?"

With a glare, he warns, "Don't turn this into the student teaching the professor."

"Before you cannot control yourself anymore? Before your discipline gets the best of you and you're compelled, determined—*forced*—to violate me in a heinous way which you will never be able to forgive yourself for? Before you break my heart into a thousand pieces because I have fallen for you—*the man who lured me in and arguably abducted me?* Who is testing who here? Answer me!"

"Run, bitch!" he howls in the shed as the tension snaps. "Run!"

I sprint into the clearing, holding my tethered wrists to my chest, as the fire beckons my eyes. It's bigger, brighter, better than it was before. The flaring intensity turns the wood into ash without regard.

He wants to burn me.

He wants to burn me down and plant his seed with the hope that he can rebuild me into his perfect little submissive that will surrender to his will and call out his name in the night.

Me—who fought for every little thing and found freedom in the crush of one boy only to lose him in the most horrific of ways. Jynx doesn't want to fight with me; he wants to fight for me, even if that means his greatest rival is me.

Jynx must singe the me that existed before he came into my world and turned everything upside down. He must flush and cauterize the infected wounds, which won't ever heal because I keep picking at the scabs with every line I fight to control.

But I won't do that.

I won't stop being me.

He won't break my heart.

He won't burn my soul.

Because I won't give him a chance.

I'll drown in his muddy waters. I will end it. Call the truce. Evacuate the scene. Never look back.

On the damp grass, I pivot to face him. "I ran, Sir."

"You didn't get far," he mentions, walking closer. "You should run farther."

"But I ran."

"Stop running, Echo," he commands, brushing his fingers down my arm. "All you're doing is running in circles, listening to the reverberations of your own echo. Stop. Running."

"Is that what I was supposed to do with the boys?"

"I knew you would run," he says, staring at me. "I just wanted to know what you'd do next."

"You're going to hurt me."

He solemnly vows, "I am. And I will not apologize for my actions.

Or being your number one fantasy. But you should go. You should run from me if it means you will stop running from yourself. But I don't think you are motivated enough to do that, so here we are."

"The lessons are getting thin."

"No," he snickers, lowering his head and peering at me. "My willpower can only last for so long."

"You want to save me from myself, when I became so independent, but we can't rewind the clock. We can't go back there. We're stuck here and now and left to deal with the shit of the past. You think that you can break me down for another man to reap the reward and eat the fruits of your labor, but what you don't understand is I won't want another after you."

I understand the true meaning of who we are to one another.

A frayed thread bound to split.

His jaw tightens. "Another man? You think there is ever going to be another man after me?"

"I fulfill your destiny; you wanted to take it further outside the bedroom window, stalking her from a distance while your hand did its business. You wanted more. You thought about it. You considered it. You dreamed about it. You fucking fantasized about it. And handcuffs stopped you."

"They were the only thing that stopped me," he confides.

With tears in my eyes, I lift my wrists as the silver shines under the moonlight. "Take off the handcuffs, Jeremiah Monroe. Be the criminal you always wanted to be. And give me my wings so I can finally be free."

"Peacocks only fly when in danger."

23

SIP. SAVOR. DEVOUR.

JYNX

TWENTY-TWO.

A damn baby to my grown-ass man.

I question what the fuck I'm thinking.

What right do I have to pursue a long-term relationship with a girl I hardly know? I want to do bad things to her—*harmful things*. I want to hurt her—*mark, stain, and bruise*—body, mind, and heart.

Since the incident a week ago with the boys, she's been staying in her room downstairs. I'm not happy about it. She belongs in my bed beside me, but we're having a spat.

222 | KAILEE REESE SAMUELS

I was a dick about the boys, but I did it for a reason. She is a loose cannon. If she returns home, I know her ad will go right back up, regardless of what she claims.

Sitting up in bed, I adjust the sheet as the mere thought of her combined with the brush of the fabric draw up a salute from the nether region. I sigh and roll my eyes.

Not tonight, fucker.

It's been the dead zone for over a week, and I don't plan on her position altering anytime soon. Stubborn as fuck youth.

With the news on the television, I sign into the Gray Market. I've been on the site all week long searching for some relief for a specific *problem* I'm having, but none of the girls—*recorded video or live*—can hold a candle to what Miss Thang downstairs does. She doesn't just spark my imagination; she dances in the blaze and begs for my participation.

My poor unattended dick is spoiled on one.

Traitor.

My cock is a defecting slut for one.

I'm watching some trio of hot girls go at it, bored to tears, and thinking about how I'd find more arousal watching some cheesy romantic film. The girls are forming a triangular daisy chain when a message randomly flashes on my screen.

> D4RK4NG3L: Do you know what it feels like to be me?
>
> $T4LK3R: Last time I checked, I've never been a 22 yo girl.
>
> D4RK4NG3L: My point exactly. The things you ask of me aren't easy. I'm constantly worried that I will misstep and do the wrong damn thing.
>
> $T4LK3R: Did you eat?
>
> D4RK4NG3L: Naw, dude :P

I laugh and shake my head, unable to stop smiling. If her two words can elicit this much reaction, I hate to think what a lifetime with her could bring. Dare I say—*elation?* She'd keep me on my toes, ensuring I stayed young and hip.

Again, not a reason for a relationship, just saying there are additional benefits of dating a youthful menace such as Echo Maines. She's a social media hound; I prefer sports with real numbers over illusionary likes.

The only thumb I want to give her is up the ass while she's riding my cock hard.

We're not even in the same generation—*she's Gen Z, and I'm Gen Y, aka one of those millennial types*—that is how bad this is. She's too young based on the half my age plus seven rule. The youngest I can date and be socially acceptable—25.

I was born a fucking rebel.

Renegade, baby.

$T4LK3R: Are you hungry, kitten?

D4RK4NG3L: Famished. Should I go lap up some
    milk on the floor?

$T4LK3R: Don't tempt me, bitch.

$T4LK3R: Sexy lingerie. Kitchen. Sit on the
    counter.

D4RK4NG3L: Sounds like you're going to eat me,
    Pops.

$T4LK3R: You're wishing, Sugar Tits.

D4RK4NG3L: Is that how we're playing this?

$T4LK3R: We can play however you want.

D4RK4NG3L: Liar. It's your way. Your table. Your
    mastery.

D4RK4NG3L: I'll spread for hours.

$T4LK3R: Top or bottom?

A long pause causes my concern until the camera turns on. She's in a sheer pink baby doll showing off every peak and curve. I close my eyes and pound my head against the headboard. "Fuck."

"Bottom, Sir."

I immediately regret calling her Sugar Tits.

The imagery is too much for the lower head to handle.

Biting her lip, she narrows in on the camera—*at first, focused on the dip of her cleavage*—and then she adjusts the angle to her gorgeous smile. "You still wanna feed me?"

$T4LK3R: You're evil. BRT.

Before leaving the bedroom, I turn on a luminous mix of techno with haunting overlays to broadcast throughout the house. I dim all the lights and pass by the mirror in my black lounge pants. I catch a glimpse of my messy brown curls and blue eyes.

"You're not a terrible looking schmuck," I mumble, stroking the week's worth of growth on my face. "You're not twenty anymore, though, and she needs more than you can provide."

I walk down the two flights of stairs to find her exactly where I want—*perched on the kitchen counter*. My eyebrows arch up as I blissfully sigh and smile.

"I was afraid you wouldn't come," she whispers, playing demure to the hilt. "I was thinking about laying back and touching myself on your marble countertops."

"You should be careful." Opening the fridge, I suggestively remark, "You could slide off with all the moisture gathering between your thighs."

"What are we having?"

"Crêpes."

After about ten minutes, she sits cross-legged. "Have you ever had Bánh xèo?"

I furrow my brow and prepare the batter. "No."

"Vietnamese Sizzling Crêpes," she says, studying my moves. "There is a really good place that has them at home."

"Do you need it?"

"What?"

"Home." I turn on the gas to heat the pan. "The culture."

"To a certain extent, I do. It's who I am. I cannot deny my heritage."

"Does it ever backfire?" I cautiously ask, not wanting to tread. I pour the batter, and it pops in the pan. "You don't look much different from any other American girl."

"America is a melting pot, so what does *she* look like?"

Her epic retaliation renders me speechless for a good minute. "You're too smart for your own good, Echo."

"In answer to your question, there aren't a whole lot of Koreans in Birmingham, but we had family that we routinely visited in San Francisco. When I moved, I easily assimilated after the first week. People are people. It doesn't matter. They either like you, or they don't, but part of that is on me. When I chose to live at the apartment complex I am in—which is probably half Asian, I accepted I would have to prove myself, not as a quarter Korean but as a human being."

Flipping the crêpe, I admit, "You scare me."

"… Why?"

"Because you don't back down."

"I don't have it in me to be weak," she honestly whispers. "Weak is for the meek; possess no peak."

"Where did you get that?"

"My freshman year, I took a creative writing class. I was sixteen, taking college classes, and feeling completely overwhelmed by everything. I decided then to fight for myself, Brandon, and anyone else I deemed worthy. I wanted to prove I could be more than a biker's daughter, but I was failing half of my classes."

"I like it," I say, plating her crêpes. "A lot."

"My Korean grandmother set a high standard when I was a child. She knew that my family was dysfunctional, and she pushed for me to get out of the mentality that my mother's neuroses stuck us in. I didn't want to let her down. I didn't want to have reached the summit only to stumble, so I decided then that there would never be a pinnacle. I would set the bar, only to keep raising it—*higher and higher*—until I was done."

"You compete with yourself."

"I do," she happily admits, smiling as I put strawberries inside the crêpe and roll it up. "That's why I put up the ad—to meet the challenge."

"And now, you've been abducted by a strange man, and you're eating his fine cuisine."

"Yes."

"Is the would-be rapist everything you hoped he would be?"

She takes a bite and stares at me. "No," she answers, rubbing her lips together. "He's far more diabolic than I ever dreamed."

"OPEN YOUR MOUTH," I COMMAND AN HOUR LATER AS SHE lays on the sleek counter blindfolded. I place the tiny piece of frozen fruit in her mouth as the piano solo carries on wistfully. "What is it?"

"Pineapple," she mumbles, attempting to chew. "It's so cold." I press my lips to hers, slurping the juicy nugget from her mouth. "Thank you."

"You must adjust your mind," I ease, letting the chill burn my tongue as the sugary acid slides down my throat. "The rest will follow."

I sip her.

"Don't move. Don't grab. Don't break my flow."

She mutters, "You're performing."

"I am. I always am—every scene, every time, without fail. You will remember the best, and I aim to please." Lifting the edge of the pink baby doll, I stare at the woman. I long for her to meet my savage. My fingers swoop over her hips and slip her panties off. With much consideration, I place a frozen blueberry on her navel. She gasps, and I grin. "Stay still."

I set out ten more, in a row, evenly spaced toward her heart as her feet wiggle. "Sorry."

"Be still."

"You're making me nervous."

"Welcome to what you do to me," I reply, taking a medium frozen strawberry. I gently place the hollowed-out core on her nipple. "Relax. Trust me. The worst that happens is I have a fruit salad on the floor."

"Jynx," she says, trying not to giggle. "What are you doing?"

"Something different."

She bites her lip. "But this is…"

"Don't drop my little blue balls now." My words cause her laughter, and one blueberry rolls off her belly and plops onto the floor. I replace it with another and cap her other nipple with a strawberry. "This is another form of practice, no different from the rest." Her lips quiver as her fingers rhythmically extend. "You played the piano."

"Until college, and I got too busy," she says with heaving breaths as the attraction heightens. We seize the lust, riding the high until we plunge into the seas with a splash. We will drown together. "How did you know?"

"A guess," I reply, loosening my pants. "I never played any instruments."

"I wasn't very good."

"But will you be good for me?"

"I will," she promises, calming her thoughts. I believe in her efforts. I quickly push two decently sized frozen cantaloupe balls inside of her pussy. "Fuck! Fuck!"

"Do you trust me, Echo?"

Her nose crinkles as she broadly smiles. "Yes!"

With a grin, I ask, "Are you good?"

"Besides that, I'm being made into a frozen fruit salad?"

I laugh. "Open wide."

"What is it?"

"Don't ask questions," I reprimand with absolute control. "Just do it."

Her pastel pink lips part, and I put the small kiwi between them

228 | KAILEE REESE SAMUELS

before stepping to the end of the counter and looping my arms under her thighs. I slowly slide her to the edge, as the blueberries roll onto the floor, and run my tongue up her slit. She moans behind the makeshift gag and my cock throbs. I buck uncontrollably, wanting to be inside of her swollen folds. I delicately suck at her tender clit, sweet and succulent.

Fresh fruit—*so fucking new.*

Her fingers ruffle in my curls and brush over my shoulders as I take her to the edge and stop. I extract the pieces of cantaloupe, lukewarm by her body, and shamelessly enjoy them. I flick the tip of my tongue against her ripened bud, needing so much more than what I can give. She wants to take all of me. But she cannot handle me.

I savor her.

My hands grip the tops of her thighs as we collide on a like-minded mission—*her orgasm.* I thrust into the air, imagining she is wrapped tightly around me as I explore her terrain in detail. I must log every freckle, scar, and identifiable point with meticulous detail.

I remove my left hand from her thigh and palm over my cock—*rock hard and ready for more than this will be.* I pump but a few times, unwarranted, without conviction.

I am sorry to disappoint you.

I am sorry to fail you, Echo.

After releasing the beast I've become enslaved to, I grab the frozen banana and penetrate her warm shelter. She's slippery with hot dew pulsing out of her like flowing nectar. I don't hesitate, fearing the thaw, as I vigorously maul her with irritating frustration—*a barricaded lasciviousness waits to bust through the dam of our desire.*

Her body rolls, finding the groove, and surrendering to the fruit within my hand.

The banana—*my cock.*

A mind is a dangerous tool.

I stay affixed to her unsullied clit with my suckling, hungry mouth. I steal in the night what is not mine. I'm a robber, a soul stealer, an extortionist—*a paradigm of mischief.*

A troublemaker, a nuisance, a criminal—*a man no woman should ever covet.*

But yet, here we are—*having fruit salad.*

Her teeth sink into the kiwi, much to her surprise. Her eyes widen and the juice pours, trickling from the sides of her lips. I yearn to lick every saccharine infused inch of her skin clean. Part of the green fruit crashes to the floor as she garbles, "Jynx! Please!"

With one hand on the banana, I mount the other to my cock as we soar to a place where nothing else matters—*where she and I exist*—alone without interference in the transmission, disruptions of the past, or miscommunications that all too often end lost in translation.

Here—*we speak the same language.*

Here—*we fight together.*

Here—*we are one.*

"Jynx," she loudly announces. "I'm going to come!"

She isn't alone, but I hold out, waiting until her quake passes, and she succumbs to the storm bringer's fury. "Take off the mask!"

I leave the banana inside of her shelter and step onto the spindles of the barstool. Rising above her undulating torso, I come, marking her flesh, icing the fruit.

With my elbow propped on her knee, I lick my lips through the hazy delusions that will fade all too soon. The intoxication is so profound, demanding my subservience to its reign.

Her body serves as the chalice and the bread—*the communion in my kink.*

She is the hallucinogen holding the rigors—*the craving of my habit.*

I don't know normal. In the process, I expand her wings, unraveling with zestful energy, and encourage her by perpetually pushing the boundary to further the limits. Through my lessons, I'm teaching her compulsion—*and I'm ruining her for anyone else.*

But I can't stop.

I'm an asshole.

I step down to wrap my lips around the banana and siphon it from her body. Walking to her side, I run my fingers through the drizzle of me. I place a piece of fruit on her lips. She readily takes it in and closes her eyes.

"Blueberries and cream," she whispers with watery eyes. She is as high as I am; the plummet will kill us. "More, please."

Glossing her sticky lips with her cum glazed banana, I order, "Eat."

She does.

And I devour her.

24

BLOW OUT THE CANDLES

JYNX

"WHAT ARE WE DOING?" SHE ASKS AS WE DRIVE INTO Columbia in the early morning on the last day of July.

"We're purchasing items for the special day ahead."

"What special day?"

I glance over to her eager, smiling face. "It's my birthday."

"Jynx!" She excitedly squeals, "Why didn't you tell me?"

"I just did!" I grab her hand, wishing she would move back into my bedroom. I could push the issue, but we'll both do better if I lure her out on her own volition. "I thought we would grill some steak and

232 | KAILEE REESE SAMUELS

shrimp, have a bottle of wine, and spend a quiet evening together as I ring in thirty-seven."

We are now fifteen years apart by the numbers.

"Mine is February 9. I'm an Aquarius."

"I know," I smirk, recalling hours of research I poured into this girl before ever crossing her path. The girl. Not her family or her past. I should've known about the viper pit I was treading into with Colton's suicide and her father's biker history. My faux pas. My fuck up. "Leo. The day is actually a present for you."

"How so?"

I exit the highway and stop at the light. "You said I didn't understand what it felt like to be you, so we're altering that. For one day, you get to take the lead—within reason. No sex."

She giggles, "Hard limit?"

"Very," I warn, snarling. "Don't push me on this, Ek."

"I won't," she whispers. "But does this mean that every birthday I get to play Mistress Echo?"

I snarl, trying not to think about the future, which is almost impossible. One minute I want to hitch the girl to the altar, and the next, I want to liberate her innocence with an insidious act, only to ghost out.

I don't know what I'm doing.

I'm fucked up, and she isn't much better. So we take it, one day at a time, and I pray for a solution, knowing it may never come as a clear, concise answer.

Not clean or neat.

But very real.

Like she is.

ECHO

I SPEND OVER TWO HOURS GETTING READY FOR OUR dinner date. Jynx is cooking and preparing to see what I have to bring to the table.

I'm fucking nervous.

My hands are shaking. My knees are wobbling. And the butterflies in my belly are on some amped up, rocking steroids, sending tremors throughout my core.

I admire the outfit I selected in the mirror—a sexy leather one-piece with a straight bodice and thin straps leading up to a collar with an o-ring complemented by a skimpy skirt, teasing with a hint of ass cheek. Jynx bought me a pair of scandalous thigh highs to go with the outfit, but he also said I could borrow any of Clementine's things.

As soon as we got home, I rushed to her room and carefully opened the plastic bins with yesteryear items. I found the boots in the picture. The ones I loved so much. They end at the top of my thigh, near my crotch, and I feel like a sexual Goddess in them.

I want him to fuck me in these boots.

I practice, pacing around the room as my blown out, tangled mess of hair bounces high up on my head. The five-inch heels give a much-needed boost, but I'm accustomed to that.

Walking in heels is not a concern.

Her feet were slightly larger than mine, so I've shoved a few tissues into the toes. She was a size seven. I'm a six in running shoes, but in most heels, I wear a five-and-a-half.

"It's just Jynx," I whisper, staring at my reflection. "And he likes you a lot."

Stepping out of the bedroom, I spot him outside. He's grilling my dinner in jeans and a loose long sleeve workout shirt.

What the hell am I doing?

I take a deep breath as my lip trembles. I make no sudden movement, tiptoeing like a cat silently crossing over the edge of a fence. I open the door, and he immediately twirls toward me.

"Hi."

"Hello," he oozes with a low rumble as his intense blue eyes scan from my face down and back up again. "You look amazing, Mistress."

My heart stops.

"I have no idea what the fuck I am doing," I admit, anxiously. "You're right. It's not easy from the other side, and I haven't even done anything."

"Give me a command," he suggests. "Name it!"

"Wine!" I shout way too enthusiastically, and he laughs. "Maybe that was too much."

"Relax." He pours the wine as I notice the outside dining table formally set with a lace tablecloth, fine china, and silver he's brought out for our special date—his birthday. He hands the glass to me. "You look stunning."

"I'm falling in love with you, Jynx Monroe."

"I know," he says, kissing my lips. "And I could say the same."

I take a seat at the table and enjoy the evening. It's warm, but a light breeze is keeping the temperature at bay. "This is going to end, though, isn't it?"

"You're asking for an answer I don't have," he replies, putting the steaks on. "But what I do know is I have a dinner date in Columbia tomorrow night with Theodore Dower from the Phoenix project. I'm not sure what he wants, but I'd like you to join me."

"Are the other *wives* going to be present?" I blurt out, stepping in a heaping emotional shit pile.

Fuck.

He smirks as his eyes spark with mischief. "Don't tell me. Freudian?"

"Fell right on in it."

His grin expands to a full-blown smile. "Dammit, girl! You know how to make a man question his sanity," he remarks, downing his wine and continuing to toy with me. "I don't know if the other *wives* will be present, but I want you there, Mrs. Monroe." He winks with a suggestive smirk gliding over his lips.

My toes curl in the boots.

God, I wish.

"You're a piece of work," I mumble.

"... Me?" His typical low tenor raises a notch with my seemingly outlandish accusation. He sticks the tip of his tongue out and laughs. "How do you want this steak?"

"Rare."

He blinks like the idea is unfathomable that a woman would eat a bloody steak. "You're serious?"

"I do know how to eat, Mr. Maines." I wink and stick my tongue out. "Dad loves rare steak. Mom wants it charred like coal."

"There's my girl," he praises. "Loosen up. This doesn't need to be strict and demanding. It can be fun and playful."

"Until I decide that I like roleplaying and want to be a succubus sitting upon my hellhound."

"I will happily get on all fours for your precious, reddened, bare ass to sit upon."

I grin wide. "You mean that."

"I do."

"So everything we have done—*from the flood to the fruit salad*—is it real or fake?"

He strides over and crouches in front of me. I avoid his penetrating gaze because we're in the early dusk when there is light out. His monster is still sleeping.

"Look at me." Reluctantly, I do. "Life is all about experiences. And wherever we end up, wherever this leads, I want you to look back and feel how much I cared about you. I don't do fake. Jynx...Jeremiah Monroe is as real as they come."

"I have more memories from this summer with you than I have from the twenty-two years beforehand."

"It's new," he says. "But no one knows how long it's going to last. More than anything on my birthday, I want you to enjoy yourself, Echo. That is what counts. Make memories. Chase the happy."

"I like that idea."

"So rare?"

"Yes!" I smile and nod.

"I'm pulling them," he says, standing up. I reach out, grabbing his balls and blinking up. He doesn't move. "Can I help you, Ma'am?"

"I like your games, Jynx."

"Good." He devilishly grins. "I like partaking in them with you."

"I SHOULD MAKE YOU FEED ME MORE OFTEN," I MENTION AS he cuts the steak. "You're very good at it."

"Don't tempt me," he counters, smiling. "I'll take all of your independence away just to care for you."

"... Is this a Dominant thing?"

"My feeding you?"

"Yes," I mutter, understanding that even though I am supposed to be leading this night, I know he is. "Tell me the truth."

"I think it can be either way."

"You're using it to garner insight into my head," I accuse with a smirk. I snap my teeth into the meat, savagely ripping it from the fork. "Well played, babe."

"I can't help it," he excuses. "I have years of experience on you."

"Natural asshole," I giggle, rising.

"Where are you going?"

I close my eyes to find the strength—*the gumption I need*—under his sensual stare. Rolling my hips, I flutter my hands along my sides and stretch them into the air as I let my body say what my mouth cannot. He backs his chair away from the table, and I hitch up the skirt, digging deep, and grinding my body against his leg. "You know you're falling for me."

"Like you cannot believe," he growls, laying his hand on the middle of my lower back as I give him a lap dance to remember. "I never knew I needed a filthy fucking girl."

"Oooh, baby," I purr, sensually gyrating on his lap. "You have no idea how dirty I want to be with you."

He lowers his head to my cleavage, inhaling my scent. "Tell me."

"What was it you said when I begged for the same—I'd rather show you? Take me to the dungeon, cowboy."

With one move, he tosses me on his shoulder, grabs the bottle of wine, and sprints up the staircase. After setting me on my feet, he tugs off his shirt and reveals a black leather harness.

I'm dumbstruck, drooling, and so out of my league. "You..."

"You didn't think I wouldn't dress for the evening?" His tongue runs over his bottom lip as he unsnaps his jeans. "I'm not a poser or an imbecile."

"Fuck!" I bounce like a wild woman and shy away, covering my face with my hands. He chuckles as I plead, "Wait!"

"Breathe, Echo."

"This is too much," I whine, sneaking a glimpse of his muscled body showcased by the bands of leather. His taut guns and rippling abs seem even more pronounced within the confines of caging. "I'm going to scream."

He swaggers closer, slowly rocking those hips and taunting every sense in me. "No one will hear you scream."

"Fuck!" I yell again as he blows on my neck. "Dammit, Jynx! You're too good at this!"

His eyebrow arches high. "Practice."

"I don't intimidate you in the same way."

"Incorrect," he mutters, pressing his lips to my bare shoulder. "You bring waves of nervousness to me every time I see you. I just control my emotions better than you."

"Do I want to know what you have on beneath those jeans?"

"May—be," he teases, suggestively. "You need me."

"More than you can imagine." I bite my lip as our eyes stay locked on one another. I slip my hands under the denim, over his hips, and discover that my heaven-kissed captor is wearing a thick double-banded black jockstrap with the harness. "Holy shit! You were serious."

"I don't lie," he mutters, kicking the jeans out of the way. "Birthday spankings for those thirty-seven bad boy years."

"Thirty-eight," I correct, free-falling into his sultry tidal wave. "One to grow on." I twirl my finger, and he shows off his backside, which is as irresistible as the front. "You'll let me paddle you?"

"Oh! Yes! Mistress!" Trying not to break character, he plays it up, placing his hands behind his back and standing correctly. "Please whip me."

I die laughing, unable to hold out any longer. When I finally get done dancing a jig in place, and all of the high pitched squeals have randomly spurted from my lungs, I point to the table and demand, "Bend over, Jynx."

It feels so abhorrent to say those words.

Somehow, I manage to respect the night's rules where I lead, and he follows—but only because he has a thing for me.

I pace over to the wall of implements and select a relatively safe looking old-school style paddle. I test the weight in my hand and catch him looking at me. He's bent over with his head propped in his palm as a smirk blooms across his cheeks. "Don't be afraid. Bring it. I can take the blows."

"Should I get a different one?"

"Are you asking what I would recommend blistering my ass with?"

I giggle, "Yes!"

"Depends. Do you want to spank me, or would you prefer to whip me, or even draw lines with a riding crop? This is on you, sweetheart. Decide what you think I deserve."

"If I did that, you'd have a ball gag, a paper sack, and a hockey stick."

With a captivating smile, he chuckles. "Whatever you fancy, but if you cover this mug, you'll miss all the good stuff that makes you drench the lace tucked between your thighs."

"How do you know I have on lace?"

"Because you're hoping I go for round two of fruit cocktail muff diving."

I blush and bend over, laughing. "You're right!"

"So bring whatever you want, and I will make sure the sweetness on my tongue at the end of the evening is your scrumptious orgasm. Let's blow out the candles and make a wish."

"Dear God..." I mumble as he innocently blinks with a deviant smirk. "I should've blindfolded you."

"What's stopping you?"

"I love the expression that manifests in your eyes," I confess, hitting a tender nerve. "They bring me comfort, like now when I have no fucking clue what I am doing."

"What's causing the nervous giddiness?"

"You. Your words. And those lips get me."

"... Really? All this and you pick my fruit slurping mouth?"

"Yes," I giggle, picking a hefty looking ruler up. "I love your smile. This?"

"Stings like a bitch in the right hands."

"Just what I am looking for," I bravely say. "You need some pain in your life."

"Dare I ask, why?"

"Punishment for all the shit you've done to me! Being a panty-melting motherfucker with no boundaries for weeks on end."

He subtly says, "I haven't made you a mother yet."

With a scrutinizing eye, I rebuke, "You haven't fucked the right hole yet, either."

"There you go," he urges with a smirk. "You've found your fire, now aim."

I stride over with his eyes glued to me. "How hard?"

He shrugs. "Test it out. You'll find your happy place. But don't wrist swing, or you'll be the one on ice tomorrow."

"... Whole arm?"

"Yes, but..." With my eyes as wide as saucers, I pop him once, and the skin flushes crimson. He breathes and clears his throat. "As I was saying, the full swing motion tends to render a harder impact. It's like anything else you swing—baseball bat, golf club..."

"Chugging back a wine bottle," I interject. "Tossing back shots."

Tilting his head down between his arms, he snorts with laughter. "Sure! Put your full body into motion."

"Are you counting?"

"So far, you have one."

"Asshole!" I pull back and strike his ass hard. "Is this arousing you?"

"Not so much the spanking, but experiencing your battle within yourself is giving me a hell of a raging hard-on."

"Fine." I drop the paddle on the table. "Show me how it's done, Master."

"It's always important to be aware of where the submissive's head is at."

"This bitch's head is going to explode in about five seconds."

"You want your bottom to feel safe and secure."

"Or, in your case, your helpless victim pleading for you to whip her ass raw and take it already because you're just too much man."

Glancing over the goods, he snickers and picks up the paddle, sensually stroking the wood like an additional appendage. "Baby, I'm not too much, man. And you were never a victim." He fires off round after round of rhythmic swats to my ass. My ass pulses with his wanton desire. I make him nervous, and he funnels the energy through his fetish. "I cannot wait to peel off those red lace panties."

"Does this turn you on?"

"Yes," he huffs, slapping the wood to my ass. "I love the power you give me."

Tears come to my eyes as the welts fester with his every swing. His breathing intensifies as sweat glistens on his skin. I understand the psychology of a Dominant, but having the courage—*the balls to do it*—is another game that I don't belong in.

Beneath the black trails of mascara tears, I smirk, knowing I failed the practicals, but nailed the mindfuckery. "… Why?"

"Because I get off on hurting you."

"Happy Birthday, Jynx!"

25

POKE. SNAP. STING.

Echo

CLUTCHED TO HIS ARM, I WALK ALONGSIDE HIS IMPOSING, confident stride through the restaurant. In my black Armani dress, I feel the stares of the well-to-do and elite. I present as the perfect mistress, trophy wife, or expensive escort for the night.

I will never change their perception.

What they think of me...

Who they believe I am...

What they conjure Jynx and I to be...

On the surface, we appear like the respected tech guru and his prized princess. I know better, but it stings in a way I don't expect. I have always preferred knowing the intensity of the bite before the burn.

This time, I don't get that option.

When I was a little girl, I used to like to play with bugs. I would let them bite me. In fact, I would encourage it. I had this crazy masochistic streak, even then at knee-high. Better to know that bees would swell up my arm and wasps would pinch for a moment and spiders...well, I barely felt them at all. Ants were the worst because even when I knew their voracious snap of jaws was about to happen, the anticipation would send a chill through my spine.

I did this with insects, arachnids, dogs, cats, hell, even humans.

I wanted to feel the bite.

Later, as a teenager, Brandon had a pet snake—I don't even remember its name or what species it was. Of course, I had to taunt it one day while feeding it a frozen mouse. The snake lunged for my arm, latching on and repeatedly striking me, three times in all. I was in the emergency room a half an hour later.

With his Grandma's pair of diamond tennis bracelets encircling my arm, I rub the snake scar near my wrist as we sit down at the table. I smile, make pleasantries, and quickly acknowledge that attending the boy's meeting was the worst thing I could've done.

To calm down, I think about the tattoo on my back, beginning a mural to reflect my yearning for things to clamp their chompers into my flesh.

All of my best friends will be there.

Every creature I can remember biting me.

I have little interest in the meeting between Theodore Dower and him, or he, who cannot keep his hands off of me tonight. If his hand slides any further up my skirt, he'll be strumming my clit.

I smile and laugh, acting the lead female role through hors d'oeuvres and drinks, but when old Teddy—*and he acts ancient*—gets up to use the little boy's room (his words, not mine), Jynx tosses a sexy glance in my direction.

"Enjoying yourself, Ms. Maines?"

I lean into his arm and whisper, "I'm thinking about how good your big...*hard*...cock will feel in my wet...*pussy*."

"Jesus Christ," he groans, licking his lips. "Is that so?"

"Yes," I reply, reaching down between his thighs and giving him a dose of his own medicine. "Mr. Monroe, I do believe you're going up!"

Shaking his head, he snickers, "You could say that."

"I want you to bite me," I ask, snapping my teeth on my lip. "Hard."

"And what location did you have in mind?"

"Everywhere," I taunt as Teddy returns. I offer a smile.

"You're quite the lovely girl, Echo," he says as Jynx tightens his grip on my thigh. "What do you do?"

"I've recently taken a position with Peacock as the head of the human relations department," I reply, giving myself an upgrade as Jynx imparts a stern glare. "I'm also doing performance coaching."

"Masters?"

"Yes, Sir, in psychology," I answer as Jynx's fingers tap against my bare inner thigh. "I'll be working from home in the fall as I plan to return to college for my doctorate."

"Psych again?"

"Probably," I say, tilting my head. "Unless I decide to go another route and work toward my MBA. I believe in Jynx and his ability to lead Peacock Consulting into the future."

"You should consider putting a ring on this one's finger, J."

"I am, Sir." My eyes beam with a shocked gaze because he just admitted his intentions in front of this old geezer, but he won't with me. "Echo is everything I ever wanted in a life partner."

Life partner?

What the fuck is that?

I want to be your damn wife, your bitch in heat, your slut on my knees, your whore that you can call upon any time—*day or night*—for a deposit of the content contained in the sack I'm gripping.

I've been reduced to—*life partner*.

"It will be good to see children from one of the Monroe brothers."

Jynx strokes his chin. "My brother will never have children."

"You and Axel should come to work for me."

His fingers gouge into my thigh as I stutter, "... In Phoenix?"

"Well, we're based all over the West Coast, but our consulting division is new, and I'd like the Monroe brothers at the helm. I'm willing to buy out whatever you've started building with Peacock. I promise to hire all of the employees, including your *girl*. And I'll put it all in writing. I'll give you more than fair market value."

I understand generational deficits, but this fucker just called me a tramp at the table. At the very least, he thinks I'm not worthy of being a freethinking woman in the twenty-first century. His antiquarian views send a searing rage through me. My blood is boiling, and my temperature bubbles over.

"Excuse me." I rush through the dining room, out into the reception area, where a bar is. I stride up the counter and pant, "I need a double whiskey, please."

I pay for the drink and walk out onto the balcony where I find an empty seat in a secluded spot. I need some fresh air. Taking a sip, I notice Jynx by the elevators and he spots me. But he doesn't hurry, taking his own sweet ass time. He sits across from me and lights a smoke.

"What's wrong?"

"He wants you to sell something you're just starting."

After gazing out into the night sky for a long beat, he focuses on me. "I never truly considered the idea of running my own business. This happened by accident, but it's not too late to shift gears and detour the direction. I think Dower's offer is worth listening to. He wants to meet with the full board of directors and me next weekend."

I repeatedly nod. "So that's it? We spend a month busting our asses, and you get the first offer and decide to pull out?"

"It's not like that," he sighs, agitated. "I did what I did because I knew I could save all of those former employees a headache and heartache if I created Peacock. It wasn't about me running a business. It was about taking care of people because that is what it's always about for me."

"Jynx Monroe with the black heart made of fucking gold," I sass, trying not to cry. "He called me your *girl*."

"He's fucking seventy-eight years old, Abby."

"Don't even," I warn.

"You won't be my girl."

"I won't?" I toss back the whiskey and stand up. "That's probably for the best!"

"Sit down."

Fuming, I give him the evil eye and purse my lips tight. "No!"

He jets up from the chair. "Sit your fucking ass down right now, or I swear I will take you over my lap, lift up your thousand dollar dress, and put on a show you will not soon forget."

I do it—*mostly cause the dress is fabulous.*

And the sexy shoes with their high ankle straps aren't too bad either.

"Now what?"

"I don't know," he says, exhaling a cloud of nicotine above my head. "I will need to consult with my head of HR, who is currently soaking in her own juices."

"May I get you another?" A waitress asks, passing by.

"Two, please," Jynx adds as I watch her walk off. "Talk to me."

"You need to get back to Teddy and his misogynistic ways."

"Abigail Renata…"

"Oh, great," I say, slumping in the chair. "We're losing ground, J."

"No, we're not. You're being unreasonable. What would you have me do?" His fingers tuck under his chin. His calm approach to battle gets under my skin just like the rest of his character's flaws, which aren't flaws at all. Jynx is flawless in my eyes. "I don't want to become my father."

"So don't," I whisper as the waitress sets down our drinks. "Do it better."

He hands her a few bills, and she leaves. "You're not listening to me. I don't want to do it at all. I did it for the employees. Those people have families, and those jobs put food on the table."

"Your heart is huge," I respond, picking up my drink. "And you deserve better than Theodore Dower. But you're the big man; you do whatever you want. We can kiss Houston goodbye."

"... We?"

"I wasn't going to go back to California, Jynx."

He moves to sit on the edge of the table. "What do you mean you weren't going back to California? What about school?"

"What about us?" I question, and he curls his lips, striving to find an answer. "You never planned on me staying past September."

"I never thought you would."

I smile and reach for his hand. "I gave myself a promotion, Boss."

"Better watch it. I'm going to give you a promotion."

"I won't be your life partner," I inform, staring into his eyes. "I'll be your wife or your bitch, but life partner is out."

"So is Old Lady," he reminds with a chuckle. "Anything else you need to stipulate, Miss?"

"Don't go there right now, Jynx." The combination of alcohol and the intensity of his gaze sends a chill through me. "You should go back inside."

He rises and extends his hand. "Come with me?"

"As your life partner?"

"No," he counters, without reaction. "As the slut that's going to suck my cock on the way to the club."

My eyes flare-up to his in a panic. "... What club?"

"His son, Edward, just arrived, and Theo wants to hit a bar," he replies. "And you're going with me."

"AM I STAINED?" I ASK AS WE LEAVE THE CAR WITH THE valet at the upscale strip club. The rain is pouring down in buckets.

"No," he says, grinning. "Nothing like doing seventy and ejaculating."

The bright lights flash, and the music thumps when I notice the line to get inside holds very few women. "What am I thinking?"

"You're trusting me." His fingers lace into mine when we walk through the door. "We're having two drinks and leaving."

Standing on my tiptoes, I crane my neck to peer inside the noisy club. "What if I want to dance?"

"On a bar? No. With me? Sure."

We follow the hostess to our private booth with a grand view. Someone paid a pretty penny for this on a Saturday night. Shots are flowing when we sit down. "Eddie, this is..."

"The girl from my wedding!"

"Yes," I laugh as Jynx smirks. "I worked at The Vinery."

Technically, I still do.

I abandoned my life because I was abducted by a crazy man who happens to be incredibly suave and sophisticated. He also owns a magnificently large cock that I want to tame or maybe I want his untamed dick to claim me, either way.

"Are you ready to come work with me, Echo?"

"I'm considering all of the *possibilities*."

Jynx blinks, hiccuping like the idea of thinking about our options is unrealistic. "I'll be honest. We have several offers on the table."

"I figured you would," Teddy adds, mesmerized by the girls. "But no other option can give you the security of an upstanding company like Dower."

Ed continues, "You don't want the trouble of getting involved with Deacon Cruz."

"He is my cousin." The anger perks in Jynx's voice. "We stand to do quite well."

My fingers dig into his leg, attempting to dissuade a bar brawl from breaking out as I stare longingly at the almost empty dance floor. I have no clue why there is a dance floor in this strip club, but a darling silver-haired couple is putting on a show. "Let's go!"

I hop up, and he quickly follows me. In his arms, we sway to the sensuous beat. "What is he talking about?"

"Cruz offered to partner with Peacock with the hope that we could build the business to compete with Dower."

My expression contorts. "This is a no brainer. Why aren't you doing it?"

"Because Cruz's money is dirtier than one of these girl's snatches," he informs, twirling me around. "And it means I will be getting in deeper with the club because it's all connected. I didn't figure you would support the idea if you knew I was growing Peacock with mob money."

"... Mob?" I whisper very low as my lip quivers. "Like bang bang?"

"Yes," he laughs, rolling his hips into me. "Like bang...*bang.*"

Oh, God, he's making light of this by seducing me.

The only other couple smiles, and we switch partners for a good minute. I don't mind. The older man is a grand dancer, spinning and dipping me. I'm far more concerned with the sixty-some diva batting her lashes at my man. Surprisingly, I'm getting very turned on by their innocent flirtations.

Reality hits like a landslide—

Jynx Monroe could be my man.

We politely part ways, returning to our respective mates. "I need out of here," I say with tears in my eyes as girls roll on stage and shake everything the good Lord gave them. Teddy and Ed are getting lap dances when I implore, "Please, Jeremiah."

Call your safeword.

"Come on." With determination, he grips onto my hand, and we escape out a side exit to the torrential storm. His jacket comes off, and he yells, "I'll go get the car. You stay here under the awning."

"Jynx!" I shout over the driving rain and thunder. I latch onto his shirt and passionately kiss his lips. His mouth beckons, wanting me just as much as I want him until we briefly separate and our eyes lock with nothing but love.

He glances around the empty backlot and picks me up, pushing my body against the side of the building. His mouth is insatiable, and I fall into the dreamy concoction that is our addiction.

Fuck the dress.

Fuck the shoes.

Fuck the Doctorate.

"Goddammit, I need you," he roars, bearing down on me. "You weren't supposed to happen, Ek. I had my life, and it was good."

"How good was it, though?"

"Not good enough!"

Propped between his frame and the building, I feel his fingers delve between my thighs. "I'm not wearing any panties."

"Fuck, you're a naughty whore."

"Do it, Jynx! Do it! Make me yours!"

He shakes his head. "I'm fucking hard as stone, but there is no way I'm letting you lose your virginity against the wall of a strip club."

"I don't care anymore," I compellingly argue. "I just want you. I want to lose it with you."

"You kids need to move along," a wrinkled man in a security guard uniform warns from his golf cart. "The place for live performance is about seven hundred miles north."

"Apologies, Sir!" Jynx respectfully relays.

"It's alright," he cackles nodding. "If my wife ever looked that good, I would've done the same thing at your age. Have a nice night!" He waves.

We laugh, holding hands and running in the rain to the valet. Jynx hands our ticket over, and I beg, "Stop thinking about the gap."

"It's easy to forget when two elders blessed us."

"Ignore the fifteen years you've been dwelling on and let go, Jynx."

He lights a smoke. "And what happens when I break your heart?"

"That just makes you a sadist with roses."

He imparts a smug grin. "And does my masochist like thorns?"

"I like things that bite."

26

LOCKED UP

JYNX

BY MID-WEEK, WE'RE STILL AT ODDS OVER PEACOCK AND speaking very little. Echo has an endless well of energy and believes in our ability to grow the business with my cousin's help. The problem with that is—I still don't know if I want to run the damn thing. It won't be her ass they're calling at three in the morning but mine.

And life as the boss is not one I ever envisioned.

Not because I can't do it, but because I don't want to do it. I understand people readily follow my lead, but that comes with a lot of responsibilities I detest. If I'm getting calls in the middle of the night, it's a technical problem, not a personal one. And that is the difference between her and me.

I don't do humans.

Or unsolvable issues.

In incremental doses, I can deal with those who speak the same geek jargon I do. Anything else is too fucking much. I don't want to hear about how clients complain that some idiot made a crass comment that got misconstrued as sexual harassment *blah—blah— blah*...I do not care. I have far more important things to figure out, and I do not want my business—*Peacock*—hinging on others. I'd rather go solo.

I'm an asshole.

And self-knowledge is important.

Despite Echo's opinion, Axel wants to entertain Theodore's offer, and I tend to agree with him, so I'm leaving early Friday morning for Phoenix. To say she is pissed might be the understatement of the year, but she's full steam ahead on hooking up with the underworld to do whatever we need.

It makes zero sense.

I spent two-thirds of my life crooked. And the other third trying to straighten the nefarious shit out. I've worked my ass off to get where I am, and I can't see shipping it down the river for the sake of the bottom dollar. We could make a fuckton of money running the machines with Deacon's illegal crusade coins. But if we get caught, my ass will be back in the slammer again.

Facts.

Been there. Done that.

Not doing that again.

It all comes down to—*how much do I trust the dynamic duo of Deacon Cruz and Sal Raniero?*

Because of our ongoing war, she's refusing to sleep with me. Even after the chemistry exploding during our romp in the rain, we returned home to a goodnight kiss at her bedroom door.

What the fuck was that shit?

I'm not even sure anymore, but I need to get off.

Preferably in her.

We're doing the evening chores—putting the horses in the stables and feeding the peacocks when she softly says, "Why do you not want to run the business?"

I stare at her in the ripped jeans and loose camisole with no bra. Her nipples peak against the fabric, and I throb. Running my hand through my hair, I sigh, "I don't want to end up in a cage."

She deadpans, "But you're an animal."

"Yeah, but..."

"He's your family," she implores, stepping closer and holding the green feed bucket. "You're running out of options."

"It's not that." I take the bucket and dump it into the shoot feeder in the stall. "You don't know how bad I was."

"What is that supposed to mean?"

"From the time Grandma bought my first computer until I went in behind bars, I was causing all kinds of chaos. And it started slow until I was running one of the backbones of identity theft and credit card scams. I was good at hiding in the maze, but doing that is very similar to kink."

Which I am failing miserably at avoiding in her presence.

I'm no longer in recovery or remission; I'm a full blown junkie.

"It's addictive," she mutters, setting down the bucket and walking to the gate where the four beautiful horses wait. "And one craving leads to the next."

"The whole thing becomes a game to see what I can get away with. I embezzled millions for—*real evil*—the kind of people you don't want to meet in a dark alleyway or on your screen."

"That's why you intercepted me."

"Part of the reason," I admit, unlatching the hook and swinging open the gate. The horses run inside. "I know the shit that's out there because I was heavily involved in that scene. Where you went on the Gray Market is the edge of a cesspool. I lived deep in those waters, and if I hadn't been arrested for stalking, I'd probably still be doing it. You should be proud I turned my life around."

"I'm not," she critically chastises. Her words hit like boulders, smacking into my flesh and knocking the wind out of my lungs. "You aren't happy."

"9 to 5 is where I am at. Happiness doesn't play into it," I reply, locking up as we leave the barn. "I'm sorry if you don't understand."

"You're smarter than working as someone else's peon."

"That may be true, but I go to work, get a real check every two weeks, and have health insurance."

"And you're miserable."

I spin back to her and yell, "Because I'm not helping my cousin figure out the best way to exchange dirty money into crypto currency?"

"Yes!" she argues.

I set my jaw, knowing she's right. "But you don't know what happens in the corral of prison."

"Did they push you down and rape your ass, Jynx?" She yips out. "Or did your cookies get stolen in the night?"

"You're a bitch sometimes."

"Thanks!" She flips me off but keeps pace with me—which considering our difference in height and stride, is almost an amazing feat. The eighth world wonder is a pint-sized, mouthy, wise-cracking girl that I long to bend over and fuck hard. "Does Axel hack too?"

"He's not as good as me," I reply as we trod to the peacock coop. "He always followed my lead."

"And he will now."

"Yeah, but I'm not traveling into that sludge. I'm not getting blood on my hands anymore. I traded that for mud on my boots."

"How did you buy the beach house, Jynx?"

"We're not discussing my finances or investments."

She fills the water containers and mutters, "Then we're not discussing our sleeping arrangements either."

I watch as she walks off.

And if I'm not careful, she'll walk out of my life too.

I EAT DINNER ALONE.

Her plate sits untouched as she claimed to be tired.

Lies. Excuses. Fake bullshit.

She doesn't want to fight anymore, and I can't say as though I blame her. I'm exhausted by her pestering efforts and in desperate need of a vacation. Somewhere cold where I can plop my blue balls in the fucking snow.

I clean up the kitchen, take a shower, turn on the flatscreen, and scroll through my email. Release is one click away with a random girl, which is bad considering the only girl I want is two floors down.

"Fuck this shit," I mumble, tossing the laptop on the bed and storming downstairs. I notice her plate, silverware, and napkin are all missing.

Thank God she's eating.

I don't bother to knock.

Her eyes widen as she takes a spoonful of the mashed potatoes. "You need to eat the meat."

"Cut it up."

I arch my brow high. "Try that again."

"Cut my meat up, asshole."

"Why are you so damned angry with me?" I question, sitting on the end of the bed. "Let's just get this out in the open."

"Your cousin is a good guy."

"My cousin is the right hand man of a mafia boss," I inform as she frowns. "The guy you were sharing your beloved flakes with…"

She quips, "He's a nice guy too."

"I'm not doing this," I reply, grabbing her plate and cutting up her chicken. "You're spoiled."

She shrugs. "… Who's fault is that?"

I shake my head. "So does this all come down to your first impressions of people?"

"Pretty much," she counters, chewing. "Teddy and Eddie are douchebags. They're going to make bank off of your skills."

"Do you like Axel?"

"I have no opinion of him." Strangely, I feel about the same. "But I know when the shit hit the fan, I watched those two run to your aid. That is something Dower will never give you. So what if it's risky? Walking down the street is risky. Deacon's not asking you to run their shit. He's offering to give you a loan to run your legitimate business. Big difference there, buddy."

She doesn't know how deep the blood flows.

I toss down her fork, and it clatters against the plate. "Because I already am. I built their whole infrastructure about four years ago and now I maintain it. That is how I bought the beach house and that is why they came. I helped them out of a bind; they reciprocated. It doesn't mean I want to partner up with them at Peacock. That's an entirely different issue, *buddy*."

"You have people wanting to be good to you," she whispers, picking up her fork and sticking it in a bite of the chicken. "And you'd rather go to work for the asshat."

"I don't want to go to jail again, Abby!"

"Why?"

"Thirty days turned into eight months!"

"Why?"

"Because I liked to fight—*a lot*. You may have picked up on the fact that I have a temper," I roar, swooping the plate onto the floor as she hurries back to the headboard. I pull her arm, diving on top of her frail body and holding her down with my weight. We're nose to nose as I run the dull edge of the razor-sharp steak knife over her cheek. "I'm a bad guy. I'm the villain in this tale. And you don't want to meet him."

"You keep saying that, but you can only restrain yourself for so long. Eventually, he will escape from the cage," she charges, closing her eyes as the tears fall from the pinch. "I'm sorry, I don't buy into your reform."

"I'm not the guy I was a decade ago."

"Because you believe you caused Celeste's death."

"No, because I haven't beaten anyone to a bloody pulp in ages."

"You're going to be an outlaw sooner or later. And you know it. I know it. You don't want me to see that though, but I do. Don't forget who my father is. I know the hot look in your eyes when you can rig the system in your favor. You enjoy corruption."

"It's a hankering I don't want anymore."

"You're praying that the summer ends before that lawbreaker reemerges, but what you don't seem to recognize is regardless of who you are, Jynx—I will love you forever. You want to be an upstanding guy at Dower or a hacker in the underground, I don't care. But stop holding back who you are for the sake of me."

"You don't know who you're messing with."

"I know you're on the verge of a relapse," she points out. "You want to give in to the shadows. Your coding and kink aren't just similar; they run parallel; they're best fucking friends. One addiction craves the other."

Lifting, I hover over her and slice the blade through the silk camisole and push the cold edge of steel against her heart. "Say it."

"What do you want to hear, Mr. Monroe? Fuck me," she sensually whispers. "Fuck me like the bad boy you truly are. Stop faking it and putting on airs that I burn right through and bring me—*your real,* baby."

"Slide your hand in your panties."

She bumps her knuckles against the erection trapped behind the fabric of my lounge pants. "I'm wet...so wet it hurts, J. Make it stop, please."

"I didn't say finger fuck yourself."

"Sorry," she says, sighing. I take the flat edge and smear it around one nipple before sucking the bud into my mouth. She writhes beneath me—bucking up and moaning, "There's something so mysteriously dangerous about you."

"Touch your clit." Raising on my knees, I trail the blade over her neck and down to the other nipple. The silver shines like a mirror in the light as her fingers strum faster against her arousal. "Don't stop now." I dip down, darting my tongue over the bud before flipping the blade in mid-air above her belly. She squeals beneath me. Her eyes widen with grave concern. With a side-eyed glance, I wink and smirk. "Be a good girl for me."

"Yes, Sir..." she breathes, rubbing faster. "I will be good."

I drop the front of my pants and graze the head of my dick against her nipple. "Stroke my cock like my dirty slut." Her slender fingers grip around the shaft as she jerks me off. With the blade in my hand, I shove the wooden handle inside of her wetness. "That's it, baby. Take it all."

"Jynx...I'm going to come soon."

I spit onto her hand, and she lubes up my dick. "Harder! Faster! Don't you fucking come without me. I want to cream all over your tits."

My hips buck in tandem with the thrusts of my arm. "I can't hold on..."

"You will," I demand, pulling out and tossing the knife onto the floor. I inch up. "Suck my fucking cock, now!"

Her lips eagerly open to receive me, and I pound two fingers into her opening. Her pussy slurps around my hand, pooling up to my wrist. Giving her everything, she rides my hand hard, and I feel her pubic bone.

We've all got skeletons waiting to become weapons, stashed in closets for the future generations—the infantry sieging four chambered vessels in a surprising stick up.

Her echoes threaten my ticker.

But I can't get enough of what she does to my pulse.

Her voracious mouth suckles, but the slippery wetness of her cunt is too much as I skirt closer to the edge. I yank out, and her hand promptly returns to pumping me.

"Don't stop! God! Don't stop!"

"Such a good bitch! Dance with me!"

"I need to..."

"Do it, sweet thing!" I howl, squirting my jiz all over her tits as her pussy puckers, baptizes my hand. "Yes! You're so fucking fantastic!"

Tears cascade over her cheeks as her hands clamp around my forearm, bringing it for a closer inspection. She blinks in astonishment at my unblemished flesh. "… You're not bloody?"

"I've only got your cum on me, baby." Beaming with an impish grin, I growl, "I'm really good at what I do, Darlin'."

27

A MOMENT ASUNDER

Echo

Jynx finally asked if I wanted to go to Arizona with him. I was reluctant at first, but his charming manner and contagious smile sealed my fate—in more ways than one, many weeks ago.

We're flying first class to Phoenix. I've never been one of these people, sipping on mimosas and making small talk while everyone else boards the plane. My fairytale unfolds with my prince sitting right beside me. I try not to pay attention to the discreet glances.

There is clearly an age difference between Jynx and me.

And if I weren't holding a champagne flute and cuddled up next to his shoulder, I'm certain the assumption would be that I'm his daughter. I lean over and kiss his cheek as one older woman's eyes bug out. When she passes by, I announce, "I love you, Daddy."

He turns toward me, trying not to laugh, as his lips curl. Laying his hand on my cheek, he kisses my lips with a quick swipe of his tongue. "I love you too, babygirl." He winks.

I spend most of the flight reading several books on cooking. They're filled with memoirs, techniques, and recipes. At one point, Jynx peers over my shoulder and mentions, "If you want to learn how to cook, I can teach you."

Teach me everything.

Please, Sir.

Don't let go.

I need many lessons.

We land and exit the plane. Jynx is the perfect gentleman, waiting for me and assuring my safety with a light touch to my back. As he retrieves our luggage from the baggage carousel, I wait by the windows, and the woman with the bulging eyes approaches.

"Hello," she nervously says, digging in her purse and handing me her business card. "I saw you with the man in first class."

"Yes, Ma'am?"

Her eyes fill with tears. "I want to tell you how beautiful you are."

I expect the—*I should find someone my age*—remark. My eyelashes flutter, stunned. "Thank you!"

"Years ago, before you were even born, I became involved with a man, twenty years my senior."

Her smile broadens across her cheeks as my mouth drops open. "… Really?"

"Yes!" she exclaims, gripping onto my arm. "I'm sorry to say I lost him last year, but I want you to know, no matter what anyone says, the only thing that matters is what's in your heart."

"How old were you when you met him?"

"It was 1975 when I met Freddy on the train. I was twenty. He was forty. We were married less than six months after meeting and had four beautiful boys, which is why I'm in Phoenix, to visit my youngest son."

Her stare was her love reflecting in ours.

Her scowls weren't hate-filled, but full of pain from her loss.

I need to stop assuming everyone is out to get us. Not everyone is like our immediate families. There are people, like his cousin and Selia, who will support our romance.

"Thank you so much," I reply with an embrace as Jynx's brow curiously furrows. He shrugs, smirks, and mouths—*what are you doing?* "I really needed to hear that."

"Have fun with him," she boasts, grinning. "He's a hell of a catch!"

She wobbles off as I mosey up to Jynx grinning. "We should get married."

He blinks several times and chuckles, "You think?"

"You'd have to stick your dick in me then."

"I wouldn't have to," he replies, carrying our bags as we walk to the exit. I nudge his side. "But I probably would...three or four times a day."

"Are you a twenty-year-old boy?"

"... With you?" He mischievously grins. "I'm better than a twenty-year-old boy. I bring the rain."

"That you do, Jynx. That you do."

I SPEND FRIDAY NIGHT ALONE.

I didn't want to be privy to Jynx selling what I saw as our future away. I had no right to feel the way I did, but it didn't change things. I ordered a pizza from room service, took a long bubble bath, and watched cooking shows. I considered texting him to see how things were going, but I decided to leave him be.

I curl up in bed with a good book and know this will be the first night we've slept together in weeks. The truth is, distancing myself from him has been the hardest thing I've ever had to do. I'm in love and want to spend every minute with him.

He returns to the room after midnight. He doesn't say a word. Not even a hello. Shutting the bathroom door, he appears a half-hour later with a towel wrapped around his waist. Water droplets splash against his chiseled chest as he clicks off the light on the nightstand.

I'm reading, but I don't complain because heaven knows we'll meltdown.

"Take off your clothes."

I set my reader on the nightstand and do as he requests. Staying under the covers, I fling my shirt and panties to the floor with a deep breath as my heart races in my chest. "Are you okay?" He doesn't answer, ripping the sheet and blankets from the bed. Literally, he balls all of the linens and slam-dunks them into a chair across the room. "Score!"

"Precisely." Pulling the towel from his waist, he tosses it down. "Spread your legs."

"Jynx..." I mutter, scared as hell.

"What are you doing?"

He crawls onto the bed between my thighs and spits in his palm. "Taking your virginity."

"... Right now?"

Stroking his dick, he says, "Yes."

"In a Phoenix hotel room?"

"You were a very naughty girl, Echo," he reprimands, pumping his fist around his cock. "You talk to strangers, run off all willy-nilly, and give yourself promotions without the boss' approval. How do you intend to rectify this situation?"

"My boss is checking out."

"No," he mutters, gently lowering on top of me. "Your boss is checking in."

Our lips narrow, exchanging warm breaths and daring fate for more. We're on the cusp, a tranquil abyss, where soaring together seems like an elusive dream. He begs for my trust, promising that he will not let me fall. Hot kisses send waves of fiery carnal lust through my skin. His determined mating ritual shifts from playboy to primal. We aren't engaging in courting games. This is real.

He is a man.

And he wants to claim me as his woman.

I finally break away and ask, "What are you doing?"

"Fucking you."

"What happened?" I breathlessly whisper.

"I signed the deal to transfer the employees to Dower and agreed to help with the initial training and integration. I will be in Phoenix for six weeks," he mumbles, nuzzling my neck. "And I called Deacon and told him to hold Houston because Peacock Consulting, my solo endeavor, will be moving in by October."

Every inch of my body turns numb in the clandestine meeting. "... You let go and kept yourself?"

"I let the parts I didn't truly want, go," he informs as his taut body rolls against mine. "I never wanted thousands of employees under my umbrella and looking to me for guidance, but what my father did was wrong."

"You didn't want them treated bad."

"Right," he confirms, suckling my breast. My body melts to his, betraying my mind, making me delirious with want. "And I could use a coach," he teases, rubbing my nipples. "That is, if you're willing to accept my job offer. All you have to do is sign your name on my dick."

I tease, "This is harassment, Jynx."

"Oh, I'm well aware," he replies, rubbing the head of his cock along my slit. "Coercion. Bribery. Extortion of bodily fluids."

"You're really moving to Houston?"

"Yes," he maintains, slicking on the seam. "And you're coming with me."

Holy crap.

This is happening.

"You're not going to fuck me."

Resting his tongue on his lip, he quickly arches his brow. "How do you know that?"

"Because it would be the end."

"You think the ending is determined by our making love?" he questions with a hint of machismo. His intimidating confidence overwhelms me. I stare into his eyes, drenched with blue, as his soul soaks into mine. "You're still not believing anything that happens after the blow. Who is the hit it and quit it here?"

"I don't deserve any of this, Jynx," I implore, crying and digging my nails into his guns. "Everything about you is surreal. You're a fantasy, a dream, a thing of make believe. This isn't romance. I put up an ad. You stalked and lured me into your world to try and save me."

His fingers caress the side of my cheek. "You're so fucking beautiful, Echo."

"After all of this time, you missed one thing—I won't ever heal."

His mouth hits mine with an unexpected ferocity as his tongue commands my attention. I cannot escape his draw, yet I know I should pack my things and run out the door. I should leave and never look back because nothing but heartache waits at the end of this journey.

His fingers hold mine as he slowly lifts my arms and places a stronghold on my wrists with one of his hands. He skirts the other one low, between our bodies, guiding his cock toward my opening.

"You seem to have forgotten one key critical point on your timeline, Abigail. I fell in love with you."

His aggressive thrust impales his cock into my hollow puddle with the force of a cannon firing. I scream from the searing pain radiating through my body. "Jynx!"

"Yes?" He smugly grins.

"Don't move!"

A proud glaze shields over his eyes, guarding his spirit from anything I could throw at him. I am helpless—captured by his body and tortured by his heart. And as much as I don't want to be, I've become his willing victim, begging for more of his provocative, endless Dominance.

He smirks, gloating in his success. "I don't plan on it, Sweet Pea."

Tears band on my lashes as I finally understand the difference between what I can do with fake plastic in my hand versus a real man —he has a mind of his own, moves when he wants, and reacts to the shallow subtle changes in my exploits.

"I cannot believe you're doing this," I mumble.

"I warned you that I was going to; it isn't my fault you didn't believe me."

"But you're inside of me..." I moan, startled by the painful intrusion. "Why now?"

"Because I need you, Echo."

My pussy stretches to accommodate the grand length and profound girth of his cock as he slowly moves with short strokes. "Shit..."

"Yeah," he acknowledges, grazing his lips and tongue from my neck to my collar bone. "We could be so good, Ek."

"I never wanted to fall in love," I cry out as he relentlessly pushes the boundary with deep throbbing strides. "You're stealing what was never yours to take."

"This isn't rape."

"No, you son of a bitch, this is an assault of my heart!" I wrestle beneath his weight, no longer fearing what is below the belt but what lies within his chest cavity. "Fuck you! Fuck you for turning this into something it was never supposed to be!"

"We're doing this."

"You can stick your dick in me and profess all the love in the world, it doesn't mean I will stay."

He scoops my body into his arms and lifts as I sit up with my legs straddling around him. His penetration swells into the chasm of my gut, and my eyes roll. He laughs. "You may not embrace the love, but you're damn sure getting my dick. Stop worrying about the future and feel me in the present."

There is no choice.

Jynx Monroe is a well-endowed asshole who knows how to wield his tool and manipulate the game in his favor. I will never be victorious in his presence. I will never vanish from the ghosts of the past as they haunt every minute of my life.

There is no beauty in the future, only ghastly reminders of my unforgivable prior mistakes. I have fleeting moments where I believe happiness exists for me, but those delusions fade like shadows in the sun.

I will never be whole.

He broke me long before Jynx.
And it's only a matter of time before I take flight.

JYNX

"STOP THINKING."

"I can't," she whines in my arms as I thrust from below. "This isn't leading anywhere."

"Do you trust me?"

"Yes, but..."

"Do you trust me?"

"Don't yell at me!" she shouts as heartbreak floods every nerve ending.

"There are no buts here, Echo," I mutter, holding her close without moving. "You either trust me or you don't."

"I want to, Jynx."

"Take it," I encourage with a stern stare. "Use my body like you do your toys when you're watching those videos. Don't think. Fuck me like a machine."

"I can't do this!"

"Goddammit! Yes, you can! Claim what is rightfully yours!"

"You aren't mine!" she argues, struggling to flee as I tighten my grasp. "You never were!"

"Yes, I am!" I furrow my brow. "You aren't getting away. We are fucking. You are fucking me."

"You don't understand!" she screams, pounding on my chest. "Colton killed himself because of me." She hysterically sobs in my arms. "I went to a graduation party that I never should've been at. I had too much to drink and he walked in as his friends and I were about to..."

"Abby...*what?*"

"We were about to have sex."

"You and…"

"Me and five other guys." Her words punch with unexpected jabs. "Colton stopped them, but not before he accused me of causing all of it."

I don't know what to say as my eyes peer down. In an almost out of body experience, I see our entanglement, woven—*stitched*—together, but fraying from everywhere. Saving this night means nothing because this was never about sex. Her heart is hemorrhaging from a night that went bad.

"Did you…"

"I chased that boy for four fucking years, but he never showed any interest. That's why I had never been kissed until you came along. That's why I never did anything. I made one move and it ended with a fucking funeral and hundreds of grieving kids and parents. I caused Colton's death! Me! Because I pushed too far!"

Slowly, I tilt upward and stare at her reddened cheeks and hazel eyes. "Did you do it? Was he right? Did you lure the boys, taunt them to the point that there was no other choice? Were you going to have a gang bang like the violent shit you get off online to?"

She weeps, "Fuck you!"

"Admit it! Stop hiding like it isn't something you crave! Stop pretending a dirty little girl doesn't exist in you!" I yell as she attempts to push me away with her forearms. "I see the way you look at me! I hear the way you call me *Daddy*!"

"Please don't do this!"

I stand firm—*a force to be reckoned with*—knowing if the scab is never picked from the wound, it will only continue to manifest, infecting her heart. She needs to bleed. And God help me, I will be man enough to take the hate she brings in her sorrow. "Tell me the fucking truth!"

"Why should I, when you've already passed judgement on me?"

"Say it!"

"Yes!" she howls, admitting her part in the foray. "I got drunk, flirted, and made sure I had all of his best friends in the room to have their way with me so he could see what he was losing out on. I wanted

270 | KAILEE REESE SAMUELS

to make him jealous! So he would know and feel guilty! I wanted him to save me!"

"Just like you wanted your rapist to do," I rebuke, shaking my head. "But the next day..."

"He killed himself!"

My jaw pops as I brush my fingers over her arm. "You played a bad fucking card in puppy love. The only question that needs answering is which one will you play now in real love? Are you brave enough to heal? Or are we too far gone?"

"He never showed any romantic interest," she wails, holding onto my arms. "I thought it was unrequited. I thought we would never be anything more than friends. I didn't know he was saving it all for me until after college. His parents found the notebooks and his sister told me about them. She blamed me! His parents blamed me! Everyone at school blamed me!"

"You didn't kill Colton," I firmly contend, slightly disoriented by her previous actions. Her demons chase me with a vengeance—she manipulated my kind to win another, but it's in the past, I repeatedly say to myself. I bargain. I make deals with the devil. I pray. And I hold on until the bitter end as I struggle, fighting for her and all that I believe we have in this love together. "Colton killed Colton. Not you. You did not kill that boy!"

"My deceptive plot to get his attention forced his hand," she mumbles, curling into my chest. With my hands secured to her back, I feel her ragged breaths and drumming heartbeat. Exhaustion takes a heavy toll, leaving me weary from her war that I never should've been involved with—I was a soldier, volunteering to do battle for a girl with a pledge to defy consent. "I wanted to be attacked to take the punishment I deserved."

I shake my head and scowl with hurt. "And you couldn't have told me this weeks ago?"

"You would've ended up hating me."

"That's where you're wrong," I whisper as my eyes fill with tears. "I was never going to leave you—*ever*. You want to believe I am only here for this, but that's not who I am. And I don't think for one second that you're the girl online."

"But I am," she cries with an agony that I don't know how to repair. There is too much blood; she's bleeding out. And every time I put pressure on one flesh wound, another one gushes. "I did it. All of it."

"You were young and naive," I stupidly excuse as the pulse flat-lines. Laying my hand on her shoulder, I lie, "It's okay, Echo."

My heart ticks, rattling with self-condemnation—*I was old enough to know better than to get involved with someone fifteen years my junior*—as I set her aside and my cock falls out. And I fall from grace, the same delinquent I always was—*disobedient and offensive.*

"What are you doing?"

"Taking a timeout," I mutter, scratching my head. "You aren't ready for any of this. You aren't ready to forgive yourself. You aren't ready for love. You aren't ready for me."

Our brief but illicit affair scars my soul at the time of death.

Her love was infectious, and I'm contaminated.

And once again, I become a phantom hiding in the pitch black of the night waiting on the unsuspecting.

28

THERE IS NO WAY

Echo

In the chair, I read the ad, which led to all of this. The words brought out a monster of a man trying to protect me with his gentleman.

And that was what Jynx was.

He didn't portray the real version of himself with me, but acted the role of a knight in shining armor to prevent from hurting me.

Why did he do it? I'll never know.

He stripped off the shield of his dickhead costume, showing a side that I imagined few had ever seen.

Raw. Bare. Free.

I blink at the man face down on the bed with his head buried in a pillow, inked and scarred and broken beyond comprehension.

With heavy tears in my eyes, I pack my things. I will never flee his kingdom. His reign. His rule. And I must make a run for it while I can —before we become something neither of us ever intended to be.

He isn't a gentleman.

And I am not a submissive.

I slip out the door with my adrenaline pumping. I cannot stop crying as I hail a cab and leave the hotel and Jynx Monroe behind. I cannot rent a car, but if I book a flight, he will wind up at the airport before I take off. And I will end up right back where it all began—*at his feet, pleading for more.*

The cab drops me off at the bus terminal, and I book the next one leaving for LA. I'm on the highway in a crowded vehicle with kids crying and people talking entirely too loud in less than an hour after leaving him. I cannot feel anything.

I got out.

I left my captor.

I turn off my shared location and block his number on my phone. Putting my headphones in my ears, I lay my head against the window and uncontrollably sob. An older woman with missing teeth and blue hair sits beside me. She offers to hold my hand.

I refuse to take it.

Don't touch me.

I hurt people.

I'm an evil, wretched soul meant to destroy everyone I encounter. I killed Colton. I cursed those boys in the room with a lifetime of guilt. I used Jynx for my manipulations, attempting to get out of the place I reside in. I used him—a would-be criminal to upend my creed. I never planned on a fearless, protective monster.

Nothing helps. Nothing heals.

There is no solution.

There is no easy answer.

So I run away.

I book a flight from LA to San Francisco and text Selia, "Can you come pick me up at the airport? I left J."

"What do you mean you left him? Why?"

I cannot talk to her about it right now, or I will end up on the floor of the bus, convulsing, unable to breathe because I'll be screaming like a siren.

I left him.

God, I cannot believe I walked out.

The blue-haired Grandma places her hand on my lap. Her wrinkled face turns to me, and I notice the crow's feet surrounding her blue eyes. They're the same color as his. I latch my fingers with hers, and I bawl my eyes out on her shoulder.

I tug out my headphones, and she asks, "Did he hurt you, child?"

"No," I reply, slobbering. "He did exactly what I wanted him to do."

"Then why are you leaving?"

"Because he deserves more than what I can ever give him."

Her fake gold and gemstone ring-laden hand presses against my dampened cheek. "Everything in its own time, sweetheart. Close your eyes. Rest your heart."

I wake up as we stop in Los Angeles.

The kindness of a stranger pulled me through the first hours of my detox from him, but the worst moments were still ahead of me. I have a two-hour wait before my flight. I roam through the airport. I rummage through stores, not buying anything.

I scan over the book section in the gift store. Romance titles etch like hieroglyphs onto the walls of my chambers as I sniffle. The cashier asks, "Are you okay?"

"Yeah, I just left my boyfriend."

I called Jynx, my boyfriend.

But what was he?

"You're young," she replies, offering a tissue. "You'll get used to them breaking your heart."

I broke my own heart long ago.

I smile and buy a bottle of water. "Thanks."

"Take it easy."

"You, too."

The activity in the airport plays out like a movie I don't want to be cast in. I haven't earned the right to be a leading lady. I certainly don't want to be an extra. I take a seat and wait as I stare at a young couple holding hands.

He always held my hand.

Monsters come in all forms.

Sometimes even tall, well-kept gentlemen with wavy brown hair and a smile to steal your breath away. I eye my phone, knowing he must be aware of my absence by now. I close my eyes as it takes every ounce of willpower I have not to unblock him.

As I hold my phone, Selia messages, "Are you okay?"

"Yes."

"I went and bought lots of alcohol, cigarettes, chocolate, and tissues."

I smile through my non-stop stream of tears. "Thank you."

"I got you."

"I know."

Thank God someone does.

Because I have to get over him.

Or maybe Deacon was right—*I have to get over myself.*

***

JYNX

***

SITTING IN THE CHAIR, I STARE AT THE BED WITHOUT ANY linens and grip the whiskey bottle in my hand. I bring the shirt she had on last night, which she threw onto the floor and forgot to pack this morning, to my nose. I inhale her scent and long to wrap my arms around her again.

"God! Fuck!" I roar, gripping tightly to the fabric. "No! Abby! No!"

My face twitches as I attempt to swallow the fact that she is gone. She cannot be gone. She must be here somewhere. I toss on some clothes and walk through the hotel. I ask the ladies at the front desk, showing them her picture. I interrogate the bellman, the cab drivers, and random guests.

Has anyone seen this girl?

She belongs to me.

I try her number again and again as I smoke outside by the empty pool. I call Selia, and she answers, saying nothing.

With a shaky voice, I demand, "Where is she?"

"Jynx...she is done," she informs with a fierce tone. "You need to let her go."

"Where is she, Selia?" I rally, begging for the return of my possession. "I need to talk to her."

"You only want to talk to her to con her into coming back."

My eyes shutter closed as I pick myself up and keep fighting through the battle. I'm damaged, wounded, and confused. "Echo Maines belongs to me. I seem to have lost her. If you find her, can you please tell her to return to me?"

"Not a fucking chance in hell, asshole."

Click.

I throw my phone, shattering the screen on the pebbled walkway surrounding the pool just as Axel walks out. He picks up the phone, handing it back to me. "... You okay, bro?"

"No," I steam, fuming. "She left."

"That would be, she escaped from the clutches of a deranged lunatic."

"I was trying to be better."

"Yeah, well," he assesses, swiping a smoke from my pack. "You cannot change what has always been."

"Do you have a purpose here other than aggravating me?"

"Yeah," he says, dropping the lighter on the glass top table. "Actually, I do. Wang is coming in from Chicago. He wants to know if he should catch a ride or if we're picking him up. He's been messaging you, but you've been non-responsive for twenty-four hours."

"I've been a little busy," I harshly remind. "Assuring he and everyone else that was involved with Monroe Consulting has future employment at Dower."

"I'm not the enemy."

"We aren't friends," I state, not caring.

"Eventually, you need to forgive me for all the shit that went down," he callously remarks. "I wasn't there when Celeste died."

I give a disdainful glance over to him. "No, but you knew what they were doing. You knew what they were doing and you didn't stop them, which makes you just as guilty as Chuck Tullen."

"I didn't rape or murder that girl," he says, stubbing out his smoke and standing up. "And I'm not the one who brainwashed a twenty-two-year-old girl and convinced her to move in with me. You played her ass and you lost."

"Fuck you."

"You don't want to hear this, but the truth is—you kidnapped Echo, making her believe she was in love, but all the while, you were toying with her emotions. You need to take a good long look in the mirror. She outplayed you and you're pissed. But you wanted the same thing you always do—*complete control*—to have your way with her—heart, mind, and body. Don't take your anger out on me. Tell me, was her tight, wet snatch worth it?"

Everything turns red—*blazing hot, bubbling with fury and pent up rage.*

"What did you say to me?" I howl, clenching my knuckles and swinging as I come unhinged, unleashing years of suffering on my brother. His attempts to dodge my swings are futile and met with more abrasive aggression as I lash out like a relentless son of a bitch. "You will never fucking talk about her that way again!"

My fists don't stop until cuffs click around my wrists.

Echo

ON MY BED, I CURL IN A FETAL POSITION WITH MY HEAD resting on Selia's thigh. Petting my hair, she asks, "What if you're wrong about him?"

I roll over and stare at her through the hazy glow of swollen eyes. "You mean what if he was really trying to change with me?"

"What if he is a genuinely nice guy with a bad boy history?"

"Then I just fucked the goose."

Her eyes close. "And what if you regret it?"

"I already do," I agonize through the loss. "But he deserves a whole person."

Her intense stare lassos a noose around my heart. "Who the hell is whole anymore? Are you aware how absurd that sounds? If someone is whole and functioning, I want their hands to bless me."

"It's too much to ask of anyone," I whimper.

"Everyone has a closet with skeletons. Yours and his, for that matter, may be a little darker than most, but it doesn't mean shit. You need to stop placing the template of the past onto to the present. You're not the graduating senior in high school anymore; he isn't twenty-five behind bars."

"Oh, God...Sel..."

"Do you need me to stay another day or two or a week?" she asks as I look out into the hallway at the bags and boxes she has packed for her new life tomorrow. I'm a horrible friend for doing this to her right now. She needs me now more than ever, and I'm crying like a newborn fresh from the womb I long to return to.

"You need to go be with Benjamin," I reassure, squeezing her hand. "I will be fine."

"You don't look like a person who is any sort of fine."

"I'll do whatever is necessary to get over him and move on with my life. I have to forget Jeremiah Monroe ever existed. He came into my world like a bomb and it's my goal to recover from the blast."

Her hand smoothes over my hair. "I know you're associating Jynx with something terrible, but you needed a change—a dramatic one. He gave you that. He wanted to make you better. Don't forget that."

"... Are you on his side?"

"I'm on the side where love wins."

"He didn't really love me," I argue, cringing through the words. "I was only a side project for him to notch his belt with. I was an accomplishment—*swipe the girl, make her fall in love with you, and keep her forever.* He didn't truly love me."

"Is that why he called me in a panic?" she asks, holding back tears. "That man on the phone was broken, Ek. I heard it in the tremor of his voice."

His sexy deep command.

I could've done anything with that voice guiding me.

"He's good. And I played right into him. I won't go back to him. I can't."

"And all of the joy he brought to you?"

I blink as the tears drip from my eyes. "I let it go. I break up with happiness too. The light only wages war for so long up until the darkness consumes her every night. Just like he did me."

Jynx

"WHAT THE FUCK?" WANG ASKS, PICKING ME UP FROM THE police station several days later. Despite my brother's broken nose and two black eyes, he decided not to press charges. I plop in the passenger seat of his rental car. "Tell me what I can do."

"I need a round of wings."

Ninety minutes later, he stares across the table at me as half-empty baskets sit with the carnage of our consumption. The beer pitcher is mostly empty. Our scantily dressed waitress walks past and drops off the check.

"You're in love," he randomly blurts out. "Fucking Jynx Monroe is in love."

"Even if I am, she left," I sneer, sitting back. "And I never chase a bitch."

"You're telling me after all of that, you aren't going after ad hoe?"

Don't tread on the sacred.

"I can't," I stutter, snarling and shaking my head. "The incident with Axel proves that I'm out of control. And as you know…"

"You hate when shit is out of control."

I lean with my elbows on the table and rub my lips together. I miss the taste of her kiss and the feel of her body beside me. "It's time to get back to being me. I did what I needed to do. Maybe she listened and learned something about the bigger picture."

"Jesus!" He rubs his face. "This is just…wild."

"It's been a hell of a summer romance, but it's time to wind it down. Fall is coming. She needed to go back to school anyway."

"Now," he says, pointing. "You're just making excuses."

"It's not though," I implore, trying to believe my own words. "We were never going to work out. She doesn't want a commitment. I'll get back to the hard ass I'm known for—*I have a reputation to uphold.* Maybe in a few months or years, we can fondly look back on the weeks we spent in the sizzling South Carolina summer."

He polishes off his beer and flops his credit card on the leather case. "You're never going to get over her."

"How do you know?"

With a brief smirk, he points out, "Because in the almost twenty years I've known you, I've never heard you talk about a woman for almost two hours. Your days as the bachelor you were are gone, whether she is here or not. She changed you, J."

I look down at the mess of our table, avoiding the truth even though it's the barrel pointing at my temple. I know Echo Maines changed me.

And I also know she left me.

29

THINGS WE NEED

ECHO

I STUMBLE THROUGH THE NEXT WEEK IN MY PAJAMAS, spending far more time on the bathroom floor and inside of my closet than ever before. I say goodbye to Selia, who was arguably the only rock I had left. She is so happy with Benjamin. I try not to think about how they'll be in Houston, where he will be in October.

Morgan got wind of my return and called several times. She wanted to know if I was returning to my job. My counselor at school checked in to make sure I would be attending fall classes. My mother messaged to tell me Dad was doing better. The most surprising dialogue came from my brother. Brandon was fresh out of rehab and wanted to sell our old childhood home that held so many painful memories.

I didn't answer any of it, but instead took to a steady pace of drinking. Not shitfaced, but a slow drip, numbing the pain.

Every afternoon at five o'clock hurts the worst because he'd appear with a smile on his face regardless of what he was doing. Hand-in-hand, we'd feed the peacocks and put away the horses.

I wonder what he is doing with the farm.

I wonder if he will sell the beach house.

I wonder if he's happy that he's free of the pest in his house, life, and heart.

I might not have meant anything to him as the grand scheme played off, set forth by me, brought into practice by him. I won't take the blame alone for this mess that we're in.

That's assuming too much…

That would mean believing that he cared, and his recovery was nothing more than a memory taped over with a bandage and the left-over sticky on his skin was remnants of a past he couldn't control.

We were through.

I had sex—*sort of*—but not enough to feel like I wasn't sitting on the fence. I even managed to fuck up fucking. I needed the explosion at the end.

But it was never coming from Jynx.

He'd meet some new girl, probably closer to his age, settle down, have kids, and a happy life, making a wonderful husband for someone else.

But she won't be me.

I curl up on the sofa in the glow of the television and flip channels. I quickly pass by all the romantic movies because I don't have time for that nonsense in my life. I land on a nature show with each segment devoted to a different species.

Under my blanket, I peek out until the peacocks appear.

He tickled me with a feather, chasing me around the yard. His laughter filled the air as I skipped around the coop. We playfully bantered until we collapsed in the grass.

His intense kiss said everything as he mounted on top of me amidst the squawking and social mingling of the flock.

"Goddammit!" I yell, clicking off the television and tugging my blanket to the bedroom. I hysterically sob in the middle of my bed. "Where are you? Why did this happen? This isn't real. He's still here. I never left the hotel."

Drool streams out of my mouth as I clutch the blanket around me. "Come back to me. Please. God. Help. Me."

JYNX

"THANKS," I SAY TO THE PIZZA DELIVERY GUY AT THE hotel. I toss the box on the coffee table and swig back another shot of whiskey. The weekends will be the most challenging part to get through because it's blatantly obvious I'm alone in the room. There is nothing but a vacant hole in my chest where she once stayed.

On the end table, my phone rings, and I lunge to answer it. "Hey..."

"How are you doing?" Deacon asks, flurried. "I'm putting you on speaker phone for a sec."

I mumble, "Misery is sitting on top of me."

"I knew a stripper named Misery once," Sal chimes in as I hear pounding in the background. "You don't want to know why they called her that."

I shake my head and snort. "I can imagine."

"You need to get moving. Go for a run. Go to the gym," he suggests as I glance at the clock—almost midnight. "Burn some energy. Before the crazy burns up your brain."

"Maybe I'll go out tomorrow."

"Nup, you *will* go." The racket in the background continues. "No maybe about it."

"What are you two doing?"

Deacon informs, "House shit."

"At this hour?"

"You don't understand," Sal replies, groaning. "It's a fucking mess."

"Tighten that. We'll teach that bitch to stay, even if it means bolting her ass down," Deacon professes with a sigh of relief. "Sorry about that, you're off speaker. He's right, you need to stop sulking."

Stroking my chin, I snicker, "I can't just bolt her ass down?"

"Well, you did drug her ass so anything is possible," he laughs as a screen door slams. I smirk, recognizing the sound. I miss home. I miss her more. "But I wouldn't recommend it in Echo's case."

"What would you do?"

"She's young. Give her some time. Don't push. Let her come back to you. If you chase her, she isn't going to get any better. She'll feel trapped like you forced her healing process. She needs to do it on her own."

"Are you telling me to play hard to get?"

"I'm saying, give a lot of slack on that leash," he offers, snapping his lighter closed. "If you need to check on her, then do it. But she needs freedom without you tugging her along. Or, you can just go abduct her ass again."

I laugh. If he only knew how many times I considered doing that the last week. There isn't much to think about behind bars. Caging Echo was better than anything else on my mind. "Do you think she is going to put the ad back up?"

He takes a breath. "It would be odd. If she does, you should forget her, because you mean nothing. Either way, you get to come here and help us. Fun shit."

"I need a place for my cocks," I snicker, grinning. "I can't leave them behind."

"Are you selling?"

"I haven't decided. You know, Deacon," I mutter, feeling a tad better about where I am. "You're more like a brother to me than Axel."

"Axel is a poon," he chuckles, and I do the same. "He always was. Don't be like him."

"That will never happen."

"You're lucky he didn't press charges," he says, triggering a thought I hadn't considered. "Bastard says anything else about Ek, let me know."

"I need to go eat dinner."

"Alright, man. Be good."

"Will do."

I click the end button and check Axel's location. He's in the same hotel I am, but I don't trust him. "He wouldn't go after her," I mumble, grabbing a slice of pizza. "… Would he?"

These are not questions I ever expected to need to answer about my brother, but he's way too much like my dad. Though I hate to say it, Echo's probably too old for him.

Axel is my biological family.

But my blood is somewhere in Texas.

ECHO

WALKING INTO THE VINERY THE NEXT MORNING, I SMILE at José stacking beer cases before the store opens. "Hey, hot stuff! Long time no see!"

"I took some time off," I nervously say. "Is Morgan here?"

"Yeah," he replies. "Did you meet someone or something? Cause you're looking damn fine."

I shake my head and passively dismiss the notion, "Nah."

I make a hasty exit, not wanting to engage in any small talk that could potentially lead to an onslaught of inconsolable tears.

"Well, there she is!" Morgan booms with a broad smile. "How are you?"

"I am okay."

"A man broke your heart," she immediately assesses, stepping from behind the counter. I spot the prominent protrusion in her lower belly.

"You're pregnant!"

"I am!" she squeals, hugging me. "I'm about four months along with Ravi's baby. We're getting married at Christmas."

"I'm so happy for you!" I mean every word, seeing Morgan so content gives me hope that love can happen for me too.

She moves to a display and plops down in the ornate metal chair. "Tell me all about him."

I shrug and smirk. "There's nothing to say."

"Don't make me bribe you with an iced caramel coffee!"

An hour later, I grin and wait for a response after telling her the whole story. Her smile twists on her face as she nods. "Tell me one thing, do you love the darker sides of him?"

"Like the fact he's been in jail?"

"Or, he likes to take the lead," she whispers before eyeing her watch. "Because it matters. I'll be honest with you, I conceived this baby during a scene with Ravi." I bite my lip as she brings clarity to everything. "This may not just be a nighttime thing with him. He may be blunting the edge because he's afraid of losing you. You need to decide if you want that much power over your life during the daytime too."

"… You think he's hiding?"

"I feel as though he is feeding you incremental doses so to not overwhelm and lose you. Ignore the age difference because I don't think it matters. Far more important is the maturity and experience difference. The fifteen years are irrelevant as a number, but very relevant in real time. Fifteen years is cradle to almost an adult, that's a huge span of time and existence."

Leaning back in my chair, I ask, "Is he worth it?"

"Only you can answer that." Her eyes light up. "But if everything you've said is true, then I think he is probably worth risking more of your heart than you have. You either trust him or you don't. There is no gray area, Echo. But don't dick him around." She grins and taps the table twice. "I have to open the shop in ten minutes. I know you're turning in your resignation."

"... How do you know?"

"Because you look like you're in love," she says as I follow her to the counter. "And he doesn't live in San Francisco."

"It's a big assumption that I can get him back."

"Only if you don't try."

I nod and hug her. "Thank you, Morgan. For everything."

"It's always a pleasure having you around. If things don't work out and you need a job," she informs, holding her belly. "Let me know. I'll need a manager soon."

JYNX

IN THE PRIVATE GYM AT THE DOWER HEADQUARTERS, I push my limits, sweating all over the weight bench.

"I will never understand women," Wang says, holding his phone, as I groan through another set of reps. "One minute, they dote on you; the next, all men are jerks."

"I take it Carly isn't handling the split well," I mumble, sitting up and grabbing the towel.

"Fuck no!" He follows me over to the leg press. Wang does not ever work out unless it involves the motion of eating or fucking. That's it. I strongly believe if he could have a bitch feed and ride him, he would have the perfect woman. And sometimes, he even whines when I decide we need to take the staircase after his favorite lunch. "Last Monday this bitch told me she wanted to marry me. Today, she posted on her feed that she's going gay."

I pause long enough to laugh and lose count in the process. "Did she say it that way?"

"Yep," he replies, showing me the post on social media. I shake my head. "She's so messed up."

"Be glad you didn't hitch her to the altar," I repeat his words with a wink. "For the record, people do not *go* one way or another. It is not a direction or a turn."

He laughs. "Oh, I know. My father never decided to go gay. He just always was."

"People are stupid."

"Says the man who just had his heart ripped out and pulverized in a blender," he replies, smirking. "You've been hating on everyone."

"No," I correct, breathing heavily as my legs hit depletion. "I'm back to my normal oppressive, gloomy state. It's not my fault the rest of the world is full of fake, shiny, happy people."

"… How real was she?"

"Too real." I stop, unable to finish my workout, which frustrates me. "I'm done."

"Are we going to meet Eddie and his cronies for a drink?"

"If we must," I concede, downing the bottle of water. "I will fake a happy for you."

"We could pretend to be gay."

I wrap my arm around him. "Wang, I love you, man. But there is no way in heaven or hell, your pole can provide what her holes do."

"You're so fucked," he mutters, straight-faced, before breaking into a hysterical fit of laughter. "Who would've thought that Jynx Monroe would ever go off the market?"

Ripping off my soaked workout shirt, I argue, "I'm not off the market."

"You're not eligible either."

Hitting the shower, I think about his opinions of my love life. They don't bother me because...*he's right.* And I'm only going one way —*straight like an arrow to Echo Maines heart.*

If that girl wants wine and romance, then I'll give it to her by the truckload. I've got cherubs, chocolate, and a brand new, beautiful, midnight blue Mustang en route to her apartment now.

In making my final appeal, I understand it may not turn out as I plan. She could reject the traditional pursuit and smack my ass down another notch into the catacombs of hell.

What do I have to lose? Nothing.

But if that happens, she'll leave me with no other choice than to give her exactly what she wants—*a filthy fucking gentleman.*

ECHO

"WHAT THE HELL?" I SHOUT AS LILY SCRUTINIZES THE SEXY piece of machinery sitting in front of our building.

"I didn't do it," she says, tilting her gray-haired-miniature-beehive-looking-do back and forth. Beneath her heavy black-framed glasses, she rolls her eyes at me. "If you don't want it...I'll volunteer to be his sex slave."

"Lily!" I remark, shocked. "We're not..."

Her stern maternal stare stops me dead in my tracks. "Even if we are, involved."

She raises a singular finger and waves it at my face. "This is not involvement. That is where you're wrong, Echo. This is commitment."

"Sweet ride!" Spencer praises on his way out. "Whatever you did for his D," he yells, walking off. "I wouldn't stop, baby!"

Lily uncrosses her arms and holds out her hand. "Give me the keys."

"No!"

"Then drive so we can get to the market before all of the good fish is gone."

"You're not putting fish in my new car!"

"Oh, yes!" she contends with her old-style charm. "I'm making you dinner before you make the biggest error of your life."

I open her door and ask, "... Not mistake?"

"I say what I mean and I mean what I say and losing this one will be an error."

"What's the difference?"

"Because now I have your attention." Her rounded cheeks perk up as she visibly smiles in my presence for the first time ever. "Your conduct and judgement in the case of this Mister are in dire error."

"Dire error?"

"Don't make me repeat myself. If you lose this one, a dire error has occurred. You will be going against the forces of nature and the fates that be."

"Wait!" I drape my arm on the door. "You're in my car. I'm taking you to the market. And you're going to criticize me about my behavior with Jynx?"

Her eyes widen as she eagerly whispers, "... Is that his name?"

Grinding my teeth, I sigh, "Yes, Jynx Monroe."

"You really nailed a bad boy, honey," she alleges, pursing her lips tightly. "Don't make a dire error with Jynx," she sermonizes like a damn opium princess lounging sensually on a silken fainting couch. With a glazed over look, she gushes, "Jynx and Echo Monroe."

This is my life.

"... Why not grave error?"

She gives a side-eyed glance and motions a cross over me. "Do not curse yourself with that kind of bad karma! Dire error, dammit! Serious! Not deadly, unless you fuck this up!"

"Yes, Ma'am."

30

THE GIVEN

Echo

After spending the last six hours with Lily, I want to collapse. As it turns out, she's been fooling everyone this whole time. The woman is a damn firecracker of energy. Not to mention, she's a hell of a cook. I walk across the hall to my apartment with a large bag of leftovers in tow.

"Ek!" Spencer says, bolting up the stairs. "Some guy came by earlier."

"Guy?" I question, unlocking my door and fearing I missed Jynx.

I didn't really have that thought.

Go away. Leave me alone. Wait. Come back.

"Yeah," he replies. "I let him inside." I gasp at my apartment, which resembles a florist with numerous arrangements. "And then I showed him out."

My heart hurts as I try not to cry. "Thanks, Spence."

"Whoever he is," he calmly says. "He is after more than a home run."

I smile, unsure of what to say. I disappear inside. "Oh, my fucking God...what the hell!" I close my eyes, but it doesn't help. I'm human, and unfortunately, breathing is required. The rose scent permeates through my nostrils, filling every inch of me with his adoration. "What the fuck am I going to do?"

I put the leftover Sanpeijiru (salmon soup) in the fridge along with the half dozen Choux buns doused in dark chocolate and filled with Chantilly cream that Lily insisted I would need in the middle of the night to keep the demons at bay.

I change my clothes and look around for something to do. I pop my earbuds in and blast Prince as I decide to make the place sparkle or pass out, whichever comes first.

"Ughhh!" I groan as I finish scrubbing the bathroom at two in the morning. I've cleaned the entire apartment, not that Selia left it in a mess. I even moved my desk and computer in her old bedroom since I didn't plan to have another roommate.

After gulping down a bottle of water, I put all the cleaning supplies back under the sink. I pass by her room—*my new study*—and smile at how good the pink and blue lava lamps look casting a sensuous glimmer around the space. I hit the power button on my computer and take a shower.

Thirty-seven arrangements—All roses. Various colors. No card.

I don't need a card.

Twenty-two handcrafted chocolates in a pink and black polka dot box—A quarter of them are missing now.

They did come with a card—"Go online, D4RK4NG3L."

Five rooms in the apartment that I have been cleaning for the last six hours to avoid communicating with Jynx.

I fucked this one up.

Bad.

Wrapped in my bathrobe, I check on the updates and punch in my password. All of my previous windows open, including the last time I posted the ad and the green light signifying my presence. I scan over my words, reading bits, and pieces out loud as I figure out what to do next.

"Natural Dominant. Alpha. Male. No nerds or bikers. Bad boys welcome. Pure ravishment, abduction, and torture scenes. I do not wish to know your name, your peacocks, horses, or Grandma's names," I elaborate, giggling and shaking my head. *"I am not looking to date, have an affair, or engage in a romance."*

"Read it again, J!"

I have 457 emails in my inbox.

I delete all of them.

"All that is required by you is a willingness to control the scene and a giant, hard cock...that you know how to use. The right suitor appreciating violent sexual encounters. I agree to struggle, play the role of victim, and provide you with a challenge. You agree to use protection, not bruise any flesh above the neck or below the wrists, and incite fear in me....or fall in love with me," I mutter as tears flourish in my eyes. *"Just surprise me."*

God, he was perfect.

A box pops up on the screen, and my mouth drops open.

> $T4LK3R: I see you.
> D4RK4NG3L: Took you long enough.
> $T4LK3R: I could say the same about you,
> Sweet Pea.
> D4RK4NG3L: I was busy.
> $T4LK3R: Big date?
> D4RK4NG3L: Yes! With a sixty-some-odd-year-
> old Japanese woman.
> $T4LK3R: Did you eat?
> D4RK4NG3L: Yes.
> $T4LK3R: Did you drive your car?

D4RK4NG3L: Yes. And so did Lily.
$T4LK3R: ... Lily?
D4RK4NG3L: My date.
$T4LK3R: Ahh. Is she hot?
D4RK4NG3L: LOL She wants to be your sex slave
if I don't.

A long awkward pause shifts the energy of the conversation. I wish I had the box of buns, course I'd probably lick and suck all of the cream.

Oh. God.

Stop thinking, Abs.

D4RK4NG3L: Thank you for all of the gifts, but
you shouldn't have gone to the trouble. It was
too much.
$T4LK3R: Do you...want to be my sex slave?

I close my eyes, scared of what my answer will bring and who we will become. I can tell myself a thousand times I am not a submissive, but something shifts inside me when he pilots. Every worry and care diminishes unless I have an unexpected breakdown while he's snatching my innocence like a pirate.

D4RK4NG3L: I don't know.
$T4LK3R: Tomorrow, a gentleman will be coming
to your door at 6 PM. He's taking you to the
theater and dinner. Wear the dress and shoes
that will arrive. Enjoy yourself.
D4RK4NG3L: ... Huh?
$T4LK3R: When he leaves, message me.
D4RK4NG3L: I do not want to date. Did you not
read my ad? I don't want a man. Any man. I
should never have been with you as long as I

was. I'm a toxic individual, unhealthy for
anyone around me, including you.
$T4LK3R: When he leaves, message me.

His light turns red. "Fucker!"

I rush to the kitchen, grab the box from the fridge, and eat half the box of buns. And when I finally cannot consume any more and I've successfully managed to throw myself into a carb coma, I curl into a ball on my pristine floor, under the canopy of rose petals, and cry myself to sleep.

One more night alone.

I SPEND HOURS PREPARING FOR THE DATE. THE BLACK dress and heels are tastefully alluring, but nothing I would pick to wear with Jynx. The dress hem is four inches too long, and the shoes are two inches too short.

I consider going renegade and whoring out to the max.

Cause why the fuck not?

After putting on fifty pounds of makeup, I cannot do anything to ease the ache within. I miss J. I want this night to be with him.

Maybe it will be him.

The idea excites me as my bell rings at 5:59 PM. I take a deep breath, not bothering with the peephole, and swing open the door. The guy, with messed up grunge-styled, spiked, black hair and hazel eyes, grins at me.

"Bran!" I scream and leap into his arms. So much for wearing any makeup as the tears stream the warpaint down my cheeks. I haven't seen my brother since Christmas in Florida. We took a long walk, smoked a blunt, and talked about the future. "When did you get here?"

"Earlier today," he says. "I've got almost three months sober. You want to celebrate with me?"

"How long are you staying?"

"Only tonight," he answers as we step inside. "I'm selling the place in Alabama."

"I know," I say, squeezing his hand. "It's okay."

"You promise?"

"We have to grow up and move on, Brandon."

He nods as I walk to the bathroom. "The guy who called me…"

"That's a long story." Staring in the mirror, I wipe my tears. He stares at our reflection. We look very similar except for our height. I can't stop crying. "One I cannot talk about."

"He likes you a lot," he implores, laying his hand on my shoulder. "Can I drive your new car?"

"Yeah. He told you?" I ask, and he nods.

"He told me lots of things, Abby."

Segueing the uncomfortable chatter, I give up any hope of makeup staying on and question, "You want a chocolate or a dozen roses?"

Like hell, I'm sharing my buns.

Or the cream filling.

He laughs. "Nah. I just want to take my baby sis out for a night."

We spend the evening enjoying the performance and sharing a pizza at a local favorite watering hole.

Brandon is sober, but he isn't well.

He never has been.

I saw the shadows looming in his eyes as we sat on the sofa until almost dawn comparing notes on our lives. It was good. But he wasn't. He was curled up on my sofa, sleeping soundly, when I went to my bedroom at a quarter to five.

At 4:58 AM, I unblock Jeremiah Abaddon Monroe from my phone and hit send on the text, "Thank you. Brandon's visit means the world to me."

"Time is precious," he quickly responds. "Enjoy it while you can."

"He's not good."

"That's why I sent him."

I roll over on my side and watch the dark skies. The sun will burn through soon, leaving a dusty rose color until the yellow blossoms.

The light he curses; the dark he worships.

In tears, I peck out, "What am I going to do with him?"

"Love hard."

"He wants out of Alabama."

"Yes."

Through a waterfall, I send, "Did you do this to get me back?"

"I don't have to do anything to get you back. You will come on your own. Or not at all."

"And what about all the gifts?"

"Consider them presents for the twenty-two years I missed."

Wiping my tears on my sleeve, I giggle. "That sounds so wrong."

"No use in denying it. You want to be my baby; I'll be your Sugar Daddy. You should get some sleep."

"Goodnight, J."

"Night, princess."

I watch as the sun crests over the horizon, melting the dark purple skies away. The phone buzzes on the pillow beside me.

"Do you want to be mine?"

I close my eyes because a future with Jynx is too much to think about with Brandon here. I can't process both at the same time. Fifteen minutes pass when I send, "Do I have a choice?"

"No."

AFTER BRANDON LEAVES FOR ALABAMA, I SIT DOWN AT THE computer with my box of chocolates to message Jynx as he requested. I stare at the bizarre name change in less than twenty-four hours.

> JYNXXX: Are you okay?
> D4RK4NG3L: What happened to your name?
> JYNXXX: I closed my account. Had to make a new
> one. :)

I furrow my brow and mumble, "You're a fucking sex addict. There

is no way you closed your account." *Something is amok.* In my messages,
I click $T4LK3R.

>D4RK4NG3L: Hi. Are you around? Someone is
>   talking to me named JYNXXX.
>$T4LK3R: I should've killed him. One second.
>D4RK4NG3L: Who is it?
>$T4LK3R: My fucking dumbass brother.

JYNX

MY JAW POPS AS I CONSIDER WHAT TO SAY TO AXEL. HE'S
impulsive, a shit-stirrer. No doubt, he is talking to my girl just to get
my goat.
I glance down, understanding I just called Echo—*my girl.*

>$T4LK3R: Let me make this very clear for you
>   since you're a fucking idiot. If you come
>   anywhere near her, I will kill you.
>JYNXXX: LOL
>$T4LK3R: Leave her alone.
>JYNXXX: You fucked it up.
>$T4LK3R: I'm going to fuck you up.
>D4RK4NG3L: Are you okay?
>$T4LK3R: Yeah, I don't want to go back to prison.
>D4RK4NG3L: That was a decade ago.
>$T4LK3R: No, that was a week ago.

ECHO

I HIT THE CALL BUTTON. JYNX ANSWERS ON THE FIRST ring, snickering, "That took all of ten seconds!"

My eyes close at the sound of his deep warm tone. "What happened?"

"I beat the fuck out of Axel and spent three days in the slammer."

I lean back in my chair. "What? Why?"

"He said some things he had no business saying."

I bite my lip and hover my mouse over the delete account button. "Are you okay?"

"Yeah."

Not knowing what to do, I ask, "Should I delete my account?"

He pauses. "You should come into my chat room and show me your tits."

I feel the blush rise on my cheeks. "I bet you'd like that."

"You have no idea how much I would love that," he playfully flirts. "Block his ass."

"Already done, *Sir.*" I grip the arm of the chair, realizing what I just said.

Sir.

"You miss me?"

"Like you can't believe," I admit, sniffling. "I'm deleting the ad, Jynx. What are you doing?"

"Getting drunk and munching on soggy tacos."

"You should be paying attention to your chatroom," I whisper, opening my robe a little further. "There might be a better taco in there."

"Yeah," he mumbles, entering the chatroom as I show off my cleavage. "That's something worth looking at for sure." He clicks on his camera—*for the first time*—and I grin as his face fills the screen. "I don't do this."

"I know! You're willing to bend," I delightfully squeal. "Where are you?"

"In my hotel suite, on the sofa."

"I wish you were here," I confess, crying. "I'm such a mess without you, J."

His lips shift from side to side, and his brow tightens. "Hold on a sec, babe."

"What are you doing?"

He squints, staring at his phone. "Booking a flight for tomorrow morning and reserving a car."

My eyes widen. "You're coming?"

"Not yet, but I will." He focuses on the camera and winks.

"Oh, my God!"

"One condition," he says, staring at me. "You pack your shit."

"What about my lease?"

"When is it up?"

I rapidly blink. "… You're really serious?"

"Yes, I'll get us a two room suite. When is your lease up?"

"December."

"I'll pay it in full tomorrow," he offers, smirking. "And you agree to date me."

I blurt out, "And what if…"

"No," he interrupts. "We're taking a second chance at this. If we decide it isn't working, I'll pay for a year's lease anywhere in the country. But!" He lifts a finger. "If things are going well, you agree to come to South Carolina with me."

"And Houston?"

He snarls. "First things first, beautiful."

"What about all my furniture?"

"Anything precious or antique?"

"No," I reply, looking around. "I have the sofa and end tables that Selia bought and a bed."

"We trash it," he says with a shrug. "Take a risk on me."

My toes curl in the carpet. "Jynx…"

"Do it, babygirl. Say yes. Let me show you the other side."

"Does this mean you'll ra…"

He scowls, and I giggle. "Do not ask me to do that to you."

"Fine. Fine."

"But I have every intention on finishing what we started until we broke down," he softly says. "It's not all on you. I fucked up. I should've handled that better."

"You're human."

He smiles, reaching up to the camera like he's touching me. "So are you, pretty girl."

"Jynx?"

"Yeah?"

"Yes, I want to be yours."

"I'll be in tomorrow morning," he replies, gazing at me. "Get some sleep. I'll see you in a few hours. I love you. And no touching what is mine."

I smirk. "Yes, Master Jynx."

31

OH. SHIT.

ECHO

MY EYES FLASH OPEN AS THE GLOW OF THE CLOCK READS—
12:33 PM. "Fuck!"

Flipping back the covers, I stumble out of bed, feeling like a haggard drifter in my pink unicorn pajamas and messy hair. I rush into the living room and screech to a stop, almost flipping forward at the sight of Jynx reading his tablet. He's wearing glasses, a casual long sleeve obsidian shirt, and lead-colored dress slacks.

Oh. My. Fucking. God.

My boyfriend is a hunk.

His lips curl upward, the dimples hinting on his cheeks. With his right foot shielded in a black leather loafer propped on his left knee, he shoots a gaze up to me. "You were tired."

"How did you get in?" I ask, glancing over at the locks on my door. "Did you break in?"

"Does it matter?" he asks, suppressing a laugh. He sets the device down on the coffee table and removes his glasses, folding them, before sitting them on top of the tablet. Everything is in slow motion as I fear losing consciousness. All of the blood in my body rushes to my pussy, convulsing, and demanding his attention. The deluge showers my panties, and I remain in awe, speechless by his sudden appearance.

He stands so much taller than I remembered two weeks ago. I feel dwarfed by his imposing stature as he rests his palms on my shoulders. His soft chocolate curls suggest his chaos, undisciplined and messy, but otherwise, he proves to be an elegant model—a dreamboat with stunning blue eyes that capture without warning. "God, you're gorgeous, Echo."

That's you.

I hold up my hands and spread my fingers wide in front of my chest. "I need a minute to process this."

He doesn't give it to me.

His fingers skim down the thin collar of my pajamas until he reaches my skin. The back of his fingers trace the curve, dipping in my cleavage, and he unbuttons the shirt. He opens the panels, exposing my breasts, only to squat low and take a nipple into his mouth. His palm gropes the other one, and I gasp at the loss of control—*my willpower vanquishing in a hush.*

"You can process after you suck my cock," he growls, rising and encouraging my kneeling with a delicate push. I don't resist. With his belt still fastened, his zipper flies down, and he tugs his cock from the cotton slit in his boxers. Placing the tip against my lip, he commands, "Take me in your mouth, sweet thing."

I don't think; I do; I perform; I react; I engage.

I spent days craving this man, and this moment, building with rampant desire and ignoring my lust—I will not fail him now. I take his hardened shaft into my mouth, gulping him back as far as possible. I suckle with long strokes from base to tip and cradle his balls, still imprisoned in the fabric, in my hand.

But it's not enough.

He yanks my makeshift ponytail—harder than ever before—and thrusts, bucking like a wild man into my willing channel. "Fuck, baby bitch!" he groans as I taste the salty pre-cum gliding over the back of my throat and spreading out over my tongue. "I'm going to come, Abby! Fuck!" he roars, gripping my head and holding me taut as he ejaculates deep into the funnel.

And like a good girl, I swallow.

The dividing lines between where his Dominance seizes and my submission surrenders are effortlessly drawn. His ragged breaths grant my entry but provide no option at calling a truce. With his huge hands detaining me at his groin, he asserts his ownership by restricting my maneuvers.

His victory march arrests me.

Eventually, he relinquishes me. I blink up and wipe the edge of my mouth with my fingers. "I know you can do better, Jynx."

He finally breaks his composure with a mammoth grin. "Not in the light of day."

My lips part as I didn't even realize. "Oh, my God... You really are changing."

Maybe I should too.

He offers his hands to help me up. The same hands that held me down, infinitely love me. "I'm trying. And I'm going to keep striving to do better. Be patient with me. And I will do the same for you."

Without any warning, he swoops his arms beneath mine and picks me up. I latch my legs around his waist, and he dotingly delves his tongue into my mouth. My fingers press to his smooth cheeks as his aftershave hits my nose, and my heart buckles. "You're really here!"

"I'm here, Echo." He confirms that it's not just a crazy dream. "But I'd like to get on the road before rush hour."

I nod. "I packed everything last night and I gave all of the flowers to Lily very early this morning. She is taking them to the retirement center today. I need a quick shower and we can go."

"I have to drop off my car at the rental place."

"Why does that sound familiar?" I giggle, unable to take my eyes off of him. "Are you driving?"

With a tilt of his head, he snarls. "… Is that even a question?"

"God, I love you, Jynx."

"I love you too, babe," he confesses, kissing me again before setting me on my feet. "Go shower. I'll take your bags to the car." I spin away, and he slaps my ass. I glance over my shoulder, and his brow flicks up. "Better behave."

"For how long?"

"The rest of your life."

I cannot restrain my smile. "This means you'll be the one guarding me."

"Damn straight, I will."

JYNX

CLOSING THE TRUNK, I STARE AT THE FULL BACK SEAT AND smoke in the parking lot. Her permanent presence in my life hosts a very real reality check. All of her things—*all of her life*—is packed inside. She isn't only trusting me, but I have chosen to take on the sometimes challenging responsibility of the young woman in the shower.

A short distance away, I spot an Asian man, close to her age, walking with his toddler son in the grass. The kid is barely able to do it on his own. But hell, if his chubby little legs aren't trying. He takes a few steps and plops on his hands. Again and again, he does this as I watch in awe.

I don't typically interfere, engaging in small talk, but something magical exists in this moment between the three of us as I'm compelled to ask, "How old is he?"

"He'll be a year old in a month," he replies. "You have kids?"

I shake my head. "I've never found the right one."

"I've been with my wife since junior high."

"You have a beautiful family. Congratulations! And good luck."

He smiles as the tot takes another tumble. "You too, man."

I hastily dart up the staircase and stop for a moment on the landing near her apartment. I take a deep breath, feeling I have missed so much, but I know—I wasn't ready.

I'm older, more capable, wisened by the time. Despite the issues with Axel, I'm calmer than a decade ago. If I had pursued Celeste and ended up marrying her, we'd be divorced by now. I guarantee this much. Years of drinking and womanizing would've sealed our fate. Add in a wreck that almost killed me, and she would've been long gone.

Nothing more than a memory.

I wanted more than she ever possessed.

I needed the passion for the girl I'm about to heist.

Because she looks at me like I'm a fucking God.

I step into her apartment with a renewed sense of purpose and find her wrapped in a towel. She is gathering the last of her toiletries. "Did it all fit?"

"Baby, it will all fit," I flirt as she grins. "If it hadn't, I would've shipped it home. There are no excuses."

"I know," she says, pulling her hair out of the towel and picking up the comb. "I agreed to this."

"If it doesn't work…"

Mid-stroke of the comb, she glares at me. "If it doesn't work, you will let me go, but until then, I'm your helpless captive." She winks.

My smile expands as a hint of blush rises on my cheeks. "Your trust means more than I can say."

"Because I'm agreeing to your kidnapping a second time?"

"Yeah," I reply, taking the comb from her hand and running it through her locks. She pivots to face me. "You deserve it."

"This love mess started because of an ad," she reminds. "I was looking for a real winner."

I lick my lips. "And I qualified?"

"Mr. Monroe, you were the cream of the crop."

"I shut you down," I admit, caressing her cheeks. "I didn't give anyone else a chance."

"You didn't need to, J," she whispers as I hoist her onto the bathroom counter. "We won't get on the road anytime soon if that look in your eye is any indication."

"Do you know how much I want this with you?"

"Why me?"

"I wish I knew, baby," I mutter, easing my finger beneath the towel and plucking it off. "I was living my life, doing fine. I didn't want or need anything or anyone. Someone blessed me with you. And showed me that I wasn't living at all."

"Jynx Monroe...are you headed toward the light?"

"Not a fucking chance," I reply with a chuckle. "Because we need my sinister ways to balance us out."

Her facial muscles tighten with concern. "Am I not sinister?"

"No," I laugh and curl my arms around her. "I know you want to think you are because you placed an ad, but that was an isolated incident, purely done to draw out the wolves from the den."

"Are you going to show me your fangs?"

"Yes," I say, kissing her wet head. "And I want you to show me yours. Bloodsports, baby."

"I'm so hungry!" she declares.

I laugh, "Does talking of blood often make you hungry, vampire?"

"It was all the cum I swallowed." Her zestful energy blooms within as she bounces in my arms. "I need a taco."

"Or three?"

"Maybe four."

"Are you sleeping the whole way back?"

"Nope, I am too excited because I get to figure out the equation of how to spend the rest of my life with you," she excitedly confides. "We won't always agree, but this is worth taking a chance on."

"I'm asking you to risk it all and come be my brat."

"I know," she says, grinning. "But there is more freedom riding on your shoulders than I will ever find alone. You're the risk worth taking, Jynx."

"You're such a bright soul."

She simpers. "And you need me to keep you level so you don't drown in dismal darkness."

"Those few days in jail, all I did was think about you and the future I wanted to chase. In some ways, it was the best thing for me. Shutting everyone else out gave me a new perspective."

Her hands press to my chest. "And what did you learn?"

"I don't trust my brother. I trust my cousin like a brother. I want to take care of you and everyone you love, including Brandon. But I can't do that if I don't know the truth. I need you to drop all the walls and trust me not to walk out on you. No matter what happened in the past."

Her eyes glimmer on the verge of a flood. "My father wasn't good to Brandon."

"The club?"

She nods. "He lost his virginity at thirteen to a club slut. He never wanted to be a part of that world because...he was a sweet boy and Dad wanted him to man up."

"... Is he gay?"

"I wouldn't know," she says, shaking her head. "Honestly, he's never been sober long enough to get to know himself. If I were to guess, my answer would be there is something going on with Brandon's sexuality, but he did everything he was supposed to do because Dad badgered him into it. He patched in by seventeen and married the girl he dated in high school..."

"She lost his baby."

"No," she whispers as the tears fall. "She wanted the club life, even though he didn't. She had an affair with one of the guys and got pregnant. The guy was eventually kicked out of the club and out of the town before moving to Florida."

I rapidly blink, realizing the extent of what she is saying—*the hidden message clarifies.* "... Your father was sleeping with his daughter-in-law?"

"Yeah, because Brandon refused to consummate the marriage." She reluctantly meets my gaze, embarrassed by the shortcomings in her family that she had no control over. "Word got around, and my mom agreed to stay married to my father because he excused her whorish ways with his own. They moved, managed to finagle their way into another Rampage charter, and life resumed. After they left, Tawny had an abortion. For two years, Brandon fought to get a divorce because she wanted everything."

My brow lines. "Was there more than the house?"

"My paternal grandparents left each grandchild a trust fund."

With concern, I ask, "How much of a trust fund?"

"Close to a half million a piece, free and clear at eighteen, but Brandon handed his over to the dealers and booze stores after the divorce. Daphne left after graduation because her birthday is at the end of June and knew my mother would burn through it faster than a match in a forest."

"Jesus," I say, taking a breath. "Do you have all of yours?"

"I do because I hightailed it off to California and paid for school with scholarships, loans, and a job. I worked my ass off for everything I have."

I shake my head. "I don't need your money."

"I know," she says, smiling. "And I don't need yours. If there was ever a shadow of a doubt that I stayed with you because of your bank account, think again."

"I never thought that, but it means a lot that you've shared this with me."

"You're trying," she mutters, staring at me. "So am I. You want to invest it for me?"

"I can help you," I offer, stunned she would trust me—*that much.* "But I want you to have control over your money."

"You don't want power over everything?"

"No," I contend, touching her jawline. "Not everything. You need to be independent within the safety of my boundaries. That is your money. Same thing with school or work. You have your freedom."

"And in your bedroom?"

"You're the tawdry bitch that I love."

"Thank you for defining the parameters."

"I've never had to do this," I admit, enlightened. "I was one and done. I've never had to think about what would happen if I had a submissive all of my own, so we're learning that part together. We must practice patience with each other, but as far as leading you—*I know how to do that.*"

"I know, Jynx. I trust you, and I shouldn't have left the hotel," she says, kissing my lips. "I'm sorry I did that to you. You deserved better. Next time shit goes south, I will Jeremiah out of it." She winks, and I smile wide. "I feel guilty about the fight with Axel."

With how good my name sounds rolling off of her wicked tongue, we're going to need a new safeword.

"Bah," I dismiss, rolling my eyes. "It wasn't the first time I've beat the crap out of my brother and it won't be the last. He is a troublemaker."

"So are you..."

"He's just a prankster," I point out, smirking. "I'm downright cruel."

"I'm hoping so."

32

REINVIGORATE ROMANCE

ECHO

WE ARRIVE AT HIS LAVISH HOTEL ROOM IN PHOENIX AT almost three in the morning. I should be accustomed to how he lives, but I doubt I ever will be.

I grew up lower-middle class; he grew up rich.

The bellman pushes the luggage cart, full of my belongings, into a bedroom. "Am I not staying with you?"

"No," he mumbles, tipping the bellman as he finishes unloading my things. He shows him out with proper etiquette. Shutting the door, he declares, "We're dating. You'll be acting as my personal assistant at Dower until the transfer is completed. We need to have a professional relationship, which means, dating."

I curiously ask, "… But staying in the same suite?"

"Yes, so I can keep an eye on you," he maintains, kissing my cheek. "Get some rest."

Instantly, I am no longer tired as I stomp into the room and shut the door. After taking a quick shower, I toss on an oversized shirt and panties, and peek outside. The main living room is dark as I sneak out and snatch the room key sitting on a counter by the coffee pot.

"Where are you going?" I hear from behind. "You shouldn't need to go anywhere."

"I want some ice because my water is warm," I reply, twisting a one-eighty as he sits in the chair with his back to me.

"The fridge under the coffee pot has plenty of cold drinks."

I crack the door and illuminate the room. I grab a water and down half the bottle before meandering over to him. "What are you doing up?"

"I cannot sleep."

"… Why?"

"Because you're here," he mutters as I blink at his bare chest. "And I cannot get your scent out of my system."

"I don't understand why we're staying in separate rooms," I complain, finishing the water. "We've been apart for so long."

"Yet you choose to tempt me in the night," he snarls with a harsh stare. "You need to go back to your room where I put you. I want to keep you safe. And sometimes that means, even from me."

"Oh," I reply, tossing the bottle in the trash. "I have no problems taunting you during the day."

He strokes his chin. "Kneel."

I gracefully fall to the floor and await further instruction. "What can I do to help you sleep?"

"Don't ask that question, Sweet Pea."

Without being asked, I lay my head on his lap, and his eager fingers brush through my hair. I set my hand on his thigh as his scent arouses me. I smell his sex, the delicious aroma of pre-cum. My mouth waters. He rapidly picks my fingers up and places them on his erection.

"Why are you resistant?"

"I'm not," he counters with a growl. "I'm not actively in pursuit."

I lift my head to look at him. "Because of what happened the last time?"

Shadows eclipse around his sharp angles as I skirt my hand up over his washboard abs. He peers over his nose and warns, "Because I will hurt you tonight."

"How do you know?"

"When you've done this as long as I have, you learn the signs," he mutters as I sit back and pull my shirt over my head. "Jesus, Echo! Don't show me your glorious tits."

"You don't need to be alone anymore."

I feel the heat of his gaze streaming over my body. "Are you wet?"

"Yes. Do you want to feel it? Do you want me to take my panties off for you, Jynx?"

His lip curls on one side. "Yes." I leisurely roll-up. "Turn around. Show me your ass."

I bite my lip and tug the lace down over my thighs, and bend. "Fuck, I can smell you." He grabs my wrist, yanking me back to his lap. My legs rest on the arm of the chair as he holds my body, cradling me. "Spread your thighs."

Tilting my head back, I offer everything I have—a bountiful feast for his perusal. "You have a twenty-two-year-old girl on your lap begging for your consumption. Don't break her heart by turning her away." His fingers skim over my nipples, tweaking each one to a peak before he slides his hand to my slit. He rubs my clit, and I gasp, "Yes, please."

"You shouldn't want this."

"But I do," I argue as he speeds up and slows down. He sends tingling pleasurable waves through me as my eyes roll back. Drool froths from my mouth—his erection throbs, raging with want against my ass. I writhe against him when he dips inside with a precise stroke. "Fuck my pussy."

"Stand up."

He yanks his pants off and latches onto my hips, guiding my body to sit upon his knees. "You're not going to let me see you."

"Not tonight," he whispers, running his finger along the contour of my tattoo. "I'm too worked up from weeks without you."

"That's why you should put me in your bed."

"If I let you stay in my room, you will never sleep," he replies, pumping his dick. His thick mushroom tip keeps nudging my ass cheeks. "I will maul you at all hours."

"That is what I am here for," I sensually reply. "To be your slut."

"Shit," he groans as the barrier breaks, and he plucks my body back to his chest. "If you don't stop, I will fuck that hot, tight pussy until you cry, Abby."

When his lips course over my shoulder, I glance back to the feral animal I've waited for so long to meet. He is here with me now—cupping the weight of my breasts in his hands and pinching my nipples. His dismal agony is filled with treacherous despair as I attempt to navigate my way to his terrain.

"What's bothering you?"

"I know you will leave me."

"You should try me." Putting my hands on the arms of the chair, I slightly elevate, inciting his cock with my damp folds, baiting his molestation in my hollow. "Come out and play, Jynx."

He grabs the base of his cock and breeches the gate. My kingdom will fall to his arsenal. With a forceful ferocity, he thrusts in hard, impacting deep and sending a shiver through my spine.

"Take all of me," he demands, bucking up. "Take it all, bitch."

"God!" I scream as my body singes, smoldering around his shaft. "Don't stop!"

His hands drop to my hips as he uses my passage for his wretched thoughts. "You need me to hurt you, babygirl?"

"Yes, Daddy!" I beckon, calling upon his army to assault every last crevice in which I hide. "Rape me!"

JYNX

HER JUICES SLICK OVER MY THIGHS AS I REPEATEDLY RAM my dick inside of her vulnerable hole. I claim what should have been mine months ago. "I wanted to follow you at the wedding. I wanted to force myself on you then."

"But you've yet to do it."

"Because I know you will leave."

She doesn't respond as my demanding fingers strum at her clit, and I pulse with short bursts into her dew. "If you had done that," she moans, sliding her hands on the sides of my thighs. "I wouldn't be this drunk on you. I wouldn't want forever."

"Can you handle me that long?" I ask, pulling her head back and wrapping my hand around her throat. "Pretty big commitment you're asking for, little girl."

"I want all of it," she urges, attempting to move against me. "I want all of you."

"That's it," I coach as she rolls. I slow my movements, giving her the freedom to fly. All the while, I keep my palm around the delicate flesh of her neck. "Take my big dick like it's the only thing you've ever wanted and the last one you'll ever need."

I won't always welcome her assistance.

But I have never had the privilege and honor of claiming a virgin.

Especially one I'm thinking about handing over my last name to.

"You feel so good...this deep inside of me," she purrs, speeding up and screwing my dick like she means it. She is chasing her orgasm. Her sluicing pulse cannot lie. She's no longer dipping her toes in the water but diving in. Her body trembles against my chest as she nervously asks, "How am I doing?"

"You're fucking like a pro now."

She giggles as I stare at how beautiful she is against me. I have never paid this much attention to anyone. They were all nameless, faceless women offering a warm hole for my dick after I'd expressed my control for hours.

But Echo counts.

"Get up," I say, pushing her off of me.

With sudden tears in her eyes, she panics, "What did I do wrong?"

Taking her fingers, I pull her back, facing me. "Straddle me."

"Jynx," she whispers as I slow the pace and thrust in inch by inch. "What are you doing?"

"Something I've never done before."

She laughs, "Fucking face to face?"

"No," I mutter with a smile. "Making love to someone I'm in love with."

"You're shaking."

"I'm a little unacquainted with this," I confess my darkest recesses and skim my hands over her back. I grab the flesh of her ass in my palms and gently rock into her wetness. "It won't always be like this."

"I know." Her lips meet mine, and everything else ceases to matter. We're all lips and tongue in hurried, savage kisses. We part for a breath, and she says, "I am so in love with you."

"Are you going to marry me?"

She nods. "I am."

My hand moves her hair over her shoulder as I kiss her collar bone. "Do you promise if I ask…"

"I won't reject you," she interjects, blinking at me. "Not in a million years."

"Will you let me put my babies in your belly?"

"Yes," she hastily says. "Many many."

"… You're serious?"

"I am," she whispers, laying her hands on my shoulders and pivoting her hips around. "I want the whole fucked up package of Jynx Monroe."

"I adore you Echo Maines," I mutter, clasping my arms around her body. "Hold on."

I stand up, staying deep inside of her and walking to the bedroom.

I kick the door shut with my toe. "I guess the future Mrs. Monroe gets to stay in her Master's lair?"

"She damn sure does," I concede, laying her carefully on the bed. "Every night, for the rest of my life." Her supple legs tether around mine as I take serious strides inside of her drenched pussy. "God, I want you so bad."

"You should come inside of me."

I pause, not knowing if she can handle the depth of my perversion. "I don't know if I can and still be a gentleman," I admit, feeling like a failure. "It's not something I'm..."

"Fuck me like your whore then," she moans, arching up her hips. "Fuck that pussy hard. Make me cry." Without any warning, I hover over and clamp my teeth to her neck as I maim her body with my own. "Oh, my God...that's so hot!" She cries out, etching her claws painfully down my back—something shifts in her as she realizes what I need. "Stop! Stop! Don't hurt me!"

I bite harder as my hand slips around her neck. I stiffen my grip and release my snap, brimming with immoral nourishment. "I'm gonna fuck you up, bitch!"

"No, please!" She bellows, struggling against me. Her arms flail, punching her forearms against my popping guns. "Stop!"

My impactful moves punctuate, stabbing into her well like a sword as every ounce of her fight spurs on my atrocious plunder. My teeth clamp into the tender flesh again. I want her so fucking bad. She will be mine. She doesn't have a choice. I will keep her trapped in my house and heart, my sex kitten.

I release the clasp of my teeth and murmur, "You like the violence! Admit it!"

I snarl, showing my teeth as her eyes light up and she grins. "You have no idea what you're doing to me." She saturates around my aching cock, shuddering with ripples echoing in her walls. "Do it!"

"Jesus! Fucking Christ! I'm going to come inside of you!" Inside of her puddling warmth, I rapidly shoot as she clutches my ass cheeks. "Fuck, Ek!"

"That's it baby, slather me in your cum." Her fingers flutter over my sweat covered back as I lay on top of her and wait until my body relinquishes control. I never pull out; I fall out. "You can take me further, Master."

"That was fucking incredible," I admit, kissing her cheek. "Tell me I didn't hurt you."

"Not at all, but if you wouldn't mind, I'll take a nightly orgasm like that, for all of my days."

"Dear God, we're fucked up," I confide as she giggles beneath me. "We're going to conceive children doing that."

"We are," she concurs, kissing me. "And no one ever needs to know about our dirty little habit, Sir. It's my secret to keep. It's my secret to cherish. But you can play harder with me."

"That scares me."

"Take it all the way," she promises as I finally slip from her folds. "Bring your cruel monster, Jynx."

"This is remarkably unprofessional."

"Your inner rebel will love it."

33

EVOLUTION

ECHO

THE NEXT FEW WEEKS BROUGHT SWEEPING CHANGES. I took the position as his personal assistant, which was wonderful because it gave me something to do. But it was terrible because every day I watched the man I craved in freshly laundered shirts and slacks —*light on the starch*—disappear into the private office behind my desk. He always smelled the same with a woodsy musk aftershave that made my toes curl and thighs dampen.

His efforts did not go unnoticed, nor did mine concerning retributive attacks. I unpacked and bought outfits to taunt, distract, and cause as many indecent thoughts in his mind as he brought to mine.

This was war.

Not in a shed or on a farm—*but in an office, full of employees.*

Our relationship strengthened in a startlingly traditional way.

He didn't force his dirty secrets on me. We rarely engaged in any sexual activity. I did sleep in his room, but our nights involved curling up in bed with a movie or a crime show. We shared romantic late-night dinners, routinely walked the park, visited art museums, the zoo, and even attended a theater show. On the weekends, we went hiking, four-wheeling, or rafting.

We had fun.

And somehow, the six-three, thirty-seven-year-old man named Jynx was my new best friend.

I started to realize outside of the bedroom—*and his Dominion*—what an amazing catch he was. Everyone in the office loved him. Strangers at the grocery store and neighbors at the hotel who were also on extended stays seemed drawn to him as well. In social circles, he was not only the life of the party but expressed genuine concern for other's well-being, at least on the surface.

He may not have liked people, but they adored him.

His demeanor enthralled me.

And I fell more in love and lust with the guy running the scenic, desolate trail about fifty feet behind me. This out of the way nature preserve is one of our favorite places to explore.

I swiftly turn down the beaten path through the dense woods. Sweat clings to my skin on the hot and muggy late August morning, and the canopy of shade beneath the trees brings welcome relief. We have only taken this path one other time. My ponytail swishes against my back as I carefully trod down the slow descent to a creek.

I never see the rock, buried within the earth, when I tumble. Hitting the dirt, I giggle at my fuck up.

"Shit! Are you okay?" He flies to my aid, towering over in his sunglasses and ball cap.

"Aside from being an idiot?" I question, sitting up and spotting the blood trickling from my knee. It's not bad. "Fuck."

"Does it hurt?"

"Not really."

He tugs off his shirt, ripping a long strip of fabric at the hem. "It's not the cleanest, but it will do. We should be done."

"I'm not done until I get to the water."

He snarls. "You've got a truckload of determination," he admires, securing the makeshift bandage to my leg. "Thank God you don't have far to fall."

I snicker, "I bounce back fast."

"Have you always been this way?"

"Yeah," I say, smiling. "Since I can remember."

"Resilient little brat." His lips curl, and he offers his hands to help me up. "Go slow when you put weight on it."

"I'm fine, J," I assure, stretching and walking in a small circle. "Let's go! We're so close!"

He extends his hand. "Lead on. I love watching that ass shake."

We continue running another mile and a half, and I don't even think about the fabric tied around my knee. Thoughts of how gallant and charming and dirty he is take up all of my attention as I spot the creek in the distance. The slope of the land shifts to a steeper, more hazardous passage as the woods close in with foreboding darkness where only speckles of light creep through the branches.

I smile wide, knowing we made it. I deem the run a success as my shoes stop at the creek's edge. A current rushes past with a heavy flow as fish gather on the sides in still waters. I glance back, scanning the area for Jynx.

He's nowhere to be found.

Oh, my God. What if he fell?

He's massive—tall and broad—and certainly, I would've heard the thump.

I take a breath and spin to run back up the hill when I collide with the ground. His grim aura ensconces over me. With an ominous tone, he warns of the impending erotically dark dance. I'm in quite the quagmire. "You shouldn't be out here running alone, pretty girl."

I scream and flail, trying to find leverage beneath his rigid frame, which is almost pointless. He spreads my thighs fast, leaving my loose-fitting shorts on, and rams his hard cock deep inside of me.

"God! No!" I cry out, striking his glistening biceps. "Don't hurt me, please!"

Thrust after thrust, he claims what is his as I howl and fight. My feet slip against the soil. His palm covers my mouth as he assaults my wetness. His corruption confiscates my every thought. My heart pounds with absolute desire to have this man, who understands the skewed parts of me like no other.

"You should never have been out here alone, dressed like that."

I'm wearing shorts and a sweat-wicking tank top. It's not like I'm gallivanting through the forest in skimpy panties, but I play along because this is what we do. I keep struggling, wiggling, and providing a challenge.

He cannot find the rhythm to come.

I make the best moves I can, on the fly, unrehearsed.

We are impromptu in our love affair with my sinfully delicious unwilling portrayals.

He gets off on it, and I do too.

This isn't sweet and tender lovemaking in nature, but a furious battle with lines drawn. I trust that he'll never intentionally hurt me, but after this scuffle, I will have bruises to be proud of—I earn the markings, wounds, and scars of his volatile passion.

I have never had a gift I treasured so much.

He finally releases my mouth, and I manage to scurry out from under him. Before I can run, he grabs my ankle, pinning my hands and securing my body down.

He's got me now.

I know it; he knows it.

His teeth clamp to my neck as I beg, "Do whatever you want, just let me live…"

It's twisted and fucked up and wrong.

But so damn right.

"I'm gonna fuck you up, slut" he roars, driving his cock inside of me again as I feel the waves of an orgasm rock through me. I close my eyes as his grunts become louder, and his pumps evolve to a primitive state. "God, your pussy is so tight. So fucking wet. Yes, fuck my dick, baby....fuck it so good!"

He comes—hard, holding me down and forcing himself upon me.

And like the curtain dropping on a performance, his monster vanishes as quickly as he surfaced. His gentleman returns, releasing my hands and staying inside of me. He gently caresses my cheeks. "I love you so fucking much, Echo."

No apologies are necessary.

No forgiveness is needed.

"You're so bad," I whisper, grinning from ear to ear. "And I will never get enough of you—*of this with you.*"

"What if I really hurt you?" he softly asks, falling out and yanking his shorts back over his package. "Will you recover? Will you bounce back?"

"Take me as far as you can," I say as he kneels between my legs and examines the wound on my knee. "I know the safeword."

"Promise me you will use it," he tenderly says. His three modes—the disingenuous asshole, the gentle soul rarely shown, and the monster never seen in the light of day—form one chaotic Jynx. "Maybe it's time to have a talk."

HOURS LATER, WE SIT IN BED WITH MY LAPTOP. WITH HIS head on my shoulder, Jynx says, "Just so you know, I haven't ever condoned the idea of discussing sex in the bedroom."

"You've never had a relationship," I rebuke, clicking on the link to the video site. "How would you possibly know if this is good or bad behavior?"

"You have a point."

"The discussions you have with one-night stands are more negotiation for the evening, not longterm viable solutions," I say as my list of 4,291 favorites pops up. "You want inside of my mind? Pick away."

"Jesus Christ," he mumbles as I hand the laptop to him. "You weren't kidding. Define your limits and fantasies," he demands, thumbing through the list. He reads every title but never plays a video. "Please."

"Help me," I urge, feeling a bit overwhelmed.

"Obviously, being tied up is a huge turn on." Pulling my knees in, I blush and confess, "Any restraint."

"What about the couple videos with women?"

"I think it's common to wonder about having sex with another woman," I admit, trying to hide. "I wouldn't even mind watching you control a scene with another woman, but I don't think I could handle you having sex with her."

"There's a whole batch of videos with several guys."

"Yeah, but I'm kind of picky. There is a fine line between hot and eww."

He chuckles. "I will never share you sexually with a man. It just won't happen. I can't handle it," he honestly confides the hard limit for him as he continues to scroll down. "I'll kill someone."

"You have a very high regard for what is between my legs considering you enjoy trespassing like a vulture picking apart a carcass."

He laughs, but his expression turns serious. "I respect you as a woman, including your right to have ravishment fantasies. My job, as your boyfriend and lover, is to enable your growth. I never want to hinder or cause you harm. I have the umbrella of consent from you, but I will push your boundaries, which is why we're having this talk."

My hand brushes over his as I argue, "You were on the border of becoming a rapist..."

"But I never did it," he contends, licking his lips. "You gave me your virginity. And no man, on my watch, will ever breach that hallowed ground. It belongs to me." He grabs my pussy hard. "I will defend it if need be because I plan on putting my children in you. You are sacred, Abigail. Your pussy is my sanctuary."

"Gosh..."

"I don't take the responsibility of what happens to your body lightly. I respect the entire scene, even if I falter. I never liked the idea of violating anyone and that is probably why I never did it. But it doesn't change the compulsion or the craving. When you fight me, my mind finds that dark place deep within where the demons live. I won't lie, it turns me on more than anything else, but never forget, you matter to me. I'm in love with you—*all of you.*"

"But there is a point where you lose control."

"I don't ever let myself become so lost in the act that I won't abide by hearing my name from your lips. You pull the plug and I pull out."

I lean forward, slightly turning, and sitting cross-legged. "And what if I decide I need a more loving Jynx? What do I do then?"

"We'll deal with that when we get there," he replies, stroking my cheek. "Do you want that now?"

"I want to know that it's not out of the question. Not that I want such, but I need to know you're open to the idea of expansion. I don't want to get locked into one way. I want a constantly changing playing field."

"Then we have to work toward that," he contends, setting my laptop on the nightstand and hitting play on one of the videos. "I'm not done."

"Keep it as long as you need," I offer, pulling back the sheet. I trace my finger along with the shadow of his cock trapped beneath the plaid pajama pants. "Dissect my psyche."

Bravely, I tug his pants down, and as promised, he accepts me as the moans from the video heighten the tension between us. My lips soar over the tip, sucking his shaft purposefully to an erection. My mouth drifts low.

"God, suck my balls, baby..."

I lick and slurp his sack as my hand strokes his cock. I straddle over, guiding him to my entrance. "You're so fucking hot, Jynx."

"What are you doing?"

"Fucking you," I moan, pulling off my shirt as his fingers skim over my breasts. "Taking what is mine. You're not the only one with expressed ownership. I may not have your virginity, but this dick belongs to me now, Jynx. And it is sacred too."

His eyes convey a desperate yearning. He wants to grow and understand. "I want you, Echo. If that means sweet and tender or rough and hard, we will figure it the fuck out."

I ride along his ridge, welcoming the intense fullness as my core burns with wanton lust. "I can never have enough of you."

His hands drop to my hips, and he thrusts from below. "Take it baby, make yourself come on my dick."

I let go.

And so does he.

34

STAY THE NIGHT X LIFE

Jynx

"I DON'T LIKE THEM," AXEL ANNOUNCES IN MY OFFICE, midday Friday afternoon. Everyone else in the world hates Mondays. I loathe Friday because everyone wants shit done before five o'clock like I'm some sort of miracle worker. Like I can one-man reprogram the entire Dower system, which even though better, is still antiquated as fuck. I've got about a dozen people wanting to talk to me, and Axel whining about heaven only knows what.

Pulling the end of the pen from my lip, I ask, "What are you on about?"

"They're no better than Dad."

"Probably not," I admit, rocking in my chair. "Wait, what do you mean?"

"I think, regardless of what they said to you, that they're going to fire our people, starting with Wang's group."

"Why do you think that?"

As I am rocking in my chair, he asks, "Honestly?"

"Yeah."

"Because I overheard Eddie talking to some dweeb down in accounts receivable in the restroom." *Great. My brother was taking a dump and eavesdropping.* "So I followed them to the stairwell where Eddie confirmed to Mike that they planned on laying off the new Monroe employees as soon as the main team leaves."

"Back up...you were taking a shit..."

"No," he laughs, barreling over. "I was jerking off because that hot little brunette, Elisabeth, in..."

"I know who Elisabeth is," I interject—because she (and her enormous rack) works in integration, and I was doing the same thing, though not in the men's restroom, five months ago. "Fuck."

I'm not sure if the image of him jerking off is better or worse.

"Yeah, we handed over several thousand employees because you didn't want to run Peacock," he replies, tucking his hand under his chin. "I'm not trying to put any extra burden on you, but everything you're doing is a wasted effort. Your deal was with Theodore, but he is handing over the business to Eddie."

"... Which means my deal is belly up," I mumble, sideswiped. "Fuck!"

I stand and bolt for the door as he asks, "Where are you going?"

"To talk to Teddy."

"You shouldn't do that," Axel warns, grabbing my arm. I glance at his blue eyes—*the same color as mine*—fearless as he ever has been.

We fight. We forget. We move on.

He knows not to push me but does it anyway. I won't deny my brother can be a prissy bitch, and a dickhead rolled into one toxic egg roll, but he isn't lying to me about this, which means Theodore did—unless he doesn't know.

I bust out the door, and Echo perks up with a concerned look. "Fuck," I overhear Axel's mumble as I wait for the elevator. I unbutton my sleeves and roll the cuffs. I glance over at Ek, gawking, and I quickly arch a suggestive brow. She blushes and bites her lip.

I step on alone and lean against the wall. I don't want any of it. I only want her, but I'm not the guy to walk away—and Goddammit, sometimes I wish I was. I don't want to stop at the wreck, hold the dying animal, or even save the girl from herself—but I have to because it's who I am. I must accept my caring nature even if I hate it—I'm an asshole with a heart.

Let me out of here.

Let my monster free.

I take a breath and step out onto the fifth floor. I smile at Delores, and she waves me through with a wink. I open his door to find the older man sitting at his desk. He doesn't bother to acknowledge me.

"We need to have a talk."

"Can we do this later tonight?" Theodore says, staring at the crossword puzzle. "I need another word for revolt."

"Mutiny."

"No," he replies, blinking at the screen. "Starts with R."

"… Rebellion?"

"Shorter."

"… Rebel?"

"Perfect!" He booms, smiling as I nod and walk out. "Take care, Jeremiah."

"You too," I reply with a side-eyed glance, walking, dumfounded out to Delores desk. "How long has he been…"

"His dementia is worse some days than others. Today is the far end of the bad spectrum. I'm not even sure why Eddie brought him in," she informs, rolling her eyes and rubbing her lips together. "Theo had bloodwork this morning and couldn't take his meds. Eddie is taking over in a month because of the decline in his father's health."

Eddie knew when we made the deal.

I lean, abruptly placing my hands on her desk, and staring at her big brown eyes. Her long lashes blink at me. "And the deal with Peacock?"

"Eddie instigated it because he didn't want to compete against you," she whispers as her full purple lips sympathetically pucker. Delores Jones is a beyond attractive middle-aged diva. Typically, I don't go for the type—*professionally or personally*—but she pulls it off like a goddess. "And I want to keep my job."

I can't do this.

But I don't have a choice.

I must do this.

"Do you want an upgrade?" I suggest, knowing the shit I'm thinking about doing crosses many lines. "You help me and I'll give you a place at Peacock."

With a hint of sarcasm, she counters, "Working for you?"

"For me or Wang."

"You're putting Wang in charge?" she whispers, tilting closer to me. "Wendlin Rile is almost as good as you." She winks. "What do you need?"

"Personnel files."

"… All of them?" she queries, and I nod. "I do this for you, and you ship me down the river to work under Eddie, I will skin your pretty hide, boy."

"Yes, Queen D."

"Ohhhh, Honeychild! We're a match made in heaven!" She smirks, typing with her three-inch talons. "That's what I'm talking about. They're sending to your remote email now."

"Thank you."

"I want a relocation package," she negotiates like a capable opponent. "And three weeks of vacation, first year."

"How about a company car?"

"Yes! Something fast!" She silently claps her hands and grins wide. "Houston?"

"Yes, Ma'am, you're moving as my executive assistant," I say, walking toward the elevator. "Thank you."

"Hey, Jynx?" she yells, and I pivot back. "Thanks for the chance."
"Anytime, pretty lady."

"LET ME GET THIS STRAIGHT," AXEL SAYS IN MY OFFICE AT
nine o'clock later that same day. "You're going to steal his talent and
hire Wang to keep them in line?"

"I'm only hiring the best," I reply as Echo giggles on the sofa,
making a list of possible candidates. "I can't let Eddie destroy that
many lives. And Wang is more than qualified."

"But you don't even want the business," he argues in the chair
across from me. "That is why we're selling our people and clients off
to Dower."

"Things change. His contract will never hold. Our specific agreement was between Theodore Dower and J.A. Monroe; he isn't competent. Therefore, it is null and void. And I can find countless witnesses
to prove that if I legally need to. As for being a hero, it's not about
that. It never was. It's about facts. Teddy isn't functioning on all cylin-
ders, and I believe Eddie is using his father as a figurehead, a fucking
puppet, to run both businesses into the ground."

"You don't have to be the hero, Jynx."

"Yeah," Echo chimes in as I stare at her beauty under the dim
office lights. "He does. If you paid any attention to your brother at all,
you would see that he is a compassionate, empathetic soul. If people
from Peacock, former Monroe employees, lose their jobs, Jynx will
wear that like a scar on his soul forever."

Axel doesn't react to her statement. "Why would Eddie want to
lose Dower?"

"That," I reply, tapping my pencil on the desk. "I don't know. But
my best guess is—he's talking to a bigger fish about buying it."

"I'm going to eat, can I bring you two crazy kids anything?"

"I already ordered Chinese for pick up in an hour," Echo responds,
not even looking up. Axel glances at me and nods with—*Damn, you did
good, bro.*

"Ms. Maines?" Axel says, approaching my girl. "I want to apologize for my teenage pranks."

"I accept your apology, but if you do it again, I will kick your ass," she says as I smirk, holding back a laugh. "As your future sister-in-law, I suggest you straighten your act up."

"Yes, Ma'am."

Wow.

"And Axel, keep your dick out of anyone less than twenty-five."

"But..." he argues, and I chuckle.

"It doesn't need to make sense," she replies, moving the stack of papers to the long table on the wall. "There are exceptions to every rule. And I'm Jynx's one."

"Fair enough." With his hands tucked in his pockets, he bows slightly and heads for the door. "Goodnight, you two! Congratulations on Peacock and the upcoming nuptials!"

I stare at Echo in the black pencil skirt and pink blouse. Her hair is pulled into a bun—formal this morning, but with the past few hours of work, tendrils fell around her face, softening her graceful edges even more. "You just told my brother that I was going to be Mr. Maines."

"I did," she says, smiling. "I wholeheartedly believe everything you've said to me, Mr. Monroe."

"Lock the door."

She strides over and flips the latch. "Anything else, Master Jynx?"

Stroking several days worth of whiskers, I grin. "Turn off the light." She clicks the switch, and the glow of the skyline pours shadows into my office. "Anything else?"

"Take off your lovely blouse, Ms. Maines."

She runs her hands over the dainty buttons and walks closer. "Should I hike my skirt and bend over the desk now?"

"Yes." I lick my lips as she moves to my side and leans over. My mouth waters at the sight of black lace panties framed by garters and stockings. "Damn, you know how to wrap a present."

"If I don't enjoy this, can I file a complaint with HR?"

"Oh, yeah, baby," I say, swatting her ass.

"God!" Her lip trembles as she moans, "Fuck me, Boss."

"Are you happy now?" I ask, unbuckling my belt and pulling it through the loops. "Be honest with me."

"About Peacock?"

"Yes."

"I'm very happy," she slowly mutters, eyeing the belt. "At everything you're thinking about doing."

"This is going to sting."

"I know." Her voice hitches. "Do it anyway."

"I wasn't asking for encouragement," I growl, snapping the leather against her ass. "I was doing it regardless."

She sensually whispers, "... Jynx?"

"Yes, babygirl?"

"The panties are crotchless."

I spank her even harder for being a naughty little thing.

With rapid, successive strikes, I deliver the pain to send her flying, soaring into the flickering starry skies and grounding out the craziness of my day.

I need her, and she needs me.

"Are you creaming those thighs, Darlin'?"

She arches her hips back, offering a delectable view of sultry legs and taut ass encased in nothing more than a playboy's delight. The four-inch stilettos aren't hurting either.

"You should explore and find out for yourself."

My hand grabs the round curve of her ass, rubbing and kneading. She'll be bruised by morning, unable to sit down comfortably—every grimace and wince from her lips will fuel my throbbing erection.

We never stop.

We are cyclical, unstoppable.

"I heard that!" she yelps as my zipper glides down. I laugh, understanding how the nuisances matter. I rub the serrated metal edge against her ass. "I know what's coming!"

"Me...in about five minutes...if you don't stop rocking those hips like a cat in heat."

"Fuck me, J...stick your dick in my tight, wet hole and give it all to me."

I shake my head. "This is about to get sloppy as fuck."

"Yes!" She bounces, accidentally bumping into the tip and using her newfound knowledge of my exact location to grind her ass against me. "Make me dirty!"

"Dear God, I'm going to hell for this."

"Not without me!"

Placing my hand on the middle of her back, I ease in nice and slow. "Are you pulling your precious car into the garage?"

"No," I snicker, seating deep inside of her flood and dropping my hands to her hips. I pound her good for a minute or two. She groans and moves back to meet each impactful marker. Papers scatter onto the floor. Pens roll away—*it's neither clean nor neat.* I pull out fast and twirl her around to me before picking her up and plopping her ass down on my desk. *This desk will never be the same.* "I'm flooring it all the way across the country for a girl I cannot get enough of..."

"Jesus, don't make me fucking cry!"

I laugh, thrusting inside of her puddle again. Her legs wind around my body like a spider consuming its prey.

The prey is me.

I stalked her to offer myself as a sacrifice.

And no one needs to know.

I pray she feasts in my love for the rest of her days.

Fucking her on my desk is part of that.

Our bodies slam against one another, finding the greater purpose to it all. And without warning, my kinky scene turns spiritually tantric —*I can't be without this girl.*

Her brilliant, luminous vibe sheds my obscure tenebrosity.

"If I asked you to marry me in Vegas in two weeks, what would you say?"

"I'd say, I'll need a ring, Mr. Monroe."

Get me out of here.

Before she sets my monster free.

THE THREAT

ECHO

A WEEK LATER, I'M IN A RENTAL CAR WITH JYNX RIDING TO Tucson for the weekend. Friday night traffic is bumper-to-bumper as we finally leave Phoenix, but I sit quietly, using the time to reflect on my life since I posted the ad. Red taillights blur in my vision as the upheavals of the past year capsize any hope of a delightful journey.

He could have been any man willing to harm, but this one-man snuck into my life. The longer I think about it, the more peculiar it seems that one of the world's unluckiest girls would strike gold with Jeremiah Abaddon Monroe.

What were the odds?

He's either the grand conductor of a masterful orchestration or a brilliantly diabolical, well-packaged man with a criminal mindset. Neither one is easy to digest, and my belly turns queasy.

This man wants to have children with me.

Is he everything I hoped for in a husband?

Have I been blind to the truth as we explored the kinship found in the kinky nooks of my mind?

I push the fear away because conjuring in my head doesn't make the imagery real. I'll play my part until his lies run dry or he loves me enough to drop on one knee.

I don't seek the truth.

I found the perfect man with his voracious, dark appetite, and lost myself.

Air fills my lungs with a deep breath as he side-glances checking on me. I politely smile, crossing my fingers that my eyes fake the pleasantries one more time. I crave fleeing the scene, not that I ever would. I contemplate leaving. I dream about escaping his grasp. I question every little thing until I'm sick and miserable.

And I hide it all.

He's been discreetly sweet-talking Dower employees into working for Peacock, proving he isn't beyond causing strife. He will do whatever it takes for the good of people, even a girl posting a stupid rape ad. He's yet to confront Eddie with his suspicions, but that doesn't surprise me. He avoids the battle, saving souls from his fury.

Wang is super excited and already in Texas scouting possible locations. Jynx doesn't want to use the building from Sal and Deacon for the headquarters.

He claims it is our space.

His hand is on my thigh as we fly down the highway. He's wearing sunglasses, a t-shirt, and jeans—sexy and dangerous as fuck. I've grown accustomed to his confident air in slacks and dress shirts. Today's attire sets off an emotional blizzard, sending me back to a rural farm in South Carolina where he was a calculated monster I chose to escape my life with. Maybe he played me.

With a shiver silencing the demons, I randomly blurt out, "What are you doing with the peacocks?"

He tilts his head and glares over the top rim of his shades. "Depends on you."

"... Me?"

"Yeah," he says, exiting the highway. "If you like Texas and want to move there, I'll relocate the cocks." He winks.

"I hope you plan on taking the fowl too," I rebuke, glancing around at the new surroundings. "Or you'll have some angry fucking cocks."

He laughs. "You've never been to Tucson."

"I've never been to Texas either," I add, smiling. His carefree attitude makes me happy, and we have fun, *so how can it be that this guy possesses deranged merciless thoughts and still manages to be this charming for this long?* "How do you know?"

"Because you're very curious about your surroundings. Whenever you're someplace new, you get this excited glimmer in your eye. I can't wait to show you everything in my world."

"I'm a little nervous. I don't know what's wrong with me," I admit, rubbing his hand. "You mentioned taking me to the club. I'm worried about being sized up and seen as less than. I'm afraid I'll never be good enough."

"You shouldn't feel that way," he assures, but his words do little to calm me. "You don't have to attend the meeting."

My lips contort from a smile to a frown to an undecided anxious sawing of my teeth against my pouty swollen lips. "You want to put me on display before people who have done this for years."

"I don't mind parading you around, but it's not necessary for me. If you want to go to the club, I'll take you. You need to remember, everyone started somewhere, Echo. No one expects you to know how to do everything. Be the submissive you are for me. Hell, you were great under Deacon's care."

That's just it—Deacon cared.

I cannot imagine all Masters come preloaded with human decency.

"He was smooth though," I argue, struggling with the idea of gussying up in fetish wear to sit by his side at a business meeting. I'm not a fool. This isn't a black-tie affair; others will be scantily dressed as well. Though I'm not sure, that makes it any better. "Not everyone is Deacon Cruz."

"I won't argue that," he says, backing down. I hope he understands this isn't about him—*but them.* "But you do not have to go."

"But you're going…"

"Because I'm meeting with one of the primary investors in Peacock," he says, clenching my hand. "You don't have to join me."

"If I don't go, I look rude or worse, uninterested in your work."

Or I'm jealous of girls who are more than capable of stealing what is mine.

I fought for him—Not them.

Master Jynx is mine.

I must defend my base.

And yes, I do mean THAT base.

I've never had a boyfriend. My itch to be his arm candy companion is fierce. I want to be the girlfriend he shows off because I'm worth it. I long to shout to the world that we're in love and doing this—*he and I*—despite all the differences, but to do that, I must find the courage to buck up and be present in all areas of his life.

The desire to be his everything manifests from caring for the farm to organizing the Peacock clients, and I yearn to present myself as his slave in a public setting. I also understand that he is serious about transitioning to an active member of Reckless Rebellion and that will put my ass in the bitch seat. I must deal with that too. But one thing at a time.

I want to have the complete Jynx Monroe package, but fuck if it's not hard.

I've never seen myself as a sexual being, and going to the club comes with certain sensual promiscuity. Engaging in our kink behind closed doors is one thing; putting ourselves out there—*presenting our D/s dynamic*—is closely akin to exhibitionism. And I'm not sure I could actually do that in a room full of complete strangers. A few of his brothers? Sure. An unknown crowd? I doubt it.

With clammy hands, I whisper, "Will I be expected to listen to other Dominants?"

"Not unless they ask for my permission," he informs with mature guidance—using the same voice that could talk me through anything. "You're my collared submissive," he reminds me as I breathe a sigh of relief. "You came to me about Deacon. Not the other way around."

"I'll think about it."

"What are we eating for dinner tonight?" He segues away from the uncomfortable discussion. I grin wide. "Tacos it is. Do you want traditional Tex-Mex or can we go out on a limb with some fusion?"

With my mind and heart in overdrive, I point out, "You sound so... taco technical."

"I'm a technical kind of guy. And I take tacos very seriously."

I blush as his eyes, which say so much about the unspoken flirtation, immerse into my soul. "We're not having this conversation, Jynx."

"What?" He chuckles, knowing he has me. "I'm a techie and a taco connoisseur now. There was no innuendo."

"Maybe not from your lips, but your pretty blue eyes say otherwise." His mischievous smile spurs on my laughter as I clench his hand. He parks the car at a seedy-looking dive. "This looks beneath you."

"Remember who I am."

"... A pervert with a pain fetish?"

Shaking his head, he exits the vehicle and warns, "I swear I'm spanking you when we get to the hotel."

"Yum. Tacos."

JYNX

"HOW IS THE SHARK?"

"Freaking delicious," she brags, offering a bite to me. I kiss her hand and take a small nibble as she challenges, "You can do better."

"If I do better, you'll get mad."

344 | KAILEE REESE SAMUELS

"Bite my fucking taco, J." I snap my teeth around the shell and steal a mammoth mouthful. "You just ate a quarter of my taco!"

I point at her as I chew and swallow. She gloats, proud of herself. "I told you! It doesn't matter that you ordered four and will never eat all of that."

"I might, they're really good!"

"You'll eat them after midnight when I'm finished having my way with you," I counter, grinning. She squeals, and I bump her leg. "I've fed you tacos for three months, I know how you are—*possessive*."

"Sounds like someone else I know," she giggles, wiping her mouth. "What are the odds you would let another Dominant borrow me?"

"Slim to none," I rudely garble, covering my mouth. Some things must be said immediately. Fuck manners. After wiping my mouth, I clasp my hands together and instruct, "You're young. I understand there is a certain curiosity with things like the rope, and I'm willing to allow you to safely explore those avenues with my presence under a Dominant I trust. But you—*going off with any other Dom alone?*—will never happen. You will not be borrowed or lent out or passed around —*ever*."

"Because you don't trust me."

Gulping back my beer, I quickly reply, "No, because I don't trust them. That was my cousin. Different argument."

"Would you let me go off with Axel?"

"Axel doesn't do this," I mutter, scowling. "Would you even want to go off with Axel?"

"No, but that isn't the point," she implores, laying her hands on the table. "I want to know that you trust me to make decisions."

"You're not independent in this realm." I glance around the relatively empty restaurant. "Your collar means that I make the decisions concerning your body."

She scoffs, "Overlord."

I smirk. "Not at all. But I won't stand by and watch you get hurt, either. I prefer protective over feudal dictator."

"Asshole," she teases.

I lean closer and growl, "I'm taking you to the hotel. Bathing you.

Tying you up. Spanking your ass over my lap. And fucking all of your holes until you cry my name, bitch."

Her eyes spark. "Keep talking dirty to me. You'll return the car with stains." She bites into her taco as I attempt to remain unaffected, which is almost pointless with my dick pounding at the word, *overlord*. She rapidly shifts gears with no warning. "How is the Ahi?"

She is hell on my transmission.

Grind the gears, youngun'.

Why be easy on the fly when we can jerk around?

"Amazing," I say, scooping a decent-sized bite into the spoon. "Eat my tuna, baby."

Her slender fingers shield her mouth in an attempt to hide the laughter I bring. "You're so bad!"

"I did nothing," I innocently remark, taking a swig of beer. "You like being with me?"

"I do," she boasts, grabbing my hand. "A lot."

"I like you too," I say, leaning closer and kissing her lips. "A whole fucking lot."

I've become a doting boyfriend.

I'm not sure how the fuck it happened.

One minute I was all about one-night stands, never going for round two, playing the field, and now, I'm seriously considering putting a ring on this girl's finger and begging her on my knees to take my last name.

Bubbly-and-spry-fifteen years my junior-can't get enough of this girl ransacked my world, unapologetically stole my heart, and captivated every ounce of my attention.

"How far is the hotel?"

"Across town," I reply, picking at my plate. "So, what does the dream wedding look like for Echo Maines?"

Her expression blossoms like a spring garden where petals cradle thick and heavy morning dew. "Don't laugh."

Setting my fork down, I assure, "I won't laugh."

She sucks in a breath and reveals, "I always wanted a beach wedding."

I smirk, rubbing my scruff, as my brows wiggle with appreciation. "… It just so happens, I know a fabulous location." With a deep crimson flush spreading on her cheeks, she tucks her chin low to her chest, but I refuse to let her shy away. I gently run a finger to lift her face. "If you want a wedding on a beach—any beach, mine or another's sands, you will have it. I promise you."

"Jynx…" she whispers, blinking. "If you want to get hitched at the justice of the peace, we can do that. Or even in Vegas."

"I only mentioned Vegas to see your reaction."

"You're an ass."

"I'm aware," I laugh, holding her hand. "But I want to give you everything, Ek."

"Sunset. Beach wedding. White dress. White suit. Barefoot. Beautiful."

"Wow," I mutter. "You really have this down. Keep going."

"Platinum wedding bands. Honeymoon someplace simple. Maybe even the beach house."

"How many people at the wedding?"

"Small, but formal, elegant, sexy."

With a dastardly grin, I inquire, "And the groom?"

"He loves me just like you."

36

A GILDED MIRAGE

Jynx

Staring at the fading sun, I wait for my date to emerge from the bathroom. She's been dolling up for over two hours. I consider busting down the door in my casual business attire—slacks, dress shirt, and sport coat.

I need to secure my place in Texas, beyond my cousin agreeing to partner up with me. This meeting at the fetish club will do that. Madame Tilda's club is a far more controlled environment than a strip club, not to mention we both know her quite well, and security is always rigorously monitored.

348 | KAILEE REESE SAMUELS

I hear the door open, but I hold back for a moment, giving her the time and space she needs to adjust. I'm shocked she even decided to come with me.

She whispers, "Jynx..."

"Holy fuck," I mumble, eyeing the sex kitten with awe. "Where did you get that outfit?"

"I ordered it with someone's help," she says, winking. "... Do you like it? I can't decide if I feel sexier than ever before or if I should take up streetwalking as a second career."

"You look fucking amazing—angelic and perfect." I twirl my finger, and she spins like a ballerina in a jewelry box before me.

The absolute brat shaped for my beast.

"Say something," she begs.

Her long, curled locks are pinned into a messy bun with wisps falling, teasing, around her beautifully made-up face. "Again. Slower."

"You're driving me nuts."

My eyes scan over the diamond collar around her neck and sheer, loose sparkling blouse revealing an intricately embroidered black and red bra. The pleated white and black short skirt leads to thigh-high lace and mesh black stockings down her feet trapped within a sexy pair of Victorian-style boots. "How tall are the heels?"

"Seven inches."

"Jesus, Echo...you look hot as sin." I rub my palm over my face. " We're not making it out of the hotel."

"Oh! To make it out of the hotel, I have this."

"That's not exactly what I meant," I snicker.

She conceals her schoolgirl uniform with a tapered red gothic cloak. "Am I alright, *Daddy?*" She winks.

"You look incredible."

"I can't go into this club looking like I have years of experience because I don't. I'm a twenty-two-year-old college student. I hope I'm good enough to meet your business associate."

"You're more than enough for me."

With a hint of panic in her voice, she asks, "Will I be out of place in this?"

"Not because of the outfit," I reply, grabbing my jacket and taking her hand before she has the chance to chicken out. "But because you're the woman the other submissive want to be and the Dominants want to take home for the night."

I glance over at her as we walk toward the elevator. I'm accustomed to her in heels, but these are significantly higher, elevating her stature and position beside me. We step onto the elevator, and she lays her head on my shoulder.

"I'm so scared."

"I know," I reassure, peering down. "But you'll be fine."

"How long will this take?"

"At the most, eight hours."

The doors open, and I latch my fingers in her hand. "Why eight?"

"Tilda's closes at four."

"Shit," she mutters as we stroll through the hotel lobby. "I can't do this…"

"Jynx!" I hear my brother's voice and tense up. I do a one-eighty with Echo by my side. His eyes flare with intrigue over her boner-inducing outfit. "Are you leaving tomorrow?"

"Yes, I'm going back home to deal with some things at the farm."

"Where should I go?" Unable to keep his eyes off of my girl, he asks, "Home or Texas with Wang?"

"That's up to you."

"I'll catch a flight to Texas tomorrow and go help Wang," he volunteers, patting my shoulder. "Have a good night! And Ek, you look fanfuckingtastic!"

"Thank you." She blushes as he walks off. "Why is he here?"

"Because he had meetings yesterday and today, bringing Peacock to a place of completion."

"Tonight is the final celebration," she guesses, muttering, as we walk to the parking lot. "It solidifies the merger."

"Pretty much," I say, opening her door and praying she doesn't ask for more details. "All the best deals happen when surrounded by hot young things."

ECHO

HALF AN HOUR LATER, WE'RE DRIVING DOWN A DESERTED road as my hands shake, and I text Bran. He has a buyer for the house and wants to know if I can help him pack up our childhood home because he hasn't spoken to our parents in two years. He doesn't want to do it alone.

Realizing what he said, I huff, "You don't like hot young things..."

Doubts creep in my veins crippling my heart's expanse.

"No," he corrects. "I said I don't like taking them to the dungeon because they tend to not listen."

I rub my glossed lips together. "... Do I?"

"Better than most," he says as a large building with golden lights shines like a temple—*his holy house of worship*—in the distance.

"That's it," I mumble, trying not to freak. "What the hell am I doing?"

"Yes, it is," he maintains, gripping my hand and speeding toward my eternal damnation. "You need to calm down."

"I can't," I whimper as he turns into the packed lot. "Oh, my God, there are so many people here."

We wait in line for the valet. "Ekky, look at me." I can't. I know this isn't right. These people are not mine. I belong in a quiet library pouring overly scholarly texts until my eyes bleed, not dressed up like a hooker on Halloween. His finger eases under my chin, demanding my attention. "You'll be fine. We'll be fine. Do you trust me?"

"Yes, but..."

"Listen to me," he says, calming my nerves. "I'm not leaving you alone."

"What if I need to go to the bathroom?"

He grins. "Then I will take you and wait outside the door. You're such a babygirl."

I sulk. "Don't insult me."

"It wasn't an insult. It was a compliment," he replies, staring at me. "You're fresh, innocent, and mine. Own this moment."

"I don't know how."

The valet waves him forward, and he pulls up. Our doors open as things start happening way too fast for my comprehension. Before getting out, he says, "Fake it."

Like faking it is so easy. I take a deep breath. "Pull your shit together, Abs. It's about to go down."

A rhythmic beat rumbles from my feet through my core as I take Jynx's hand and step out. "Are you being my brave girl and leaving the cloak in the car?"

"I am," I reply, tossing it in the backseat. He offers his arm, and I slip my fingers around his elbow. I wish the skirt were more Amish-style, skidding along the pavement and not showing off peeks of my ass cheeks with every sway of my hips.

"Hello, Mr. Monroe," the attendant says inside of the door. She fastens a black band onto his wrist. "Who is your lovely companion?"

"This is Pea."

He snarls at me. "Welcome to Madame Tilda's, Pea," she warmly greets. "If you need anything, look for someone in one of the bright neon yellow shirts."

"Thank you," I reply, staring at my red wristband as we walk down a slight incline to two double doors. "Why the red?"

"You're a collared sub; white is an available—*uncollared*—sub," he shouts, pulling a red lace masquerade mask from his pocket. "It's Saturday," he replies, placing it on me. "A great night to experience this."

"Is this required?"

"Unless your Dom takes it off."

The door opens.

And so does every fantasy I ever dreamed.

WITH MY HAND SWEATING AGAINST HIS PALM, WE WALK through the exclusive member's only club. The noise thunders through my entire body, feet to fingertips, as a hostess escorts us to the second-tier. The lights project whirling, dynamic flashes of white.

We skirt past several tables, but a woman in a black full body catsuit, gyrating with all of her curves, ensnares my focus. I search for a red or white wristband but am taken aback to see her wearing a black one as we move past to a table in the far corner where a man waits, alone, in a suit.

I'm not ignorant. I know women can be Dominant, but the notion breeches the levee as I imagine submitting on my knees to her every desire. I shove the thought aside, refusing to pay it any more attention. I have my Master and he is the only one for me.

Jynx pulls out my chair like a perfect gentleman. I awkwardly sit at the end, staring down at the table as the two men face one another. I feel the heat of his gaze flowing through my skin. I want to plunge my body into an ice bath.

The stranger extends his arm toward me and lifts my chin. "Head up, beautiful."

"Sorry."

He shakes Jynx's hand from across the table, and while I find it rather odd that he didn't stand, I think nothing about it. "I'm pleased you're finally coming back to your family."

"It's time," Jynx says with a humble tone. "The past is in the past, but I don't think for a minute that everyone will be happy to see me."

"Probably not," the man agrees as I note his well-kept hands. They're pampered, unfit to work on an engine, with slim knuckles and long fingers. They appear soft and manicured. He's handsome, older than Jynx, with slicked-back black hair and an imposing, strict focus. "If it were a different time and place, I'd tell you to avoid it."

"I understand, but I need your resources available to me."

"Don't let mistakes happen again," he sternly warns. "There won't be a second chance."

"I'm aware, Sir."

I blink between them, not breathing and realizing this is not just any meeting. This man is a mobster—and an important one at that. And Jynx is promising to stay sane and on the level.

The man clearly doesn't understand the monster Jynx keeps caged.

"How old is Abigail?"

"Twenty-two."

"Better than last time."

I shiver, feeling as though I may hurl. Jynx keeps secrets hidden in the dark, but I must be stronger, braver, and more determined. "How old was the last one?"

Two sets of eyes—green and blue flare to me—as if I wasn't supposed to speak at all. Jynx clears his throat. "It was right before the wreck. I did some things I shouldn't have done."

Feeling a bit petulant, I ask, "How old was *she?*"

He doesn't answer, but the man does. "Jynx was not the only one to blame. She was a tramp making her way around the club, rebelling against her parents and taking advantage of the situation. Old enough to know better, but not old enough to vote."

Fear silences as truth screams.

I may pass out. My head spins, dizzy, whirling—knowing what all I have given up for this predator to exploit me. Clasping my hands in my lap, I straighten my posture and mumble, "And was he involved with her?"

"Only for a minute," the man snickers. "Jynx was warned, punished, and took off on his bike before running into a concrete barrier."

I nod, concealing my feelings as Jynx assures, "She didn't matter."

"But the accident did," I whisper, sensing the purpose of his intent. There was no accident. He failed a suicide attempt.

The man bravely lays his hand upon mine under the table. "We all make mistakes, Sweet Pea."

My heart stops when he says my pet name.

"We do," I reply, rubbing my hand against the fabric. "And I don't want Jynx Monroe to be a major trauma upon my heart."

It's too late for that.

"He won't be," he replies with a generous smile. "This man sitting here is not the same man he was then. Are you the same person you were a decade ago?"

"No," I emphasize, knowing how much I have changed. "I'm not the girl I was at twelve." We all laugh. "Or my teenage years for that matter."

The man soothes my worry, but he doesn't alleviate Jynx's guilt.

Lights dim in the club as the crowd goes wild. The dance floor clears as four people—*two men and two women, including the one who we passed as we entered*—are clad in leather with whips, starting a jolting performance. I stare longingly, wishing Jynx would shepherd me into his darkness.

"You're fascinated," the man mutters, still holding my hand. "Has your Master whipped you?"

"Not like that."

"He should," he informs, stroking my fingers. "Jynx is a master whip snapper."

I blink at Jynx. His lip curls up with a crooked grin as his brows lift high. Pieces of his true identity surface in the light. I examine them underneath a microscope and wonder if his name isn't the glaring admission of who he is—bad luck, set to influence, and destroy. Maybe Jynx's game is nothing more than a hoax like his nickname.

With sass, I persist, "You should tell him that despite his past age-related issues that he has permission to love a girl properly."

"May I take her for a spin, Monroe?"

Jynx glances away and licks his lips as my breathing increases to such a rapid rate that I fear hyperventilating. His broken blue eyes meet mine, and I know everything is not what it seems.

This stranger is someone important to him.

And this meeting wasn't a celebration but a warning like a father to a son.

Stay out of trouble.

Don't make me bail you out.

Listen to the head on your shoulders, not the demanding snake in your pants.

"That would be her choice."

I should want to know who this man is—*before agreeing to a scene with him*—but I'm so hurt by the unspoken truths that I no longer care. *Things said but not said.*

My skin tingles as they await my answer. I don't give a shit what Jynx thinks. I'm pissed and punishing him for the words he didn't say. "Yes, please," I reply as Jynx camouflages the heartache with a daring snarl. I pour salt into the wound of those critical, overlooked details left unsaid by adding, "Whip me, Sir. And call me Abby."

Jynx's jaw tics.

"Very well," he says, smiling as Jynx pulls out my chair. I note the cane held tight in the man's hand as he rises. "I will meet you in room six. I'm a little slow."

We walk, past the bar, to the private dungeons.

Once inside, Jynx stares at me. "I'm sorry."

"Who is he?"

"A mob boss," he replies.

"I gathered that much!"

He licks his lips as I turn away. "She was seventeen and a mistake."

"Because she was seventeen?" I furiously yell, full of contempt.

"No, because it got my ass suspended from my cousin's club," he says, forcing me to face him. "After my uncle beat the fuck out of me."

"How unfortunate for you! How many women have you coerced? Or you know, let's just call vermin what it is! How many bitches have you raped with all that hatred you stash up in your heart?"

Not exactly true, but I only know how Jynx is with me.

Undisclosed. Cryptic.

Shrouded in a cloak of secrets and half-truths.

Refusing to acknowledge my tirade, he warns, "You need to stop."

I do not listen.

"How many times did you follow in Daddy's footsteps Jynx?"

His fingers swipe across my cheek with an angry sting. "Do not ever talk to me that way again. It was one time. One mistake. And I will not be burned at the stake because she was a fucking whore and as guilty as any of us. Do you want to know how many guys in the club had her?"

356 | KAILEE REESE SAMUELS

"I don't give a shit about those guys or that fucking cunt," I sass, pressing my hand to my cheek. "And I shouldn't give a shit about you either. You ran your bike into the wall. Admit it!"

"Abigail!"

"Don't fucking Abigail me!" I vehemently roar. "You didn't tell me!"

He backs up, threatening, "We're not having this meltdown now. This is a discussion we need to have in private."

"When would you prefer to have it, *Sir?*" I sass, unrelenting. "When can I schedule an appointment?"

"You know, there are lots of things you haven't told me either."

"What the hell is that supposed to mean?"

"It doesn't matter," he mutters, walking toward the door. "I'll be waiting for you, like I promised. Enjoy your time with Dominic Gennaro."

37

HANGING ON BY A THREAD

ECHO

JYNX LEAVES, SLAMMING THE DOOR AS DEVASTATION flutters through my heart. My eyes weep with regret at the harshness of the things said.

Things said but not said.

I'm full-blown crying when the strange man opens the door. He's not as tall as Jynx, but with a lean definition, he boasts a grand air. He isn't a man to mess with. My breathing turns erratic, and my feet sweat in the boots.

He politely asks, "Are you okay?"

I slide to sit onto the oversized padded table and hang my head low, ripping my mask off. I shake through the calamitous ache. "Not really."

"I'm sorry you didn't know about his issues," he says, stepping closer. "It was my fault. I shouldn't have brought them up with you present. But we don't need any problems when he returns to Texas. I don't like drama. I needed to confirm that he would behave before extending our hand to facilitate his venture."

"Was he in Texas when it happened?" I peer up, needing something to cling to—anything, a fraying thread. I'm drowning in the seas, swept away and stuck between the obstacles ramming into my body. I'll live through the flood, but I won't survive the wreckage impacting my spirit with the vengeance of a landslide.

"No," he replies, standing before me. "We were at my house in New Orleans for the holidays. I walked in on them."

"So the deed was done," I acknowledge, crying harder. "He was... fucking this girl. He had his dick inside of her when you walked in."

I search for air traps to breathe before I suffocate.

This man brings oxygen and warm hands.

"You need to know a few things about Jynx. He's a great guy..."

"But he has a bad habit of not revealing things that matter," I interrupt as his finger presses to my lip. I refuse to stop, leaning back. "He should've told me. We had plenty of time on the farm."

"Silence, little one. Listen." His smooth tone and gripping gaze force my attention before dropping his hand. "He isn't the type to ever focus on one woman. You're the first. If that doesn't tell you something about how he feels for you I don't know what will. I've known him since he was a kid because his dad was in business with my dad."

"Jynx is *mafia?*"

"No," he hastily replies and hands me his handkerchief emblazoned with a DMG. "Jynx's father, Montgomery Monroe, handled multiple Gennaro books and investments for years. I know Jynx by association, but he spent plenty of time in the club in New Orleans."

Tears cannot wash away this kind of pain. We're not making it out of this one. "How did he end up there?"

"He ran away at sixteen to his uncle—Deacon's father—who owned Reckless Rebellion." My lip trembles as I glance around the room. "With his uncle's encouragement and an RR cut on his back, Jynx went back home to South Carolina to finish school. He stayed until his uncle passed away, and then he went to mourn in Tennessee with some of the other club members. He was always finding trouble at home because of an overbearing, meddling mother and an absent father. His grandmother and the club raised that boy."

I pause and blot my tears. "... Did you know Clementine?"

"I did," he answers, smiling fondly. "I was in her dungeon a time or two. Before you, Jynx used and discarded women like fast food packaging. You're the first one he's placed on a pedestal and honored like his queen. Don't doubt his intentions, even if the delivery isn't what you expect. That young man..."

Rubbing my nose, I snicker, "He's thirty-seven."

"When you watch them grow up, they're all young men, Echo," he informs with a steely gaze. "Jynx has been to hell and back. Drinking, drugs, women, accidents...jail—he's done it all. But he'll never be bad to you."

"You're defending him even though you showed up to lay down the law."

He smirks and caresses his finger over my cheek. "Because that is what a good father figure does. He's present for his boys, no matter what. He never allows loneliness or despair to creep into their world. He keeps them up on the rails. So chin up, Buttercup. Rise above this bullshit of the past."

"His dad and brother..."

He lifts his finger to my lips again. "His father has a problem and as for Axel, I'm still working on him. I'm not allowing you to dismiss Jynx because the situation is uncomfortable. Your reaction is unnecessary."

"Not uncalled for though," I point out, arguing. "I have every right to be concerned."

"But not like this," he consoles with a tenderhearted stare. "You're special and you need to trust him."

"He doesn't like younger women, but yet..." I shrug as my emotions collapse in a quandary. Jynx clearly has an issue, and until stalking me, he managed to sequester those feelings. I don't know how I feel about becoming...*being*...his source of addiction. "How long can we reasonably last until the lust runs out? Until I am thirty, maybe? When he spots some hot young thing with perky breasts and no kids and I'm nothing more than a memory to him, what do I do then? How far do I let this go before knowing Jynx Monroe will only butcher my heart in the end?"

He sighs, deeply and fully. "And what if, he never does that? What if, he is in love with *you* until the end?"

His fingers linger on my cheek, comforting, endearing, before grazing the pads over my neck, encircled by the diamond halo symbolic of my subservience. He gently traces the leash to the dip in my cleavage as he parts the folds of my shirt. I say nothing as I unfasten the blouse and dismiss the fabric from my flesh. His hand never leaves my breastbone, flattening against my heart.

I glance up to find the curious fire burning inside of the man. "How old are you?"

"Forty-eight."

I unclasp the bra and remove it from my body. "Tell me what he sees. Make me understand that I'm worth the risk to his sobriety."

His hand cuts a distinct path around the upper curve of my left breast, to the side, and cups the weight in his hand. He lowers his head and closes his eyes as I stop breathing with another man's touch.

He isn't Jynx.

He is a foreigner...an intruder...an immigrant to my unchartered lands.

My borders are not closed.

At least, not for this one. I have fallen into a peaceful acceptance where I must trust his wisdom and guidance to see me through the arduous journey to the man I love. I will not traverse this magnificent range without this stranger. This stranger who I have become one with. This stranger who has dried my tears and told me tales inches me ever closer down the path where the man I love resides.

The tenebrous passage is a darkened tunnel into a mountainside or a subway with no power—*I cannot see a goddamned thing*—and yet, I sink into the rhythm of his lead and follow along, a needy pilgrim seeking refuge in the night.

I won't make it to Jynx's encampment tonight, or even tomorrow, or next week, or maybe even next year, but if I stay close, he'll help in my plight and allocate the necessary resources to ensure I reach my destination.

Somewhere in the cage of Jeremiah Monroe.

He loves me; this, I do not doubt.

But if we're merging, bridging the gap of fifteen years and tons of experience, we'll need hardhats for excavation and a mediator to handle our challenges. And this—*mobster before me*—with his fine tailored silk suit and Italian leather loafers is offering to be my tour guide into hell.

"Will Jynx be working for you?" I whisper as his eyes slit, and he glances up with a menacing leer, a God with a bulldozer from the underworld sanctum.

"That's a difficult question."

He's volunteering to be my tunnel rat, exposing me to things unseen, things which terrify good earth-dwelling mortals. He is not of this world. I'm being cordially invited into their chambers as a scared sacrifice with their pledge to keep me safe.

I try the question another way. "Will history be repeating itself, Capo?"

His lips perk with a touch of a smirk, playful, almost bashful. He's dangerous, this man. He plays a wicked game. "I am no Capo, sweetheart. I am but the historian of relics and figures."

"Hands clean and notches on the belt?"

"You could say that." He smirks.

Lifting an inquisitive brow, I accuse, "You librarian, discipliner. You, with all of that, cleave into my world without warrant or validation. How can you leave me like this?"

"I'm not abandoning you." He chuckles once, deep and foreboding. "You're club royalty."

"Fallen from grace," I admonish, knowing the toll my father's philandering took on not only his reputation but the family name, including me. "I'm not welcome anywhere, by any club, in the South."

"Deacon welcomed you."

"To join his bandwagon of criminal outlaws and mischief makers in the mafia?" I rhetorically blast with the force of a nuclear bomb. "Why would the daughter of a Rampage VP want anything to do with the mafia?"

His thick, burly eyebrows lift with a declaration. "Because you need protection."

"I'm a college student—soon, a doctorate student. I do not need your security detail, Mr. Gennaro."

"But you do because everyone knows what your father did."

"My father is a bad man...but he is still my father."

"Your father raped Tawny—brutally, horrifically, in front of you when you went home for the holiday. Fireworks blasted with beautiful colors in the sky while the seeds of abomination planted in your mind."

I shake my head and squeeze my way past the sanctimonious thug in his expensive threads. Lucky, he still has them. Mine are unraveling, eaten by moths, and left to decay like peacock feathers in the jungle-like sun. "I'm not doing this with you."

He latches onto my arm. "The hell you aren't!"

Shit. He's stronger than I imagined.

He pushes me face-first onto the table, lifts my skirt, and strikes my ass with his blasted cane. "Stop!" I bellow. But no one can hear me. "Don't do this!"

"No!" He yells with conviction. "You don't get to swindle my boy into falling for you and bolt when things get tough!" He pops the wooden cane against my ass again. Harder than before. The welts burn on my butt cheeks. "Daddy wanted you to watch so you knew what a real man should do! His brothers held you down and made you bear witness to the villainy so you wouldn't end up like Brandon!"

"Fuck you!"

"We can do that too, sweetness," he charmingly warns, popping his belt off. "I can show you if need be!"

"No, please! I belong to Jynx!" I beg, sobbing, knowing what I just said, claiming him as my owner. My legs are threatening to give out from under me as I barely hold onto the table. "I promise to be better. I promise I won't put up the ad again. Please don't rape me!"

And only then do I know the reason for his lesson.

He lunges, hovering over my back and whispering in my ear. His warm, whiskey tinted breath crashes onto me. "What I want you to do, is promise to be good to Jynx. That is what I want. I need you to slow down, take two deep breaths before you jump off the cliff into the ocean. Before you decide this relationship is over and you break his fucking heart, make sure that is what you really want to do. Because I will be cleaning up that mess of a man and there won't be any coming back on my watch. We do not have a revolving door."

With drool and snot bubbling onto the black leather, I whisper the only thing that makes sense. "Spank me, Daddy." My words drip like honey rushing through the ravine where Jynx resides as I stand with my escort to the other side.

This time—*he truly could be my father.*

Twenty-six years separate our experience, distancing, as he volunteers to cauterize the wounds of my past, flushing them with his blood, and rending new scars for his minions to tend.

This is my sundering; this is my reawakening.

His belt shoots out of the loops, and soon I'm met with lash after lash of permeating heat rising, festering in my body. Every welt bites worse than the last until my core glows with the embers of love. This isn't about crossing Jynx, but serving another and growing from within.

A strange man that Jynx believes in, pushes that boundary, and propels my inner reflection. He doesn't restrain but delivers fucked up, precision strokes like a machete to the thick underbrush. He provides the fuel that I burn through faster than a rocket launching.

We're getting somewhere, but this will take time and healing.

The journey is long with demons crossing, haphazardly at will.

"Did you like what you saw that night?"

"I hate you," I whimper, unable to stop crying as he callously impacts my buttocks again. "I hate you so much."

"Did his moves foster all the hate you felt, Abigail?"

"Yes, to everything! I'm a terrible human being. And do you know what? I don't deserve Jynx or this or any of it! You should've just let me die to a hoodlum in a dank alley! I didn't ask for a merry gang to hold my hand in the dark."

"But you did," he alleges, rubbing the bruises. "You cried out for help. And we answered the call."

"Fuck all of this. I can't do it anymore. Just let me go back to being mediocre and quiet. Just let me get back to being me."

"This is the new you," he contends, slipping his hand low and running over the damp lace between my thighs. I struggle to understand how all of this happened from one stupid mistake. "And she is so fucking beautiful."

The belt singes against my rump like I'm being sawed in two at a circus. Only the blade isn't a trick, but an agonizing pulse, ticking in my veins. "Please just let me go and forget it all ever happened. Let me have a tombstone so Jynx doesn't have to fight my war. I'm not worth this much trouble. I'll never be good enough."

"Not a chance, doll." He breathes as his belt buckle clanks against the floor. His hand moves off of my back, releasing the pressure. I stand still, barely breathing, waiting on his next move as he confirms my worst fears, "You belong to Jynx and his brothers now."

I clutch my things and dash for the door. I toss the sheer blouse over my breasts and make my way from the private dungeons to the club. I hate navigating anything, so I'm slower than I would like to be as I scan the crowd for Jynx. The man with his cane won't be able to chase after me. Jynx will.

In the middle of the dance floor, I spot his foreboding frame arched around a girl in red leather. They're bumping and grinding, having a good old time, while I embarked on a deliriously intense scene with a delusional madman.

I want my top.

I need my Dom.

But he's with her.

I am alone, crying, lost, as the thread snaps.

And I am gone.

Spotting a neon yellow-shirted member of Madame Tilda's team, I grab her arm and plead, "Can you show me to the exit? I need to catch a taxi."

38

SUICIDE HOTEL

JYNX

I NEVER SAW HER LEAVE.

Fuck.

I pace, waiting for my car from the valet, not knowing how long she's been gone or where she went. In the amount of time I've wasted on them fetching my vehicle, I could've run to get it and been halfway back to the hotel by now.

I cannot escape the past, who I was, or what I did. I won't deny any of it. I've paid for my sins—time and time and time again. Trouble finds me. It's in my middle name. I'm the archangel of the abyss, the king of an army of locusts residing in the pits of hell as I champion destruction.

That is who I am.

She refuses to see the truth.

Her go-to option is always to flee, escaping the path of pain. In some ways, her father taught his daughter well with his ongoing misbehavior. The fear gave her wings, but no one ever taught her the proper way to fly. She should never have been anywhere near me. And as for her father, he should be six feet under, for ever scarring his baby girl like that.

My babygirl. Mine.

Anger oozes from every pore.

Lord, help me.

With an arrogant snarl, Dom says, "You need to calm down."

My temper blazes, so close to the surface that heat blasts my cheeks, bubbling and oozing from the crimson paradise. "What did you say to her?"

"Everything she needed to hear, Jynx. Your avoidance of admitting you know the truth will kill this relationship. She needed to know that we knew about her father."

"I didn't know until you told me this week on the phone. I didn't research her family. I was blindsided, distracted by twenty-two." Lighting a smoke, I mumble, "She's going to run."

"She will," he concurs, setting his hand on my shoulder. "And she will boomerang back because she knows this is where she belongs. You're her home base. Echo belongs to you, and whether she claims that—isn't your choice to make. You know she is yours."

"I should never have done this."

"What other choice did you have?"

"It doesn't matter," I say, popping my jaw. "I knew better than to get involved with someone so young. I'm starting at square fucking one in training her—trust me, stay, behave."

"And isn't it just lovely that she is so much work? So fresh and new?" He questions not giving me time to respond. He's a ridiculous advocate for age-gap relationships. "You'll have this girl custom fit to you in no time. Unblemished. Unmarked. Not tainted with anyone else's bullshit except the past she brings with her—what a glorious place to be!"

Gripping the bridge of my nose, I criticize, "I should never have taken Katie up on the offer to dance."

"You were dancing, not fucking or having a scene," he assuages, bringing on a much-needed reminder that I did nothing wrong. I crave controlled comfort with a submissive. "Besides if your dick didn't get hard dancing with Katie's rump grinding on you, you've got the answer to every question a man will ever have. And in your case, they all begin and end with Echo Maines."

"Where are you headed?"

"Probably back inside to see if Katie is interested in a lap dance." He smirks.

I snort as my car pulls up. We embrace, and he kisses my cheeks. "I'll see you in a few weeks. Don't panic. Think. You aren't out of the arena until security kicks your ass to the gate."

"I'm the villain on my knees praying to a devil I don't have faith in."

"We all are, son," he mutters, patting my back. "We all are."

I speed like I'm on the racetrack behind the wheel of my drag car. The rental place keeps giving me these piece of shit sports cars that middle-aged men rent for their weekend affairs.

What the fuck am I talking about?

I'm the middle aged man having a romantic affair with a pretty young girl with a Southern accent and a taco fetish. And I'm the son of a bitch dogging this car out.

But I won't abuse her holes for two nights.

I'll use her love to shelter my sins for a lifetime.

ECHO

"Thank you," I say to the taxi driver as he drops me off at the front door of the hotel. I already slipped my bra back on in the car ride here. I'll only look like a cheap hooker for the five-second run through the lobby. "I'll be right back."

I rush into the crowded area where a wedding reception overflows with formally dressed folks. I get stuck, caught in a traffic jam of bodies cramming together as they make their way to the entrance of the party at the far end of the hall. I veer through with a continuing mantra, "Excuse me! I'm sorry! I need to get past! Thank you!"

"Echo!" Axel shouts, leaving the front desk, with his bags in tow. He glances around suspiciously. "Where is Jynx?"

My mouth opens and closes. I don't know what to say. "We had a fight. I need to go. I don't want to talk right now. Everything hurts."

His fingers latch around my wrist. His blue eyes—the same color as Jynx's—pluck every heartstring I have. "... Do you need anything?"

"To get the fuck out of here as fast as possible," I whisper. He releases me with concern brimming in his eyes. I cannot help him. I can't even help myself. I run.

In less than ten seconds, he'll be texting Jynx.

In less than ten seconds, Jynx will know I'm leaving him for good.

I hit the elevator button and wait as a horde of people pass by. Happy families gleefully laugh when I spot the bride and groom outside of the reception hall.

The girl could've been me.

His eternal lover would've been me.

Mrs. Monroe should've been me.

I blink my tears away, afraid of the thoughts in my mind. I have to go—*I don't have a choice.* He didn't tell me. I found out by accident.

And I didn't tell him how much I taunted those boys to win Colton over.

He found out in my breakdown.

Someone hit rewind. Take me back to the moment when we were racing on the highway where I soared with freedom on his shoulders because there was no other choice.

The elevator doors slide open, and I close my eyes as I ride up to the sixth floor. I pull my room key from my phone case and slide it in the lock. Stepping inside, I spot Edward Dower sitting in a chair and pointing a gun at me.

"How the hell did you get in here?" I shrill, terrified. "What do you want?"

"Lock the door." He stands up and tilts his head. "Where is Jynx?"

"He's downstairs ordering food," I lie, hoping, praying that he believes me. Calm down. Breathe. "He'll be right up."

"You're lying," he replies, walking closer to me. "Your mascara stains tell tales, Abigail Maines."

"And you're fucked in the head," I remark, turning to the door to leave. "You can't do this!"

He's behind me in an instant, putting the barrel to my head and pressuring, "I will kill your ass dead with one shot, bitch."

Do not call me that.

You are not my Master.

Tears stream down my cheeks as he gropes my breasts. But they aren't mine anymore; they're Jynx's.

Fuck. I'm so screwed.

Why do I always run?

His cock hardens as he puts me in a chokehold and throws me on the bed. "Please don't do this!" I scurry back to the headboard as I beg for his mercy. He shows none, undoing his belt and unzipping his pants. He runs the gun over my leg and points it at my sex, pressing the metal into the indentation of my soaked panties. "Please do not do this!"

Memories I dreamed of—*a marriage with a filthy fucking gentleman that I love, gorgeous laughing children, and a blissful life*—flash before my eyes.

"Kaboom!" He gloats, laughing maniacally.

"Eddie! No! Stop!"

"That's what you're going to be saying in a minute," he brags, kneeling between my legs. He's going to rape me. The thing I begged for—*asked for*—and now, it's not the same. He's not Jynx. This cannot be happening. This isn't real.

Someone wake me up. The picture-perfect fantasy faded like a painting in the rain until there was nothing left but an undecipherable smeared canvas.

Help. Me.

Someone, please.

Help. Me.

"God! Don't do this!" I yell as he thumbs at my slit. "Please don't do this!"

I wanted one man inside of me for the rest of my life, and this is not him.

He isn't Jynx.

I fight.

With a roar, I rock my hips, knocking him away. He ricochets as I lift my leg, nailing the spiked heel of my boot into his chest near his shoulder. Blood pours all over him, me, and the bed—but he doesn't stop. His anger magnifies as he slaps my cheek and punches me in the gut. His assault with his fists is relentless. I have never felt this much pain. And he is a meek little man.

Nothing like my beast.

I can only imagine the damage Jynx could inflict.

"You don't have a choice, much like I didn't have a choice to lose all of my best employees due to that traitor of a scumbag boyfriend you hang out with. He took what was mine; I will do the same to him."

He throws his rounded body on top of me and grinds his blubber against me. Bile burns the back of my throat. I'm going to puke. There is nothing romantic or kinky in this moment. I want to die. I want to kill myself.

This man is making me feel this way.

This is how much it hurts.

Just give me the gun and I'll do the fucking deed so you don't have to.

His hand rips the lace panties I bought for Jynx to shred.

For some reason, that one little thing—pisses me the fuck off. "You, motherfucker!" I hiss and push with all of my might as he tries to enter me. We're struggling, wrestling, but he isn't very good at seizing the opportunity. He is no Dominant, I know. "Don't do this! This will eat your soul for the rest of your life!"

His cock brushes against the inside of my thigh, and a harrowing scream erupts from my lungs as the door jars open.

"What the fuck are you doing?" Axel shouts, tossing him onto the floor. "That is my brother's future wife, moron!"

I blink in shock.

... Axel?

"He has a gun!" I cry out, sitting up and cradling a pillow to my chest. My whole body trembles. "Oh, my God..."

Axel may be a prissy dickhead, but he's throwing punches like he was born in a boxing ring. *Holy fuck.* He grabs the gun, setting it on the bed. My fingers snatch it fast as I think about pulling the trigger and checking out.

Make it stop.

Make it all stop.

"Did you come to kill my brother?"

"It's none of your concern."

"What the fuck is going on?" Jynx howls, running inside. Fury fills his blue eyes as he spots my torn panties and understands exactly what is happening.

"Help!" I barely squeak out. "Me."

Axel is distracted by his brother when Eddie lands a swing to his jaw and lunges up. His upright position is fleeting because the iron fist of a monster clocks the man in the skull repeatedly until he drops to the ground. Jynx straddles over the top of him as red splatters everywhere. "You son of a bitch! I will kill you for even thinking about hurting her!"

There is no battle.

There is no war.

Eddie is a portly man and serves as no competition to Jynx's aggressive, combative nature. He will kill him. I watch in horror as the man I love morphs into a monster with annihilation on his mind. His target doesn't move, but Jynx doesn't stop the pound of knuckles to the man's grisly flesh.

Without warning, the police enter the room. It takes four brute sized men in blue to tether the behemoth of Jynx Monroe.

The cuffs click around his wrists.

And I will never forget the sound.

I hide, peeking from behind the pillow and understanding how right I was to be leaving. I cannot love such a vicious man. He would never hurt me. But if I stay with him, I must accept his anger issues, even if justified. Even if deserved.

"I love you, Sweet Pea! Don't go! I'll get out of this tomorrow!" he begs as they jostle him away. I say nothing because there is nothing left to say.

We're flawed, fucked up, and bound to fail.

Better now than later, when more hearts are on the line than mine. A skirmish breaks out near the door as he struggles against them. "Abby! Stay! Please! Stay!"

I don't process this love.

I shut down because outlaws bring cruelty.

I was born to bleed, raised to run, and determined to die alone.

39

THE MINUTES AFTER

Echo

SOME MINUTES ARE NEVER FORGOTTEN.

The police extract Jynx Monroe from my life. They're large, superheroes without capes. My heart hurts and my stomach curdles, the bitter tang burning the back of my throat. I sit with my arms wrapped around my legs, curled in a small ball near the wall, watching, waiting. Their powers are mystical, transformative. Silver cuffs glimmer like a magic wand, casting a spell on me.

I am *finally* free.

376 | KAILEE REESE SAMUELS

And then my entire body turns uncomfortably numb.

Shock sets in as words blur into a sludge-filled diatribe. The hour-long haze is behind me. Axel takes his jacket off, wrapping it carefully around my shoulders like I'm a child caught in a storm. He never leaves my side and does most of the talking, except when the female officer conducts her interview—bits and pieces resonate with the punctuated thunder of a drum line marching through my brain.

She respectfully asks, "How did you meet Jeremiah Monroe?"

Does she need this information, or is she just being nosey?

"A wedding," I lie, faking a brief smile. "In California."

"And how long have you been together?"

You're pushing me, woman.

"About six months."

Her look of condemnation is more than I can handle. She is a woman for chrissakes. Yet, she scans over my outfit, and immediately, judgement comes into play. I steer away from the obvious—the attempted rape, the gun at my temple, the barrel nudged into my damp undergarments.

Digging deeper, I protect what is mine even though I cannot possess him—the sexy stalker with dimples and contagious smile, the rusty chains looped and locked around my ankle, the feel of his giant cock ramming into my ass without lube or any invitation to do such.

He was not Eddie Dower.

I don't want to be making the comparisons.

But they happen naturally without provocation.

She thanks me for my time. A different woman in black pants and a white shirt asks to examine me. I do not shy away. I have nothing to hide. Nothing for which to be ashamed. Her voice is light, friendly, like an elementary school teacher—*Let's all take out our spelling books. Line up for lunch, children. Keep your hands to yourself.*

No pushing in the hallway.

No cornering the girl in the bathroom.

No luring her under the bleachers.

The rules jumble into a flagrant mess until we're all persecuted for having a little fun.

I had been harassed and bullied.

By luck, I graduated high school at seventeen without ever being touched or kissed. I was a virgin blessed by the guardian angels of my deceased siblings.

I was one of the lucky ones.

I was one of the rare ones.

I was conditioned that boys—the generalization of the entire sexual male population—possessed a rapturous charlatan within.

From my maternal Grandma's warnings and Mom's horror stories to the old lady's dissing on the shit their husbands pulled, I was taught all of the bad things men did. Never in the rallying bitch sessions was I informed that men could also do good things—rushing to my aid in a flood, picking my ass up when I fell, and collecting every tear like a badge held close to their hearts.

Or beating up the man who tried to rape me with his bare hands.

Balance didn't exist in my upbringing.

I was expected to behave, following in their denouncing footprints and pledging my loyalty to vaginas everywhere. Still, in the guise of good grades and perfect attendance, I was a rebel, always searching for dick.

After all, the honor roll student was a biker's daughter.

Meet me in a chat room; I'll talk dirty.

Be flirty and playful; I'll show you my tits.

Strangers—perfect strangers—who I never had to see in real life. Younger guys. Older guys. Cute guys. Ugly guys. Muscle bound guys. And fat guys too. I didn't fucking care.

Give me attention.

Make me feel something other than wanting to be dead—*anything, please*. I'll trade demons for ghosts any day of the week. I'll march into battle with a man, wearing my best heels and no bra before I'll come close to rehashing the past.

The constant emasculating of men from the women in my life made me revolt. I shunned women, proudly wielding boy's blue.

I was a traitor.

Heretic. Heathen. Renegade.

Or, according to my mother's philosophies, a girl in dire need of an exorcism by holy fucking cunt juice. Baptize me, sisters. But lesbianism was frowned upon. They'd moved on to vibrators with apps and decadent porn scripture in the lands of the fictitious man while harboring so much hate for real men that my skin crawled.

Fuck that.

I liked playing with the boys, teasing and taunting, but even more than that, I adored their wide range of conversations, which varied from sports to movies. They didn't sit around and complain about the opposite sex all day.

Eventually, I acquired a few like-minded dissenters from club kids and pep squad girls to my college study group and my roommate, Selia.

I wasn't about hating anyone.

And I don't like associating with people who do hate.

I dug love—*that was some shit I could really get behind*—loving everyone, animals, nature, and the world around. I broke the template of my upbringing, but I still hadn't healed the scars. I was working on it, but it was a slow process, and systemic infection was rampant.

And I lacked patience.

Unlike Jynx, who had enough patience to stroll right on into sainthood.

At my core, I was socially inept, incapable of bridging the distance between online and real. I wanted one of those perfect strangers to steal me away in the night and make my past disappear—from my sibling's graves to the grunts my father made while ejaculating in a helpless victim.

Just make it all disappear.

Wave the fucking wand.

Make it go away.

Begone!

I needed something catastrophic to happen to me. Something to jar me out of thinking about killing myself day in and day out because the haunting ghosts were real. What better way to chase them away than with an angry demon from hell?

My solution—*Rape me!*

Jynx's moves were spectacular and brilliant. His handsome model physique masked his inner fiend, and I never realized what nasty things could happen by placing the bait.

I managed to acquire a sadist who trapped me, and I fell in love with him.

Love hurt much worse than bruises.

He did things to not only make me forget but change my entire outlook for the rest of my life. Instead of contemplating ways to end it all, I filled my head with the possibilities of his endless love. I was hiccuping on the past but jonesing for a fix of his authority.

Feeding the craving is all I think about.

Nothing else matters.

But is it love?

His hands dripped with red—defending me, protecting me, guarding me. I was his possession. He was my obsession. And in the darkness, we found passion. My eyes close tight as the blood pressure cuff cinches around my arm.

"I don't want romance."

"Do no harm doesn't exist in my vernacular."

"I'm not innocent. I've never raped or killed anyone. Or abducted anyone until you."

"I desperately want to fuck you into next week."

"I advise taking you to the hospital," the medic says as I return to reality, abandoning the fantasy of Jynx Monroe. It hurts. I hurt. "Your blood pressure is elevated."

Jynx was ripped from my world.

Of course, my blood pressure is elevated, idiot.

Eddie is taken by airflight to the hospital, where he is pronounced dead on arrival. And I spend most of the night cradled in Axel's arms in the emergency room. No rape occurred. No kit was needed. I have major trauma with deep bruising to my torso, so I'm kept overnight for observation and released the next morning.

Despite his delightful charm, begging me to stay, Axel agrees to pack a small bag at the hotel for me. He drives me directly to the airport after I'm released from the hospital.

Gripping my hand, he stops in the unloading zone. "Are you sure, Ekky?"

"I'm sure if I don't get away from this life that he will destroy me."

"I really wanted you as my sister," he softly confides, squeezing my hand. His eyes well with regret. "We would've taken care of you."

"I know," I say, crying. "But I can't be this girl. I need stability and Jynx will never be able to give me that. It isn't who he is and it's not fair of me to ask him to be something he isn't. I can't make him change who he is. Thank you for showing up at the hotel room when you did, and not bothering to knock. Good luck with everything, Ax." I lean over and kiss my would've-been-brother-in-law on the cheek. "Thank you for saving me."

"We always have one another's extra room keys," he divulges, shaking his head. "But I didn't save you. Jynx did that all on his own. I called him and he told me to get back up to your room. Remember, I said you were bad news in the beginning." He grins, and I giggle. "If you ever need anything—*anything at all*—call me. Or better yet, call my asshole of a brother."

"He killed a man Axel."

"There is a first time for everything," he remarks with a solemn nod. He isn't proud or displeased with his brother's actions. It just is. "And what better reason to be behind bars than to have saved a woman, especially one as genuine as you. You're a keeper, Echo. You don't believe it or want to hear it, but it's true."

"… Will he get out?"

"I'm sure he will," he says, tightening his brow. "It was self-defense. The investigative team found weaponry that Eddie had stashed in his car. He was coming to kill Jynx and planned to destroy

Dower Headquarters tomorrow morning. Jynx saved a hell of a lot more lives last night than yours."

"Oh, my gosh..." I cover my mouth, comprehending the depth of Eddie's despair. "Jynx saved them."

"Yeah. And you tell me I don't know him." Poking my arm, he says, "*That* is who he is."

"How did he find out where we were?"

Gripping the steering wheel, he snickers, "My brother has a reputation. Every weekend for months, he spent at Madame Tilda's. Eddie knew he'd be in Tucson, probably checked into the nicest hotel there. My brother isn't a challenging profile, just hard as fuck to get to open up. He is a creature of habit, clean and neat, never straying far from his center."

"He wanted that center to be me," I mumble in a shower of tears. "God, what am I doing?"

"Making a decision to impact the rest of your life."

I pull the handle of the door and exit the vehicle. The humid air cloisters upon my skin with a light sheen of sweat. I accept the nightmare of my existence will never end. "Take care of yourself, Axel."

"I love you, sis."

I smile. "You're not too bad yourself."

I cry all the way home to Alabama.

The dream of Jynx Monroe is finally over.

But I fear my recovery will never end.

JYNX

"SHE LEFT ME."

"I think she'll be back," Axel mumbles, packing her things, my things—our things together. We planned to put things in our house, like the vase I bought from the museum gift shop and the large hand-woven tapestry we purchased at the open-air market on some dusty two-lane road. She wanted to frame it for the entryway of the beach house.

We were making plans.

Plans, together.

For our future.

With my hand clenched around the bottle of Stoli, I ask, "What the fuck am I going to do now?"

Tossing another handful of nuts in his mouth, Axel chews and waves his hands about in an exaggerated fashion. "You're going to get out of that chair, go take a shower, and let me take you to the airport. I'll get all this shit shipped to..."

"Texas," I answer, filling in the blank. "I'm only staying in South Carolina long enough to secure the farm. A week or two at most."

"Do I want to know how much in debt we are to the mob?"

"No," I reply, tucking my fingers beneath my chin. "I will take care of it."

"It's not money they want."

I nod, moving my jaw from side to side. "I'm aware of what they want, but I also did them a favor."

"Yeah," he says, nodding. "And you stupidly fell for her. I warned you to stay away. This one—I knew she was going to fuck your head up. The Jynx you were, living life and having fun, he no longer exists. You're going to have to figure out how to be a new you without her."

"I thought your dumbass said that you believed she'd be back?"

"I do," he replies, zipping a row of tape over a box. "But on the off chance that I'm wrong, you need to be prepared."

I tilt my head low to my chest and slightly shake the idea of losing her away. "I never thought I would be sitting here without her by my side."

"She's left before," he points out. "What's changed?"

With tears in my eyes, I stare at my brother. "She's never made it to Alabama before."

"You're slightly proprietorial."

"She is my girl—*my possession*—mine."

He blinks, concerned. "You may need to get some help for this."

"I don't want any help," I say, shooting out of the chair. "I want my Echo back."

"Then listen," he mutters, laying his hand on my shoulder. "You'll hear her."

40

ALABAMA BURNS

ECHO

THREE DAYS LATER, I'M PACKING UP MY CHILDHOOD HOME in Alabama. Brandon told me that I would be helping him. Shall I repeat that?

Told.—Helping.

He's been at work, the bar, God knows where else—but anywhere other than here, not helping me for three days. I saw him once. He picked me up at the airport, dropped me at the house, showed off the stack of unbuilt boxes, tissue paper, and multiple rolls of tape, and then he left with—"Let me know if you need anything else."

What. The. Fuck.

I am not the help.

I'm beyond angry as I wrap the plates up from the kitchen. The house is crammed with my parent's life—pictures, clothes, records. Everything remains in the house as I left it four years ago.

Rampage threatened my father after the incident.

Get out, or we're coming after you.

Ken and Mindy Maines acted like fugitives on the run. They rushed home, grabbed one bag each of clothing, and drove their two cars to just outside of Tallahassee, where they started over again.

Clean slate.

Nothing of the past.

Except for one thing—*my teenage sister.*

Daphne was beside herself and the worst off of all of us. She was starting to come out of her shell, preparing to go to high school, and they swept her away like an unexpected tornado in the middle of the night.

New city? Daphne would adjust, they contended.

New school? She would learn to accept, they said.

New friends? She'd find plenty, they argued.

She stayed alone in her bubble until graduating. She didn't have a choice. She was thirteen.

I considered running to her side, but that also meant living with my parents in Florida. I had managed to get out a year before. Like hell, I was going back.

I had made it out.

And eventually, Daphne did, too.

At seventeen, I graduated early with a year and a half of college-level coursework under my belt. I moved to California with my Aunt Josie and Uncle Moe, my father's younger brother, who was nothing like him. I attended on-campus classes and worked my ass off at the café. I stayed with them until my eighteenth birthday when I promptly moved into the apartment I had—which I no longer do because I stupidly trusted a man.

I carefully fold the tissue paper over each plate, but I yearn to smash them to bits. Take a hammer and wreck the place—just like they did our lives.

I drop the safely wrapped plate into the box and cry as it shatters.

"Oh, dear God," I whimper, falling to my knees. "What happened to who we were? How did we get so lost?"

I had gone home—to Alabama, for the first time in over a year. A steaming hot summer awaited with Rampage's Independence Day celebration, and as the VP of the club, my father and his family were expected to attend.

Dad was involved with the club since before I was born.

In another box, there are faded pictures of him holding me when I was…a baby, a toddler, a child, a pre-teen, a young lady…all on his bike with him. I vowed after I left to never sit on another motorcycle.

I had attended lots of club functions. I wasn't a biker party virgin. I knew the shit that went on and eschewed interacting as much as possible. Of course, by my teens, that earned me the reputation of being a snob, but I never wanted anything to do with club life.

I was the one random blue iris sprouting up in a cornfield.

And I stuck out like a sore thumb.

My short height and small disposition did nothing to help me with those boys either. I was picked up, tossed about, poked fun at, and generally made to feel that my place—whether I wanted it or not— would be in the bitch seat behind a young Rampage boy.

Ugh.

If Jynx had shown up into my world with a Harley and a cut, my heart wouldn't be in shambles because I wouldn't have given him the time of day.

I didn't want to lose my identity—*the identity I fought hard to discover* —to a man like that. I liked preppy, professional-types, and athletes, and even bad boys were okay if well behaved.

I held a grudge against grungy bikers.

The night boasted barbecue, bottles, and kegs of beer on red and white checkered table cloths. Like family night, but quadruple the size because everyone was in attendance. I found a quiet spot, away from the crowd, and read because that was what I always did.

With fireworks exploding in the sky and old-school rock music blaring, I was cornered, grabbed by two of his best friends, and taken to a stockroom in the clubhouse where my dad was waiting.

My mother was off gossiping with Daphne and the rest of the club because that is what she did. I don't know where Brandon was, probably off getting high and wishing he was anywhere else in the world.

One of Dad's brothers brought Tawny in, and I cried in horror as my father showed his daughter how a woman should be treated. His hostile attack went on for over an hour. I wasn't a stranger to the violence and misogyny in his world.

I knew it; he raised me in it.

And I avoided it and him until I made one critical mistake—I went to the bathroom alone. He wouldn't let them assault me, so in some emotionally crippling, dependent way, I trusted him.

But I was fearless and *helpless* standing there as he pumped his hips, and she fought against him. Two held her down as my father mauled her. I was so slight; it didn't take two men to hold me down.

One would do.

I felt the man behind me, with his burly, inked arm around my chest, grow hard against my ass. He bucked a few times and peered down at me. He grinned with his stained brown teeth and beer-infused breath. We both knew he wanted me. And we also both knew he'd never live to see another day if he tried.

In his mind, my dad could be the attacker, but he'd never condone the victimization of his little girl. And to this day, he believes he did nothing wrong, yet he condemned Jynx for being a biker.

He has never acknowledged how much his mistreatment hurt.

Dad strode up, drunk and belligerently wagging his finger in my face with his pants dangling loose on his waist. "That is how you should be treated! This is what real men do!" He slapped my cheek, and the group went on their way as I froze, staring at Tawny. "Don't marry anyone like your pussy ass brother, Echo Renata!"

Tawny was young, maybe a year or two older than me. I stared in shock at her for a long while, comparing her and me, and praying I never ended up needing a booster by spreading my legs. I eventually handed her a towel. "It was my fault. I pissed your father off by telling him he needed to raise Brandon better."

In my father's eyes, he had one child.

And she was me.

"This was not your fault," I said, quietly crying. She shrugged it off, and I suspected, though never confirmed, this wasn't the first time she'd been the party favor. "You should tell Gus."

"Yeah, maybe if I did, I could end up being the Prez's old lady."

I walked out, understanding we weren't all that much different —*she and I.*

I wanted Colton to love me, but he never would. His dogmatic Christian faith wouldn't allow any such action to occur until after college in the marital bed. I pushed the boundary, lost my friend, and would suffer from the guilt of his suicide for the rest of my days.

Tawny wanted a real man—a biker, not my drug addicted brother, who, by luck, happened to wear a Rampage cut. They had dated in high school, but with much-altered versions. Her future revolved around becoming an old lady and mother, while my brother wanted to wear heavy eyeliner and black trench coats like some Goth kid, which was fine—nothing against the Goths—but Bran was never meant to be a biker.

Dad put his only son in the club even though he was as much of an outcast as I was and didn't deserve the cut. I knew the guys shared the women, snorted the drugs, and liked to party, but my brother was in a different league of scumbag.

Since his late teens, he suffered from an addiction to heroin, liked hanging around degenerates, and squatting in homes. But anytime I needed him—*prior to the incident*—he was always there for me.

He was my person.

And I want him to be my person still.

But who he was before—*that guy left town when shit went south.*

I imagined Tawny ratted out Dad to Gus when she found out the night was never going to end with my father's spawn, who would have been my half-sibling, growing in her belly.

Despite witnessing the crime of my father, I didn't hang around for the fallout. If I could distance myself from my father, I had a fierce independent streak. I called a taxi, went to the airport, and reserved a seat on the next plane home—to California. I slept in the airport. No one called. Not my parents. Not Brandon. Not Daphne.

I walked to the end of the driveway and swore that I'd never return to Alabama because that night was more gut-wrenching than anything I had ever experienced.

At least, until I met Jynx Monroe.

And he *administered* pain like I'd never known.

Alabama ain't got nothing on a man with the devil in his name.

I SCAN OVER THE BOXES AND WONDER WHAT THE HELL TO do with all of the shit. We'll need to rent a storage unit until one of us gets settled. I'm sitting on a box and eating pizza when Brandon walks in. Nice of him to show up now that I'm done.

Asshole.

He opens my pizza box and steals a piece. And something about that little arrogant move pisses me the fuck off. I rush to my feet and yell, "Where the hell have you been?"

"I had work," he garbles, shoving the pizza in his mouth. "You know that." I fume, chasing after him as he walks through the house —like he is inspecting my work. "You did good."

He turns back toward me in the hallway, and I slap the hell out of him. Keep in mind, I'm barely five feet tall, and he is almost as tall as Jynx. Wanting to pick a fight with someone, I seethe, "How dare you!" I stomp off.

"What the fuck did you hit me for?"

I gather my things as he follows me into the bedroom. "You tossed me out of your life, didn't bother to make time to help me, or for that matter, communicate on any level. You're still a goddamned drug addict. You can't look me in the eye and tell me you aren't using again!"

I didn't need confirmation in a cup; the black circles around his eyes were enough.

"Where are you going to go?"

"I don't fucking know," I hiss, angrier than I've ever been. Shoving a few of my things into a duffel bag, I inform, "I'll figure it out. I always do. Don't worry about me." I grab my tennis shoes in the living room and sit on a box to put them on. "I'll go back to California and see if I can get my life back. You should return to rehab."

With his hands in the pockets of his black hoodie, he rocks between his feet. "That is why I needed you," he mumbles, almost inaudibly. "I'm checking into some place called Arietta Farms in Texas."

I blink, stunned like he just smacked me across the face with a dead fish. "You're going to Texas?"

You're stealing my life?

You're going to be that close to Jynx?

Again—How dare you!

"You were supposed to be there."

"I thought you were fine when you came to California, but as it always is with you, Bran, it was another fucking lie. You've got one chance to tell me exactly what you did. I know damn well this wasn't because one visit from a stranger changed your tune about everything!"

I know. I have a few friends in Texas all on my own.

I know.

He rubs his lips together and glances away before sitting down on the box across from me. "Back in January, you called me."

Standing up, I hastily remark, "I call you all the time. You never call me back."

"Yeah, well you told me what you were doing online. And I knew why you were doing it. I had to do something to stop you."

"What did you do?" My house of cards shakes, tumbling to the ground as the truth quakes in my soul. The reverberations are real and almost knock me off balance. I shake my head in disbelief, screaming, "What did you do, Bran?"

"I went and talked to Gus."

"You talked to Gus? You went back to the compound after they threatened our family?"

"Dad raped my wife! It wasn't the club's fault! You need to stop blaming everyone but the one who instigated it, Abby! Dad did that to teach both of us a lesson!"

"It only taught me one thing," I sass, grabbing my jacket. "To never trust a biker."

"It was Dad's fault!" He roars through the house. "Are you blind, Daddy's Little Girl? Daddy who gave his princess everything she wanted. Daddy who loved his precious girl. Daddy who named you Echo. He is responsible for what happened to Tawny. He did that. Not you. Not me."

"Fuck you, Brandon!" I spin away, and he grabs my arms, pinning me against the wall. "He didn't give me everything I wanted. He gave me piano and ballet lessons and a fuckton of absent father. That is what he gave me. And he kissed it all better by giving me shit to occupy my time, so he could go stick his dick in the hooch of the month."

"I don't know when I will see you again, and no one else in the world is brave enough to put it out there in front of you."

"Yeah," I whisper, snarling, and holding back the tears. "There was one."

"You need to accept that Dad's version of love for you is pretty damn fucked up. He isn't a man you should be respecting or looking up to and I know you still do. He had the heart attack and you ran to his side. Just like always. You're either running away or running to Dad. Why don't you stop and think, and then run to someone who does matter and who is worth looking up to?"

Everything stops as I'm suddenly forced to deal with my feelings for Jynx all at once. I don't know how to stay. I run at the first sign of distress. And I don't know if that will ever change—that is why I left. Jynx deserves more than a girl always on the run. He deserves more than a fucked up mess who doesn't believe she can stay, fight, and win.

"My relationship with Jynx Monroe does not concern you."

"You're with Jynx because I asked Gus for help and he contacted his supplier who happened to know a hacker. And do you know who that guy is?"

"You son of a bitch!" I twist my forearms and shake to get out from under his frame. But my drug-addicted asshole of a brother doesn't budge. He stands firm, taking my blows and demanding I open my eyes. I finally give up the struggle. "You fucking told someone! You betrayed me!"

"I told Gus and his supplier." He releases his grip and points to his fingers. "I asked for help, Abigail!"

"And his supplier's name just happened to be Deacon Cruz."

"Yeah," he confirms as tears stream over my cheeks. "It was. I called him and I begged for help because my bat shit crazy sister wanted someone to kill her because she couldn't stomach the idea of killing herself after Colton died."

"You're such a fucker!" I cry, babbling incoherently. "It was all a set up, rigged to make me stop. Jynx was never supposed to stay."

He rolls his hazel eyes and huffs, "I did it because I love you, Abby. And you deserve a lot more than what you were wanting. You deserve love."

"No! I don't! I never did!" Glancing up, I spot the tears in his eyes. "I was the replacement child for Alan, nothing more. Dad wanted another boy and he got me. That is why I became his biker *brat*."

He sighs, ignoring my need to segue the conversation. "Jynx was only supposed to figure out how to remove the ad. I didn't know he was going to..." He looks for the words, waving his arms around like the answer will land on his fingertips. "I didn't know he was going to fall in love with you. I didn't know he would be so damned perfect for my sister. Before you walk away from him for good, you need to take a breath."

"I already walked away from him," I callously say like the bitch I was born to be. "And now, I'm walking away from you."

"Abby, please!"

"There is nothing left to say. Good luck with selling the house, rehab, and the rest of your life. I'm going to live mine."

41

CAN WE GO BACK

JYNX

MY EYES SLIT OPEN AS THE SUN STARTS TO FADE INTO THE horizon. The brightness blinds my eyes, prohibiting my sleep. "Fuck... the cocks!" I stumble out of bed, wishing I could return to the dream I was having. Echo and I were on a tropical white sand beach.

I still hear her laugh.

I still see her smile.

I trip over the pile of clothes, grabbing onto the dresser, and knocking over the tequila bottle. "Goddammit!"

I throw a dirty shirt on the puddle to soak up the mess.

She's been out of my life for three weeks.

October is almost here.

And I'm moving next week. I should've been there last week, but I ran into some trouble with a guy named Jim Beam and his best friend, Jose Cuervo. They dueled my ass nightly and kept winning by a wide margin.

Don't bet on me.

Foolish moves.

I fire up a smoke before tugging on my jeans. I need a shower, a shave, and maybe something to eat that doesn't come in a bottle. I hurt—*all over*. I pop a couple of acetaminophens and grab the uncapped whiskey bottle off of the nightstand. I wash them down and grab my ball cap.

Fuck the shirt or belt.

I zip down the staircase to the wrecked house. Grandma would kick my fucking ass if she knew how bad it looked. I slip on a pair of flip-flops by the side door and head out to feed the animals. I should've kept the Ag boys on until I left, but I stuffed a wad of cash in their palms, thanked them for their help, and let them go in one sentence.

I. Am. An. Asshole.

Riding the four-wheeler out to the horse stalls, I feel her arms around me. I kill it and grieve, moping with my hand covering my face. I'm not a man who cries. More bluntly, I don't ever cry. But fuck if she hasn't got me. She is inflicting severe damage now.

"God, I miss you," I sob, breaking down and feeling all the pain of losing her. She isn't here. And she isn't coming back.

Where is she?

I don't have a fucking clue, and neither does anyone else. No credit cards. No plane tickets. No re-emergence in California.

Nothing.

I'd worry about her if I didn't know her, but she'll put up a fight. I keep telling myself she doesn't need me. She'll be okay without me. And it's probably all true.

Echo doesn't need me.

I want her to need me.

"Fuck!" I bellow, kickstarting the four-wheeler. I wipe my eyes on the back of my hand and barrel toward the barn, full speed ahead. It won't kill me like I wanted the cement wall to do when I was twenty-seven.

But I even fucked that up.

I grumble and groan, dismounting to gather the cocks and fowls' feed. I ride out to their pen and dump the bucket of chow. I freshen the water as they squawk in protest at the missing girl who used to chatter with them.

I'm surrounded by peacocks and lost without one girl.

"You guys should go to Dermot's parent's house," I say, snarling. He owns the feed store in town and offered to buy the whole flock from me. I doubt they'll stay put anywhere they go.

This is their home.

I wanted to be her home.

She flew away because she was in danger.

Just like a peacock, my Sweet Pea, flew away from me.

She was in danger too.

And it was all my fucking fault.

Regardless if I move them to Texas or sell them to Dermot, they'll feel displaced and out of sorts. They'll spend the rest of their lives trying to get back to where they belong.

"Just like you."

Shit.

She won't. She isn't a damn bird. She's a girl with a mind of her own.

And I don't think she is well trained enough to return to me.

A few months was all it took for her to screw me over completely. I'll be looking for her—*forever.* I'm part of a mated pair, and my partner has gone...*missing.*

Ignore that it never should've happened because she was too damn young; the simple truth is that it did.

And now, all I want is her.

"Be good ladies and gents."

She always wanted to stay longer with the peacocks. Sometimes, we would. Far too often, I had work waiting in the house, and I would cut her short. I will never have the chance to do that again. And even if I did, I wouldn't rush us along. I'd prop next to the coop and relish in her playing with the birds she felt spiritually connected to.

I hop on the four-wheeler and drive the long way around the property, out by the lake. Immediately, I stop, jarred by the sight of a gator sticking half-way out of my lake.

"Where the hell did you come from?" He spots me, not moving. We're in a stand-off—*he and I*—and on the other side of him is the shed where she stayed.

She isn't there.

First place I checked.

I stop every day, paying penance for my sins and begging the disciples of darkness to bless me with one gift. "You're a big, beautiful boy. You can attack me if you want, but my girl's spirit is in that shed over there. And that, my friend, is where I am going."

With determination, I point, and he seems to understand, scooting back into the water and disappearing without incident.

"Go feast on a cotton mouth or snapper turtle."

I speed past the lake and park. Unlocking the door, I spot the chains lying on the floor and close my eyes as the flashback haunts my mind.

In my Phoenix hotel room, I asked, "What do you mean—a girl wants to be assaulted?"

"I mean, this kid's sister is off her rocker and asking to be raped. The ad is up on the Gray Market," Deacon said, smoking like a chimney on the phone. "Can you see if you can pull it down or something?"

Or something.

I scratch my forehead and lay on the bed. The pillow still smells like her perfume as I grip it to my chest.

"You want to abduct her?" he asked, shaking his head as I met with him outside the hotel in New Orleans. "You shouldn't be doing this. You're getting in too deep."

"It's too late for that. Are you going to help me or do I need to bind and gag her all the way to South Carolina?"

"I'll help you, but you're going to be the one needing help if you lose her," he advised, handing the pills to me. "Make sure you want to do this because if you fuck up, she will destroy you."

I hate how right he was.

My hand clutched around the pill bottle. "How do you know?"

"Because you're a predator, Jynx. And you won't admit it, but you've been stalking her for months. Her brother wanted the ad taken down, and you decided to usher this thing in a fucked up direction. She's yours. And this mess is on you."

I remember picking her up out of the car when we finally arrived. She was out of it. I didn't know what to do with her, so I did the one thing I knew she couldn't get out of—a shackle and chain on her foot in the shed. It wasn't the best situation, but neither was her option.

We were both bad—searching for a way out. She found hope in an online post, and I rekindled my addiction by hijacking her life.

Neither of us was getting out unscathed.

Her wounds, my scars...we were a mess of hurt and misery, but somehow, it worked. She had the light in her eyes, tempted by my dreadful ways. I guarded the doom and reveled in her emanating rays.

I toss the pillow down and straighten the bed. "I love you, Echo Maines."

With a smirk, I see the look in her eyes as I thrust into her ass. She believed in me.

"I want an honorable man with a closet full of skeletons."

"I possess those; I possess you."

Tilting my head back, I rub my eyes. "There's no coming back from where we've been. And there is no getting over you." I mournfully walk out of the shed, shut and lock the door. I press my hand to the wood. "I'm sorry I took you. I'm sorry I broke you. I'm sorry I ruined you."

The sun sets, shooting off a generous splash of tangerine and flamingo in the sky. She loved dusk with a passion. I stop off at the barn to feed and water the horses. I'll clean the stalls tomorrow. I said that yesterday too. I should call someone to help with the horses.

I should call someone to help me.

But who would understand what I'm going through?

I abducted a girl, and now, I'm disheartened because I lost her. Fuck you, asshole. Fuck me. I fucked up.

I'm just lucky she didn't file charges against me. She had every right. I took her. I coerced her. I fell in love with her and refused to give her up. And I did terrible things to her every night in the darkness.

In the light, she forgave me.

Because I am a gentleman with a decent body, a friendly smile, and kind regard, she pardoned me for the spoils of the midnight hour, and I punished her body until dawn for being so damned beautiful.

Hell, I miss her.

I SCOUT OVER THE HOUSE, WHICH RESEMBLES A BACHELOR pad. Grandma really would kick my ass for this. "I have to clean this shithole up because I'm moving in four days." I grab my phone, turn on some music—Kanye West's *My Beautiful Dark Twisted Fantasy*—and blast it.

I start with dumping one suitcase from Arizona directly into the washing machine. I hit the kitchen next containing twenty-one days of dishes—coffee cups and silverware, mostly. I empty the fridge with all the leftovers I've stashed.

Picking up the living room, I fill one trash bag and start another. I grab one of the booze boxes—*there were three - a box for each week - I'm balanced after all*—and fill it with the empty liquor bottles.

I clean the bathroom to a spotless shine, change my sheets, and collect the laundry from my room. I vacuum and mop. I clean until I smell like damn Lysol and bleach.

"I'm certain I didn't wear all of these clothes," I mumble, looking at the four laundry baskets full. "Shit..." I sigh, knowing there is no way I'm finishing it tonight. Stripping off my clothes, I toss them to the growing heap and grab a bottle of water from the fridge before heading upstairs. I pass by the double doors on the second floor. "I'm packing you up tomorrow."

I haven't decided if I'm selling the farm.

The beach house is on the market—*cheap.*

I turn on the shower and smoke a cigarette, wishing I had something more. I don't. I know better. Addiction is a nasty thing. But tonight, it would be nice to cut the edge off. I stare at myself in the mirror. "You need to shave and go for a run."

I decide not to put off one of those.

Twenty minutes later, I realize how bad I look as my pasty skin holds the dimples I cannot hide. "Tomorrow, you're eating." I point at myself in the mirror. "No excuses. Need to get back up on the horse." I nod and step into the hot, steaming water. "Damn."

Pressing my hands to the tiled wall, I try to remember the last time I was in water. It's been at least a week, probably when I puked the gin. I love goddamned gin. Unfortunately, it doesn't like me. Course, I drank the entire bottle in a matter of two hours.

I lather myself up twice and stay in the shower until I run out of hot water. I let the cold blast my skin and let out a deep, guttural roar. I have got to get her out of my system.

Hit me with something.

As long as it doesn't have a pussy.

Please stop raping my heart.

I'm begging.

I feel infringed upon, violated, assaulted.

She's penetrating my soul and threatening to end me. I cannot let her do this to me. "I'm Jynx Monroe. I hit Echo. I quit Echo." I repeat it about a hundred times as I dry off and toss on a pair of loose, thin gray lounge pants. I grab my laptop from the bag, click on the flatscreen, and sign into Gray Market.

Nothing.

Her ad isn't up.

I search for her name to see when the last time she was on was. Her account has been disabled or deleted by the user.

The user.

Who was using who?

Who abducted who?

I close my eyes as wetness clusters on my lashes. "Goddammit, Ek! Where are you?"

I check my phone.

Nothing.

I check my email.

Same.

She's gone.

I stroke my bare cheeks with one hand as I poke around in places sane people don't go. I will never be one of them. "You're somewhere. I know you are. You're too drawn to the dark."

I find zero leads. Not a clue. I shake my head. "You went to Alabama." I pull up the address for her house. "You're not going to Texas via Birmingham, asshole." I sigh. "Message me. Give me something."

Nope.

I wind up on nasty porn, stroke my dick less than a dozen times, and call it a night.

My balls ache.

But not nearly as bad as my heart stuck in the cage.

RIDE LIKE YOU MEAN IT

JYNX

"WE'VE GOT THE PERFECT SPOT," AXEL SAYS THREE DAYS later on the phone as I pack up most of Grandma's house. "Problem is, it's halfway between Austin and San Antonio, but it's cheap."

Cheap—*there is a word I actually like in this instance.*

But I'm surprised to hear it coming out of Axel's mouth. I was expecting some grandiose, golden, and crystal palace that charged six figures a month.

"Why is that a problem?"

He pauses like I should readily know the answer. "You're moving to Houston."

"I'm not running Peacock!" I insist, moving her old books from the case to the box. "Wang is leading it, not me."

He laughs. "You say that until the phone call comes at three in the morning, and he whines, Jynx, fix it!"

I roll my eyes because he's right. "Then I guess I move. I'm not worrying about this right now. I've got a fucking morgue of memories to deal with."

"I'll call you later."

"Hey, Ax, sign the lease."

"I'm not signing the lease, chump muffin. I'm buying the damn building. It's cheap."

"Fine, whatever," I say, scooting a box of fragile knickknacks out of the way. "Make it happen."

I bought sheets to cover the antique furniture, and now a fright of ghosts inhabits the home, scaring me at every turn. The first night I had the living room covered, I walked downstairs to get a drink in the middle of the night and just about pissed myself.

It's eerie, everything changing shape.

The house has looked the same since I was a boy. It's unnerving to shift perception. It's also very good for my psyche.

I leave in two days, but I'm running out of room in my truck. I've been trying to figure out how to drive my truck, tow the Mustang, bring my bike in the back of the truck, and still manage to get half of what I don't want to ship. I've about decided it's impossible.

Taking a breath, I make a whiskey and coke before assessing what is left to do. I light a smoke in the kitchen, feeling a bit closed in by all of it.

Leaving South Carolina was never in my plans.

Under my hand, the phone buzzes with a text from the real estate agent. He's taking a couple out to the beach house this afternoon and needs the keys since we did the listing over the phone.

"Fuck," I mutter, glancing at my watch. It's just before noon. The construction crew packed up and left when I halted completion since I was putting it on the market. No one else has a key but me. I swallow the rest of my drink and text him back—*"Meet me at the house in two hours."*

I open the junk drawer, which I still haven't gone through, and grab a set of the beach house keys. I toss my Reckless Rebellion hoodie on and pluck the keys for the Harley off the hook. The car is already loaded on the car hauler, and the truck is full of boxes. I don't have anything else to drive. I mean, I do...but...

I grumble, "I don't fucking have time for this today."

But I need to sell the house.

Not for the money.

The memory—*or would-have-been memories*—implicitly conditional with an existential improbability to never occur.

Yeah. Beach house needs to GTFO of my life.

I lock the house and carefully pull the bike out of the garage between the two cars—my drag car, which I moved up from the shop and is being freighted tomorrow, and her Mama-mobile, which I have no idea what the fuck to do with. Running back inside, I grab the keys and decide to drop them off with Dermot.

He took the flock to his parent's place; he'll take her keys too.

I sold the peacocks because I cannot keep them.

It hurts.

And everything that hurts is going away.

I had Axel drive her new blue Mustang to Texas. I plan on stripping it out and building another drag car.

Remove the source of pain.

The horses are being professionally transported later this afternoon. Deacon offered to let them stay at his farm until I get settled. If I sell Grandma's house, I'll have to hire movers or come back or maybe both. I haven't made up my mind yet.

And that is how one man disassembles almost seventy-five years' worth of love and devotion—one day at a fucking time.

I fire up the bike on a pleasant day. There is a hint of fall in the air, and the ride will be brisk on my cheeks, reinvigorating me, which is a good thing because I have a ton of shit to get done.

Stopping in town, I fill the tank with gas and veer next door to the feed shop. I walk inside as Amelia greets, "Howdy, handsome!"

"Hi, beautiful," I warmly say, kissing her cheek and pulling off my sunglasses. Amelia is Dermot's sister, and I've known her forever.

Almost twenty years ago, Dermot McElvaney was the drug dealer in our small town. My gang made him a ton of money. Dermot and I are the only ones still left in this town. We never made it out, so we have a pretty significant history of fistfights, bar brawls, and good times. He's probably my best friend. "Is Dermot here?"

"Yep, he's out back with Madison," she says, grinning. Madison is his older sister. I don't know how much of my spunk she's swallowed, but back in the day, it was a lot. "They're unloading a hay shipment."

I never tapped Amelia because she was a good girl, unlike Madi, who was open with twenty-four/seven drive-thru service. Madi liked assholes—and not my kind of an asshole, either. Abusive guys were her forte, but they only landed her with many bruises, broken bones, three ex-husbands, two kids, and one very pissed off brother.

Thank God Dermot was the only son.

I meander through the tack and feed shop his grandparents owned. He's local with deep roots like me. Despite being born up north, Grandma secured my spot in being a small town, Southern gent. I was as good as native.

I spot Madi and her bright red hair standing in the open trailer of a semi-truck. She's pushing bales to the edge and struggling to do that as Dermot and an employee stack them on the carts.

I hop up in the trailer and finish moving the bales as Madi goes to help a customer inside. She suggestively smiles, but I ignore her. Not a chance in hell I'm going around that worn out block. I'm better than that. God only knows what diseases linger there.

Dermot and I finish up quickly, and he asks, "How are you doing?"

"I need you to do me one more favor," I say, following him over to the fence where he lights up a smoke. His fully inked sleeves cover the scars of our youth—his battles were hard-won between the needle and the vein. He's been sober for fifteen years now.

I don't feel like I'm even sober now.

I'm drunk on a girl I cannot have. Pulling the keys to her car from my pocket, I drop them in his palm. "I need you to get these to her if I call you."

"You steal her car?"

I tried to steal her heart.

And I failed miserably.

"No," I snicker. "She left it here when we flew out to Phoenix. We broke up. She left. I don't have a clue where she is, but I imagine she'll want them back eventually."

"I got you, man," he replies, puffing on the smoke. "If you need some help out in the Lone Star State, holler at me."

I nod. "I will."

"I'm a phone call away."

"I know," I mumble, tossing my sunglasses on. "But you know Deacon, he doesn't drop the ball. I need to go. The realtor has someone interested in the beach house."

"Take care, brother." He embraces me. "Don't let the girl drag you down."

"Never," I lie, accepting that it is too late for that. I'm tied to her heart and being jostled through the crevasses of a cranky, glaciovolcanic hell. "I just need a change of scenery for a while."

"You won't ever come back," he points out. "And I wouldn't blame you. Hell, I may wind up trailing your ass if things don't pick up around here."

I turn back to him. "Do you need some money?"

"No, it's not about money. I need decent help. That's why I've got both the girls working with me now."

"I'm not selling your animal chow."

He laughs, and we part ways as I start the journey toward the ocean. I've done this trip so many times; I can do it blindfolded. I take backroads, avoiding the highways. A few leaves are falling on the perfectly crisp fall day.

I think about the past, the town, Dermot, my grandma, and the cows grazing in the fields I pass—anything to keep my mind off the one who has me so tied up in knots.

I can't think. I can't eat. I can't sleep.

Her absence is the worst fucking case of withdrawal ever.

I arrive shortly after one and hand over the keys. I don't make small talk—not interested. Just sell my fucking house, and the painful *would-have-been* memories contained therein. He checks to make sure they work, and I spot the grand curved staircase where she once stood.

The moment blasts my heart like a tidal wave, locking all of my emotions up. I'm safer being a coldhearted, cruel bastard than a caring soul.

We shake hands, and I nod at the house as I put my helmet back on and ride away.

I don't cry.

I grieve.

STOPPING AT THE END OF THE DRIVEWAY, I GRAB THE LAST day's worth of mail at the farmhouse. It will start being forwarded tomorrow.

J.A. Monroe no longer lives here.

I don't live where the mail is being delivered either—342 Del Rio Canyon Road in Little Bee, Texas. I've never seen the place, but tomorrow, I'm officially a resident.

I straddle onto the bike, slowly pulling down the gravel path. I wonder how long someone has to live in Texas to be considered—*a Texan?* It's kind of cool sounding. *'I'm a Texan.'* Hell of a pickup line. All the girls will think I wear boots, jeans, and a cowboy hat while toting around a massive cock. Well, one out of four ain't bad.

Dear God.

Axel will be wearing giant silver belt buckles.

I shake the thought away and park next to the truck. "I've got to figure this out. How do I get you, Harley, inside of you, truck bed, with all the boxes?"

"You use my car," Echo mutters, revealing herself at the edge of the garage.

I drop the mail. "Fuck." I bend down to pick it up.

"Which part makes you say fuck?" she asks, stepping closer. "Dropping the mail or me?"

I glance up, still low to the ground, and gaze at her smiling face. Her freshly bleached blonde hair shimmers with the sunlight on her back. She appears like an angel, a gift from the heavens above, sent to rescue me.

"That all depends on you, I suppose." I stand up, but she's too close. I dodge around her and walk toward the garage.

"I need my car keys, Jeremiah."

I spin back with a wolfish grin. "You need more than keys, Darlin'." She giggles and chases after me as I unlock the door. "Where have you been?"

"Do you want the truth?"

"Yeah," I say, smacking the mail down on the kitchen counter. It snaps, and she jumps. "Because I've been worried fucking sick."

"I've been hitchhiking since I left Birmingham." She could not have told me anything worse at this point. "I ended up going to New England. I stayed there for about a week until I finally found a sweet little couple who took me to Tennessee and let me stay in their basement for another week. Then, their daughter drove me down to Miami where we stayed for a week. She dropped me off here on her way back home."

I blink, unamused, and ill-prepared to deal with her dangerous stunts. I have a good mind to grab her arm, drop her leggings, and blister her ass until she cries. And to top it off, I'll fuck her ass just as a reminder as to who owns her.

"You're serious. Aren't you?"

"When your future spouse is a techno geek, you don't pull out a credit card."

And now, on top of everything else, she is blaming me.

True, but still.

"I see."

"My brother sold the house for cash and gave me ten grand."

My mouth drops open at her absolute stupidity. "You hitchhiked? With ten grand in your purse?"

With an innocent expression, she whispers, "Some of it was sewn in my jacket and tucked in my panties."

That's it.

My fingers latch onto her arm and push her face down on the kitchen table. I yank the back of her pants down and wallop her with a hefty palm. "You do not go hitchhiking across the country!" I scold, striking her sweet—*God, she is so sweet*—delicate flesh. My mouth waters. My dick hardens. Everything in me is on fire and set to explode at any moment. "Never ever again!"

Tears drip from her eyes. "But it brought me back to you! And I'd never rode in an eighteen-wheeler before!"

Oh. No. You didn't.

With one hand on her back, I use the other to snap my belt off, rip it through the loops, and welt her ass red. She is screaming, crying, and I lose it with one tug of my zipper. Grabbing my surging shaft, I thrust into her swollen pussy lips and moan, "Goddammit, Abby! Do not ever leave me again!"

My hand smooths over hers, resting flat on the table, and she lifts her fingers, lacing them into mine. My other hand grabs her hip, and I piston deep inside of her wetness until she whimpers, "Fuck me, Jynx. Fuck me harder."

And I lose it fast, coming like a rocket and depositing all of my milky seed inside of her warmth. I don't care if she comes right now. She's in trouble—*big trouble*—and her punishment isn't over. I lean over, nuzzling her hair and kissing her neck. "I love you, bitch."

"I know you do, asshole."

I fall from her folds, and she flips over. I set her on the table and stare. "I can't believe you're here. I can't believe you came back to me."

"I needed time to think about things. And I realized how much I love you beyond all of the shit. I want to live my life with you. I need you by my side." Her hands run over my shoulders and land on the RR emblem on my left pec. "You're a biker."

"I don't qualify for your ad."

"I know," she mutters as mascara drips over her cheeks. "That's why I rewrote it. I'm now looking for Natural Dominant. Alpha. Male. Nerdy biker—a professional-type of bad boy. I'm seeking him for pure ravishment, abduction, and torture scenes. Plenty of personal communication is expected for a lifetime commitment. And he must provide lots of tacos."

I grin wide. "... Is that so?"

"Yes, Sir."

"And you realized all of that while in an eighteen-wheeler?"

"Actually," she says, smiling. "I came up with that when I was in New Jersey heading to Tennessee. I was a bit broken for the first week. I cried a lot because I saw you take a man's life."

"I did that for you," I interject as she bravely places her finger on my lips.

"I know that," she whispers. "But I never wanted you to feel like you had to change for me or even defend me."

"That's what a boyfriend does."

"Well, I know that now, too. I never had one of you before."

Holding her in my arms, I laugh. "... A boyfriend or a stalker?"

"Both!" She giggles, and I kiss her lips again for the first time. I start slow and sensual with little pecks until I can't take anymore. I slip my tongue inside of her mouth, and her hands ease under my hoodie. We're hot, smoldering, and so needy for one another. I take everything she offers and demand for more like a greedy bastard. "Take me to bed, Jynx. Make love to me in the light."

I scoop her into my arms, not questioning or fighting. "You're still in trouble," I remind, marching up the staircase. "And you're not getting out of it."

"Neither are you, Jynx."

THE SLIP OF SAND

JYNX

I WAKE WITH HER SNUGGLED BESIDE ME. I SPOON MY BODY around hers, providing plenty of warmth. Her blonde hair is spread out, twining around my bicep. She secures my place to her heart with every breath from her lungs. And I will never get enough of Echo Maines.

I made love to her for hours in the light yesterday.

Not fucking—*passionately wild lovemaking*.

Rolling toward my chest, she sleepily grins. "How long have you been up?"

"A bit," I reply, stroking her cheek. "You were tired."

"You have stuff to do today?"

"First off, I have to go retrieve your car keys from Dermot," I inform, staring at her radiance in the early morning light. She shines in my shadows. "And then I need to finish packing."

"I'll help you," she offers, pushing on my shoulder. I ease over onto my back as she crawls on top of me. She readily straddles me—owning every bit of her sexuality and her relationship with me. "We can load up my car and I will follow you to Texas."

"Not a chance," I counter, rubbing my hands over her hips and encouraging her behavior. I invite her once with a gentle rock of my hips and a flick of my brow. "I love following that ass."

"I'll need directions," she whispers, batting her lashes and reaching between us. Her slender fingers guide me to her wetness. She isn't timid or afraid of me at all, and I love that about her. She's aggressive, going after what she wants with gusto and vigor. "I tend to get lost."

"You're doing a great job of finding exactly what you're looking for right now."

She blushes and giggles as I arch up and slide in a bit more. I offer her my hands, and she grasps them, lowering onto me. "That's easy when you're pointing north with a big cock."

I laugh and snarl. "Do you have any idea how much I love you?"

"I have an idea," she says, smiling. "But you should know, I ran out of birth control pills a week ago."

My only reaction is a grin. "Are you trying to trap me, schoolgirl?"

"Would I do that?" She winks, leisurely riding my cock with rhythmic sweeping motions from base to tip. "It's not like I like you."

"That's enough from you," I playfully tease, sitting up and kissing her sweet lips. "If I get you pregnant, you'll have to stay with me."

"Mhmm," she moans. "Because I wouldn't be capable of caring for a baby by myself?"

"Not at all," I boast, wrapping my arms around her waist and rolling my hips from beneath. "I know you can do it. The point is I don't want you to. You're mine. The baby I plan on putting in your belly is mine."

She eyes me. "... Possessive much?"

"Quite a bit, actually."

"We'll need to practice a lot."

"Of course!"

"How many kids do you want?"

"I'd never actually thought about having children," I honestly admit. "I was always concerned with avoiding them until you came along. You broke me."

"Maybe I fixed you!" She softly smiles but turns rapidly serious. "Are you sure you want them with me?"

"Echo, the first time I looked in your eyes at the wedding, I knew I wanted you to be the mother of my children. I will take a boy or a girl or twins or whatever we're blessed with, but the one thing I know is I want to have children with you."

She glances down as a blush rises on her cheeks. "We're really doing this?"

"We are," I confirm, inching closer to her lips. "You're my girl."

She rolls her body against mine, and a minute later, she drops a much bigger bomb than possible offspring. "I want to ride on your bike."

My brows tighten with concern. "... You what? I thought you were the anti-biker?"

"I met this really great guy and he loves riding, so I have to make sure the seat fits my ass."

"Ahh, I see," I reply, holding back a shit-eating grin. "Because you may not fit?"

"Right!" She nods as her hazel eyes sparkle at me. "There are things I need to work on healing, and this is a big one. There is not a better man for me to latch my arms around while doing sixty."

"Do you mean that? Do you really feel that way?"

"I do," she hastily says. "Just don't call me your old lady because I'm not ready for that yet. And I don't know if I ever will be. The phrase has a long history of being a painful thing in my mind."

"I'm a rather mature, patient fellow." I promise, "Those two words will not come out of this mouth, but you never have to worry about me doing something dumb. I waited years for you to show up. I will be loyal, loving, and doting on you until my last breath."

"Will you defend my wish to not be called such by your brothers?"

With my complete focus on her, I shake my head. "You never have to ask me to defend you; it will just happen, I assure you. The incident in Tucson can easily occur again, but honestly, my cousin will probably beat me to it and make the point very clear one time. That will be the end of it."

"So we'll ride?"

"We will," I agree, stealing her mouth for my lascivious needs. "But first I'm making you come on my dick and then I'm bathing you in a nice, hot shower."

"I could get used to this."

"Please do," I seriously say. "Just know, if you toss me a positive pregnancy test, I will be twice as bad."

"That would mean you're coming too."

"Oh, baby, I'm going to come in you forever."

Есно

I SIT ON HIS HARLEY SEAT WHEN HE HOLDS OPEN HIS RR hoodie, and I slip my arms inside. He zips it up and asks, "When was the last time you were on a bike?"

My lips twitch, thinking. "Probably thirteen, maybe fourteen."

"It's been awhile."

"Yeah, once I hit those teenage years, I didn't want to ride with my father anymore because it started to take on a symbolism of the club, his cheating, and my mom's subsequent behavior. I never knew her not being crazy, but the more self-sufficient we became, the worse she acted. She loves club life and ignores his shit. Unfortunately, I couldn't."

"I don't think that's unfortunate," he says, plopping a helmet on my head. It's way too big. "You're smart enough to recognize bad situations and not put yourself in the middle of them." He straddles onto the bike. "If you get nervous or need to stop, let me know."

"So I can tell you to stop the bike, but not stop driving your dick into my backdoor?"

"Pretty much," he replies, putting on his sunglasses and smirking. "Hold on, gorgeous."

He starts the bike, and I feel the rumble travel through my core. I ease closer to him. "Is this okay?"

"Get as close to me as you need to," he politely invites, glancing over his shoulder. He wants me to be comfortable in his presence, even if I am throwing a hissy fit. "You aren't going to bother me. Just go slow if you plan on grabbing my dick."

"How do you know I will grab your dick?"

"Your name is Ekky and you're twenty-two," he snickers as we slowly drive on the gravel. "They're coming to get the horses later today."

"You'll be back in time," I reassure, feeling his hard, warm body against mine. We reach the end of the driveway. "Where are the peacocks?"

"I sold them."

In an instant, I'm utterly heartbroken. "... You did?"

"And I am working on selling the beach house too," he informs as I frown. "I needed to get rid of everything that reminded me of you."

"Is that why you packed Clementine's house? Are you selling it?"

"I haven't decided yet," he says as I rest my face against the back of his neck. "I can do whatever you want. And we can start our muster of peacocks. The best chance for their survival is to stay near home. I hope they don't come back here, but they might."

My eyes threatened to spill as I babble, "You sold the peacocks."

"We can rebuild our ostentation of peacocks."

I grab his balls and taunt, "Smartass." He laughs, stopping at the end of the drive. "Don't be a pussy pulling out just on my account."

"I don't plan on it," he snarls, lowering his shades and peering over his shoulder. "And I don't ever pull out."

By the time he exits the feed store, I'm begging for more of his ride like a sex-starved kitten. I enjoy the long trip down the backroads until I recognize where we are.

"Jynx? Why are we at the beach house?"

"I need to say my final goodbye," he says with a hint of sadness, driving down the blacktop road to the magnificent house. "I got an offer on her this morning."

Before we've stopped, I pull off my helmet and question, "Are you taking it?"

"I don't know," he replies as we stop in front of the steps on the circular drive. The old, dilapidated house has been torn down. The pristine yard is landscaped and looks nothing like what I remember.

"Is the inside still unfinished?"

"For the most part," he informs, extending his hand to me. "They finished the walls, but we omitted a lot of the trims and details for the final owners to choose."

"Can I see it one more time?"

"Of course," he says with a smile as we climb the steps to the front porch. I turn around to the ocean view, and he unlocks the door. "I'm going to miss the water."

The house is clean and neat, smelling of paint and varnish. I run my hand over the smoothness of the ornately carved wood handrail on the staircase and meander through the house with him following me.

Though instead of a house tour, a melancholy feeling takes hold, like visiting a cemetery. I walk the three levels, peering in every room. He stays close, and I whisper, "I want to see the water."

Through the gardens, a stone path leads to wooden planks set within the sand as I gaze with wonder out to the sea. I bravely pull off my shoes.

"It's gonna be chilly," he warns, smirking. "Don't get too wet."

"It's hard not to when you're around." I wink.

The waves rush around my feet, and I bite my lip. "When I was a little girl, my father used to go for weekend rides. He loved the water, and it didn't surprise me when they moved to Florida. I never liked the ocean because it seemed so much bigger than me, like it could swallow me whole. And I remember, he used to dip my feet in the gulf and I would scream like I was being murdered. But he insisted on doing it anyway and laughing at my cries."

"I won't ever laugh at your cries, not your real ones at least," I whisper, knowing how hard it is for her to open up. Because it is hard for me too. "Do you still feel like the seas will consume you?"

"No," I whisper as he walks up and wraps his arms tightly around me. "I have you to protect me. Nothing will ever hurt me again. Not like he did. I want to be brave enough to have my wedding on a beach. I'm tired of being the victim of his emotional abuse; I want to be a survivor."

"I won't let anything happen to you ever."

"I know," I mutter with puddles forming in my eyes. "That's why the girl who is terrified of the water is standing in the Atlantic Ocean with her boyfriend holding her. You're part of this culture, this place, and I don't know how I feel about you moving away from it."

"Texas has the Gulf too."

"It's different," I say, realizing what all he is giving up. "Why are you doing it?"

"You want the truth?"

"Yes," I say, nodding. "Please."

"Because this place as fond as I am of it, holds a lot of bad memories for me. I want to start over somewhere new with you. Not your home. Not my home. Our home, a neutral ground with no history."

"And only your cousin to bail us out of trouble?"

"My brother too," he says with a crooked smirk. "There won't be a lack of good family."

I walk, just a few feet away, feeling the sand slip beneath my feet. He trusts me, letting me go alone as I process the idea of our new lives together.

We aren't starting. We already started four-plus months ago at a wedding. This is our love story, and we're writing every page. Every day is a new memory, another page.

"It's so amazing," I marvel, glancing up at the beautiful white house with teal shutters. "Why don't you keep it for a vacation home?" I spin back to Jynx and find him grinning and lowered on one knee. "Oh, my God..." I cover my mouth as the tears shower against my cheeks. I am ugly crying in front of a fabulous man. "What are you doing Jynx?"

"Abigail Echo Renata Maines, you are the most incredible woman I've ever met. And when you left, I swore if I ever saw you again, this would be one of the first things I did. I don't want to ever lose you again. I don't want to spend another minute without you by my side. I need you in my life like I've never needed anyone else. And I want you to be my wife. I want to give you my last name and my life—every good and bad memory from here on out, I want them to be with you." He stops to open the red box and pulls the stunning diamond halo ring out. "Will you marry me?"

I freeze. "Shit." I turn away and bounce in place for a minute.

"... Ekky?"

"Hmm?"

"Let the scream out."

And I do.

I yell like a siren calling the seas to her side.

When I finally calm down to take a breath, I smirk like an innocent angel with the devil on my mind and shout, "Yes! Yes! I will marry you Jynx Monroe!"

I hold out my hand, and he slides the ring on my finger. With a boyish grin, he confides, "I've never done this before. I never thought I would."

"You did fine!" I giggle as he stands and picks me up high into the air. "I'm a bird!"

"Don't stop sailing in those skies, beautiful."

"I snagged a hell of a catch."

His brow lifts, and his dimples pop as he restrains his amusement. "You think?"

"I know," I say as he spins me round and round on the beach. "God, you had me feeling terrible with you acting all sad about selling the house."

"Nah, I turned the offer down and took it off the market this morning."

"You're such a dick!" I tease, swatting at his biceps. "And you're brilliant with me."

He closes his eyes and pulls me close. "I'm crazy in love with you, Ek."

"I'm crazy in love with you too, Jynx. You're my everything! You're my perfect match and I cannot wait to call you my husband," I squeal in his arms again. "I'm going to be Mrs. Jynx Monroe!"

"Yes, you are!"

He sets me down and picks up my shoes. We stroll on the beach, hand in hand. "Hey, since you're my best friend. I need to tell you a few things, J."

"Yeah?"

"I'm gonna marry a biker."

With a deep sigh, he shakes his head and warns, "You need to be careful with those types. They can be dangerous."

"He's also my stalker."

His head jets back as we pick on one another. "Gosh, he must be a real mess."

"And he abducted me!" I continue, making big eyes at him. "He kept me in a shed and did things to me in the dark and then during the day, he was a damn gentleman! I fucking fell in love with this guy!"

With grand exaggeration, he questions, "You did?"

"I did," I giggle. "His first smile stole my heart."

He proudly snarls, trying not to break his composure. "I was only supposed to convince you to take the ad down, but ..."

422 | KAILEE REESE SAMUELS

"You're a bad boy," I interrupt with the declaration and point at him. "Admit it now. Own it. You are a bad boy!"

"I am. You are marrying a bad boy. And I'm hitching a naughty hot young thing to the altar."

"I must be his excuse for a midlife crisis."

He rebounds, "Sugar Daddy much, brat?"

Laughing, I bite my lip and stare at the rock on my finger. "My bad boy has really good taste in jewelry." I grin wide, knowing how bad my cheeks are going to hurt come tonight. "I'm going to smile so much I won't be able to suck your cock later."

"Like hell, bitch."

"Oh, God...yes!"

"Jump!" He commands, lowering down as I leap onto his back, and he carries me piggy-back style to the house. He locks the door, and I kiss his neck.

"I love you, Jeremiah."

"I love you, Abs." He winks. He sets me on the bike and fastens the helmet on my head. "No taking it off early!" He scolds.

I salute with my middle finger, and he snarls. He carefully drives to the road—*the end of our chapter in courtship*—opens her up, and we soar —flying away from the danger.

We'll never be apart again.

We're a mated pair.

44

SO MUCH MORE

JYNX

FOR TWO DAYS, I FOLLOW MY FUTURE WIFE IN HER MAMA-mobile across the southern United States. We spend hardly any physical time together but stay on FaceTime the whole way there. We stop in a hotel in Lafayette, and I buy her a box of cheap tacos. She gobbles them up like a good girl. We don't make love because we're fucking exhausted and ready to start our new life—together in a new place.

New locale. New faces. New friends.

Same Jynx and Echo, but without the bullshit of our past to interrupt our love. Staying brought the risk of interruption, with potentially marred bones being thrown from the closet at every turn. We were running from the skeletons as fast as we could.

For me, it made sense to leave South Carolina. The only reason I stayed so long was because of Grandma, and somewhere deep inside my heart, I knew she wouldn't want me living her life. She would've wanted me to live my own life and be making new memories, especially if I found the perfect girl.

I did.

And I wasn't even looking for her.

The next morning, we stop for coffee and kiss as I fill up our gas tanks. We drive the final four hours to Houston. Leading our way to the address, I pull up to the locked gate, and she whips around me, parking just past the driveway.

Our new home is a hundred-year-old, red-bricked building in the rundown industrial section on the outskirts of town. The old-style sign is painted in a black rectangle at the top with giant white letters, Banks Arts & Co. I glance over to the bustling two-story warehouse across the street with a sign marked, Ever Hope.

Stepping out of the truck, I recheck the address as Echo walks up. "... Is this it?"

"It's the right address," I reply, pointing to the warehouse. "I know that for sure because my cousin grew up there. "

"Deacon grew up in a warehouse?"

"It used to be a clubhouse," I inform as flashbacks of his birthdays hit. They weren't bad ones—full of triggers, but happy times with plenty of good memories. I was four years older than him. We didn't come to Texas often, but I remember every visit. I pull out my phone and call him.

He answers on the first ring but says nothing. A dog barks, and a baby cries in the background. "Sorry about that," he says, winded. "Did you make it? What can I do for you?"

I hesitate and snap a picture to send in a text message. "Am I at the right place?"

"Yeah. Temporary code on the gate is your birthday backward. You can change it when you get upstairs."

"So where do I go?"

"Wherever you want," he chuckles as a beeping noise goes off. "Sorry, microwave. I have an angry hellion crying for lunch. We're giving you the building. Technically, my loverboy is giving you his building, but yeah..."

"... The whole building?"

"Yeah, it's a really long story, but Sal doesn't want it anymore because it holds some bad memories. If you decide you don't want it, let me know. We'll take it back."

"What is this place across the street now?"

"They make lingerie!" Echo excitedly chirps, doing her little bounce dance and showing the website to me. "I have a few EH pieces!"

Deacon laughs. "Yeah, we own that too. The top floor of the loft is finished out like a house, floors two and three store fabric and shit for EH, and the first floor is the garage. Enjoy yourselves."

"Did the horses make it alright?"

"Yeah, they just got here last night," he says, mumbling. "Sal is out riding now."

"So, top floor?"

"Yep. Call me after you've slept. I've got a business proposition for you."

I snicker, "Does it involve lingerie? Because that is something I could really get behind."

"No," he chuckles as Echo spins and shakes her ass at me. "But I'm sure he'll sell you some points if you want in," he snickers as the baby gurgles. "Just don't unpack everything."

"Is he going to want the building back?"

"Nah, he's over it, but we had an idea this morning over Denver omelettes that might work better for you considering Axel bought the building out in Godland."

I laugh. "I told him I wasn't working for Peacock."

"You're right. You're not," he maintains, snapping his Zippo closed. "Someone else wants to hire you outright and make you a partner."

"Okay, this is too much for my head at the moment."

The mafia is calling my name.

And coming for repayment.

"I told you—*later*," he chuckles, exhaling. "Go take a shower. Unwind with your fiancée. There is a list of all the good restaurants that deliver in the kitchen drawer. Tell them you're my cousin. They'll take good care of you."

"Thanks, bro."

Echo blinks at me. "... The whole building?"

"Yeah," I mutter, awed by their generosity, comprehending what it all means—*the mob owns me.*

"You were only supposed to get her out of the mess she is in."

"It's becoming more than that. I want her," I said to my cousin. "And I need some help."

"We only agreed to do this for her brother because Echo was Rampage royalty," he informed. "If it had been anyone else, I would've said no, but I owe one of their charter princesses a favor."

Deacon was in debt too.

And I knew I would be if they helped me get Echo Maines.

"Can you help me?"

"Yeah, but it's going to cost you the rest of your life."

I shook my head. "I don't fucking care. I need this girl."

"We could use your skills."

"Whatever it takes. Deal."

I glance up at the daunting four-story piece of architecture. "They own Ever Hope too."

"Your cousin and his gay lover...*own a lingerie house?*"

Lighting a smoke, I snort as the idea seems to blow her mind. "They own a lot of things to launder money through, sweetheart. And he isn't gay. He's bi and married to a woman."

"Oh," she whispers. "Is she pretty or some old hag he uses as a front?"

"Um…" Furrowing my brow, I question, "Does this matter?"

"I want to know *everything*, Jynx."

I glance over at the high fence surrounding the warehouse. I see the visions of Deacon and I running in the parking lot that we pretended was our kingdom. There used to be an alcove near the building's garage, and it served as our fortress. The lamp posts dotting the lot were fake trees, and we battled massive monsters like beetles. One time, we beat a snake to death with two metal pipes we stole from the shop. We were reckless rebels of the concrete jungle.

"We call her Sal's hot wife," I admit the details of the boy's club. "She's half English, half Japanese, and runs her own mafia."

She rapidly blinks like I spit in her eye. "So he works for her?"

"No, he has his outfit, she has hers, and my cousin has the club," I say as she looks baffled by the idea. "Deacon and Sal partner their businesses together."

She gives a scrutinizing stare with much concern. "… Who is the biggest?"

"She is—by far—right now, but that could change."

"You should work for her," she blurts out as I laugh. "She knows what's up."

"I cannot go to work for the opposing team," I inform, unable to stop smiling. "Shall we go check this out?"

"Yes!" she excitedly squees. "We're on a grand adventure! But you should still work for his hot wife."

I'm not sure why she is encouraging this.

His hot wife is not my type.

I prefer to be the only one in bed with a pair of balls.

I like my women, demure and undefiled.

"We are having a grand adventure," I reply, pushing in my birthday backward. "And, no."

"Damn you're old, 1983. Are y'all going to refer to me as Jynx's hot wife?"

"Probably, Miss 1998."

"That's much better than old lady."

She grins, and I kiss her lips. We hold hands, walking back to the curb. "You pull in first."

I watch as she carefully backs up and swings her car into the small parking garage. She runs back out and hops up in my truck. I didn't get her door, and I feel like an ass about it. *Yeah, yeah. Gentleman.*

"What if the F-250 doesn't fit?"

"I'm not thinking about that," I reply. She grabs my phone, sitting in the console as I tilt my head with dread. "It's not gonna fit."

"Deacon says it will if you hit it directly in the middle."

"Even with the trailer?"

"Yep!" she declares with huge eyes and a shrug. "He says pull straight in."

I snark, "I never pull in crooked."

I back up and swing it wide as she booms, "Holy shit, you're good!"

"Age, baby," I flirt, grinning, and she pokes my arm. "Takes a certain amount of crazy to do this."

"Fuck!" she yelps. "That scared the hell out of me! My feet are sweating!"

I shut off the engine and look around. "We are tight in here. Hold on. I'll come and get you." I weasel out the door and shut the cage door for the garage before obtaining my soon-to-be bride from the truck. "M'lady?"

She slips her hand in mine. "I'm so happy, J."

"You're not alone." I smile.

I grab our overnight bag, and we crank up to the fourth floor in the antique cage lift. The pulleys squeak on the quaint, stylish, and chic elevator. Her hand brushes over the exquisite relic detailed with curves, swirls, and birdcage inlays.

She mutters, "This is either going to be a dump or a bachelor pad."

"I'm trying my birthday again," I say, opening the door as we stop. "Let's hope it works."

The mechanics click, and I cautiously open the door as Echo peers inside. "Jesus…"

"Yeah," I snicker, glancing around at the tranquil space. "Welcome to the mafia."

"… It was theirs?"

"Yep, well his…" I walk over to the garage door inset with mirrored tiles and push the button outside. My cousin warned me it looked like a stalker's lair though I wasn't sure I believed him. The whole place is sleek and sexy black with chrome finishes and heavily lacquered dark woods—beyond clean and neat. "Thank heavens there's a rail."

This is OCD to the max.

I'm in nirvana amongst the shadowy creed, but I'm not sure she is comfortable.

"And they're giving it to you?"

"No, they're giving it to us," I correct, running my fingers over the gothic-style guard rail emblazoned with fleur de lys. I nod once. "This is a hell of a homecoming gift."

I am eternally indebted.

I will never get out from under them.

One look at Echo, though, and I don't give a shit. I'll play dirty if it means keeping her on her knees.

She doesn't yet know; they own her too.

And I'm not sure I'm ready to tell her that. I may do the work, but we're a package deal. If I am in, so is she.

"Sky lights and tin ceiling!" She peers up, and her eyes twinkle at mine. "This is all ours?" Immediately, her expression contorts at the sight of the floor to ceiling black metal rack with an enormous horizontal brace three-quarters up. "What is that?" She tiptoes closer, tilting her head. "… Jynx?"

I stroke my beard and snarl. "That is where we pray for forgiveness from our sins."

"Oh, my God…it looks like a cross."

"Our fetish is our religion."

Grabbing her phone, she mutters, "He's fucking insane!"

"Who are you texting?"

"Who do you think?"

"One of the boys, my guess is Sal."

"He says there is a remote control on the back wall," she replies as I hold it up and toss it to her. I don't know if his efforts are sincere or he's manipulating her with friendship to win her over. I wouldn't put either past him. "This is beyond. So...someone gets in this thing..."

"The harness," I instruct, filling in the blank and halting my laughter. "And they go up. It's a custom suspension rig."

"... You knew?"

"Deacon mentioned it, but we don't have to use it."

Her voice quivers, "Have you used one before?"

"Not quite like that one but yes," I candidly reply. She needs to know the extent of my spirituality before we travel any further down this road. "Many times."

"With?"

"Flavor of the night," I bluntly say. "Never twice. Never any place I cared about. That was reserved for someone special, someone I was waiting on."

"If I had been eighteen..."

"Don't go there," I mutter, stepping closer. "Because age means nothing in terms of my steadfastness to the craft. If you had just graduated high school, I would've too."

A veil of innocence emerges on her face. She knows what I would've done and the kind of predator I am. Still, she stays, infinitely curious, and testing my game. "Are you a bad man, J.A. Monroe?"

"Yes, Ma'am," I confess, "I am."

"And you never got caught?"

"One time was enough." I mumble the excuse, "Stalking."

"But you didn't learn your lesson."

I devilishly smirk. "Ask the question properly, Abigail."

"How many girls..."

"Quite a few."

She gulps. "Is there an age cut off?"

"Yeah. I like tits, ass, and pretty red lips. My preference is young women—*any kind*—thin women, fat women, white women, black women, a quarter Korean women. Any woman as long as she looks like a young woman." I motion an hourglass with my hands and wink.

"Are you a predator?"

"Yes, I am," I admit.

Covering her mouth, she understands my addiction and why I tend to avoid anyone under thirty. One taste. One hit. And I am right back on my drug of choice.

"If you lost me..."

"I wasn't going to date anyone under forty," I reply, having thought it out. "I was going to be some older woman's boy toy."

"But it isn't your fancy."

"Twenty-two seems to fancy me a lot."

The intense moment lingers, and she takes a breath. "It's kind of warm in here."

Raising a brow, I bait, "It's not going to get any cooler."

"How high are the ceilings you think?"

"At least twelve feet, maybe more," I say, staring at her, absorbing it all. She taps the button, and her mouth gapes open. "... Are you okay?" I know she's not. This is a lot to handle—from the new environment to the criminal underworld I am about to be heavily involved with again and the truth of who I am. "One step at a time, babygirl."

"Ahh..." she pauses, enamored and shocked by it all as the harness goes up. "And you do what exactly when you're up there?" Taking a random guess, I open one of the drawers off to the side and smack the whip against the floor. She jumps with fright. "Oh, God!"

Her naiveté shows. And my dick pounds with an awareness of her youth. I step closer, and her breaths quicken. "Do you want to play, Echo?"

"Shit just got serious, Sir."

"We don't mess around with our daily devotionals."

"And I'm the sinner because I don't speak your native tongue."

The back of my hand brushes over her cheek to her neck. I slip my fingers into her blouse and fondle her bare breast. I rub my palm over her nipple. "You can immigrate. We have a ritual for that."

ECHO

WE'RE SITTING ON THE TILED FLOOR OF THE OVERSIZED shower with the hot water pouring on us. I watch the water droplets splashing against the glass as I consider what all I have agreed to.

The glittering diamond on my finger catches my attention. Between the droplets and the facets, the rock dances, sparkling with his love as tears cascade over my cheeks, blending into the surroundings and disguising the dread.

"You're having doubts," he mumbles in my ear. His arms are loosely wrapped around my naked body. "I can hear you even when you don't say a word."

"What if I am wrong and cannot do this?"

"You will do this," he replies, kissing my neck. "You don't have a choice anymore. I won't let you go."

"What if, I was wrong and I cannot be with a bad boy?"

"You won't do that because you would be lying to yourself. You love me. It's just been a lot to digest today."

I close my eyes as his hands graze against the sides of my breasts. "What if, the club or the mob is too much for me to handle?"

"It isn't," he smugly contends. "If you can handle months with me, then there is nothing new to handle."

"But there is," I argue as the smokescreen of tears thickens, and I cry harder. "Not only are you about to be involved in some very illegal activity, you apparently like them young."

"You aren't old," he interjects with a ferocious snap. "You're letting all of the external forces intimidate you. Control your mind. Focus only on me. Let the internal force be your guide. Listen to my voice, Echo."

I push away, not wanting to be seduced by his sensual words.

"How can I when there is a giant black cross in my living room where people get whipped on?"

He gives me a side-eyed glance. "Just say it, already."

"Say what?"

He calmly replies, "Stop letting your curiosity get the best of you and say—Will you please whip me, Jynx?"

I eye him harshly. "What? No Sir or Master needed?"

"I don't need the honorific for you to know who I am, Darlin'."

"I just don't know if I'm good enough for all of this, Jynx."

"You're good enough, baby," he contends as I stand up and stare at the man I have fallen so hard for—his chestnut curls, ocean blue eyes, and *that smile with those dimples.* My eyes skim over his inked arms and damp chest hair to his washboard abs and flaccid cock sheathed in the foreskin. His legs stretch out, showing off his sinewy thighs and deliciously muscled calves.

"No, I'm not," I whisper, fighting his will. "And I never will be."

He rises, standing so much taller than me. I glance up as a peasant —a pilgrim—an ignorant disciple, begging him to teach me. Despite my fears, I cannot say the words.

"It's me who should be worried, not the other way around. Don't be scared. Tell me what you want, Abigail. Tell me what you need. Say the words and I will provide."

With water splashing over my body, I am baptized in his darkness and claimed by the demons of his unrest.

"... Will you whip me, Daddy?"

His lips upturn to a smirk as I blink down and notice the pronounced arousal of his shaft. "It's about time." He swiftly latches his arms around me and pushes me into the wall. "Are you a naughty girl?"

"I'll be the best slut you ever had, Jynx."

"You already are, Mrs. Monroe." He briefly smirks, offering reassurance that his gentleman is very much present despite the filthy fucking that is about to happen. He gets off on the style of play, and luckily for him—I play broken and insecure with ease. "Your safeword..."

"It will always be Jeremiah."

"Fair enough," he replies, lifting me onto his shoulder. He swats my ass and grabs a couple of towels. "And your name will forever be bitch."

"Because I am Jynx's hot fiancée?"

"No, because you're the bitch that managed to tie me down. It's never been about disrespect. If anything, as my submissive, it is as much an honorific as the Sir you worry about saying."

"And you'll always be a cocky asshole."

"If I'm not, then I'm failing at my only job."

He sets my wet ass on the dining room table and covers my body with the towel. "And that is?"

"You, princess."

45

GOASSLSCHNALZEN

ECHO

WITH MY HAIR BRUSHED AND PULLED IN A TAUT BUN, I wait with the harness hanging on my body. I nervously peer up, understanding that not only will I be elevated to a new height, but come face to face with his Dominance. I know that he has been my Dominant, but this is an advanced form of play. The significance leaves me tingly from my toes to the tips of my fingers.

He walks out of the bedroom in a loose-fitting bluish-gray tank top and black pants. And he smiles—*one of those drool-worthy, panty-melting grins.* "You okay?" he asks, sucking on something. "You seem tense."

My head tilts inquisitively as I whisper, "What do you have in your mouth?"

"A mint," he politely says as his eyes blink up to meet mine. "Do you want one?"

I laugh. "We're about to have a scene?"

"Yeah and I'm anxious as fuck."

I wrinkle my nose. "... You?"

"Yeah," he contends, pulling a mint from his pocket and unwrapping it. He puts the disc on my tongue. "You don't get to corner the market on nerves."

"How often do you get nervous?"

"Not very often," he says, tightening the straps on me. "But I'm in love with you. You're a game changer."

His private confession isn't what I expect. "Aren't I supposed to be the one having the therapy?"

He fastens two matching ankle cuffs to my feet. "That's where you're wrong. If it's done right, this is as much about me as you. There is balance. If there isn't balance, it isn't BDSM. It's not always fifty-fifty, but I am in this with you."

"What about the random one-nighters?"

"That," he says, fastening a collar around my neck. "Never has the same appeal. Because I don't have the emotional connection with them. It's strictly a power trip, but there is still a balance. With you, this is intensely intimate."

"You're such a gentleman." I smirk.

His brows dart up fast. "That's what you keep telling me. I'm not going to argue, but I know you're scared and I want you to have fun."

"You get clothes," I point out and glance down. "Is that to hide the raging boner?"

"Pretty much." He leans in and softly kisses me. "How high do you want to go?"

I take a deep breath. "Take me all the way up."

"Okay, but I'm bringing you back down. What do you want me to do?"

"I want you to whip me and show me who Master Jynx is."

He licks his lip as the smell of peppermint calms me. "But you're sleeping cuffed to me."

My eyes fill with tears. "Not letting me run off?"

"Not a chance in hell."

Closing my eyes, I whisper, "Take me higher than I have ever been, Jynx." He pushes the remote, and I lift about three feet before I say, "Hey, J?" He stops me.

"Yeah."

"I fucking love you."

"I fucking love you too, babygirl." He hits the button and grins. "Stop holding your breath."

I glance down at him as I reach the top. "How did you know?"

"It's a common problem. You'll get yourself more worked up than necessary."

I look out the massive industrial pane windows. "The view is incredible."

"So I've been told."

"Have you never been up here?"

"No, I'm too tall. This ride has a height requirement that I don't meet."

My body relaxes as I giggle under my breath, "Are you serious?"

"It's only built to hold between four-ten and six feet because the previous owner is a short motherfucker at five-ten."

I laugh and gently swing on the ropes. "And your cousin?"

"He would never do this, way too much alpha in those sneakers," he replies, taking a drink of water. "But he's like six-one. Hold your mint between your teeth."

He rotates me with my back to him. "Jynx?" The quick-release drops my body, paralyzing my breath and sending my stomach to a new location in the back of my throat. He stops me about a foot off the ground. "Jynx, what are you doing?"

The whip cracks to my left and rapidly to my right. "Worship."

Dear God.

My lip quivers. My body trembles. He detaches the D-clips from the armholes, releasing and removing them. My hands cling to the ropes as I balance in thick belts wrapped around my waist and between my legs. "What if I fall?"

"You're a foot off the ground," he interrupts. "You're not falling."

I glance over my shoulder. "I meant in love with doing this."

"Then we need to get you back on the pill because I don't play lightly."

I bite my lip and prepare mentally for his first snap. He brushes the tip over my back, and I notice the mirrors on the closed garage door and in front of me. I can see myself, and him—*everything*. "Someone has a thing for watching themselves."

The loud crack sounds to my right side on the floor. He's taunting me—*teasing me*—building up the tension. It's all in my head, I think. *The mental fuck.* Until he strikes me once, and I shut my eyes. "Open them."

I do. And I stare at his reflection—*dark, foreboding, intimidating*—purposefully driven to bring pain to my body. My hot fiancé is a dangerous man with a sculpted body and calculating mind.

I am so in love with him.

He flicks the whip again, searing the tails across my back. I'm hot, slipping into a drunken space where nothing matters, and it is so good. He tosses another and another until I've lost count, and the only thing that matters is he and I are sharing in this precious, perfect moment.

"Take it," I purr, rolling my hips in the harness as the slickness trickles between my thighs. "Please, Sir."

He doles out a few more, some of which sting, and drops the wretched and wonderful beast on the floor. "That's enough for now." He hoists me out and sets me on the platform bed beneath the skylights. I feel so small in his arms as I protest, "Are we done?"

"Not even close," he replies. "But you'll be emo mush if I keep going."

"But that is where you pray."

He grabs a long, thin stick with a popper at the end. "Coachwhip. And I can pray anywhere."

Rubbing my nipple between his thumb and forefinger, he arouses it to a peak and reaches to do the same to the other. I close my eyes, distracted by the sensation of his fingers, and never see the nipple clamps.

"The hell!" I open my eyes to the deviant grin of a monster. He tugs the shiny silver chain between them. "Oh, gosh..."

"How good are you?"

"I'm very good, Jynx."

"Face the wall over there," he says, pointing to the vacant space on the side of the cabinets near the suspension rig. I quickly do as he says. The wall is perpendicular to the mirrored garage door, and I see myself—with black cuffs on my neck, wrists, ankles, and black clamps adorning my nipples. "And do not move. What are you thinking about?"

"That I look incredible."

"You do," he praises with his deep, sexy tenor. "The perfect little doll to thrash and trash." The blazing bite of the coachwhip on my ass sends my hand to rub the flesh. "Hands up on the wall. Spread your legs."

He runs the tip over the length of my slit and I ask, "Are you hard?"

"Very."

"And what are you thinking about?"

Pacing closer, he breathes against my neck and cackles, "How much I want to hurt you."

He gently tugs on the chain between my breasts. "They should be tighter," I complain as he flips me around and demands, "Open." Placing the whip between my teeth, he slowly increases the pressure.

My eyes flare at his, and I moan, "Enough."

"Just a little bit more."

"Bastard!"

"Don't ever tell a sadist you want more pain."

He retrieves the whip, and I growl deep in my throat. "It's too much."

"No, it's not. Mind over matter. Push yourself. Embrace the pain. Run to it, not away from it."

Tears form in my eyes as I look at him. He tilts his head and lifts his brows with an evil fascination. I turn away, sniffling, understanding the routine.

"It's too much!"

His hand grips my shoulder, spinning me back into the wall and pressing down. He rips the zipper open on his pants and angles himself. "Suck my cock. And watch those pretty lips swallow me in the mirror."

I open my mouth, and he grabs my hair, which tumbles out of the bun. He shoves his dick deep into my throat. I stare at the girl, on her knees, submitting to this man, and lust replaces the ache in my nipples. They're burning, almost numb, but all I can focus on is how much I want him to touch my pussy. I want his lips on my throbbing clit and his fingers fucking me. I reach up to cup his sack, knowing he won't be long.

He yanks my head back by my hair, seizing control of my movements. I am his sexual puppet meant for his pleasure.

"What?" I pant as my eyes water. "Say something."

"You're fucking beautiful." He dips down and passionately dives his tongue into my mouth. "Watch carefully." His fist clutches around his cock, and he pumps it hard and fast—*violently so*. His heavy, ragged breaths snag in my heart with each thrust. "Open your goddamned mouth, bitch!" He grunts hard and shoots his hot cum down my throat and over my face. "You're mine. And that is what I am going to do to your pussy."

Without even a beat, his finger slips into the hoop on my neck collar, and he tugs, pulling me to the bed. He strips off his shirt and lays down flat on his back as I whip my tongue along my top lip to clean up his mess. I wipe the wet spots with my finger and lick them.

"Did you think I'd say no?"

"Sit on my face," he randomly demands. I blink, stunned by the request. He sees the hesitation in my eyes. "Grip the headboard to balance and sit your swollen little cunt on my lips. I'm kissing you from clit to ass."

I straddle over his sexy mug, totally uncertain about this move—

feeling like a power shift. He's offering to let me regain some control. I refuse, lowering, but his hands tether to my thighs, driving me down. He sucks my hard little nub into his mouth and gently nips before sliding forward and fucking my opening with his tongue.

When he swirls around my puckered asshole, I understand his gospel and beg for more. His supercharged boost elevates my standing with him as I find the melody in his maelstrom and automatically move on my own.

He slides his thumb into my ass and uses his other hand to pull the silver rein latched between my nipples. We're moving as one, chasing the storms, and embracing the debauchery.

"I'm going to come, Jynx!" I'm on my own, flying full speed ahead into danger. "God! Fuck! Don't stop!"

And then, he moans, vibrating the whole deluge of my wanton undercarriage from ripe clit to hungry hole over and over again.

"Yes!" I howl out like an animal as I discover who I am, what I am capable of, and who I am meant to be. "Suck my orgasm out of me!"

I am an animal just like he is.

He focuses on my clit as the massive full-body tremor erupts through me. Waves of dew flow from my body, drowning his face, and I slow down to take a breath.

But he is Jynx, and I've come to know he is far from through. Tossing one leg over, he escapes, drops his pants, and mounts behind me like a primal savage. He winds my hair around his palm and pulls, bucking his hard cock into me.

"You like it rough, little girl?"

"Yes!" I cry out as he fills me. Just when I think I cannot take anymore, he thrusts deeper, slapping our thighs together and resonating in my core. No one else in my life will ever mean this much.

He reaches around and pulls the clamps from my nipples one at a time. It burns. "Are you going to be my whore, Abigail?"

"I will be everything you need! I want to be your submissive!" I retaliate, and he smacks my ass hard. "Please, be my Master! It's all I want!"

442 | KAILEE REESE SAMUELS

He slows down, pounding my puddle with the entire length of his shaft. "Your pussy is so goddamned good—*so goddamned good.*"

"This is going to take all night."

He calmly corrects, "No, this is going to take the rest of our lives."

A WEEK LATER, I STARE OUT THE WINDOW AT THE ROLLING fields as he drives. With my hand laced in his, I peek over and smile at the man I've fallen in love with—Jeremiah Abaddon Monroe. He's a techie freak, a hacker, a biker, a hell of a Dominant, and a dangerous man. I didn't get everything I asked for; I got something better. Something I seemingly forgot ten months ago.

A gentleman.

My "rapist" must be a gentleman with a kink streak a mile wide.

I scoffed at the idea of being submissive for so long because I never found the right partner. He showed up, and everything clicked like magic. People influence one another. People change and grow.

There isn't anything I won't let him do to me.

He lifts my hand to his lips and kisses my fingers.

This man loves me.

How rare is that?

So we're a little off, fucked up in how we play, but we're soulmates fated from the beginning.

Apparently, he's saving biker royalty—something I have dismissed for a long time. I didn't know until three days ago, but my father helped start Rampage MC many years ago in Arkansas. I didn't even know my dad ever went to Arkansas. The pages of our history sometimes fall out of the book and get lost, and we hope and pray that someone hands them back to us. Someone must know the story.

A guy named Jynx did.

As we sat naked in bed, with me feeding him pecan praline ice cream, he researched for hours in his glasses and messy hair.

I needed to know why I was on the radar of his new boss.

And now I do.

We made a decision based on our escapades to put off having children for a while. Before we left South Carolina, I swallowed the little tablet to erase the slight chance of a baby preemptively stealing some of our fun away. In Houston, I visited a doctor, received bloodwork, and had an IUD implanted.

It's not time...*yet.*

And we have plenty of time.

The truth we both knew is that we weren't ready because we were too into one another. I cried for about thirty minutes, questioning the what-ifs that ultimately he deemed to be my decision. I was young, and we had plenty of time. I gulped down the mature decision and swore to be the best Abigail Maines I could be for me, him, and our future.

I met the man of my dreams.

And I can slow down or speed up the story at any point because it is *my story*, my history, that I am building day by day.

Under Jynx's spell, I regained control of everything because I trusted him. I wouldn't recommend my way to everyone, but it worked for me.

I like rough sex.

And he certainly fits the bill.

We pull through an open gate and stop outside of a grand Victorian estate. "Is this it?"

"... I think so?" he cackles, running his hand through his curls. "I'm feeling a bit of déjà vu."

He's scanning his phone when I spot Deacon exiting the garage and grinning at me. "J?"

"Huh?" He looks up. "I was just about to call. I'm on my way to open your door."

"I think someone is going to beat you to it," I inform as Deacon does. "Hi!"

He offers me his hand—*his dirty biker hands*—and I take them. I welcome them. I embrace him. He isn't my father, and neither is Jynx —*he is something so much more. He is the Daddy of a spoiled brat.* "How are you doing?"

"I'm good!" I reply as Sal emerges from the garage and gives Jynx a bro hug. We're going to be okay. We're going to fucking make it. And it's going to be one hell of a trip. "I'm glad to be here. Thank you for inviting us!"

"You look amazing!" Deacon compliments, playing with the tips of my hair. "This light blonde really pops your eyes!"

Sal twists his ball cap around and opens his arms wide as I walk over. He lifts me off my feet a few inches and kisses both of my cheeks as I spot my Mustang in the garage. "This is your house."

I look at Jynx, who is grinning mischievously. "You knew!"

"I did," he admits, bashfully. "And I knew you would love it."

"But but!" Sal excitedly says, holding my hand and refusing to let go as we rush toward the garage. "The best part is this!"

I gasp at the wire and wood box with four baby peacocks. "Jynx! It's the start of our pulchritude of peacocks!"

"We could call it a pride of cocks." Sal wiggles his brows and picks one up, placing it in my hands. "They're yours." He digs in his pocket and hands me the keys. "And so are these."

"Whose house is this?"

"The whole property is mine. I'm having another house built past the tree line in the valley by the creek."

"Are y'all going to live there?"

"She says y'all!" Deacon gushes, patting Jynx on the shoulder. "Do it again!"

"Y'all!"

"Naw, *y'all*," Sal mocks in his best Southern drawl, "will share the property, but you won't ever notice the neighbor. Trust me. You have seven hundred acres."

"Holy shit!" I spot the girl exiting from the house with long, dark hair. I shove the peacock at Sal and walk over. She's a little taller than me but not by much as we meet in the middle of the garage and stare at one another. Her blue-violet eyes blink at my hazel ones as she imparts a stern gaze. "You're Sal's hot wife."

"If you ever do something so incredibly stupid again, I will hurt you. And you will regret ever crossing a woman."

"Yes, Ma'am." Her expression softens, and she embraces me. Her hair smells like a lavender bouquet. I'm utterly bewildered by her enchantment. "Can I come work for you?"

"We can talk about that in a few days." She winks. "I'll need a resume."

I turn back to the three boys lined up in a row. "That is a whole lotta trouble."

"You have no idea," she giggles, gripping onto my arm. "Good luck! May you have plenty of sparks and lots of ice!"

FOUR WEEKS LATER

46

RUNAWAY

Jynx

ON AN OVERCAST DAY, SHE SITS OUT ON THE BACK PORCH, tied to a wooden chair as I pace barefooted in jeans. I wouldn't have answered the call, but work has taken on a new urgency. I have lots of days off, only to end up working for a week straight with little sleep.

The job is spastic.

And I love it.

I run my finger along the red binding that I've got to silence her crowing. She has been biting the fabric for over two hours. "We'll come over tonight for dinner to discuss it further." Her big hazel eyes stare with anticipation, excited that I might actually get off the phone, so I can finish what we started. "Yep, seven o'clock. I remember where it is and I'll tell Axel to get his ass over there too. Later, bro."

She wildly blinks and groans as I untie her mouth. "Oh, my God... can I have a drink?"

"You were such a good girl!" I praise petting her ratty blonde hair and giving her a drink of my water. She gulps, and water spills out the sides of her mouth. "I'm so proud of you."

"Whew!" she sighs. "That was a long one."

"Are you ready?"

She licks her lips as I stare at her pretty fall dress. "Yeah, I am ready."

"Do you need anything?"

"Your fat cock in one of my holes."

"We're going," I reply, flicking open the blade and pressing the shiny metal to her cheek. "What do you want?"

"Please, don't hurt me!" she begs, turning on the tears. "I'll do anything you want!"

I lower the razor-sharp blade and pop a button off her dress.

"Are you aware of how much this one costs?"

I smirk. "You seem to think I care, Abs."

"Good thing I ordered two."

"Can we get back to this? We have a dinner date in four hours and I need to come inside of you."

"Yes, sorry!" Her watering eyes return as she struggles against the thick rope binding. "Please let me go! I promise I won't ever tell anyone what a creep you are!"

I can't find my mojo.

I shake my head, laughing, and dropping to my knees. I put my head in her lap. My arms wrap around her legs, and my fingers grip her butt. "A creep, really? Give me something better than that!"

She spits at me. "Fuck me, asshole."

"You want to get mad about it?"

She grins as I sit back on my heels and stare at how beautiful she is. "How many takes of this scene do we need?" I tuck the blade under the ropes and carefully sever them from her body. "Run, bitch, run!"

"Old man!" she baits, hopping up and dashing past me. "You'll never catch me!"

From the outdoor kitchen cabinet, I grab and fire off the gun toward the target—*yes, I really did set it up that close to the house for this express purpose*—and tuck my feet in the running shoes before slipping on the ski mask. Good scenes take some forethought.

"Like hell, girl."

We're running fast.

She's a good distance ahead and darting into the thick of the trees. She'll head for the creek because that is what she always does. We've done this same scenario, minus the phone call, about a half dozen times. The gloomy day serves as the perfect backdrop for an assault in the deep woods.

God, I love this woman.

I veer around the thicket of wild blackberries—I made that mistake one time. By the time I found her, I was scratched all to hell and bleeding.

Good times.

Scaling down the hill, I stop suddenly at the sight of her. She's at the water with a young doe just on the other side. I'm surprised she didn't run off with the gunshot. They're acclimating to my wayward choreography.

Echo glances over, pressing her finger to her lips, and smiles as the doe takes a drink from the swollen creek. I pull off the ski mask and quietly walk closer. She is watching the doe, and I am watching the golden light pour from her kindhearted soul.

We cannot plan for every outcome.

"You're beautiful, Mama."

I grin and touch her hand. "So are you."

A noise in the woods distracts the doe, and she runs off. "We aren't done, fucker."

I chuckle and touch her cheek. "I spent a good twenty years being wild and you tamed me."

"I swear if you do not shove your cock in me soon, I'm going to be the assailant. And I'm a nasty fucking girl who is not afraid to take what I fucking want, dickhead."

My eyes drift off to the side as I consider that idea and raise a brow. "I would so be down for that."

"Jynx!" She swats at me, and I grab her hands.

I stick out my tongue. "Do you want me to corrupt your light?"

"Yes! I do!" She pivots to run, but I grab her arm and force her to the ground. We do not play gently anymore. "God! No!"

"You're getting my dick, bitch."

She swings punching and clawing. Our battles have inched up a few notches. I'll take her blows because of the love she brings. With my weight on top of her, there is no way she can escape.

I hastily unzip and lift her skirt before grabbing my cock and thrusting inside. She screams, and a chill runs through my spine. I cover her mouth with my palm, and she bites me hard. I rip her motherfucking dress open, tug her bra down, and latch my mouth to her tit. I suck and bite at her nipple as she pushes against me.

"Jynx..."

"Take my big cock in that tight, wet pussy."

"Harder!" she bellows, shifting gears again. I follow—*this time.* "Give it to me harder!"

I pin her hands down in the leaves with one of mine and wrap the other around her delicate neck as I buck my hips fast. "You like it rough, Darlin'?"

"Choke me, Jynx...Choke me *harder!*"

"I'm going to come soon, baby." I tighten my grip and let her hands go so she can pull against my strangulation. It's so good. I'm so hard. And she is so fucking wet. "Shit...I don't want to go yet..."

Her hips jet up, taking me. "Come inside of me," she musters out. "We'll do it again in the shower."

"... You promise?"

"Swear," she says through gritted teeth as her moves tantalize the beast in me. "Give me your milk."

"My dick is giving your pussy a sloppy, wet kiss." I continue thrusting, taking us to the edge. We fly as I tighten my chokehold and come with a roar. I shoot my load deep inside of her shelter—*my secret hideout*. She moans in ecstasy beneath me, and I hover on my forearms as we wait for the collision of loving waves in her passage. "I'm crazy in love with you, Echo."

"I love you too, my filthy fucking gentleman."

"God, that was so damned incredible. You were so wet." I fall out of her and sit back, looking at my blood coated dick. "Honey, you finally got your period."

I dip the tip of my finger in her and smear blood on my cheeks. "Am I the kill and you're the hunter, now?"

"Sure," I snicker, licking my cum and blood covered finger. "Tasty!"

"You're so bad, Jynx Monroe."

"And you love me this way."

MS. SAMUELS NOTES #30

BTEPD

Thank you so much for reading Jynx and Echo's story. I hope you love it as much as I do. It has been an honor and a privilege to work with these characters for the last eighteen months. If you have the time, please consider leaving a review.

I could talk for hours about this book and how much it meant to me. However, I think I will leave those conversations in a more private setting over a bottle of wine.

I have written 30 "dark romances"—for lack of a more specific genre. I don't believe every story needs a happily ever after with a bow on it, so I push the boundaries a little with the "romance" part of that equation needing to end with a HEA/HFN. I tend to be on the other side where you can have a romance, and it ends, but the book is still a romance.

I get the general public does not agree with this.

We're socially married to rainbows and unicorns.

I'm not.

I won't ever be.

I want black, gray, and white rainbows and flaming icy pegicorns (pegasus + unicorn).

A story is still valid as a romance even if one or hell, both, of the H/h, dies. We can grieve "dark" and still have love "romance." I'll argue that with anyone. Even in death, a romance can yet exist—as long as one keeps the flame lit.

So, I started thinking about these two words we toss together quite frequently—*dark romance*. And I examined what they meant to me. My thoughts traversed to a somewhat dangerous place because I realized that so much of what we consider dark romance, even some of my work in the standalone pieces — *She/He* and *Poppy* — have centered-around this oppression and subsequent elevation of women.

And well, I couldn't do that again.

I might...at some point, but not within BTEPD.

I don't discriminate on beating characters—*male or female*—up. Fling them against the wall to see if they bounce or cry. Sounds silly, but sometimes, it's the truth.

I wanted to break dark romance into two words—
dark + romance.

So, we have dark, twisting elements spiraling around, but at the core of that, we have this romance, which skirts close to a sweet romance at different points in the book.

I wanted the elements—dark + romance—separated—*isolated, if you will*—so the shadows of light and dark magnified. That was the hope.

I never know what the response will be, but ultimately I wanted to give you, Dear Reader, three things in BTEPD—dark + romance + a helluva lot of fun.

I've written some pretty dark shit. I didn't want this to be so dark that you capsized or felt the need to set it aside—*those books have their time and place*—but I needed BTEPD to bring a whole lot of love and enjoyment into the current gloomy climate.

**I'm not trying to change the world;
I just want to give you a couple of hours to
breathe and be you.**

I always aim to do that—*I am an entertainer, an artist, a writer*—but I also accept that the sex + violence in my mafia series, TAT— *a Tomb of Ashen Tears,* can be intense. And I love TAT for that very reason, but at the same token, I wanted BTEPD to ease up from that level of grim.

Various monochromatic hues in my dark prism.

As for the characters, I was blessed to have Jynx and Echo because I am acutely aware after three million words that you don't always receive complete characters in a package that are ready to talk. Sometimes, I have to dig, and that's okay, but it's a blessing when they come pre-assembled and ready to go.

Jynx Monroe was a complete asshole to *me* in the beginning, but for the most part, he ended up being exactly what *she* wanted—a filthy fucking gentleman.

Echo Maines stood out in my studio/laboratory/cage as possessing a unique strength. She was one of the rare characters, tapping on my shoulder and saying, "Write me, please. Make time for me. Let me audition!"

Of course, I rolled my eyes.

Go away and come back in five years.

Well, the pesky little thing wouldn't hear of that.

And finally, S & D said, "Let's see what she has to say."

I'm like whatever. I'm on your journey. This isn't mine. I gave up years ago trying to understand how we end up where we go or why.

I don't write meek women, but damn Ekky brought spunk I didn't expect for a character so young on my canvas. She delivered a strength that I more than once compared to Iris during the composition process. Echo was truly a gift to me.

I'm glad the boys gave her a shot. ;)

I was compelled by their story, falling into my hands, eighteen months ago.

BTEPD genuinely started with just a simple idea—*what if a girl posted this ad?*

And I won't debate that here—for right or wrong, that was what was handed to me. I could've taken this in a very dark, seedy direction, but I didn't want to do that because of this whole oppression thing I had running in my head. I wanted to uplift and twist it into something obscure—*what if he wants to save her?*

What kind of guy would do that?

Turns out—a pretty fucked up one who practices chivalry.

The whole process has taught me so much about myself. I have said, writing Jynx changed me. And he did. He closed the blinds and we had some long ass heart to hearts. I'm not ready to talk about those changes yet, but they're coming.

Blame Jynx. Blame Sal. Blame Deacon.

BLAME JOHN.
I made you a promise, and I intend to keep it, Sir.
Words, Sir.
I will deliver your words.

Specifically to my TAT girls, #RANIEROFANGIRLS, I would like to mention the timeline on this story coordinates, *or should*, with TAT7 during the summer of 2020.

While bringing some of our current real-life issues into the mix with TAT, I have intentionally chosen not to do such in BTEPD because I wanted the primary focus to remain on Jynx and Echo.

To preserve their atmosphere's integrity, I captured this romance in an idyllic setting—without the proper safety protocol that has been needed in 2020.

Yes, Sal will be wearing nothing but a mask soon. Woo! :D

I tease, I tease.

I would never have done this book without a much-needed push from some extraordinary people in my life. You know who you are, and I love you all immensely. Your encouragement, notes, words —*sometimes my words you repeat back to me*—your teasers, the LOVE that you give me MEANS the world to me, and I cannot thank you enough.

YOU are why I hit publish.

I scribble the words, writing every book like it's my last book—every time.

And I will continue to do such for YOU.

Because **YOU** deserve my best.

Thank you again.

Peace. Love. & Sal.

@ the farmhouse,

kailee xx

December 4, 2020

P.S. Thank you for the trip! South Carolina was lovely, and I learned so much in the darkest hours. I'm headed back home to Sal and Cruz in Sugargove for *Forbidden Sins* (TAT6). I must be going before I'm late. The keeper of tomes is waiting for me. xx

Join Kailee for water, wine, or whiskey at

KaileeReeseSamuels.com

Made in the USA
Middletown, DE
04 September 2021